Finding Matt

Escaping the Past: Book One

by

Suzie Peters

First Published in 2017
by GWL Publishing
an imprint of Great War Literature Publishing LLP

Produced in United Kingdom

ISBN 978-1-910603-36-9 Paperback Edition

GWL Publishing
Forum House
Sterling Road
Chichester PO19 7DN
www.gwlpublishing.co.uk

Dedication

To S.

Chapter One

⤸∞⤵

Matt

I drum my fingers on the desk, and take yet another sip of dark, strong black coffee as the iPad warbles to itself, and then cuts off once again. Is that the fourth attempt, or the fifth? I've lost count now.

"Luke…" I say, out loud and exasperated, to no-one other than myself, since I'm alone in my office at six o'clock on a wet mid-February Friday evening. I've been trying to FaceTime with him for over half an hour and, while I've got a reasonably good idea what he's doing, I wish he'd screw around on his own time, not mine. Pressing the connect button, I decide to give him one last chance, and then I'm going home and I'll call him later – even if it means waking him up in the middle of the night. It'll serve him right. Leaving the tablet to try and make the connection, I wander across to the coffee machine to freshen up my drink.

"Hi," says a disconnected, but familiar voice. "Where the hell are you?"

"I could ask you the same question," I call from across the room.

"Oh, you are there, then." I can hear the smile in his voice, even though I can't see him.

"I've been here, trying to call you for the last half-hour. Where have you been? As if I didn't know." I sit down again and lift up the tablet, so he can see me.

"Hmm. I think I preferred it when I couldn't see your face. You're scowling at me." He sounds pained but he's grinning.

"Well, it's six o'clock, it's wet, it's Friday and I want to go home."

"Oh, quit moaning, would you? It's eleven here, and it's also pouring with rain, but I'm not whining like a baby, am I?"

"No, knowing you, you're probably getting laid," I snap.

"Not yet, Matt. Give me time. I only landed here this morning."

I glance at my watch. "You mean you've been in London more than twelve hours already, and haven't found some unfortunate woman to drag to your bed yet?"

"Hey. I never have to drag them anywhere… They come willingly – usually at least three or four times, and always screaming for more." He grins again and winks.

"Okay. I get the point." I want to turn the conversation away from his overactive libido and onto more serious topics. "How did the meeting go?"

"It went great. That's one of the reasons I didn't pick up earlier. I haven't stopped since I got here. I checked that the team were okay, that their accommodation was dealt with, and we went and had a look at the venue. It's spectacular, but I left Paul to deal with things there."

"Just as well. You know what he's like if you tread on his toes." I imagine Paul, our chief designer, shooing Luke out of the way while he bossed everyone around.

"Then I met up with Grace and Jenny for a drink as planned and we talked through things, which took a bit longer than I'd thought, so I came back to the hotel, had a late dinner and a long bath, which is where I was when you called."

"You have been busy, haven't you?" I drip sarcasm. "And what have you arranged with… um… Grace and Jenny?" I note he's on first-name terms already and I wonder if that easy familiarity should make me nervous.

"I've said that we want the logo and website designs created within the next two months, and the build completed by the end of July. I showed them our ideas and they're okay with what we've got in mind and the schedule. The contract will be drawn up by Monday, when you get here, so you can meet them and sign on the dotted line. I've set up the meeting with them for early Monday afternoon, at their offices, then our show is on Tuesday morning, but we've got time to meet some buyers before flying off to Milan on Wednesday morning. Paul is flying out on Tuesday evening with the rest of the team to get set up there."

"Our Milan show is on Thursday, isn't it?"

"Yep, why?"

"I'll stay for the show, but then I'm coming home, and you'll have to do Paris by yourself. My mom's taken a turn for the worse, so I can't be away for too long."

"That's fine. I'll cope. Paul does most of it anyway. I'm just here to glad-hand the buyers." We both know that isn't true. Yes, Paul works hard getting the shows right, but Luke does a lot more than he's suggesting. That's one of the reasons the business is doing so well.

"So are you gonna fly back home on Friday?" he asks. "Or will you try for a Thursday afternoon flight? Our show's in the morning..."

"No, Friday will be fine." He doesn't ask any more about my mom, and I'm grateful. It's a weird position to be in. She's never been my favorite person, but now she's dying, the sense of duty with which she raised me has kicked in big-time.

"What were they like?" I ask.

"Who?"

"For heaven's sake, Luke... The two women at Richards Cole Design, how were they? I know you're jet-lagged but can you try and stay focused, just for a bit longer. Are you sure you haven't got someone there with you?"

"Positive. I sure as shit wouldn't be talking to you if I had. They were..." I sense he's searching for the right words. "Married... both of them, and one of them was even pregnant... I mean, what's a guy to do?" He smirks.

"Luke," I bark. I know I sound testy, but I really do want to go home now. Except I have to stop off at the hospital, which is why I'm being so cross with Luke... it's not his fault.

"Okay, okay. They were keen, and interested in the products, but they queried the lack of names and identities for the range."

I'm confused. I thought these women would understand. "What do you mean? The brand has a name. You explained that this is completely separate from Inspirit? That this is a whole new venture for us?"

"Yeah, I went into the background of the company." He sounds impatient. "I told them that sportswear has been our thing for over eight years, but we've branched out because—"

"Tell me you didn't give them too much detail about the new fabrics?"

"Matt, what do you take me for? They signed the NDA before we even gave them the brief, remember?"

"Yeah, sorry."

I can tell from the look on his face that he knows I've got a lot on my mind... He doesn't say anything else for a few seconds. "Look," he continues, "I know you think I'm just here to check out the talent, but I spent a lot of time this afternoon speaking with Grace. Jenny contributed as well, but it was mainly Grace doing the talking. If you want me to be honest, I think she's the brains behind the outfit. I explained the concept of the lingerie range without giving too much away, but Grace's point was that Amulet, while being a separate company from Inspirit, only applies in name to the brand and that the ranges should all have a complete identity of their own. She understood that each range will be named after a gemstone or mineral, but she didn't think that was enough. Everyone does something like that. She'd come up with some concepts and designs, showing an individual identity, logo, layout, color scheme, and so on, for a couple of our styles. They're good – really good. I know this would mean a lot more work for them, so they might just be trying to increase their own pay check, but it seemed like a good suggestion to me." He looks pleased. "It sets us apart. We've got all the names for the first season's ranges mapped out, but we hadn't thought of them each having an actual design and recognizable identity of their own. I left the meeting feeling really inspired by Grace's ideas. I tell you, Matt, these two women are bright, they took everything on board and, to be honest, I thought their concept was worth considering."

I think about it for a second or two. "Hmm. They sound like they've really thought it through."

"They have. Plus, they're talented, the designs are amazing; and they're women… and, let's face it, we're surrounded by men – mainly suits – most of whom are so mired in checks and balances, they wouldn't know one end of a crotchless thong from the other."

"We don't make crotchless thongs, and we never will but, apart from that, yeah, I hear what you're saying. They give us a different perspective. But then, why do you think I selected their agency from all the others? They're in London for Christ's sakes. I could have made life a lot easier for both of us by choosing a Boston-based, or at least US-based organization, but I liked the idea of having a team of women working for us on this. I also liked the fact that a European point of view might give us something else over our competitors," I explain.

"Well, it seems as though you might be right."

"I really hate the fact that you're surprised by that. So, is everyone who works there female? Aren't there employment laws against that?"

"Who knows? Frankly, who cares. Jenny and Grace are the only full-timers and they own the business, so I guess that's how they get around it. Everyone else is a freelancer, but Grace assures me that they only employ women."

He yawns and I decide to take pity on him. It's eleven-thirty in London, but he's been awake for so long, he's probably lost count of the hours. "Go to bed, Luke," I say. "I'll meet you at the hotel on Monday morning."

Grace

Why, oh why did I think it was a good idea to drive into London on a Friday afternoon? Well, I know why, of course – because we had to meet Luke Myers and because Jenny's ankles are swollen and she didn't want to chance the tube, but the traffic has been dreadful all the way from the South Bank to Richmond. I've dropped Jenny at her house and it's quietened down a bit now I'm on the motorway, probably because I'm a good hour behind my normal schedule. It's raining, just lightly – that annoying rain, where the windscreen wipers squeak with each swipe, but you still have to use them, because if you don't, you can't see properly.

I sigh, wishing I could delay my journey, find a reason not to go home. Jonathan is due back from a seminar in Dublin and, as always, when he returns from time away, the thought fills me with fear. It's not tonight I'm dreading... it's not like it used to be. He'll be tired, so he'll order an Indian take-away, open a bottle of wine and crash out on the sofa. Tomorrow morning will be completely different. It always is. I shift in the seat, anticipating his complaints, the blows, the pain, the usual excuses. There's nothing I can do about it. It will be the same as it ever is.

Changing lanes to overtake an articulated lorry, I turn on the stereo and select a CD. Oh...How ironic is that? I've chosen Adele's *Rolling in the Deep*, a song which Jenny has been humming to herself all the way out of London. It's a song she's been singing and whistling to herself, on and off, since it came out. It's an obsession. An annoying one. Today, I've let her off this disturbing habit, because today has been a good day for the two of us – a very good day. Jenny and I have been worried for some time; business has been dropping off and, for the first time since we started Richards Cole Design, nearly five years ago, we've been wondering if we did the right thing, leaving our jobs at big London agencies, and setting up by ourselves. We have a few loyal customers, but this contract from Amulet to design and build a website for their new lingerie range is going to save our bacon. We decided not to celebrate tonight, but to save it for next week, once the contract is signed – we don't want to jinx the thing when it's so close we can almost taste it.

The meeting went well with the American, Luke Myers. He was just how I'd imagined he'd be from our phone calls and emails: tall, attractive and flirty. But, he seemed to like our ideas, despite Jenny's fretting that we were overstepping the mark by making suggestions, rather than just sticking rigidly to the brief. They want to employ us because we're women, so I figured we'd give them our opinions – except Jenny's one that women don't always like wearing thongs that actually split you in half when you sit down, and that sometimes sensible cotton knickers are just more comfortable. I wasn't sure a manufacturer of luxury lingerie would want to hear that. He made lots of notes about the comments we did put forward though and, hopefully his boss, Matt Webb, will like the ideas too. Oh well, we'll find out when we meet him on Monday afternoon, I suppose.

I pull off the motorway and head towards Ascot. Our house is just outside the town. I say 'our house', but it's Jonathan's house really. I've been married to him for four years, but I still consider it to be his house, because it is. He bought it around eight years ago, I think, two years before he even met me. It's his style, not mine and very little of what's in the house belongs to me, or is of my choice. I'm not complaining; I've learnt not to.

I turn into the driveway, noticing out of the corner of my eye that there's a police car – a Range Rover – parked outside the house opposite. Because the road is so narrow, it's parked very close to Nathalie's front hedge. I hope everything's okay with her. Her husband left her about six weeks ago, clearing out their personal bank account and winding up his company at the same time. I know he'd been suffering from depression, and I really hope nothing bad's happened. I park up. Jonathan's car isn't on the driveway, but he's probably put it in the garage. He's very precious about his beloved Porsche. I grab my bag and walk up to the front door, putting the key into the lock and only then hearing the footsteps behind me. I turn round just as I'm twisting the key and see the two police officers, one male and one female, standing a few feet away from me. I wonder if they've come to ask for my assistance with Nathalie. Maybe they're wondering if, as a neighbour, I can help them out…

I smile and open my mouth to speak, when the the male officer says, "Are you Mrs Cole?" I nod my head. "Your husband is Doctor

Jonathan Cole?" I nod again. "Would you mind if we come inside?" he continues, not taking his eyes from mine. The look he's giving me doesn't make me think of Nathalie any more.

I open the door and step into the house, bending automatically to pick up three envelopes that are lying on the floor. They're all addressed to Jonathan. The two officers follow and I close the door behind them. The three of us stand awkwardly in the large, empty hall, dominated by the ugliest abstract painting which hangs on the far wall, until I remember my manners and usher them into the enormous sitting room, turning on the wall lamps as we pass through the entrance. Soft light bathes the room, which is almost entirely white, except for the accents of dark grey. On Tuesday, I bought some bright yellow roses, which are in a glass vase on the coffee table. Jonathan will hate them, but I needed something to brighten up the drab room. They'll be dead soon anyway.

"Please, have a seat," I say, putting the envelopes on the table next to the vase. I'm surprised by the echo in the room. Does it normally echo like that? Or have I just never noticed it before?

"Thank you," the female officer replies and, after they've both sat down, their dark uniforms contrasting with the stark whiteness of Jonathan's huge sofa, I take a seat on the small, bloody uncomfortable, designer chair opposite them. She looks at me. "I'm afraid we've got some bad news," she continues and turns her head towards her colleague. I do the same.

"It's your husband," he says, still looking at me with eyes which I can now see are a brilliant blue. "I'm afraid he's been in an accident."

I feel a strange sensation running through my body. "What happened?" I ask, going to get up, expecting them to tell me which hospital he's in, and maybe that they'll take me there in the Range Rover.

"I'm afraid his car was involved in a collision on the motorway... with a petrol tanker," the officer is saying, although his words start to merge and mingle, and I sit back in the uncomfortable chair again. "There was an explosion." I hear the word 'explosion' and I know. I know he's dead. They don't need to tell me. "I'm afraid your husband didn't survive." He tells me anyway.

They're looking at me with pity on their faces, which feels odd. I'm not sure how I feel, but I certainly don't deserve their pity. I stare into the empty void of the room, at the numb blankness of my life. Is this really how it's supposed to feel when your husband dies?

Chapter Two

❦

Matt

This feels kind of like déjà vu, except now I'm knocking on Luke's hotel door, instead of pressing a button on my iPad. The net result is just the same, though... total silence. We definitely arranged to meet here; I know we did. He messaged me his room number to save time, so I know he's meant to be here. I've called his cell three times and sent five text messages, and here I am still, standing in the hallway, hammering on the door. It's already gone eleven o'clock, and our appointment to sign the contract is at two-thirty... and where the hell is he?

I'm about to give up and go check with reception whether I've somehow got the wrong room or something, when the door cracks open and he peers out.

"Jeez, Matt," he says, drying his hair on a towel, while another hangs from his hips. I glare at him. "What's the damned door ever done to hurt you?"

"It's not the door, Luke. It's you." I barge past him into his room. "We arranged to meet up this morning, remember? It's now after eleven and you're still not even dressed."

"We're not due in Richmond for over three hours. It'll only take an hour to get there – tops. Just chill."

"Why haven't you answered my calls, or my messages?" I flop down in the chair by the window. It's uncomfortable, really uncomfortable, at least it is for a guy my size.

"My battery died." He looks sheepish.

"You have your charger, don't you?" He nods. "Don't tell me, you switched it to silent." He doesn't reply. I just look at him.

On reflection, this chair's too uncomfortable to sit in, and besides, I think I'd rather stand and intimidate Luke more effectively. I'm a little taller and slightly broader in the shoulder than him and right now, I feel like using those advantages. I'm just getting up again, when I hear a noise, like something being dropped into the bathtub, coming from the closed door on the opposite side of the room. I look across at him. "Please tell me that isn't what I think it is."

"That kind of depends what you think it is..." He's grinning at me now, but I can't grin, or even smile, back.

"Luke..."

"I know, I know." He's trying to sound placatory and it's not working. I'm really not in the mood for this.

I stand and cross to the door which leads out onto the very familiar hallway. "Get rid of her," I say, between gritted teeth. "I'll meet you downstairs in the bar." I glance at my watch. "In fifteen minutes."

As I open the door, he mutters, "We couldn't make it thirty?"

"No!" I bark back at him. As I turn to look, he's smiling and holding up his hands in surrender to my foul mood.

"What's really wrong?" he asks, taking a sip of coffee.

"I don't need this, Luke."

"What? What am I doing that I don't usually do?"

"Nothing, I guess." I sigh.

"Maybe you need to get laid too."

"I have." *Just not very recently.* And suddenly we're being a little too serious... too personal.

"Yeah, right. You need to let up on yourself; remember that you were the victim. None of it was your fault, Matt."

"I'm *not* a victim." I go to get up, but he grabs my arm and drags me down again.

"I didn't say you were 'a' victim, but 'the' victim. There's a difference." I think about what he's said, but it doesn't make sense.

11

Nothing that Luke has said on this subject for the last two years has made sense; not to me, anyway. I know he means well. It's not his fault if I can't get my head around it.

"Sorry," I say and and I mean it.

"No, I'm sorry." I know he means it too. "If you're not ready, you're not ready."

"It's not that," I say quietly. "I'm just..." What's the word I'm looking for? Scared? No. I was, but after two years, and a few out of character, meaningless one night stands to prove a point to myself, I realise I'm not scared any more. I'm done with scared. Now I'm... waiting. Waiting for someone who's worth taking that leap of faith with. I don't want casual or meaningless anymore. I want special. And until I find that special someone, I'll keep waiting. "Can we talk about something else?" I say. "Tell me about Grace and Jenny."

"You've read their website?"

"Yeah, so I know the official story."

He shrugs and takes another sip of coffee. "Well, I don't know much more."

"Okay, so they went to art school together, they're both in their late twenties?"

"I think they're twenty-eight."

"And they started their company about five years ago?" Luke nods. "That was quite young..."

"Says he who started his business at the age of twenty-two." He has a point.

"They've done some fairly prestigious work, but looking at their client list and portfolio, nothing really big for the last twelve months or so."

"Sounds like a reasonable assessment."

"Do you think we're taking a risk putting our business with them?"

"If I hadn't met them, I might think so, but now I don't. Grace Cole, in particular, is exciting to be around."

"How many times, Luke..." The warning tone is in my voice again.

"Not like that. I'm capable of thinking about women professionally, you know… well, sometimes." He smirks. "And besides, I told you, she's married."

"Definitely off your radar, then."

"Yep. I'm never breaking that rule. No woman's worth the hassle."

"And Jenny Richards… she's pregnant?" He nods again. "How pregnant? I mean, if she and Grace are the only two permanent employees, is she going to disappear to be a mom, and will Grace be able to handle everything on her own?"

"I asked that question myself." He looks pleased with himself. "Bet you didn't expect that, did you? Grace was very reassuring. I know it could be bullshit, but I don't think so. She was… genuine. I can't think of a better word to describe her."

My stomach is still feeling as turbulent as the last hour of my flight in from Boston, so I order a salad for lunch and manage to eat a little of it while I watch Luke consume a steak and fries, which would probably look and taste delicious, in normal circumstances. However, at the moment, nothing is very appealing.

I'm surprised that I start to feel better once I've eaten and, after another coffee, we catch the train to Richmond. This morning's storm has passed and the sun has come out, and although it's cold, we walk the short distance from the train station to their offices.

The street we walk along is filled with shops – mostly chains, although there are some independents too – and lots of coffee shops. A mix of old and new buildings, it's quieter than central London, and there's a really relaxed feeling about the place. Halfway down the street, we take a right turn and at the end we come out onto a small green, surrounded by leafless trees. Grace and Jenny's office is off to our left.

Set above a delicatessan, the entrance is at the side of the building and, once we've been buzzed in, we climb some narrow stairs, at the top of which we're faced with two doors, one to the right, marked 'Reception' and another which leads to a hallway. We take the door to the right, which opens into a bright, airy room with a huge picture window. There's an old wooden desk facing us, a few pieces of paper scattered untidily across its surface and, along the wall to our right, there's a large couch, which looks like the most comfortable piece of furniture I've ever seen. It's worn, and soft and has deep red covers, and I'm tempted just to launch myself at it and lose myself in blissful sleep… it would sure be different.

On the wall above it are three photographs of a wooded park, filled with trees, taken at dawn, I think, with a mist rising; one featuring a deer, which seems to be looking straight at the camera. They're breathtaking images in a simple but beautiful room and, I'm surprised that, considering we're in an office, it feels more like a home.

We stand and wait, but no-one comes – although they must know we're there, since someone let us into the building. I look at Luke, who shrugs his shoulders. After a minute, maybe a little more, the door on the far side of the room, next to the couch, opens and a pregnant woman appears, with a cell phone clasped to her ear. She's quite short, with blonde hair, tied up in a pony-tail, and no make-up. She's wearing black leggings and a big chunky blue sweater, with a pretty pink scarf tied around her neck. She smiles at us, but it's not hard to tell she's either been crying, or is suffering from a severe lack of sleep – or maybe both. Her eyes are red-rimmed and she looks pale. I glance at Luke, but he just shakes his head and we wait.

"I know, but there's really nothing I can do right now," the woman says into her phone, and waits while someone speaks. "Well, fine. If that's your attitude, so be it." She hangs up the phone and flings it on the desk, leaning over it for a minute before looking up at us. "I'm so sorry," she says and her eyes are filled with tears. It's hard to know what to do, so we do nothing. She sits down in the chair behind the desk, and waves in the general direction of the couch, which we walk over to, and sit down on, waiting. "Mr Myers," she continues, then looks at me. "Mr Webb?" I nod. "I tried calling you, Mr Myers. All morning."

"Oh," Luke replies. "I'm afraid my battery died."

The stare she gives him makes me wonder if my face had looked like that a few hours ago.

"Is there a problem… Mrs…?" I ask.

"Sorry…" She gets up again, comes over and holds out her hand to me. "I'm Jenny Richards. Please call me Jenny."

"Nice to meet you, Jenny." I take her hand and shake it gently. She seems as though she's about to break, so a soft touch is probably best. "Has something happened?"

"Yes, I'm afraid so." She goes back to her seat, flops into it, crosses one leg over the other and, weirdly, takes off her shoe and starts rubbing her foot. "I'm sorry," she repeats, and tears start to well in her eyes. What the hell is going on here? Where's her business partner and why is she leaving this poor, clearly upset, pregnant woman to deal with everything? I'm starting to dislike Grace Cole and I haven't even met her yet.

"Is there anything we can do to help?" I ask, uncertain what I think we have to offer.

"Oh… sorry…" It's almost as though she'd forgotten we're still here. "No, there's nothing."

"Why were you trying to contact me?" Luke asks, seemingly as interested as I am in finding out what's behind her strange behaviour.

"I needed to cancel today's meeting. If I'd been able to get in touch, I could have saved you the trouble of coming out here."

"But why do you need to cancel?" I ask.

"Because Grace isn't here," she replies. Now I'm even less impressed. Okay, so I suppose she might be sick, but… "Her husband was killed on Friday." Shit. That'll teach me to judge someone… As she says the words, a single tear falls onto her cheek. "I feel really bad for messing you around like this, but I did try to call."

"It's my fault," Luke says.

"I'm so sorry." I speak at the same time. I get up and go over to her, taking a handkerchief from my inside jacket pocket and handing it to her. That's one of the few things useful things my mom drilled into me: always carry a clean handkerchief. A very practical piece of advice for a mother to impart to her only son. Jenny smiles up at me, taking the handkerchief, and at that moment, the door through which she entered opens again and a man, wearing jeans and a check shirt appears.

"Jen," he says, not looking up from the tablet in his hand, "I've got no idea what I'm doing with this thing." She smiles at him just as he looks up and notices us, then turns to see her with tears in her eyes. "Hey, come here." He throws the tablet onto the couch, next to Luke, and takes the few strides to lift her into his arms, holding her head against his chest and smoothing her hair with his hand. He's much taller than she is and she fits neatly under his arm. It's an intimate scene, in which we feel like intruders. He pulls back slightly and looks down at her. "It's all a bit too much, isn't it?" She nods and he turns to us. "I'm sorry, gents. I'm Dan Richards, Jenny's husband." While keeping one arm around her, he holds out the other to shake hands with me and Luke, who gets up from the couch and comes across to join us. "I assume Jenny's told you?"

"About Grace's husband, yes," I say, still feeling a little stunned.

"How did it happen?" Luke asks.

"A car accident... It's awful, really awful. He was a doctor – well, a surgeon. A bloody good one, too."

Jenny's nodding her head. "He... He was such a lovely man, so kind and considerate, so good... with his patients."

"He and Grace were really close," Dan adds and Jenny starts crying again. Dan holds her tighter.

"How is Grace?" I ask.

"She's in a daze, really," Dan replies. "I don't think it's sunk in yet."

It feels awkward encroaching on their time. They've obviously got a lot to do.

"We'll get out of the way," I say. "I can see you have enough to do without having us here." Jenny looks up, a little startled.

"Would it be possible to re-arrange your meeting for another day?" Dan asks. "When things are a bit less stressful?"

"Yes, of course," I say, without even thinking.

He gently lowers his wife back into her seat, kisses her forehead, and goes back to the couch to pick up the tablet. "I think there's a calendar thingy of some kind on here," he says. Luke goes to stand next to him and touches an icon, bringing up the calendar app. "Well, that was easy!" Dan smiles. "What day is good for you?"

"We have to go to Milan on Wednesday," I reply, thinking as quickly as I can, "but I can come back here on Friday, just for the day – if that works for you. Luke will have to stay on in Milan, but I was planning on heading back to Boston then anyway. I can divert here first and then I'll go home on Saturday, if you're okay with seeing me on Friday?"

Dan looks at Jenny and she nods her head. "I doubt Grace will be back at work by then, but we can get her to sign the contract in advance, if you don't mind. We'll take you out for dinner, if you have time?" I can't help but like this man and I nod my head.

"I'll e-mail you once I've confirmed the flights." I think through altering my plans. It'll be okay. I'll make it okay.

On the train back to London, I turn to Luke. "Are we making a mistake continuing with them? We can't afford to go wrong on this... Should we just have walked away?" I ask.

"I have no idea. You were doubtful before, but with Jenny being pregnant and Grace now grieving for her husband, it could be an issue placing the contract with them."

"Yeah, but pulling out now seems like a real shitty thing to do."

"Well, I guess you've got the week to think about it. If you still feel doubtful, you might just have to pull out... shitty or not." He pauses for a long moment. "What about your mom? I know you wanted to get home on Friday."

"I'm only delaying by one day. It won't matter."

I turn and look out into the darkness, seeing myself reflected in the smeared glass. As usual of late, I don't like what I see. But for the first time in years, I'm not pre-occupied with my own problems, my failings or disappointments. It makes a change.

Grace

I feel guilty about missing Monday's meeting with the Americans, but there just seems to have been so much to do. In fact, I feel as though

I've have spent the last few days on the phone, talking to various people I've never even heard of before. It's actually quite pleasant today to be driving up to London to see Jonathan's solicitor. He called me yesterday afternoon, saying he needed to see me and, being as he had a free slot this morning, and I was desperate to get out of the house, we arranged that I'd come up to his offices in Hammersmith, near to the hospital where Jonathan worked. It seems odd to think that tomorrow will be Friday again and Jonathan will have been dead for a week already, and so much has changed in that time, including the flowers that Jonathan would have hated, that adorn the living room, sent by patients and friends... Sometimes compassion and kindness are the hardest emotions to accept and I've found myself curling inwards just to avoid the reality of having to question my reactions to other people's sympathies. Because I do question them, all the time.

Sitting across from him, Malcolm Anderson is younger than I'd expected. On the phone, he'd sounded about fifty, but he's probably only around thirty-five, quite short, maybe only an inch or two taller than me, with blond hair. His eyes are pleasant, and kind, although once we've shaken hands, taken our seats and the tea has been brought in, he keeps them focused on the file in front of him.

"It's very good of you to take the trouble to come up here, Mrs Cole," he says.

"It's no problem."

He coughs, and I sense a rising awkwardness. "This is a little unusual," he begins. "Normally, I wouldn't read the will of a deceased client until after their funeral, but in this instance, I'm obliged to make an exception." He coughs again and takes a sip of tea from the bone china cup beside him. "Your husband," he continues, "made a new will, just over a year ago."

This is news to me. "I didn't know."

It's as though I haven't spoken. "I am the sole executor," he says, "and he made a very particular request, that on his death, his ashes were to be scattered on a beach in Wales..."

"Wales?" I splutter.

"Yes. At a place called Llangrannog, to be precise."

"Why?"

"He didn't specify a reason." He turns a page of the document in front of him. "Moving on to the specific provisions," he continues. "This is very awkward… Your husband left his entire estate to Miss Beth Jameson."

"Beth?" I recall the theatre nurse who's worked with Jonathan on and off for the last three years. She's been to the house a few times, and to various parties at the hospital that I've attended. He's never shown, or expressed any particular interest in her.

"Yes."

"Why?" To me, it's the most obvious question.

"I can't say."

Can't or won't, I wonder, but I don't comment.

I sit staring at the man, not knowing what to expect next. "I'm afraid, Mrs Cole, that this will include the property in which you are currently residing."

"You mean…? You mean I'm being turned out of my own home?" *Jonathan's home, Grace… It was never yours, remember?*

"Well, Miss Jameson has kindly said that she won't be asking you to leave immediately. She's suggested a three month period for you to find somewhere else to live…"

"How generous of her." I can't help the sarcasm.

He ignores it, and me. "There are the other two properties to be dealt with as well, although I believe she's thinking of keeping one of them, to live in herself."

"What other two properties?"

"Your husband owned a flat in London and a house Wales."

Wales again? "I had no idea."

Once more, he doesn't comment on my remark. "So, shall we agree on the sixteenth of May as a date for you to vacate?"

"I'm sorry… do you mean to tell me I have no rights whatsoever."

"Under the terms of this will, no. You can contest it, of course."

I stand abruptly. "No. I won't be contesting it. And don't bother with the three months' notice either. I'll move out at the weekend, then she's welcome to his bloody house. She's welcome to all of it."

I turn and storm out of his office, not looking back.

I've ended up at the hospital where Jonathan used to work. It's not by accident either. I want answers.

"Can you tell me where I can find Michael Williams?" I ask the lady on the reception desk.

She looks at her computer screen, taps a few keys and says, "He's on the fourth floor. Radiology."

He's the only one of Jonathan's friends I can think of asking any of the questions that are rattling around my head.

The lift takes ages to get to the ground floor, and then a crowd of people get off before I can enter and press the button for the fourth floor. At the reception for radiology, there's a lady booking in for a scan and once she's moved away to the seats to wait, I ask to see Michael.

"He's in his office," the lady says. "Do you have an appointment?"

"No. I'm… I'm a friend."

She raises her eyebrows, noting my hesitation.

"Well, if you give me your name, I'll call and let him know you're here."

"Can you tell him Grace Cole is here to see him. Tell him it's about Jonathan."

"Very well." She looks like she thinks I'm wasting her – and his – valuable time, but she makes the call, listens and then replaces the receiver.

"He says he'll be out in a minute." She nods towards the chairs in the waiting area and I thank her and go and sit down.

It's actually nearly ten minutes later before I look up and notice him standing in front of me.

"Grace," he says softly. Right from the beginning, I tried to get along with Jonathan's friends, sometimes to my cost. Michael is one of the few I wasn't accused of sleeping with at some point during our marriage. I stand and we shake hands before he guides me into his office.

It's a fairly standard hospital room, with a wood veneer table, an examination couch, a comfortable chair for him and two uncomfortable ones for his patients. The view out of the window is dull. It's started raining again.

"How are you?" he asks, sitting opposite me. In his late forties, he's tall, probably best described as lanky, and has a full head of steel-grey hair.

"I'm… in shock." I think it's the best way of describing my current state of mind.

"That's hardly surprising. I mean, it was—"

"I don't mean that," I interrupt. He looks confused. "Well, obviously Jonathan's death was a shock," I clarify, just to be polite, "but I've just come from his solicitor's office."

"Oh, yes?"

"Yes. Did you know, he left everything: the house… well, his houses… his money, all of it, to Beth Jameson."

"Oh."

"Oh? Is that all you can say?" He doesn't reply, but starts to fiddle with a pen on his desk. He knows something and he's trying to work out how to tell me. "What is it?" I ask eventually.

He sighs. "There's no easy way to say this, Grace, but Jonathan and Beth… They'd been having an affair for over two years."

Well, that explains a lot. "So? He had affairs all through our marriage. Lots of them." He winces at the harshness of my tone and words.

"She was different, Grace."

"How?"

"He fell in love."

I laugh. The feeling is quite frightening, because I'm suddenly uncertain if I can stop. "Love?" I manage to say, "Jonathan? Don't be ridiculous."

"It's true. I'm sorry, Grace… but… Beth's pregnant."

I stare at him. "Pregnant?" I whisper. He nods. "With Jonathan's baby?" Even I can barely hear my own voice. He nods again.

"I'm sorry," he repeats.

"How pregnant is she?" I ask. I wonder if maybe it's a recent thing, if maybe he might have been trying to persuade her to...

"I'm not sure exactly. I think it's due in the spring... May, perhaps?"

So, she's about six months pregnant, then... I stand, surprised that I'm not more shaky on my feet. He gets up too.

"Are you alright?" he asks. "Do you want me to do anything?"

"No, I'm fine." I go to the door, then turn back to him. He's still standing at his desk, staring at me. He doesn't know what to say and neither do I, so I open the door and leave.

Chapter Three

Matt

The walk to Grace and Jenny's office isn't anywhere near as pleasant in the darkening rain. Nonetheless, I ignore the row of cabs lined up outside the station because I want to check in with the hospital to see how my mom is doing. When I get through, the nurse is abrupt – they usually are, I've found. But the news is essentially 'no change', which is a good thing. My mother would regard it as yet another failing on my part if I missed her death. I bought an umbrella at the airport, so I'm not drowned, but I'm feeling about as gray as the weather by the time I arrive and I'm still no further forward with my thoughts about the contract I might be about to sign. I'm let in by Dan, who's waiting for me at the top of the stairs, so I leave my dripping umbrella at the bottom, and join him.

"I'm sorry to get here so late," I say as I reach him. "The flights out of Milan were a bit limited. I'd hoped to be able to fly out this morning, but there was nothing available."

"Don't worry about it. We're in the meeting room today," he says, shaking my hand. He takes my coat, and disappears into the reception just for a moment, returning empty handed.

"How is everything?" I ask.

"A bit better than it was." He opens the door which leads down the corridor and allows me to pass through. "Keep going to the end," he says, following me. There's another door straight ahead, and I move down, passing a small kitchen and the men's room on the way. I open the door and step inside to find Jenny sitting at one end of a large rectangular wooden table, the grains on its surface giving away its age. She stands as I enter and reaches over to shake my hand.

"Thank you so much for putting yourself out like this," she says.

"It's really not a problem." I sit on the chair Dan offers, with my back to the door. The chairs are ladder-backed, with really soft cushions covering the seat. They're surprisingly comfortable.

"Would you like tea or coffee?" Dan asks.

"I've never acquired a taste for tea, but a coffee would be great." He leaves the room and returns a few minutes later with a tray, containing three cups on saucers, a cream jug and a sugar bowl. Handing me a cup, he offers the cream and sugar, but I decline. I've always preferred black coffee and I take a sip. It's delicious and strong, which is just what I need.

"How are you?" I ask Jenny, hoping she won't object to the intrusive question.

"I'm okay." She smiles. "I'm really sorry about the other day."

"You've got nothing to apologize for. I can't imagine how difficult it's been."

"Well, it's nothing compared to how hard it's been for Grace," Dan says, sitting opposite me and adding three spoons of sugar to his coffee before stirring it. "I went to see her on Wednesday. She's signed the contract, but she was rushed off her feet dealing with people, and she was having to go and visit Jonathan's solicitor yesterday, although she hasn't told us yet how that went."

"Yes," Jenny continues. "She's putting a brace face on it, keeping busy, but it's only because it hasn't hit her that he's never coming back. I think after the funeral will be the worst time." I hear the crack in her voice as she finishes her sentence. She still seems very upset.

"When is—?" My question is arrested by the opening of the door behind me and we all three turn. I hear Jenny gasp and Dan leaps to his feet. I get up as well, automatically, but unlike Dan, who moves forward, I stand still and stare and I know I'm staring, and there's damn all I can do about it. The woman who has just entered the room is breathtaking. I think she's very possibly the most beautiful creature I've ever seen. What am I saying? I don't *think* anything. There's no doubt about it. She's tall, but not too tall. She's wearing a soft, knee length dark gray sweater-dress, which clings where it needs to, with a v-neck, above which hangs a delicate silver necklace. Her mid-brown, shoulder length hair curls delicately around her face, with whiskey colored flecks that catch in the light. Her skin is flawless and fair, and she has high, delicate cheekbones and perfect, full lips, touched with just a hint of dusky pink gloss. But, even as I take in all of that with little more than a glance, it's her eyes that really grab and hold my attention. Some people might call them hazel, but they're not. They're honey-brown: sweet and rich, warm and – I have to admit it – incredibly sexy... They're the kind of eyes...

"Grace..." Jenny says and suddenly I'm back in the room and I don't know how to react. Have I really just been checking out a woman whose husband died a week ago... a week ago today?

"Yes?" Her voice is gentle, like the breath of an ocean breeze. *Seriously? Cut it out, Matt.*

"What are you doing here?" Jenny sounds a little cross.

"Um... working? Look, I know I said I'd take a couple of weeks off, and I know I've already signed the contract, so I didn't have to come in today, but I was up here anyway..." She pauses. "I had some things to take care of." She glances at me. "I'm so sorry," she says, "I haven't introduced myself. I'm Grace Cole."

"Matt. Matt Webb," I reply, holding out my hand. She takes it and I feel her smooth skin, her long fingers gripping mine firmly, and a bolt of electricity passes through me... It's all I can do not to shudder. *Enough, already.* I turn and pull out the chair next to mine, and she smiles and sits. As the corners of her mouth turn upwards, I notice there's just the hint of a sparkle in her eyes and I have to remind myself to close my mouth before I sit down next to her. There's probably about a foot between us, but as I resume my seat, she twists toward me and her dress rides up fractionally, so I can see just a couple of inches of leg, and that's it… I'm hard… I'm bone hard. *Oh, get a grip, man.* I haven't reacted to a woman like this since… well, since forever. How inappropriate am I being?

"Would you like a coffee?" Dan asks her.

"No, thanks, Dan." She turns to him. "That's very sweet of you, but I'm fine."

"Why are you up here?" Jenny asks.

Grace stills. I sense this isn't a question she wants to answer in front of me. "I… I just had some things to do," she says.

"Like what?" Is Jenny really going to push this? It feels insensitive, and Grace looks pained.

"I'm really sorry," I say. "I'm exhausted after my flight, and we've still got the contract to go over…"

"Yes, yes, of course," Jenny sits up straight. She hands me a copy of the contract and I take another glance at Grace as I turn over the first page. She's looking down at her hands, which are clasped in her lap. I notice they're shaking. Whatever's wrong, it's obviously something that's affecting her deeply. I wish I could take her hand again, but this time to comfort her, to let her know it will get better… eventually.

We start going over the details of the contract and, within a few minutes, Grace joins in the conversation and any doubts I might have had on Monday soon disappear. That's got nothing to do with her sad, beautiful eyes, or her gentle smile, but everything to do with her ability to do the job I'm asking of her. Yes, she's stunning, but she really knows her stuff and I like that.

Jenny is nervous about the payment terms – that much is obvious from the way she keeps avoiding it, and changing the subject whenever we get onto finances – but it's fine and I tell them so. They've asked for interim payments, which is understandable for a small outfit. They can't afford to wait until the end of the project to get paid. I get that and I'm okay with it.

"I'll have my finance people send you the necessary forms." Grace looks at me, puzzled.

"What forms?" she asks, a frown settling on her face.

"You need to fill in some forms for the IRS… The Internal Revenue Service? In the US?" She's still looking a little bewildered. "It's not a big deal," I say. "It's just a formality, but we're not allowed to pay you unless you've completed the forms. It's to do with taxes… so it's very boring, but really not that hard. It won't take long and as soon as it's set up, we'll make the first payment." I smile at her, trying to look suitably reassuring that we've done this before, which we have, numerous times.

She smiles back and seems to have relaxed a little. I guess she's got a lot on her mind, and doesn't need any more obstacles in her life.

Once the contracts are signed, she gets to her feet and says that she's tired and she's going home. We all rise too and Dan offers to drive her back to her place, but she's adamant that he and Jenny need to take me out for dinner, as planned.

"I'm fine," I say. "I'm a big boy. I can look after myself." *What the hell made me say that?*

She smiles again. "Honestly, I just want to go home, sort out a few things and then take a long soak in the bath." *Oh, I really wish she hadn't put that image in my head…*

"Are you sure?" Dan asks.

"Absolutely." She turns to Jenny. "I'll call you later," she says.

They hug, then Grace turns back to me and shakes my hand, telling me she's looking forward to us working together. Then she's gone and the room seems suddenly duller, but maybe that's just because it's completely dark outside now… *Yeah, of course it is.*

I let myself back into the hotel room. Dinner with Jenny and Dan was good. We went to a really nice French restaurant by the river. The food was great. Jenny was a little quiet but Dan and I talked about his business as a property developer, the state of the economy in the US and the UK, the sportswear business, sports in general, but not Grace. Maybe she's one of those people who keep themselves to themselves. I can relate to that and, after everything that's happened to her, she's entitled. As much as I want to know more about her, I'm glad her friends respect her privacy. And anyway, I'd like to find out about her more directly… by getting to know her for myself.

It's not too late, so I call Luke on his cell and, for once, he sounds like he's alone. I tell him that the contracts are signed.

"You're okay with using them then?"

"Yeah. I feel better about it now I've met Grace."

"She was there?" He sounds surprised.

"Yes. A little warning might have been nice, though."

"Warning about what?"

"That she's so… so beautiful."

"Why, what did you do? Oh God… Look, I know you're out of practice, but don't tell me you were drooling. It's very undignified for an adult male to actually drool. You know that, don't you?"

"Shut up, asshole. I wasn't drooling, but I did have to keep telling myself that she's recently – very recently – widowed."

"Was that before or after you fell over your own tongue?"

"Piss off, Myers."

Grace

The drive home is dull. It's stopped raining, but it's getting misty, so I'm going slowly… or is that just delaying the inevitable? There's still more packing to be done. I started last night when I got back from London and I should be able to finish most of it tonight, with any luck, but I'm exhausted. Sleeping on the sofa doesn't help, but I can't bring myself to sleep in any of the bedrooms. There are bad memories in all of them.

As I pull off the motorway, I think about my disastrous morning. I drove up to Richmond to have a look at a flat I'd found on the Internet. It was the only place available online that I can afford, and it was awful. It was so damp, there was water literally running down the wall of the bedroom. The problem is, I think I'm going to have to sell my car, so I need to find somewhere fairly close to the office, or at least commutable by train, so I spent the next few hours trawling round local estate agents, but most of them just looked down their noses at me when I told them my budget. I need to do some more research, maybe have a look at other areas and see if there's anywhere cheaper, but not tonight… I can't face anymore tonight. I make my mind switch off from thoughts of Jonathan, Beth and my current predicament and focus instead on this afternoon's meeting. Matt was nothing like I'd expected. But then, what had I expected? He's strikingly tall. I'd say he's probably six foot six, with broad shoulders and a muscular build, which made it hard not to notice how his light grey suit fitted him so perfectly. He's got short, dark, dishevelled hair and a lovely, warm, kind smile that touches his grey eyes, and I guess it's that warmth and kindness that surprised me the most. I suppose I thought he might be a bit angry with us for re-arranging the meeting, and having to divert his flight home, but he was really considerate and sensitive, especially when Jenny was being so intrusive. Why did she keep pushing me like that? And in front of a client… it was very unprofessional.

Jenny phones at ten-thirty. I knew she wouldn't be able to wait until I called her. It's been a busy evening. I've finished packing my clothes and personal items and found some boxes in the attic, and started packing my books. I can do the rest in the morning. I'm not taking anything else. While I've been packing, I've made the decision to give up searching for somewhere to live for the time being. I'll stay in a hotel for now, and deal with it all next week, after the funeral. It'll probably make a huge dent in my credit card having to stay at a hotel, but what else can I do? I certainly can't stay here.

"What's going on?" she asks, not bothering to even say hello first.

"It's a long story."

"Well, I've got a hot chocolate and my feet up, so fire away."

So, she's set up, all nice and comfy and expects me to just unburden, even if I don't really want to… marvellous. Does it never occur to her that I might not want to talk? "It's the house," I say. I'm sitting on the sofa, sipping wine from a plastic cup. I bought the wine on the way home, together with a microwave lasagne, which I ate from the carton. For some reason, using anything that belongs to Jonathan – well, Beth now – feels wrong. I'll throw the whole lot in the bin when I'm finished.

"What about the house?" she presses.

"I have to move out."

"Why?"

"Because it's not mine."

"I don't understand."

"Jen," I say, trying to sound calm. "I don't really want to talk about it, but Jonathan didn't leave me the house… or anything, for that matter, so I've got to leave."

"What? Now?"

"I'm going to move out tomorrow."

"You can't… I mean, where will you go?" I tell her my plans between sips of wine. "Sod that," she says. "Come here until you get yourself fixed." It's kind of her, I know it is, but do I really want her asking questions and interfering all the time? Do I have a choice? I might need my credit card for the deposit on a flat… if I ever find one.

"Are you sure?" I've asked the question before my brain has even had time to process the potential pitfalls.

"Of course. Dan'll come down and help you move your things in the morning."

"Shouldn't you check with him first?"

"He'll be fine."

Jenny has a knack of organising the people around her and Dan tends to just fit in with her plans. I think it's easier that way. No, that's unfair of me. He loves her very much.

"Okay… as long as you're sure. It'll just be until I find somewhere."

"I can't believe he did this to you. It's so unlike him."

Really? You think so? "It was a shock when I found out yesterday, but now I'm not even that sorry. I never liked this house anyway."

Chapter Four

Matt

I've run my fingers through my hair so many times, I know it'll be standing on end. It's never usually that tidy, but after the workout I've given it these last few hours, it must be a mess. I don't care though, because I'm beyond frustrated. I look at my screen again and raise my right hand towards my head before lowering it again. I can't blame my hair for the problem, so it's no use doing it any more damage. I get up and cross to the full-length window, and look out over the skyline. My office has a spectacular view of the Charles River, and the glittering water ripples in the early-April sunshine.

I hear the door open behind me. Only Luke would enter without knocking first.

"What's up?" he says, coming to join me.

"What makes you think anything's up?"

"Your hair for one thing." He raises his eyes to look at it and smirks.

I don't bother to smooth it down, but turn back to my desk. "It's these layouts Grace has sent through." I sit down and he comes to stand next to me.

"The logo designs were really good, so what's wrong?"

"The website just isn't working out how I thought it would." I scroll through the pages.

"That one's not bad." He points at the screen and I stop.

"It's not quite there, though, is it? It's like she hasn't quite got the feel for what we want."

"Have you tried speaking to her?"

"We've been sending e-mails back and forth for the last month, ever since we approved the logos for the ranges, but…"

"Ever heard of the telephone? It's a fairly new device… allows you to communicate directly with a person in another place, using speech…"

"Luke, you are a prick sometimes."

"Call her, Matt – better still, FaceTime her. If you can see her reactions to what you're saying, you might understand each other better." He pauses just for a second. "Besides, it's been, what… a couple of months since you set eyes on her? Go on, man, you know you want to…" I don't look up, but I know he's grinning. He moves around and sits opposite me. "Give yourself a break." His voice is suddenly serious. "It was over two years ago…"

I don't say a word, but lower my eyes, staring at my desk.

"Okay, I'm not going to talk about it," he continues, "but you need to stop being so hard on yourself."

"Even if that were true – and I'm not saying it is – are you actually suggesting that I should go after Grace? Her husband's only been dead for seven weeks."

"I wasn't counting." He goes silent for a minute. "Maybe the timing is a bit wrong, but what you've been doing, shutting yourself away… it's unhealthy… and it's not like you. You did find her attractive, didn't you?"

I nod my head, unable to deny to myself or my oldest friend the effect Grace had on me, or the fact that I haven't been able to think about much else since meeting her.

"Doesn't mean she wants anything to do with me though, does it? She might find me abhorrent."

"Yeah, I know. That happens to you a lot, doesn't it?"

"We only spent a little over an hour together. We know nothing about each other."

"There's only one way to fix that…" He leans forward. "You need to move on, Matt… properly."

I look at him and realise he's right. "Okay," I relent. "I'll arrange to FaceTime her."

"Today?"

"I don't know. I'm in meetings until four and she might have plans this evening." *I hope not.*

"And she might not." He gets to his feet and walks to the door, turning back right before he opens it. "Just one thing though…" he pauses to get my attention. "Do something about your hair before you speak to her. She'll be able to see you too and right now you make a scary picture."

She connects straight away.

"Hi." Her voice is just as soft as I remember. The picture delays for a couple of seconds while it focuses in, and then I see her and it takes me a moment to realise I need to stop staring, start breathing, and speak.

"Hello," I say. "How are you?" *Lame, Matt, real lame.*

"I'm okay."

"I'm really sorry the call has to be so late."

"That's fine. It's only just after nine here."

I glance behind her and notice the photographs of the park hanging on the wall. "Are you still at work?" I ask, before I can stop myself.

"Yes, but it's okay." She smiles, and leans over to her right, picking something up from the floor, I guess. "I have wine." She holds up a glass to me before taking a sip.

"Lucky you. What is it?" I ask.

"It's a Verdicchio. Nothing expensive, but I like it. Actually, this one's really quite good…" She's looking at the glass. "It's light… a little bit of almond, a little bit of citrus… very drinkable." Always a good quality in wine, I've found. She seems to know what she's talking about. Am I intimidated? Hell, no. Am I impressed? Maybe… Just a little. "Do you like wine?" she asks, and leans over, presumably to place the glass on the floor next to her again.

"Of course." I smile. "But it's a little early still here." And I raise my coffee cup just to prove the point.

"Oh dear. Well, I think I've got the better deal."

"Undoubtedly."

She sits back, and the light shifts, making her hair glow, highlighting the different shades of russet and caramel.

I'm distracted. "Those photographs," I say, trying to take my mind off her hair, and her eyes, "I noticed them when we came to your office the first time. They're beautiful." *Like you.*

"I took them a couple of years ago," she says. "Very early one autumn morning."

"You took them?" Now I'm even more distracted.

She nods her head. "Photography is a hobby. I'm nowhere near good enough to be called professional."

"I beg to differ. Seriously, Grace, they're good." She looks embarrassed. "Why black and white?" I ask, so she can talk, rather than feeling awkward.

"It's more atmospheric, although the one with the deer does look good in color too."

"I'd like to see it… if you don't mind."

"I'll look out the original and e-mail it to you."

"Thanks." We stare at each other for a moment.

"So, these designs," she says and I drag myself back to reality.

"Yeah." I glance at the print-outs which I've spread across my desk. "They're so nearly there," I say, "but…"

"There's something missing, isn't there?"

"You knew?"

"Yes. They don't feel right to me either, but I had to send them across, or you'd have thought we'd been sitting on our hands doing nothing all this time, but I'm not happy with any of them." She looks away and I can hear a rustling of paper. "The fourth one," she says. "The one with the feathered background…"

"Yeah. Luke and I thought that was closest to what we're looking for."

"But it's still not right." She leans forward again, resting her chin on her upturned hand. I want to reach out and run my thumb gently along her bottom lip, and it's so close, I almost could, except she's three thousand miles away and the image before me is just on a screen. She'd be able to see me do it too and I'm sure she'd wonder what was wrong with me… if I'm as crazy as I'm starting to think I am.

Grace

I knew the designs were wrong… and now I'm wondering if it was it a mistake to send them. Usually, if I'm not happy with something, I work on it until I'm comfortable and then I let the client see it, but this time, I've gone back and forth, over and over, and nothing's been quite right. It's not like I've been that distracted. Okay, living with Dan and Jenny has been tense at times, mainly because Jenny won't let up with the questions and comments about Jonathan, but I've found a flat now, although it took longer than I'd hoped to finally find something within my budget, and I'm moving in this weekend. Despite all that, staying at their place had its advantages; I've spent more time at work, just to avoid going back there in the evenings, so, if anything, I've been more focused than I have in years. Still, no matter which way I looked at it, the designs haven't been working for me, So, I talked it through with Jenny yesterday, and we decided to let Matt and Luke have a look.

"Maybe it's an American-British communication 'thing'," Jenny suggested and I wanted to believe her; believe that maybe we were reading too much into the brief and they'd be overjoyed with what we've produced. I've never worked with a client I've known so little about, and that could be part of the problem; I don't know Matt's tastes. I know nothing about him. Perhaps that's why I sent the designs over… to get some feedback; some idea of what he does and doesn't like.

At this point, I can't imagine he likes me very much. I'm being very unprofessional. I haven't said anything in a while and now he's looking at me as though I've completely lost my marbles. Or maybe he thinks I'm drunk. Is that why he asked about the wine? It's my first glass, and

I've only had a couple of mouthfuls, so I'm still sober – sober enough to know I'm stuffing this up royally.

If I'm not careful, we're going to lose this contract and, probably, our business with it. The man is kind, patient, considerate... but he's got a company to run and he needs his website designed and built by the end of July. It's already the first week of April.

"You got all the samples, didn't you?" I hear him ask.

"Yes, we've had them for ages. They're lovely." I don't mention that there was no way either Jenny or I could try any of them on, if that's what had been intended. Jenny's obviously a little too pregnant, and I'm not a US size four – which is what all the samples were – not even in my wildest dreams.

"But they didn't help?" he asks and I focus in on him again.

Clearly not. "They should have done..."

He's shaking his head. This is not good.

"Give me a minute," he says and disappears from the screen. Where's he gone? I can hear something in the background and it takes me a moment to work out that he's pouring liquid. He must be getting another coffee. I'm not being dismissed just yet, then. While he's gone, I take another gulp of wine and replace the glass out of sight just as he sits down again. "Sorry," he says, "I need the caffeine."

"No problem." I don't know what else to say except, 'I need the alcohol', but that's probably unwise. I feel as though the ball's in his court. He has the power to keep us on, or fire us now and find another agency, while he's still got time.

Meanwhile, we're sitting, thousands of miles apart, connected by technology, neither saying anything. Should I offer to step down? Can we afford to do that? Will Jenny kill me? Very probably. But do I care...?

"I have an idea." His voice cuts through my thoughts.

"Hmmm?" I can't even form words now and my hands are shaking. Thank goodness he's not here with me. *Please, just don't fire us.*

"Would it be possible...?" He hesitates and I wonder what he's going to ask. He's staring at me now and I can't help but stare back, directly at his mouth. It's distractingly perfect... I wish he'd just ask the question, whatever it is. Put me out of my misery. He shakes his head just a little. "Would it be possible," he repeats, looking down at something on his desk, "for you to come to Boston?"

Oh. I didn't expect that. It takes me a few moments just to gather my thoughts. "Come to Boston?" Dear God, now I've turned into a parrot.

"Yes, you see, I'm thinking that you could meet Paul, our designer, see the design process, and look around the factory if you want. I can arrange a showing for you, so you can see all the ranges on actual models, rather than just the photographs and samples we've sent you. These are completely new fabrics, Grace; it's a whole new concept and I'm wondering if I've not given you enough to work with."

He's blaming himself? I don't feel happy about that. "This isn't your fault, Matt. If I'd felt I didn't have enough of a brief, I could have... well, I *should* have told you."

"That doesn't matter now. The point is, can you fly over here?"

Can I? I think about it... We're not exactly rushed off our feet. Jenny has just completed a brand identity for a client of hers, and no doubt we'll wait ninety days or more to get paid for that, as usual. There are a couple of brochures to finish off, but other than that, we're light on work – except for Matt's business. He's been paying us regularly, so we can just about afford the air fare, and Jenny can hold the fort, as long as I'm not away for too long. She gets easily tired these days. "I'll have to check with Jenny," I say, "but it should be fine. When do you want me to come?"

There's a moment's hesitation. "As far as I'm concerned, you can come whenever you like," he says. Is it my imagination, or did his voice just get a little deeper, and did the corners of his mouth turn up, just a fraction? No, it must have been my imagination... or maybe it was the connection.

"Well, I'm moving into my new flat over the weekend," I say. "Can I e-mail you on Monday and confirm a date?" Do I need a visa? I have no idea. I'll check that out before I message him. He nods his head.

"You're moving? Really?" he asks. He seems surprised.

"Yes."

"You're selling up?"

"Er… No." Now he looks confused. Do I want to explain? Well, maybe some of it. "It's complicated. The house isn't mine. Jonathan's house, that is. It never was really, but in his will, he left it to… someone else, so I've found a little flat near the office, which I'm going to rent. Dan is helping me move in there tomorrow."

He looks even more confused. "You don't think…?" He starts his sentence and then stops abruptly and I can tell from the expression on his face that he wishes he hadn't begun.

"Think what?"

"Nothing."

"No… go on."

"It's just that they say, when someone dies, you shouldn't make big decisions too quickly afterwards… Couldn't you arrange to hang on a bit longer, rather than doing this so soon? I'm sure whoever owns the house now would understand."

I want to laugh, but I'm scared that if do, my laughter will turn into hysterical tears. I shake my head. I can't tell him that his suggestion would mean staying on in what is now my late husband's mistress's house. But more importantly, neither can I tell him that this is the first step in restoring myself, piece by piece, because I haven't told anyone that yet. I know it will take a long time – maybe a lifetime, and maybe I'll never be completely whole again – but I refuse to be defined by what Jonathan did to me. I won't give him that final victory, so I'm making a start, because every journey has to begin with a first step.

"I'm so sorry, Grace," he says when I don't reply. His voice has such sincerity that it almost hurts to hear him speak. "It's none of my business."

"No," I manage to say. "Don't be sorry. I can't explain it at the moment, but this is the right decision. I'm doing the right thing. I know I am."

"I hope so. I really hope so," he murmurs and I catch something in his eyes, right before mine blur.

"I'll speak to Jenny," I mutter, looking down so he can't see my face. "And I'll e-mail you once I've got a date to come over."

"Okay. Look, I really am sorry," he says. "I didn't mean to intrude."

"You didn't. I'll be in touch." I hold up my hand in a kind of wave, but really I just want to hide my face as I disconnect the call, before I embarrass myself. Tears stream down my cheeks but it's not because I'm sad. It's because a man I spent roughly an hour with a few weeks ago, has shown more kindness to me from three thousand miles away, than my husband did in the entire six years I knew him.

Chapter Five

Matt

After the FaceTime call ended the way it did, I'd fully expected Grace to e-mail me and tell me she couldn't come after all. I had expected her to use Jenny's pregnancy as an excuse. I felt like such a jerk. She was clearly crying, and I was to blame for being so insensitive. If it wasn't for the fact that she'd have thought me even more of an idiot than she probably already does, I'd have jumped on the next flight to London, just so I could say sorry properly. She was obviously pleased to be moving home and I questioned her decision. What's it got to do with me anyway? It seems odd that her husband left his house to someone else, but I know sometimes families can be weird – look at mine. Maybe he was forced to leave his property to some distant male relative or something. Stranger things have happened and it's not my business to pry.

I was so relieved when she sent me a message the next day, attaching the photograph we talked about. She's right, the colors are incredible, but I agree with her, the black and white version has more atmosphere. My relief was complete when, on the Monday after our call, she sent another e-mail to say she'd be flying in today, and waiting a little over two weeks to see her has just heightened my anticipation. We've e-mailed since, and phoned. In fact I often find an excuse to contact her, but there have been no more FaceTime calls and the image of her eyes, filled with tears, has haunted me since that day. As her visit has gotten closer, I've found myself growing more and more impatient to see her again.

I decided as soon as I heard from her and got her flight details that I'd drive to Logan and pick her up myself. She's landing at one-thirty, so I figure I'll take her for a late lunch and apologize in person for upsetting her. I'll need to leave at about twelve-thirty to allow for traffic and parking, so I brought forward our sales meeting to ten, to make sure it's over by twelve.

Just as everyone is filing out of my office, my cell phone rings and I glance at the screen. "Shit." It's the hospital.

Luke is standing in the doorway and stalls, turning to face me. He ushers everyone out, then closes the door and comes back, standing in front of my desk as I connect the call.

"Hello? Matt Webb speaking." I listen. *Why? Why, today of all days?* "Okay, I'll be there as soon as I can." I hang up the phone.

"What's happened?" Luke says.

"That was the hospital."

"Your mom?" I nod. "Is she...?"

"No, not yet."

"But they think she might...?"

"They think it's quite likely." I glance at my watch.

"Go," he says. "I'll collect Grace." I'm still torn. I could make it to the airport and drop her at her hotel, then go over to the hospital. I could do that, couldn't I? Of course I couldn't. I'd be failing in my duty. I grab my jacket from the back of my chair. "Is she booked in at the Summers?" Luke asks as we both head for the door.

"Yeah," I snap. I'm borderline angry, but it's not his fault.

"I'll check her in and let her know you'll pick her up for dinner." I look at him. "Whatever happens, you've got to eat, Matt – you may as well eat with her."

It's at times like this, I remember why he's such a good friend.

The journey to the hospital is slow, but I'm in no rush. I think I'd almost be relieved to get there and find I was too late. Considering that my mother was at death's door nearly three months ago, she's hanging in there. And meanwhile, my life's on hold, as I visit her every night after work. I'm aware that sounds heartless, mean, ungrateful… but then I've met my mother.

When I arrive, I'm buzzed into the reception. This is a very expensive private hospital; they don't let just anyone in here. I walk down the wide, thickly carpeted corridor to my mother's room, wondering what I'll find. The door is open and there's no-one attending to her. She seems to be asleep, so I sit and watch her. She's sixty-five, I think, but she aged a lot when my dad died nearly three years ago. Really, at her age, she should have years left in her, but cancer has taken its toll. It was a heart attack with my dad and the irony of both of those facts is that my parents have always been incredibly healthy. Neither of them smoked, or drank, they exercised and ate well. Maybe it's that thing called Karma…

She opens her eyes and turns her head to look at me and I see the disappointment before she even speaks.

"Oh, it's you," she says.

"Hello, Mother." I don't stand. I don't hold her hand, or lean in and kiss her. Why would I? The woman has never shown me an ounce of affection in my life.

"Where's the nurse?"

"I don't know. Do you want me to go and find out?"

"No, don't bother." *Why ask, then?* "Why are you here in the middle of the day? Shouldn't you be working?"

"They called me, Mother. Told me to come in."

"Oh. Yes… I was feeling very poorly this morning. I suppose they thought…" She turns to look out the window. "It's sunny again."

Seriously? They got me down here so I can discuss the weather with her? When I'm done here, I'm going to find whoever's in charge. I can't keep doing this.

"Look, if…" I begin.

"While you're here," she interrupts, "there's something I want to talk to you about." I know precisely where this conversation is going and I wish I'd gone with my first instinct of picking Grace up at the airport, rather than coming here. "You know what your father always wanted."

"He got what he wanted from me," I say, not disguising the bitterness.

"That was just business – a business which you nearly ruined with your fooling around." Oh, she had to bring that up, but then she never fails. She takes a deep breath. "You know there was always more to it. Your father didn't live to see it happen... I'm still here."

"Mom... What do you expect me to do? They gave you two months to live three months ago." The words are blunt, but true.

"I want the same as your father wanted." Her lips form into a thin line.

"That's not possible and you know it."

"Why?"

"Because I can't grab a woman off the street and marry her, and somehow miraculously produce a son and heir in the next few days, or weeks, just to please you. Even if I could, you still wouldn't be satisfied, because any woman who'd make me happy wouldn't be good enough for you."

"Are you trying to tell me that, at the age of thirty, there isn't a single woman in your life?"

I don't reply for a moment, thinking of Grace's tearful, beautiful, honey-brown eyes. I don't want her poisoned by my mother's influence. "No, there isn't."

"And whose fault is that?" she spits. "If you weren't chasing around after models all the time... getting yourself in the press..." She starts coughing. I sit and watch her. "We introduced you to plenty of nice young women," she continues, once she's calm. "Surely..."

"Yeah, I remember them. All of them." I recall the parade of old money princesses my parents processed before me, none of them worth spending time with. I can't remember a single one of them who didn't bore me rigid from the moment we first met. None of them interested me, none of them made me smile for no reason, or made me want to fly three thousand miles, just to apologise for being a jerk. They didn't have eyes that sparkled, hair the color of leaves in fall, skin like delicate porcelain and lips so perfect I could…

"You're not concentrating, Matthew." No-one calls me Matthew, except my mother.

"I'm sorry."

"What for?"

"Everything. All my shortcomings." I know it won't be enough. It never is.

"All we asked of you was that you make a success of yourself in business, that you marry well and have a child."

"I achieved one of those things. The business is thriving."

"One out of three is not a great track record, Matthew." Her disappointment is palpable. She turns away again, waving her hand. "I'm tired now." And just like that, I'm dismissed from her presence.

Outside, I check my phone. Luke has sent a message to say that Grace is at her hotel and I'm meant to pick her up there at six. It takes away some of the sting of my mother's words.

As I get into the car, I call a little Italian restaurant I know, not far from Grace's hotel and book a table for six-thirty. The food there is great, but it's also quiet and that means we'll be able to talk.

I can't face going back to the office, so I go home, change into sweats and a t-shirt and go for a run.

Pounding the pavement in the middle of a Wednesday afternoon is a strange experience. But my mind is full of strange thoughts, so it feels appropriate. I wonder, not for the first time, why my parents bothered to have children, or a child, to be more precise – other than to 'carry on the family name', as if that was so great.

It was made clear to me from an early age what was expected of me: success in business, marriage to the 'right' woman, children – a dull carbon copy of my father. I met Luke at college and my parents most certainly did not approve of him, or his background, or the fact that he was a 'bad influence'. He showed me how to live a little, that was all. Of course, he lived a lot, and still does, but he's always been good at that. Don't get me wrong, I've had my fair share of women, at least until recently, but nothing like Luke, and nothing that's lasted.

I turn into Boston Common and slow down a little. Sitting on a bench is a man, with a little boy beside him – presumably father and son. It looks like the boy has fallen over and the father is comforting him. I never had that kind of intimacy with my dad. It's alien to me and I run on past, speeding up until I feel my heart hammering in my chest.

Grace is waiting in the lobby, wearing a knee-length fitted black dress, with short lace sleeves and a sheer lace panel at the bottom. I don't think it's a designer label – at least it's not one I've seen – and I like that. So many of the women I used to date spent their lives chasing the next fashion trend, and forgetting about what actually looked good and made them feel comfortable. She's tied her hair up loosely, but there are a couple of wavy strands hanging down, framing her face. She's not wearing much make-up and she looks… well, perfect. I force myself to move forward and accept the hand she's holding out toward me.

"Matt," she says, and her breath whispers across my nerve endings.

"Grace," I reply. How can one word, just one word from her lips, and the touch of her hand make me feel so alive? It's like coming into the light, after the darkness of my day… well, my life, of late. She shouldn't be able to make me feel this good, and every time I think about her, I have to remind myself that she's not available, not yet anyway. She needs time to get over the death of her husband. "Shall we head off to the restaurant?" I suggest, and she nods her head, smiling. Then, as she passes through the door that I'm holding open, her arm brushes against mine, and I inhale her scent. It's like I'm in a rose garden, on a summer's afternoon, and I know at that moment, with a startling clarity, that I'll give her all the time she needs, however long it takes, but that for me, the waiting is over. I've found what I've been looking for. I've found my special someone. It's a sobering, but strangely satisfying realization.

Outside, it's a warm evening. "The place we're going to isn't far. We can walk, if you like?" I offer.

"That sounds nice." She looks up. "Gosh... the buildings," she breathes, looking around and turning a full circle. Her face is radiant, excited.

"Um, what about them?" I glance upwards.

"They're so tall."

I laugh – I can't help it. She's cute. "Have you never been to the US before?"

"No."

"Well... welcome to America, Ma'am..." I put on my cheesiest accent and she giggles. It's a sound I haven't heard before and I like it. I mean, I *really* like it. A lot.

Grace

"How are the scallops?" he asks, just as I've put a piece of one into my mouth.

"Hmm..." I nod and make the right noises until I can swallow. "They're delicious. How's the ribeye?"

"It's good. But I eat here quite a lot, so I knew it would be."

I glance around the restaurant. The wall behind me is brick-faced, the one opposite is painted white, and dotted with framed Italian landscapes. The front and back walls are made of glass panels, but Matt told me when we arrived that, when it's really hot, they open these up, so the whole restaurant becomes more 'al fresco'. It's not busy, but not empty either, which is just how I like restaurants. There's nothing worse than being the only people in a place and feeling awkward, but I'm tired and really not in the mood for a noisy crowd. In fact, I'm so tired that I can't believe it's only just after seven o'clock and I have to remind myself that, for me, it's midnight. So I'd normally be asleep, not eating mouthwatering sautéed scallops. My eyes come back to rest on Matt. He's wearing a darker grey suit tonight which, I have to say, looks even better on him than the one he wore in London. From what I can see, his white shirt seems to cling to his broad chest and the mid-grey tie just kind of brings the whole outfit together. In the flickering candlelight, he looks... well... he looks gorgeous.

"How did the move go?" he asks.

"It went well. It was easy really. I had so little to take, Dan could fit it all into his car. Actually, I think my whole flat would fit into Dan's car if you put the back seats down." He laughs. "It's the tiniest flat ever, but I've got almost no furniture, except a sofa and a bed, so that's probably a good thing."

"It isn't furnished then?"

"No." I hesitate just for a moment. "This is a fresh start for me. I wanted to get my own things." Did I really just say that to him? I still haven't explained that to anyone else, but there's something about him that makes him easy to talk to. I wonder if it's his eyes...

"I can appreciate that." He finishes the last of his meal and places his knife and fork neatly on his plate, wiping his mouth with his serviette before placing it back on his lap. He looks across the table at me. "Sometimes you just have to do what feels right for you, don't you?" he says and he looks at me.

"Yes, you do." His eyes are shining, staring deep into mine. The moment is broken by the waiter coming to take our plates. He asks if we want dessert, but for once I'm too tired to consider anything sweet and we both just order coffee before the waiter leaves again.

"What made you go into lingerie?" I ask him. Matt is very masculine, and lingerie... well, isn't. I'm intrigued.

"We didn't start off in lingerie," he explains. "We started off in sportswear."

"Oh yes... I remember Luke explaining about that when we met him in London. Okay, so what made you go into sportswear?"

"I used to work out a lot – when I had more time," he says, smiling. "It used to annoy me that the clothing was always either comfortable and looked really bad, or the other way around."

"So you designed something that worked both ways?"

"Me personally? No. I'm just the money. But I met Paul – our designer. He introduced me to Josh, who creates our fabrics and we got talking… and it kind of built from there. The lingerie is a new thing, which developed by accident when Josh came up with our newest fabrics."

I twist my wine glass between my fingers. "I see. It sounds like you have a good team. So, how does Luke fit in?"

"Officially, he's in charge of our sales department. Unofficially, he's my right hand."

"Do you need one?"

He grins. "Quite often, yes. Usually when I don't even realise it. I guess it's like that with you and Jenny?"

"Sometimes." Even as I answer, I know that isn't true. It might have been a few years ago, especially when we were studying together, and when we first started the business. We were inseparable then, and told each other everything, but she changed not long after that, a few months before she met Dan. Or maybe it was me who changed. That probably makes more sense. After all, I was married to Jonathan by then… and that's when everything changed.

We leave the restaurant once Matt's paid the bill. He insisted, despite my protests. Outside, it's cooled off and I regret not bringing a coat, or at least a cardigan, but before I can even make a comment, I feel Matt's warm jacket being placed around my shoulders and I look up.

"Thank you, but won't you get cold?"

"No, Ma'am…" He's doing that dreadful over-the-top, drawling American accent again and I can't help but giggle as we start walking down the road.

Before we get to the corner, I feel something vibrating just below my left breast, and look up at him. "I think that must be your phone?"

He looks down at me and realisation dawns on his face. "Sorry," he says and stands awkwardly. He can hardly go feeling into the inside pocket of his jacket when I'm wearing it, so I reach in, find the phone and hand it to him, without looking at the screen. "Hello, Matt Webb?" he says, holding the phone to his ear, and I wander to the side of the pavement, looking in a shop window, to give him some privacy. "What, now?" I hear him say. There's an impatient tone to his voice, which I haven't heard him use before. "I came over earlier and she was fine." There's a pause. "Okay. Tell her I'll be there in an hour." He hangs up and, in the reflection of the window, I see him put the phone in his trouser pocket and look up to the sky, before he comes to join me.

I don't ask him anything – it's got nothing to do with me.

"Sorry about that," he says.

"Don't be."

"That was the hospital." I turn to look up at him, but I'm still reluctant to ask. "It's my mom." He gives the information freely.

"Oh, I'm sorry. I didn't realise she was ill." I feel guilty. I've had such a lovely evening with him. "But... what are you doing? You should be with her, not here with me." A strange look crosses his face. "Go," I say. "I can make my own way back to the hotel." I start to take his jacket from my shoulders.

"No way," he says, pulling it back into place. "I'm not leaving you here."

"But—"

"Come on." He holds his hand out and, after just a second's hesitation, I take it. His skin is warm and soft, but not too soft. "I'll see you back, then I'll drive over there."

"What's wrong with her?" I probably shouldn't have asked that, but... well, we've been talking openly all evening, so it feels okay.

"Cancer," he replies and I feel my throat closing.

"Oh." He stops in his tracks, pulling me up with him.

"What's wrong?" he asks. I can't look at him. I know the tears will be forming in my eyes and he's seen me cry once already, even if that was from a distance. I shake my head. "You lost someone?" he asks.

"My mum and dad," I croak out.

"Both of them?" he says and I feel his fingers squeeze around mine.

"My mum died when I was eighteen, a couple of weeks before I started at art school." I've found my voice again. "Dad went just a few months after Jenny and I started the business."

"I'm so sorry, Grace." There's that incredible sincerity in his voice again.

"I always felt it was odd," I say, not really knowing why I'm telling him this. "My dad was devastated when mum died. When his cancer was diagnosed, I always felt he was just hanging on until I got on my feet, till I was set up, and then he went to be with her again." The tears are back, but I manage to blink them away.

"It sounds like they were great parents," he says.

"Yes, they were. They were so happy; they appreciated every day they spent together, everyone around them, everything they had."

"You were lucky."

"Yes. I was, wasn't I?" I look up at him, but he seems very far away all of a sudden. "Is your mum…?"

"Dying? Yeah… Yeah, she is. She was diagnosed about three months ago, and told she had two months to live. Unlike your mom, she'd never win any awards for mother of the year, though." *Oh*. He's thoughtful… sad. I keep quiet. It feels as though he needs to talk, and me interrupting isn't going to help. We start walking again, more slowly. "Neither of my parents would have won awards," he continues. "They gave me strict instructions on how to live my life, but I gave up trying to please them years ago, when it finally dawned on me that nothing would ever be good enough, even if it was exactly what they were asking of me." He sighs and I'm scared to say anything. "Sorry." He turns to look down at me. "You don't need to hear this."

"It's fine," I say, leaning into his arm. He leans back, just a little. It's comfortable. I like it. "I take it your father…?" I'm not sure how to finish the sentence.

"He died nearly three years ago." He looks up at the sky again. "We had a strange relationship." He pauses. "My father was a very successful businessman, a self-made millionaire. We lived a privileged life; a huge house, holidays in Europe, servants. Hell, I didn't really see much of my parents until I was old enough not to be an embarrassment. But I was well educated – I'll give him that."

"And do you live like that?" I ask him. "In a big house with servants?" I hope he doesn't. It sounds so sterile.

"No. I live in a two bedroom apartment across the other side of Boston Common, opposite your hotel. I never wanted the kind of life my parents had. It doesn't mean anything... there's no substance to it." I can't help but smile.

"Anyway," he continues, smiling back at me, "when I graduated, my dad called me into his study and told me his plans, and it became very clear it wasn't something I had a choice about." He stops talking, just for a moment, I think to catch his breath. "He made me a loan of five hundred thousand dollars to start my own company. Can you imagine it? Five hundred thousand. I was twenty-two years old and, at the time, I was thrilled. I thought maybe this meant he did take me seriously after all. I wondered if he was going to help me build my business, mentor me, you know, like a proper father. I wondered that for all of about thirty seconds. Then, he pulled a contract out of his desk drawer… There were terms attached to the loan, you see." I look up into his face and, even in the street lights, I can see the hurt still lingers. I feel my mouth dry as I picture a younger Matt, still with slightly messy hair, those fervent grey eyes and strong jawline, full of enthusiasm and hope, having that sucked from him by an uncaring, cruel and vindictive parent. "The interest rate was pretty steep," he continues. "And I had to repay the whole sum within five years, or the company would become his outright." I hear myself gasp, even though I've been trying really hard not to react in any way. I'm not sure he's heard me though, because he just carries on speaking. "In the meantime, although I could choose what the company did, he had the final say on all major decisions... who I hired, how I ran the business. Once the loan was repaid, the company would be mine to do with as I pleased. I sensed all along that he anticipated failure, which just spurred me on to succeed." I want to say 'Good for you!', but I remain silent. "I worked…" he says, "I worked damn hard. I paid him back, in full, in eighteen months and the first thing I did once the company was signed over to me, was to hire Luke. I'd known him since college and my parents hated him just because he was brought up on the wrong side of town. A couple of years later, I made him a partner."

"What did your dad say to that?"

"We never spoke about it. Once I'd repaid the loan, we never spoke about business again."

"Isn't that a bit odd?"

"No. He resented the fact that I'd succeeded."

"But surely that's what he wanted, wasn't it?"

"No, I don't think it was. And as I got older, he especially resented that I was more successful than him… quite a lot more successful. You know, I think he really hated me for that." His voice is hushed, almost as though it's the first time the thought has registered with him. It's sad that he doesn't know how it feels to have that unconditional love from a caring mother and father. At least I had that.

"So, you and Luke own the company jointly?" I want to change the subject; keep it focused on him, not me, but take away that sad look on his face – if I can.

"No." He turns to me. "I have the controlling interest, but Luke has my back." He suddenly looks serious, like he's remembering something. "He's proved that more times than I care to think about, so I gave him a twenty-five per cent share. Like I said, he's my right hand. He may not be perfect, but his loyalty is second-to-none, always has been. I think that's the kind of thing that should be rewarded."

I realise all of a sudden that we've stopped walking and we're standing outside my hotel. *How long have we been here?*

"You should be going," I say. "Your mother will be wondering where you are."

"And you must be exhausted." He glances at his watch. "It's nearly one-thirty in the morning for you."

"That would explain why my head feels like cotton wool."

"I'm sorry I've kept you talking for so long."

I take his jacket from my shoulders and hand it back to him, my hand brushing against his chest. It's solid muscle and I shiver as I pull back, which must be because the chill night air is settling around me already. "You've nothing to be sorry for. Nothing at all. What time do you want me to come to your office tomorrow?"

"I'll pick you up," he says. "Say, nine-thirty?"

"There's no need to do that. I can get a taxi."

"No, it's fine."

"But what if… I mean… there's your mother to think about."

He hesitates for a minute. "If I can't make it, I'll get Luke to come, but I'll text you if there's a problem, and one or other of us will meet you in the lobby."

"That's very kind of you." We stand awkwardly for a few moments, but I'm really fighting sleep now and I'm starting to get cold. "Well, goodnight then," I say.

"Goodnight, Grace."

I'm just about to switch off the light when I hear the really annoying beep of my mobile phone, telling me I've got a message. I turn and take it from the bedside table. He's written:

— *I just wanted to thank you for tonight. Hope I didn't bore you too much. I had a great time. Thanks for listening. Sleep well. Matt*

Oh. He's so… I click in the message box and type:

— *I had a wonderful time too, thank you. Enjoyed listening. Hope your mum's okay. See you tomorrow. Grace*

As I'm about to replace the phone, I pause, press a few buttons and, without hesitating, select a ringtone for him. It's the perfect choice and, besides, I really hate that annoying beep. Then I turn over and fall straight to sleep.

Chapter Six

Matt

No-one except Luke knows the background to how I started my business, or about my dad's involvement, but for some reason it all just spilled out of me last night, and it felt good to tell Grace about it. The fact that we were holding hands, that she leaned into me and that she kept looking into my eyes might have had something to do with that. I also liked the fact that she seemed... I don't know... relieved, I guess, that I don't have the kind of lifestyle I was brought up into. That's not who I am, and I want her to see that. I want her to get to know the real me.

When we said goodnight outside her hotel, I really wanted to kiss her, but it's too soon, I know it is, and the last thing I want to do is scare her off.

I park up and walk to the hotel lobby, feeling like I've got a spring in my step for the first time in months – no years. *No, it's forever, and you know it.*

She's waiting, sitting in one of the chairs and, as she stands, I can feel the air being sucked out of my lungs. Will she ever stop doing that to me? God, I hope not. I've only seen her wearing dark clothes and I'd assumed she'd adopted some kind of mourning for her husband, but I guess that's just been the luck of the draw, in terms of her clothing choices, because today she's like sunshine. She's wearing a pale yellow dress, with blue flowers around the neck. It's nipped in at the waist with a narrow blue belt, then flares out into a full skirt, which shows off her perfect hourglass figure. She's left her hair long, touching her shoulders, again with just minimal make-up, and has a smart brown leather messenger bag over her shoulder. She smiles as I walk toward her.

"Good morning," she says.

"Hello." I want to tell her how beautiful she looks, but she might think I was being too forward. *One day, Matt, one day...* "Are you ready?"

She nods her head and I hold the door open for her. As she passes through, I notice that the back of her dress features a cut-out panel, showing a diamond of bare skin. I want to touch it, to feel her softness, and I run my hand across my chin, just to check I'm not actually drooling. As Luke says, it's very undignified.

My car is parked around the corner and, as I click the button on the key fob, I hear her gasp.

"This is yours?" She turns to face me.

"My one real luxury," I reply, going around to the passenger side and opening the door for her.

"It's beautiful." Her eyes graze over the bodywork before she lowers herself into the black leather seat. "A DB9," she breathes and I look down at her, still holding the door. "It's just my dream car, that's all," she explains, grinning up at me. I close the door and walk around to the driver's side... *Oh, how perfect is this?*

I climb in next to her and fire up the engine, revving it, then letting it purr.

"That sound..." she whispers.

"It's amazing, isn't it?"

"It's so nearly perfect." She turns toward me, smiling.

"Only 'nearly' perfect?" I pull out into the traffic. "What's wrong?"

"The color, of course. A DB9 should be gray, dark gray."

"So, dark red is no good, then?"

"If someone gave it to me, I certainly wouldn't give it back... but I might have to consider a re-spray." She's grinning so wide, it's hard not to join in and suddenly we're like two kids just out of school as I cruise down the street.

We're stopped at lights when I hear a female singing voice, coming from the footwell of the car. I glance at her and she reaches down. "Excuse me," she says and pulls her cell phone from the side pocket of her bag, cutting out the song as she connects the call. "Jenny?" she says quietly. "Is everything okay?" She pauses, then her face takes on a serious expression. "Okay. Sorry about that. Why didn't he just call me on my mobile? Well look, if he calls again, can you tell him I'll ring him when I get back. I'm sure it's not that urgent." She listens, then smiles. "Yes, that'll be fine, thanks... Yes... Of course. I slept like a log... It's amazing." She glances across at me. "And you won't believe this," she says into the phone, "but Matt's driving me to his office in his Aston Martin DB9." There's another pause. "I know!" She almost squeals the last word and, for some reason, I find myself puffing up with... what is it? Pride? Satisfaction? She giggles. "No, it's red, but you can't have everything. Look, I'll call you later... Yes, of course I will. Bye." She hangs up and puts the phone back in her bag.

"What was the ringtone?" I ask. I'm intrigued and, although I'm also curious about her conversation, and I'm dying to know who 'he' is, asking about that feels pushy. Besides, I'm just as interested in finding out about her tastes, musical and otherwise.

"It was *Rolling in the Deep* by Adele."

"And that's your ringtone?"

"Only for Jenny."

"You give people individual ringtones?" Now I'm even more fascinated.

"Some people, yes. Not clients, just friends, people I know well... or, um... who are important to me." Is she blushing?

"How do you choose the song? Or do your friends get to choose their own?"

"No. It's always my choice. Jenny's is because she's been singing that song for years now and, as much as I love Adele, you can have too much of a good thing. It's become a bad joke between us... hence the ringtone. Dan's is *Swing Low, Sweet Chariot*, because he's rugby fanatic and sings it all the time, especially when England are playing – well, whenever they're winning at least – which would be fine, except he's tone deaf. It's awful." She's smiling again. "Generally, I suppose they're just based on the person involved… something that suits them, or suits how I feel about them…" Her voice fades.

I'm dying to ask if she's set up a special ringtone for me, whether I'm 'important' enough to her, or if I fall into the 'client' category, but I don't because I think I'll be real disappointed if she says she hasn't.

"Did your husband have one?" *Oh, crap. Where did that come from?* I'm pulling into the parking garage beneath our offices. "I'm so sorry. You don't have to answer that. I shouldn't—"

"His was *The Winner Takes It All*," she says, her voice just a whisper.

I don't reply, because I don't know what to say. I can't remember the song, but I'll check it out later. I park the car in my space and climb out, without saying another word, then walk around to her side to let her out. As I take her hand and she stands, I just say, "Sorry," again, and she smiles up at me. I read a book once, years ago, where one of the characters was described as having a 'sad smile' and I've always thought that must be impossible… until now.

It's been a busy day for Grace. I introduced her to Paul and Josh and she spent a couple of hours with them, looking through the designs, getting a feel for the fabrics, while they explained how we developed them, without giving away any of the trade secrets. Then we ordered in lunch, and I showed her around the rest of the offices, so she could meet everyone. We decided to skip the factory. She didn't feel there was anything to be gained by going over there – apart from another ride in my car. She laughed when she said that, which was good and I think I'm forgiven for my thoughtless questioning this morning.

Now, we're in our showroom, and Melissa, Rachel and Crystal are showing off the different ranges for her to see. Grace is sitting beside me, with a sketch pad on her lap and a pencil in her hand, but the page is blank. I'm worried. This was supposed to help, but I'm not sure it is, and I'm concerned that I've upset her, reminded her of her unhappiness, her grief, and maybe that's why she can't focus. Melissa, who's been with us the longest of these three, and is a pretty redhead, with the most precocious three year-old daughter and a dentist for a husband, steps off the runway, wearing nothing more than a plum coloured bra and matching briefs, and comes over to us.

"This isn't working for you, is it, honey?" she says to Grace.

Grace looks up. "I'm sorry," she says. "It's not you. I'm just not…"

"You're not feeling it?"

Grace shakes her head.

"I've got an idea," Melissa says. "Give us a minute, boss?" She looks at me and I shrug and nod my head, wondering what she's got in mind. She grabs Grace by the hand and hauls her to her feet. Grace turns and places her pad and pencil on the seat, then follows Melissa to the corner of the room, where a door leads through to the changing area behind.

I've got no idea what Melissa's doing. After a few minutes, I get up and pour myself another coffee and go to stand by the window, gazing out across the city. Recalling this morning's conversation, I take my phone out of my pocket and go to my iTunes app. I search for and download *The Winner Takes It All*, which turns out to be by ABBA. I have a set of earphones in my office, so I go along and fetch them, plugging them in and setting the track to play as I walk back to the showroom. The lyric is utterly heartbreaking. Was this her marriage? Did he take so much from her? It sure sounds like it from this.

I'm feeling a little shocked as I pull out the earphones and fold them away into my pocket. I'd assumed she was happy with her husband, but this song tells a different story. Were they splitting up before he was killed? That wouldn't make losing him any easier, I guess, but it might explain the situation with the house, maybe?

Unless I'm reading too much into it, of course. It could be that it's just her favorite song, which means she'd naturally give it to the man she loves; or perhaps they heard it together somewhere and it kind of stuck, or they had their first dance to it. It's a weird choice for a first dance, but I've known weirder. *Dead Ringer for Love* springs to mind… but that was a very, very odd wedding all round, so Meatloaf and Cher kind of fitted in.

I glance at her bag, which is lying over by the chair. Her phone is still in the pocket and now I'm dying to know. Without considering the consequences of disappointment, I click on the 'phone' icon of my cell, and call up her details. It connects automatically and I wait a couple of seconds, until I hear the sound coming from her bag. What I hear is a melodic tune, classical and quiet... I'm not familiar with it and I imagine it's probably her usual ringtone, the one for clients and 'unimportant' people. I hear voices from behind the door and cut the call before Grace can hear her phone ringing, replacing my cell in my pocket.

The two women come back into the room. Melissa is now wearing a black silk robe, and Grace looks just as she did before. I'm confused and it must show on my face.

"Aw, bless him," Melissa says and she and Grace look at me conspiratorially. I feel at a distinct disadvantage. "He's just dying to know what we've done." Melissa leans into Grace. "It'd be fun not to tell him, but I just can't do it... He's way too nice. If it was Luke, I'd make him suffer."

I laugh. "Go on then, tell me."

"Grace is wearing items from the Onyx range." Melissa smiles. Grace is blushing, but the two of them are staring at me and I wonder if my tongue is hanging out. I bite it, just to be certain... nope, it's still firmly in my mouth. Of course, I have no idea which items she's wearing and I'm not about to ask. I've messed up too many times already.

As Grace climbs back into my car an hour later, I notice that she's tentative in taking her seat before settling in, but I don't know why. On the drive back to her hotel, she's quiet and I'm not sure what to say, just in case I say the wrong thing. I'm still confused about the ABBA track, wondering about her marriage, and – if I'm honest – a little disappointed that I didn't warrant a ringtone of my own.

We're sitting in heavy traffic when Grace's phone rings. It's the default ringtone, the one I use, because I've never been bothered to change it, and my mouth drops open. Before I can really process the thought, she answers the call and I notice her shoulders dropping and her whole demeanor changes.

"Yes, Malcolm," she says into the phone. Who's Malcolm? I'm guessing he's not a friend – he didn't get a ringtone, although I evidently did. I smile, but it quickly fades. Her voice sounds kind of weary, but business-like and clipped. Whoever this guy is, she's not keen to talk to him. "I know. Jenny called me earlier. I did ask her to explain to you…" She waits, her leg twitching. "Do we have to do this now?" she continues. "Well, I didn't pick up the messages because I'm not there. I'm in Boston." She listens for a few moments. "You're kidding me… No, of course you're not. Can I call you…?" She sits upright, listens for another couple of seconds and then says, "Okay, Malcolm. Stop right there… No. Don't bother." She's raised her voice. Man, she's mad at the guy. "I thought as he'd given them to me, they were mine to keep… but clearly not. I'll return them to you at your office as soon as I get back. I assume you can wait until then?" She pauses for a moment. "Good… Goodbye Malcolm." She disconnects the call and puts the phone down on her lap, resting her head back on the seat and breathing hard.

"I apologize for that," she says after a while.

"Hey, don't worry about it." I glance across at her as the traffic starts to move again.

"That was Jonathan's solicitor."

"I see." It's all I can think of saying.

"There's a problem with his… with his will."

"Oh?"

"Yes." She looks upset. "Do you mind if we talk about something else?"

"Sure. Where do you want to eat tonight?" She hesitates for a moment. "What's wrong?" I ask. Is she trying to tell me she doesn't want to have dinner with me? Has this Malcolm guy upset her that much? Or is it me? Is it one of my many misdemeanors that's caused a problem?

"Would you mind…" she says, and I grip the steering wheel a little tighter, bracing myself for the letdown, "… if we ate at the hotel?"

I wonder if she can hear me breathe out, if she notices my knuckles loosening. "Of course not, if that's what you want to do. I can come back around six?" She's due at the airport early tomorrow, so I'm assuming she won't want a late dinner.

"That sounds great. It's not that I didn't enjoy going out last night… and please don't think badly of me…" Is that even possible? "It's just…" What is she trying to tell me? "I was looking at the hotel's menu while I was waiting for you this morning, and they have the most amazing looking trio of chocolate desserts. You know, where you have three little tiny puddings, but they're all chocolate? Just looking at the photograph made my mouth water and I've been thinking about it all day." She pauses for a moment, a smile forming on her lips. "I mean… obviously I've been thinking about the project most of the time, but this is chocolate we're talking about…"

Her excitement is joyous. "I'm guessing you like chocolate?"

"Doesn't every woman?"

"No. My mom hates it. But then she would." I grin at her as I pull up outside her hotel.

Although it's only a few minutes' drive to my apartment, I'm not even halfway home when my phone rings, the boring, default tone, which makes me smile when I remember that Grace has given me a ringtone of my own, even if I don't know what it is. Without thinking, I press the button on the steering wheel to take the call.

"Matt Webb."

"Matt?"

It's Grace. Is something wrong? "Hi. Are you okay?"

"Yes. But you called me… earlier this afternoon? I've got a missed call on my phone."

Oh shit! "Um… yeah. Well, I did. It was a mistake." How pathetic do I sound? "I meant to call someone else, but I hit your number by accident." *Really?*

"Oh, I see. That's alright then. As long as everything's okay. I'll see you soon?"

"Yes. I'll be back at six."

Grace

I don't even know why I'm surprised. It's not like I was going to keep the bloody jewellery anyway, so what does it matter? It all dates back to before we were married, when he used to make gestures, buy me things, like expensive jewellery. It reminds me, for a moment of a time when I still had hope; before he took that from me, along with everything else. I'm not attached to any of it; I was going to sell it once I'd got a bit more settled into the flat, but I suppose it's the principle, really. Malcolm has told me, rather in the tone of scolding a naughty schoolgirl, that I shouldn't have removed any of it from the house. Jonathan kept the receipts and insurance documents, and valuations – he would – and I've got no proof, according to Malcolm, that any of it was given to me as a gift. I find it hard to believe that I have to prove it, but I suppose he's right. He is a solicitor, after all and I really can't be bothered to argue about it any more. Maybe it's for the best – one less link with Jonathan has to be a good thing, after all.

I'm going to do some work before I shower and change, while everything from today is still fresh in my mind... I think I've got a couple of ideas.

As I take my first mouthful of the chocolate dessert, I'm not disappointed. This one is a chocolate and Earl Grey mousse, with a cardamom sorbet on top, and I know really should open my eyes, but I just want to savour it, uninterrupted, for a moment longer. When I do look up, Matt is staring at me, a smile on his lips.

"Sorry, I can't help it. This is pure paradise on a plate."

"Good."

"Are you sure you don't want anything? I feel like such a pig sitting here eating this all by myself."

"I don't really like desserts, but I'm enjoying watching you." He takes a sip of his coffee and I dive back in to chocolate bliss.

"How can you not like desserts?" I ask, between mouthfuls.

"I guess I don't have a very sweet tooth. I've always preferred more savoury things."

"You don't even like chocolate?"

"Not really, no."

"Well, that is odd." I take another taste… It's so good. What's not to like?

When I've finished all three desserts and managed to avoid really embarrassing myself by actually licking the plate clean, I look up to find he's still watching me.

"I meant to tell you earlier," I say, placing the spoon down on the plate at last. "I'll get the hotel to launder this lovely underwear I've got on, and I'll get them to return it to your office tomorrow."

"Keep it," he insists.

"I couldn't. I know how much it costs."

"I'd like you to."

"You don't even know what I'm wearing. It could be the most expensive things in the range for all you know."

"I don't mind. Keep it."

"Thank you." I shift slightly in my seat and smile to myself. Jenny would be laughing her head off right about now. The thong is so comfortable, and nothing like her description. I've never worn one before, but Melissa sized me up with one glance, took it off the rack and handed it to me. She was being so friendly and kind, I would have felt foolish giving it back to her. She sort of made the assumption that I'd be familiar with wearing one. I suppose I also I wanted to see if Jenny was right, but despite feeling tentative when I sat back down at the office and then when I climbed into Matt's amazing car, I'm barely even aware I've got it on. Melissa explained while I was changing, that was why she wanted me to wear it for myself, so I could understand how different this underwear is to anything else. My experience with luxury lingerie is limited – actually, it's non-existent – but I can see what she meant. It's wonderful. But it's not quite as wonderful as that chocolate dessert. Matt is looking at me again.

"Do you have to dash off?" I ask.

"No, why?" He raises his eyebrows.

"Because I've been sketching out a few ideas since I got back. That's probably why I didn't have time to change. I got started, and the next thing I knew, it was ten to six, and I'd run out of time. I've got them here, in my bag." I reach down to pick it up.

"Why don't we have a drink in the lounge and you can show me in there?"

"Okay. It'll be more comfortable."

"You're not uncomfortable, are you?" There's a hint of something in his voice, but I'm not sure what it is.

"No, I'm fine." His lips curve upwards and I wonder, just for a moment, if he's thinking about the underwear. I remember Jenny's comments again and smile. If only he knew.

We go through to an enormous bar area and sit in a large red leather sofa. Matt orders a brandy for himself and looks at me. I just want a coffee. I'm flying home tomorrow morning; I can't afford a hangover. Once the waiter has delivered our drinks, I reach into my briefcase and pull out my sketch pad, flicking through the first three pages.

"That's it!" Matt suddenly says, leaping closer to me on the sofa and taking the pad in his hands. "That's exactly it!"

"It's hard to tell from a pencil sketch, but I think it's right too."

"Can you work this one up?" he asks, excitedly.

"Yes, when I get home. I'll do it as soon as I can and send through some sample pages."

"This is great." His eyes are alight and he stares at the page. "Thank you." He turns to me.

"You should really thank Melissa. If she hadn't come up with the idea of getting me to try on the products, and if I hadn't, therefore, realised how incredibly comfortable a thong can—" I stop dead. Did I really just say that out loud?

As if he senses my acute embarrassment, he looks back at the sketch and lowers the pad onto his lap. "Do you know what I like best?"

I clear my throat. "No, what?"

"It's not girly... the design, I mean. I didn't want anything overly feminine, or floral or frilly for the website. I like the fact that, while our products are really sexy, they're also very comfortable, so women want to wear them all day, every day, for themselves, not just to please a guy. And what you've done here, it kind of captures that."

We finish our drinks and it's still only eight-thirty, which feels a little early to say goodnight, or goodbye as it's going to be, since I'm taking a taxi to the airport in the morning, as Matt has a meeting.

"Do you want to go for a walk?" he asks, and I wonder if he can read minds.

"I'd like that." *I'd like that a lot.* "Can you hang on while I take my bag upstairs?"

"You can leave it with reception and collect it later," he suggests.

"Oh, okay."

We move out to the lobby and he takes my bag from me, handing it in to the man behind the reception desk.

Outside, it's chilly, but I've got a cardigan on, so I'm okay without Matt's jacket tonight. He takes my hand, just like last night, and steers me to the right and down a long street and, then left and, before I know it, we're at the river. We walk along the path for a while, until Matt stops and we lean against the railing, looking out across the water. The lights from the buildings on the other side twinkle on the inky surface of the river and it's magical.

"Can I ask you a question?" he asks, looking down at me.

"Yes." I don't even hesitate. *How odd.*

"The ringtones on your phone..."

"What about them?"

"When I called you earlier," he says, "your phone was in your bag and I heard it ring. It wasn't the default tone." I'm really glad it's dark, so he can't see me blushing. "Is that a ringtone you've set up for me?"

"Yes."

He pauses. "Okay... well, I understand Jenny's and Dan's..." He doesn't mention Jonathan's and I'm so grateful. I don't want to explain that. "But I don't even know what that piece of music is... the one you've chosen for me."

"It's Elgar," I say, swallowing hard. "It's called *Nimrod*, from his *Enigma Variations*."

"Why choose that for me though?" I can feel him looking at me, but I keep staring out across the water. I can't tell him why I chose it. That would mean explaining how important he's becoming to me and I'm not ready for that. Not yet.

"Would you... would you mind if I didn't tell you? At least not right now. I'm sorry, it's just..."

"Hey, it's okay. You don't have to tell me anything." His voice is gentle and kind, and he doesn't say another word, he just takes my hand and we walk along the riverside in the moonlight.

Chapter Seven

Matt

I've dropped Grace back to her hotel, and we said goodbye. Just like last night, I wanted to kiss her... well, actually, I wanted to do a lot more than kiss her. As it was, we shook hands. It wasn't anywhere near enough.

I'm still not ready to go home.

It's been a magical evening. Watching her eat that dessert was incredible... the expression of ecstasy on her face when she closed her eyes and took that first bite of chocolate... I want to see that look again, but I want to see it when she's in my arms, with my name on her lips.

As for discovering that she's wearing the Onyx thong... The thought of that tiny triangle of sheer black lace, barely covering her... well, let's just say I'm glad I was still holding her sketch pad and could move it to my lap to hide how my body responded to that image. I don't think she noticed.

Then, walking in the moonlight with her, looking out over the river. She looked so bewildered and sad, which is understandable, considering her husband's only been dead for a few months, but... I don't know, I thought there was more to it than that, especially with the way she reacted to my question about the ringtone... Or maybe it was just the moonlight, and the moment. Or maybe I'm reading too much into things... again.

I want to hear that piece of music properly. Even if she's not ready to tell me, I need to try and understand why she chose it for me, so I wander back to the river, to where we stood. Leaning against the railing, I download *Nimrod* onto my phone then plug in my earphones, turn the volume up and let it play. It starts quietly, but even at the beginning, I can feel something and I close my eyes, blocking out my surroundings, wanting – no, needing – to focus on it, to focus on her, on trying to work her out, on feeling her with me still. Slowly, relentlessly, the music builds. It fills me completely and I let it, and as it reaches its breathtaking crescendo, my skin tingles, I take a deep breath and I open my eyes to find the scene before me is a blur. I don't cry; I've never cried – not once – and I'm not actually crying now, but it's close. It's real close. I shake my head. It's just a piece of music… A piece of music that Grace – for some reason – thinks appropriate for me. I wish I knew why.

I let it finish, then I find the song that's been playing in my head ever since I first met her, the one I keep humming in the shower, in the car, when I'm running, cooking… lying awake at night, thinking about her. I listen to it and it's perfect. I have no idea how she made the ringtones for her phone, so I check on the Internet, download the first app I come across and create a ringtone for her. I want to know when she calls or texts; when she needs me. I want that link to her. I know what this song means to me, even if I don't know what *Nimrod* means to her. And I don't care if it's a little slushy and sentimental. She'll never hear it anyway.

It's been four days now since Grace was here and I've missed her. I've really missed her. I've called or e-mailed her every day, for one reason or another, mostly for no reason at all, other than the need to connect with her, but this afternoon, we're going to FaceTime. I'll get to see her and I'm childishly excited.

She smiles as soon as the connection clicks into place.

"Hi," she says. "How are you?"

I want to say 'better for seeing you', but I settle on, "I'm good, how are you?" *Very formal.*

"I'm okay. Did you get the designs I sent over?"

"Yes. They're perfect."

"So, we can start the build?"

"Definitely."

"Great." I notice that the background behind her is different. "Is this your new apartment?" I ask.

"Yes, would you like a tour?"

"Sure." She gets up, holding what I presume is her laptop, and turns it around, so I can see. Her voice is now disconnected.

"This," she says, "is the kitchen, living and dining room. I told you it was small." She wasn't kidding, either. It's tiny. The kitchen takes up one corner, with units made out of what looks like oak; there's a small table with two chairs by a glass door, which I presume leads either to a garden, or a balcony. On top of the table is a vase of flowers. The colors, even in the dim electric light of the late evening, are magnificent and I wonder who gave them to her. Before I can dwell, she turns, and I see a fireplace, with an array of candles in the hearth, a small sofa with a coffee table set in front of it and a TV. I'm guessing it's an older property, maybe in a converted house, or something like that. She sits down again and her face reappears on the screen, and I gather I'm not going to be allowed to see the bedroom.

"Nice flowers." Okay, I'm fishing, and I know it.

"Aren't they? I saw them in the market today, and I couldn't resist," she says, a smile crossing her lips. Why do I feel so relieved? *Like you don't know the answer to that one.* She seems happy, relaxed in this place. It suits her.

"You have a lovely apartment. It suits you." I've really got to stop my mouth from repeating my thoughts without filtering them first. I'm going to get myself into so much trouble.

"Thank you. I like it." She glances around her and her eyes shimmer.

"Are you going to be at your office tomorrow?" I ask.

She raises an eyebrow, seemingly confused by my sudden change of subject. "Um, Yes. Jenny's got a hospital appointment, so I'm in all day. Why do you ask?"

"I've arranged to have a small surprise delivered to you. I didn't have your home address, so it's being sent to your office."

"This sounds intriguing, although I'm not sure I like surprises…" Her voice is really sad.

"It's taken me a few days to organize, but you'll like it, trust me."

"Okay." Is she saying she trusts me? I hope so…

My inbox announces I've got a new e-mail at just after ten in the morning. I see it's from Grace and the subject is 'Paradise at my door'. I grin and click to open it.

'Dear Matt,
What can I say? A mere 'thank you' seems so inadequate. I have no idea how you did this, but – thank you. Thank you so much.
Grace
p.s. In case you're still wondering, I gave you Nimrod, because it's my favourite piece of music.'

Oh my God. My ringtone is her favorite piece of music? I hit the reply button straight away.

'Grace,
The pleasure was all mine. It was nothing, really. Summers is a chain, so I called their London hotel and they let me speak to their head chef. He was very accommodating. He said he'd have to make a few changes (I think the sorbet was going to be a problem, not surprisingly), but I hope you enjoy the desserts as much as you did here.
Matt.
p.s. I'm honored that you gave me your favorite. Thank you. This feels like scant repayment but in return, here's part of a favorite of mine:

She walks in beauty, like the night
Of cloudless climes and starry skies,
And all that's best of dark and bright
Meets in her aspect and her eyes.'

I wonder if it's over the top, or too obvious, but hit 'send' before I can think on it and change a word, then I open my iTunes and find *Nimrod*, clicking the play button and leaning back in my chair. So, I didn't just get any ringtone... I got her favorite—

"What's putting that smile on your face?" Luke asks. I hadn't even heard him come into the office.

"Nothing." I sit up straight.

"Yeah, right." He stops. "And since when do you like classical music?"

"Since a few days ago."

"She's really gotten under your skin, hasn't she?"

"Who?" I ask, trying to sound nonchalant.

"That bullshit's not going to work on me."

"What can I do for you, Luke?" I ask.

"Okay, I get the message... you don't want to talk about it. I've arranged a meeting for two o'clock with Josh. Once we've spoken to him, Paul will be able to get started on the new range."

We decided a couple of weeks ago to start a small range of men's underwear, just to compliment the women's one. Josh has been working on something new for this. As yet, no-one outside of the four of us – Luke, Josh, Paul and myself – knows about it, but an idea is formulating in my mind, even as Luke stands in front of me.

"That's fine," I say to him.

"You're really not going to tell me what's going on, are you?"

I shake my head, but I'm smiling.

"She's good for you, Matt," he says quietly. "You haven't been this happy in ages."

"I know. I'm just..."

"Stop over-analyzing," he interrupts. "If it feels right, just go with it." The e-mail pings again and I glance at my computer screen. "I'll

71

leave you two alone," he says, walking away from my desk. "But I'll be back later, with Josh… If you and Grace could try and finish your e-mail assignation by then?"

The subject on the message this time has been altered to 'Paradise in my inbox' and I laugh out loud as Luke closes the door behind him. He's chuckling to himself and I don't care. I click on the e-mail like a love-hungry, love-struck school kid. *Did I just use the word 'love' then – twice?*

> 'Dear Matt,
> *That doesn't sound like nothing. It sounds like you went to a lot of trouble, and probably expense. Thank you again.*
> Grace
> *p.s. Chocolate and Byron in one day. It's too much.*'

I suddenly feel regretful. 'Too much'? We haven't arranged a FaceTime call for today, but I pick up my iPad and find her details, hoping I'm not interrupting anything. 'Too much' makes me wonder if she's upset, if I've gone too far. The call connects and she comes into focus.

"Did you know it was Byron, or did you have to look it up?" I smile at her.

"I knew." She's smiling back but her eyes are glistening a little and I wonder… "That was—" I hear a crack in her voice. What have I done? Was it really 'too much' for her? "I think that was the nicest thing anyone's ever done for me," she says and now I can see a tear trickling down her cheek.

"Hey, please don't cry," I say, leaning forward. I feel so helpless.

"Sorry."

"And don't be sorry." God, I wish I was there, or she was here, and I could kiss away that tear and hold her. "You gave me your favorite piece of music. The least I could do was give you a poem."

"But it's such a lovely poem."

How can I tell her it's perfect for her? "Is it your favorite too?" I ask.

"No."

"What is?" I want to stop her tears, but also get to know her better, in the hope I can make things right somehow.

"A piece by Christina Rossetti, called *Remember*."

"I don't know it. Wait a second, I'll look it up." I keep a hold of my tablet with my left hand and use my right to search for the poem on my laptop. It comes up and I quickly read it. Dear God, I think that's about the saddest thing I've ever read. "Is it about death?" I ask and I wonder if she's thinking about her husband.

"Some people think so, but others think it's actually about a relationship breaking up. I guess it means whatever you want it to mean – like a lot of poetry." She's really down – even though I sent her chocolate desserts. Maybe it's the poetry? Maybe it's her memories? As long as it isn't me…

"I have a proposition," I say, remembering my idea from earlier and trying to distract her. "A business proposition, that is." I don't want to make her nervous.

"Oh yes?" She rubs the back of her hand across her cheek, to wipe away the tears.

"I can't really go into much detail yet, but we've got a new men's range we're about to embark on and I wondered if you'd like to be involved. We need a logo and website, just like before."

"But we haven't finished with the lingerie build yet."

"I know. Look, if you don't think you can handle it, I'll understand."

"No, it's not that, it's just – well, you're putting a lot of faith in us. We haven't actually completed the first job yet, and you want us to take on a second? What if we let you down?"

"I don't think you will." Her eyes stare at me from out of the screen. *Say yes, Grace, please?*

"Okay, what do you need me to do?" I feel lighter, all of a sudden.

"Can you come back over again?"

"Um, I guess so. When?" *Right now? Right now would be really good.*

"Paul should have the first set of designs ready in about two weeks' time. You can meet with him and discuss the range. We might have a few samples ready by then, I'm not entirely sure."

"I'll have to check with Jenny. She's due to give up work around then." Damn, I'd forgotten about that.

"Okay."

"I'll talk to her tonight and let you know tomorrow."

"Good."

She takes a deep breath and coughs. "There is one thing though, Matt." Her face is really serious.

"What's that?" Why am I so nervous?

"I'm not trying on the samples this time… not for anyone." Her mouth twitches upwards and I laugh, and so does she. Thank God for that.

Grace

"I was really sorry about your mother," I say, sitting back into his exquisite car.

"Thanks. And thank you for sending the flowers. It was thoughtful of you."

"It felt inadequate, but I wanted to do something."

"It's weird… I know I should feel something, but I really can't."

"There's no right or wrong way to deal with it." He looks across at me but I can't read his expression.

"How's Jenny doing?" he asks, changing the subject as he pulls the car out of the parking space.

"She's enormous, although I'd never say that to her face. I can't believe she's still got four weeks to go. She looks fit to burst."

"And she's okay with you coming over here?"

"Yes, she's fine. In any case, I'm going to have the run the company single-handed for a while once she stops work and after she has the baby, so she can hardly complain about me coming here on a business trip for a couple of days."

"Does she know what she's having?" He steers out into a stream of traffic.

"No. They wanted it to be a surprise."

"I get that." I'm taken aback. I wouldn't have thought this would be something to which he'd have given any thought. "Some things shouldn't be over-planned. Planned, yes, but not over-planned," he says, as though he knows what I'm thinking.

"No, indeed." Babies, pregnancies – planned or otherwise – are not really something I want to talk about. I look out of the window. It's hotter than I'd expected outside but the air conditioning makes it feel cool inside the car.

The traffic is light and we're at the hotel before I've even realised it. He parks in their underground car park and helps me out, before fetching my bag from the boot of his car, then we go up in the lift to the reception. I check in and he declines their offer of help with my luggage, saying he'll carry it, so we go back to the lift and once inside, he presses the button for the fourth floor.

We're silent on he way up, but I'm already flagging and really I just want a lie-down, and maybe a bath before dinner. If I don't, I know I'm going to face-plant into my starter, let alone make it to dessert. When we reach the door, I use the card to enter.

"Come in," I say and he follows me.

The room is beautiful, as before, with a wide bed, a sofa under the window and a desk in the corner. The adjoining bathroom has the biggest walk-in shower I've ever seen, and a bath that would fill my bathroom at home. Matt puts my bag on the bed.

"I'll let you get settled," he says.

"Thank you." Is it me, or is there an awkwardness between us? "Is everything okay?" I ask. I hate atmospheres. I've lived with them for too long. I don't go looking for them any more.

"Yeah," he says. "I just…" He hesitates, opens his mouth as though to speak, then closes it again.

"What is it, Matt?"

"It's nothing… It's just… Are you okay?"

"Me? Yes, I'm fine."

"You were sad – upset – when we spoke on FaceTime."

"I'm sorry. I was just struggling a bit, that's all, but that was ages ago, and you cheered me up in the end." He smiles.

"Good. As long as you're sure…"

I move towards him and put my hand on his arm. "Yes, I'm fine, really. Thank you for asking. And thank you again for those desserts."

He smiles down at me, covering my hand with his. I like the feeling of his touch.

Dinner last night was good. The earlier atmosphere, or awkwardness or whatever it was, had vanished and we spent most of the evening laughing, which was nice and just what I needed after my flight. We laughed mainly about the differences between our two cultures, and some of the language variations, but also about the merits of cricket, rugby, and football – or 'soccer', as Matt insisted on calling it – against baseball and American football. I don't understand baseball at all, despite his lengthy explanations, and he's said he's going to take me to game to convert me. It's so not happening. But I'm definitely going to drag him to a rugby match when he next comes to London. I'll have to see if Dan can get hold of tickets to Twickenham…

We've had a busy morning. I've met up with Paul, and also Josh, and had lunch with Matt and Luke, who did nothing but flirt. Matt kept scowling at him. I think he was perturbed that Luke wasn't being entirely professional but I didn't mind. I wouldn't trust him further than I could throw him on a personal level, but he's okay, as long as you're not 'interested' in him. I think he could easily break your heart, if you tried to get too close though.

Now, we're back in the showroom, awaiting a very short display of the new menswear range. They've only got a few samples and Matt has arranged this, so I can hopefully get some ideas. I'm nervous and uncomfortable, but I can't tell him that, or explain why.

The door opens and I have an uncontrollable urge to run. I manage to stay seated, but it's a battle of wills… all of them mine.

Two men walk out, wearing just skin-tight trunks. They're both tanned and oiled, broad shouldered, and with muscles like I've never seen, except in adverts. Also, they seem to have been chosen for their obvious 'attributes', in terms of the fact that the trunks don't leave much to the imagination. They're tight... very tight and I can see *everything* in outline. I don't know where to look, so I focus on the blank piece of paper in front of me, glancing up every so often when I sense they've turned around.

They walk up and down for a while, and then Matt gets up and stands in front of the raised platform, talking about the fabric, the fit, the styles. I can't look at him either, so I try to sketch something. He stops talking and seems to be watching me, waiting. Did he ask me a question? I have no idea. As the silence stretches out, I wonder if I should make an excuse and run to the Ladies' for a few minutes... or years, but then he dismisses the two men and comes to sit by me again.

"Is everything alright?" he asks.

"Yes." I know my voice sounds abrupt.

"Do you have everything you need?"

"I think so."

"Okay." There's an uncertainty in his voice that I don't like. This isn't his fault and I really want to tell him what's wrong, but I can't. "I can take you back to your hotel, if you like. Then I'll take you out to dinner tonight?" It's a question, not a statement, and there's a definite hint of doubt in his voice.

"Yes, that would be lovely." I don't want him to think this has got anything to do with him, so I smile across at him and see the hurt and confusion in his eyes diminish a little.

"Are you sure you're okay?" he asks, and reaches across the dinner table, taking my hand in his. Once again, it makes me feel good, and I turn my hand over so our fingers clasp.

"Yes, really." How can I tell him that I've never seen any man naked – or even semi-naked – except Jonathan... and that the sight of those men made me want to run and hide? I didn't know those men; they were strangers and I felt terrified of them, even with Matt there. But I can't tell him that. I don't know him well enough yet to share any of it… to tell him what Jonathan did. That he destroyed me physically and emotionally; wrecked my self esteem, my dignity, my confidence and my hopes for a happy marriage and family. And, as if that wasn't enough, he got his lover pregnant, and left her the house we'd shared, as well as everything else he owned, leaving me pretty much penniless. The secrets rolling around my head are likely to drive me insane, but I can't tell him any of it. "I'm fine." I manage a smile and he smiles back.

"They do a great chocolate cheesecake here."

"I didn't think you liked desserts?"

"Ah, but Luke does. He recommended it when I told him of your addiction."

"It's not an addiction," I protest, half-heartedly.

"Okay… habit, then."

"Well, that makes it sound so much better."

"Hey, if you enjoy—" He stops talking abruptly and his face pales. He's looking over my left shoulder and I turn instinctively, just as a blond man approaches the table, and comes to stand between us, glaring at our joined hands. I look up at him. He's wearing jeans and a shirt, with a casual jacket, so he can't be a waiter here. He's not that tall, but he's standing so he feels intimidating, made worse by the thunderous expression on his face. I feel uncomfortable, so I withdraw my hand from Matt's and place it on my lap, just as the man turns to me.

"Can I help you?" I ask, surprised by the strength in my own voice.

"Do you have any idea of the risk you're taking, lady?" he says.

"Um, what risk? I'm having dinner…" Who is this man? I glance at Matt, who's now so pale, even his lips seem to have lost their colour. He's just staring at the man and is rooted to his seat, and suddenly I wonder if they know each other.

"But you're not just having dinner, are you? You're having dinner, with Matthew Webb." He's raised his voice. This is so embarrassing. And it's clear he knows Matt – he knows his name. So I guess Matt knows him too. I look across at him, urging him to stop this, but he does nothing except continue to stare at the man.

I can feel my eyes stinging, but I sit upright and face the stranger again. "Look, I have no idea who you are," I say, "but I can assure you that this is a business dinner."

"Yeah, well I know how Matt Webb does his business, and I'm telling you to watch out, lady. He'll fuck you, then he'll fuck you over... then he'll—"

Matt suddenly leaps from his chair.

"That's enough!" he bellows and I freeze. "Get out of here, Tony," he hisses, through gritted teeth. They're glaring at each other and the memories flood back. The fear I haven't felt in months returns with their anger. Whatever their relationship is, I don't think it's anything good, and it's certainly nothing to do with me. I can't be a part of this; can't even watch it. Seizing my chance, I grab my bag from the floor and run, straight out of the door.

Luckily, there's a taxi just passing and I hold up my arm, flagging the driver down. He stops and I jump in the back, giving him the name of my hotel, despite the shaking in my voice, which is matched by every muscle in my body.

It only takes minutes to get there and I fling twenty dollars at the driver and run for the entrance, straight into the lift and up to my room. Once inside, I crumple to the floor. I've got no idea who Tony is, or how he's connected to Matt. And I'm more than confused about what he said. I've been working with Matt for months now and he's been nothing but kind, considerate and attentive, friendly, and always, always a gentleman. I don't want that man's words to be true. Matt's different, I know he is. He has to be... because I'm really starting to like him.

I'm still on the floor when I hear the knocking on my door. I glance at my watch. It's only been fifteen minutes since I got back here, but my legs are already stiff from where I'm curled up, and I'm not sure if I can stand. I'm not sure I want to.

"Who's there?" I ask, although I already know the answer.

"It's me." I hear Matt's voice. I don't reply. "Can I come in?" he asks.

"I don't think that's a very good idea."

"Please, I need to explain." Maybe he does, but do I want to hear what he has to say? I put my head in my hands. Do I want to hear? Yes, I think I do. I want to know if he's the genuine man I think he is, or if I've got him wrong too... I struggle to my knees and crawl to the door, opening it a fraction and crawling back, leaving it for him to come in.

Chapter Eight

Matt

Iopen the door wider. Grace is on the floor just inside and, as I kick the door closed again, I fall to my knees beside her. I want to hold her and tell her it will all be okay, but I can't, because I'm not entirely sure it will be, so I kneel back, then sit, my arms resting on my knees. I don't take my eyes from her face. She's sitting with her back against the wall, her arms encircling her bent legs; very defensive.

"I'm sorry," I say.

"What for?" she asks.

"That scene."

She doesn't reply. She's waiting. I knew I'd have to tell her all about it one day, I just didn't think it would be this soon. I thought there would be more time; that I'd know for sure how I feel about her – although I've got a pretty good idea – and that I'd have some clue as to how she feels about me. Now I'm just going to have to take that leap of faith… and hope I don't crash.

"I owe you an explanation," I say.

"You think?"

Okay, she's angry as well as defensive. I don't blame her. "Yeah."

"Who was that man?"

"His name is Tony Owens."

"And how do you know him?"

"I don't, not really," I admit.

"Well, you could have fooled me. He seemed to know enough about you."

"No, Grace. He thinks he knows me, because I dated his sister for a while."

"He doesn't seem too happy about it."

"That's not surprising."

"Why?"

"Because it all went wrong… And he blames me," I add.

"Why?" she asks. "Why does he blame you, Matt?"

I stare down at the blue carpet between us, reliving those few weeks. "Because he thinks it was my all fault," I begin. "In a way he's right. I should never have even started the relationship in the first place. Brooke was a model, you see… She wasn't a regular, but a girl we'd hired to do a one-off job, because one of our girls was sick. I've got a strict policy about fooling around with the models, mainly for Luke's benefit, but it was me who screwed up. She…" I look up. Grace is staring at me. "Do you really want to hear this?" I ask. She hesitates, then nods her head. I take a deep breath. "Okay. It was a show we were doing at a sports venue about two and a half years ago. She… she stayed behind when the others had gone. I don't really know why she did that, but she did and… well, I'm not proud of what happened next, but – in my defense – she instigated it." God, that sounds awful, even if it is true. "I'd have been happy to leave it at that – a one off that should never have happened – but she kept contacting me, calling, sending messages. Eventually, after a couple of weeks, I gave in and we started dating. She was okay to be around, I guess, but it was never serious as far as I was concerned. After a few weeks, things started to change… she became really demanding, really possessive. She wanted to know where I was all the time. It was too much for me. It was making me miserable. I finally put a stop to it when she turned up at my apartment. I don't even know how she found out where I lived… I mean, I'd never invited her – or any other woman – back to my place, but she was there waiting for me one night when I got home from work. She made such a fuss outside, I had to let her in. She was crazy and I had to tell her I couldn't see her anymore. She didn't take it well. It got… ugly."

"What happened?" she whispers. The look on her face has changed, and I realise with a sickening thud to my gut that she's afraid; but surely she's not afraid of me, is she? *Why the hell would she be scared of me?*

"She lashed out at me…"

"And did you… did you hurt her?"

"Hell, no! She tried to hurt me, Grace, not the other way around. I raised my voice, not my fists. I told her to leave. I made it very clear I didn't want to see her again – and why. I was blunt, but that's all. She… She pulled a knife from her bag…" I hear Grace cry out, then muffle the sound, but I don't want to look at her. "I tried to talk to her to start with, but she kept lunging at me, and laughing. I managed to grab her arm, eventually, and knocked the knife out of her hand. That was the only time I touched her, I swear."

"What did you do?"

"I called Todd."

"Who's Todd?"

"He's a friend of mine… A cop… I didn't know what else to do. I wasn't sure I even wanted to press charges, but he pointed out that she could come back, and maybe bring a gun the next time…"

"So, what happened to her?

"She's in prison."

Grace nods her head slowly. "How long for?"

"Not as long as you might think. It was complicated… And she had a good lawyer. She claimed that we'd been living together, that I'd… that we'd talked about marriage and that I only broke it off with her because I'd met someone else. That isn't true at all… none of it. We'd only known each other for a few weeks; I'd never even spent a whole night with her, let alone lived with her and I certainly never mentioned love, or marriage… We were never that serious. They created a whole fiction around our lives… around my life, and it didn't seem to matter what I said, they had an answer for it. They'd covered every angle."

"And was there someone else?" she asks quietly.

"No. I'm not like that… I don't cheat. Hell, I haven't even dated anyone since it happened … well, not properly. I couldn't…" I stop. I was about to say that I couldn't trust another woman enough to have a relationship, but then I'd have had to tell her how that's changed; how meeting her has changed everything… and I don't think she's ready for that.

She looks at me, like she's thinking about something, although at least the fear in her eyes has faded. "It seems unfair that they could treat you like that… in court, I mean."

"It was. But there was nothing I could do about it."

"And tonight?"

"I haven't seen Tony, or heard from him since the trial. But I guess he believes Brooke's side of the story. He thinks I got what I deserved and blames me for what happened to her, then and since. The sentence she got was light, but it should never have…" I still can't bring myself to look at her. What must she think of me?

"You blame yourself, don't you?"

"Yes, a little. Like I said, I shouldn't have started the relationship in the first place."

"There's something else, isn't there, Matt?"

How does she know? I nod my head.

"Do you want to tell me?"

"Yes, but I'm not sure how to…" I've never been able to explain properly, even to myself, how it made me feel…

"Well, just tell me what happened." Her voice is so soft.

"It started with the publicity over the arrest and then the trial. It didn't look good. I was worried about the business. You can imagine the headlines. I thought it might ruin us… and my mother, well she had a field-day. But, afterwards, once Brooke had been sentenced, this journalist just appeared out of nowhere… He'd been working overseas, so he'd missed the trial, but it turned out he'd dated her for a while a few years before, when they were both at college. She'd gone a bit crazy on him too, but without the knife, and he wrote an article about the trial, exposing her for what she was… A couple of other guys came forward with similar stories and a second article appeared. It seemed there was a pattern to her behavior."

"Surely that exonerated you?"

"Yeah, I guess, and from the business point of view, it definitely helped. Everything picked up again and, within a few months, it was like it had never happened. We got back to where we were before, and then came up with the idea for Amulet and things have gone from strength to strength…"

"So what's wrong?"

"The story… the article… it was picked up by some of the bigger, newspapers, and one of them ran a series on domestic abuse against men… They came and interviewed me. I didn't feel I really fit the category. Yeah, Brooke was violent, but I could've defended myself, if I'd chosen to. I didn't like the way I was portrayed. I got letters of support, and sympathy – from women as well as men – some of which made me feel uncomfortable. Their stories and mine were so different. Some of them had been in violent relationships for years, and they were thanking me for 'going public' with my story. I felt like a fraud. I guess at least I wasn't being portrayed as the bad guy anymore, but nothing felt right. It seemed to me that people were looking at me differently. I tried moving apartments, partly to escape the reporters – my new place has better security – but mainly for a fresh start. Even that didn't really make much of a difference. Suddenly I was a victim – or I was being made to feel like one. I wasn't happy about that – I'm still not. I put myself in that position. It was my own fault. Being made to feel like the injured party… I felt… weak." I've never said that before, never even really acknowledged it. I look up. She's staring at me.

"Matt, you need to let up on yourself a little."

I stare right back at her. She's repeating exactly what Luke's been saying to me for months, but hearing it from Grace makes a difference and, for the first time, I really start to wonder.

Grace

I gaze across at him, although he's gone back to looking down at the carpet. How can he feel like that? It's all wrong, and I can't just say nothing...

"Being attacked in your own home is the most terrifying thing..." I tell him. I should know, but I'm not about to reveal that. Besides, my situation was very different. "It leaves you feeling vulnerable, threatened, insecure..." I need to stop talking before I say too much. "You can't blame yourself for what happened. You went out with the girl. You didn't ask, or expect her to attack you. You're not at fault. She's responsible for her own actions. And you... you have to put that night and its consequences where they belong – in the past. You need to forget her and what happened to her and what she did to you, and move on with your own life, otherwise she and her fancy lawyers have won." I take a deep breath, staring down at my hands. "As for being made to feel a victim... That was the view of strangers, so what does it matter anyway? No-one but you can determine who and what you are. I think you need to stop worrying about how the world sees you, and maybe try to see yourself through the eyes of the people who *really* know you, the people who really care about you... They don't see a victim, or a weak man. They see the same thing I do. They see a strong, kind, caring, gentle man."

I look up and he's staring at me. He stands and takes a step towards me. And suddenly, I've had enough... I'm talked-out, drained, exhausted. And, although he doesn't know it, it's all much too close to home... I feel like I'm brimming over. I've reached a point where, if I have to take on anything else, even if it's just a touch or a look, or a single word of kindness, I'll overflow; I'll burst. And then I'll break. I can't do this... Whatever 'this' is.

"Please, don't." I hold up my hand and he halts.

"Grace?" His voice is soft, concerned.

"Please, Matt. I'd like you to leave."

"But…" He's really confused. I don't blame him.

"Please…"

He pauses for a moment. "But you're flying home tomorrow," he says.

"Yes."

He seems to want to say something, but stops. He looks at me for a long time, but he doesn't speak again. He goes to the door and opens it, passes through and closes it quietly behind him.

I haven't slept at all. I've tossed and turned all night long, thinking. I didn't like the way things ended last night. Matt opened up to me, and from the sound of it, he hasn't done that with anyone. I suppose I should feel flattered, no honoured, that he chose to tell me. Despite everything that's happened to him, he must trust me a lot to do that, and I know how hard it can be to trust someone. Let's face it, I've never spoken to anyone about my secrets.

He's not to know that I'm carrying around so many of my own problems, the idea of dealing with someone else's is just too much right now. I'm not strong enough yet.

I'm due to fly out this morning, but I can't just go home and leave it like this. He's got a meeting at eight, which is why he couldn't take me to the airport. I've worked out that I can get the taxi to take me to Logan via his office and I can stop by before his meeting. I know he'll be there, even though it's only just after seven; he told me yesterday that he'd have to get in early today. This is the right thing to do, isn't it? To explain why I asked him to leave, at least. Even if I can't tell him the rest of it, I can tell him that. I can explain that it's just all a bit too much right now. I don't need to give him details and I'm sure he'll understand… Because I certainly can't fly home feeling like this.

Riding up in the lift, my doubts are surfacing again. What if he's not alone? What if he won't listen to me? What if he won't even see me? I did just dismiss him out of hand last night… Perhaps I should just go home after all. Or maybe I should call him first? I step out of the lift. I know I'm nearly at his office door, but if I call, I can at least check if he's alone before I go in. Yes, that's the best thing to do. That will avoid any unnecessary embarrassment, and if he doesn't want to see me, I can pretend I was never here.

I call up his details on my phone and wait for the connection. His office door is just around the corner. Wait... I can hear a piano playing and then... that's... that's Joe Cocker, isn't it? I'm sure it is.

The song cuts off as he answers. "Grace?" I can hear his voice through the phone and in my other ear at the same time. "Are you okay?" He sounds so worried.

"Um..." I speak quietly, hoping he won't be able to tell I'm in the corridor. "Yes... I..."

"Where are you?" he asks.

"Outside your office."

There's a pause. "Okay," he says, sounding confused. "Come on up."

"I am up."

I wait for him to say something, but instead he appears in front of me. He looks tired, but smart, although his hair is tousled, and he's just wonderful, and I realise for the first time how much I want to stay here with him. How much I want to feel safe in his arms... *Well, that's a new thought. Where did that come from?* We both hang up.

"Why—?"

I don't let him finish his question. "I wanted to explain... about last night." Why the hell are tears forming in my eyes? I'd planned what I wanted to say. I've been thinking about it since before dawn, and tears weren't part of it. "But I wasn't sure if you were alone, or busy..."

"I'm not alone. Luke's here too, and a couple of guys from the finance office." Oh, I'm so glad I called first. He takes my hand. "Come with me." He leads me along the corridor to another room, opens the door and lets me go inside first, before closing it behind us. There's a large conference table in the middle, surrounded by too many chairs for me to count.

"Shouldn't you be at the airport?" he asks.

"I've got a few minutes. I just wanted to tell you that I'm sorry. I understand how hard that must have been for you last night and I shouldn't—" *Swing Low, Sweet Chariot* rings out from my phone, which I'm still holding. "Damn. I'm sorry, have to take this." He nods, then runs his fingers through his hair as he turns away, walking to the other side of the room to give me a little privacy.

Chapter Nine

Matt

She's here… she's actually here. She came to me. I was going to give her time to get home, then call her later on this afternoon, to talk things through, and maybe see if she'd let me fly over to London at the weekend to see her. I sure as hell wasn't going to just walk away from her, not for long anyway. I don't know yet what's going on between us, but I'm not ready for it to end. I don't think I'll ever be ready for it to end. Why does the thought that she's standing here, in my boardroom, that she came to me, make me feel like a king? *Calm down, Matt. She only came to explain. Her explanation might end with, 'I never want to see you again', so stop reading things into this that aren't there.*

When I left her last night, I went down to the river. I walked for a while, then I sat on a bench, and I stayed there until just before dawn. I couldn't believe I'd blown it, or that the look on her face when she asked me to leave hurt so much. It hurt more than anything else in my life… more than anything Brooke and her lawyers did to me. I reasoned and reasoned with myself that I'd had to tell her… that I've probably wanted to tell her since the beginning, really, not because I was concerned about what she'd think of me if she found out, but because I thought, I hoped, she'd understand. And she did; she got it… she got all of it. Grace is the most incredible woman I've ever met. With just a few words, she made me feel strong and safe at the same time, and I haven't felt either of those things in a long while. All I wanted to do was thank her for listening, for being there and understanding, and making me feel better about myself, but then – and I have no idea why – she told me to go and, until about two minutes ago, I feared that might be it for us. And now she's here... *Please don't let her say she never wants to see me again...*

"But she's alright isn't she?" Her words intrude into my thoughts and I turn. "Thank God for that, Dan." She leans back against the wall, looking up at the ceiling. "And the baby?" Has something happened to Jenny? I start walking back toward her. "That's good," she continues. "If I get back in time I'll come and see you all before I go home... Yes, I will... Thanks for letting me know... Okay. Bye, Dan." She hangs up. I expect her to explain the call, or maybe just carry on our conversation where we left off, but she doesn't do either of those things. To my surprise, she slides down the wall, falling to the floor, and sobs into her hands, her whole body shaking. I take the last three strides across the room and pull her to her feet and into my arms. She stiffens, just for a blink, and then unfolds and lets me hold her properly, her hands resting on my shoulders, her tears soaking through my shirt onto my chest. It's the first time I've held her and nothing about it is registering like it should. I can't think about anything, except that I want to help her. I've never seen anyone cry like this; it's like she's falling apart in my arms and I don't know what to do to make it better. We stand like that for a couple of minutes before she leans back a little. I keep hold of her, my hands on her waist, and she doesn't seem to object.

"Talk to me," I say. She shakes her head. "I can't help if I don't know what's wrong."

"Sometimes you can't help," she says, looking up at me. Her voice is sad, not bitter. "You can't make it better. No-one can."

"Please, Grace. Let me..."

"No, Matt."

I wait for a minute. "Is this about last night?" I ask.

"No." I believe her.

"Is everything okay with Jenny?" I ask, thinking about the phone call.

"Yes," she says. "She had the baby."

"That's a little early, isn't it?"

"Yes, but they're both fine. The baby's got to stay in hospital for a few days, but she's a good weight, considering." That's good news. It doesn't explain her tears.

"She? It's a girl, then?"

"Yes. They're calling her Lily."

"That's pretty." Why am I making small talk about babies' names, when I know there's something really wrong? Something she doesn't want to talk about. "Grace…" I murmur quietly.

She looks looks away. "I have to leave," she says.

"But…"

"I'm out of time… I'll miss my plane." She's right. I let her go and stand back. She picks her phone up from the floor, where she dropped it a few minutes ago. "I've got a taxi waiting downstairs." I wish I didn't have this meeting. Could I bail on it and go with her to the airport? Luke set it up and he'd probably kill me, but it's my company, after all. These guys have flown in from LA, just to see us, though. It would be really rude not to be here. Shit. I'm so torn. "You need to get on with your day," she says.

"I can take you…" Can I? Not really, but…

"No. It's fine. You're busy. I'll… I'll call you when I get home."

"Okay." Why did I say that? It damn well isn't okay. It's the polar fucking opposite of okay.

It feels like there's so much we're not saying. Both of us. Not only has she not told me what she came here for, but I've got no idea what just happened, or why. And now she's here, I want to tell her how I feel about her; what she's done to me, and for me, but I can't – not like this. The silence stretches again until she turns away. She's leaving, but I don't want her to go. I want her back in my arms, I want to know this isn't over before it's even begun, and I want her to tell me why she was sobbing like her heart was breaking.

Grace

The flight attendant has just topped up my coffee for the third time. I think she's feeling sorry for me. The fact that I haven't stopped crying since boarding two hours ago might be a clue to how I'm feeling, but as for explaining it? Out loud? Well, that's not going to happen any time soon.

I couldn't tell Matt what the phone call meant. Explaining that would have been impossible. How could I tell him that hearing Jenny's news, which should have been happy, reminded me that Beth's probably due to give birth around now too, or maybe she has already… to my husband's baby. It was a stark reminder of what he did to me; how much he hurt me; how much he took from me. It's such a mess. I thought I'd come further than this, but I feel as though I've taken so many steps back over the last couple of days.

The tears start up again.

"She's beautiful," I murmur. I'm surprised she's not in an incubator and I say as much.

"She's perfectly healthy," Jenny explains. "Her lungs are fine and she's doing well. They just want us to stay in for a day or two."

"As I said on the phone, it was Jenny who they were more worried about," Dan says from his chair by the bed.

I look across at him. "Yes, but you didn't give me the details. So, what happened?"

"Oh, nothing…" Jenny shifts the baby in her arms and Dan gets up to take the bundle from her.

"Nothing, my arse," he says. He holds the baby towards me and it would be rude to refuse to take her. He places her in my arms and she feels warm, snuggly. I'm so sad. I'm happy for them, of course, but I'm so, so sad at the same time. All the 'might have beens' fill my head…

"She lost a lot of blood," he continues and I look up from Lily's tiny face.

"Stop fussing," Jenny says, trying to sit up. Dan moves back to her and helps lift her. "Anyone who says this is easy is lying," she smiles. "It bloody hurts!"

"You were… amazing." Dan looks down at her, moving a hair from her forehead. I want to run from their intimacy.

"I can't wait to go home, I know that much." Jenny looks up at me. "She's so perfect, isn't she?" I nod my head, pretending I'm loving the feeling of a baby in my arms. "How was Boston?" she asks.

"It was fine," I say. "But, I've come back with a lot of work to do."

"Well, don't expect me to help," she says. "I'm planning on doing bugger all for a while… except looking after that gorgeous little thing." The look in her eyes is of pure love.

I glance at the basket of pink flowers on her bedside table and the little teddy bear, in a pink gingham dress sitting beside them. "That's cute," I say.

"Oh, I know. You'll never guess who they're from."

"Who?"

"Matt."

"Matt?" I repeat. Jenny nods.

"They arrived this afternoon," Dan says.

"Isn't that sweet of him?" Jenny adds and I nod my head, because it is. It's really sweet.

At home, I sit for ages, staring at nothing. It's nine-thirty in the evening and I'm so exhausted I can hardly think. But it's more of an emotional exhaustion than anything else. My body clock is all over the place and I'm not sure whether it's morning, noon or night. Going to Boston for just two days is very confusing. I don't have the opportunity to adjust from one time zone to the other before I have to come back again.

I haven't eaten, and I can't really be bothered, but I need to call Matt. I said I would. I open my laptop and go to the FaceTime app. I don't want to just phone him. It's too impersonal. I want to see his face, not just hear his voice.

I call up his details and click on the connect button. He picks up straight away. He's in his office, leaning back in his chair.

"Grace," he says. Just hearing him speak is soothing to my nerves.

"Hello. Sorry it's so late."

"It's not late here, but you must be tired." Perhaps that's his subtle way of saying I look rough around the edges... or just rough.

"Yes, I am. I went to see Jenny and the baby before I came home."

"How are they?"

"They're well. The flowers you sent were lovely. I don't even know how you found out which hospital to send them to, but that was really kind of you."

"It's fine." He seems to be waiting for something.

"Thank you," I say... because it's the first thing that comes into my head.

"What are you thanking me for?" He looks surprised.

Where do I start? "For this morning..." I don't know how to finish the sentence.

"I wish I could've done more to help."

"You did help. I'm sorry... I shouldn't have fallen apart on you like that."

"Grace... don't apologise."

I know he wants me to tell him what it was all about, but suddenly I'm back to where I was in the hotel room. I'm filled with the fear that he'll ask one too many awkward questions, or that my exhaustion will get the better of me and I'll give something away – something I can't take back. Something that'll ruin everything between us; and I really don't want that.

"I'm sorry," I say, yet again. "I really need to sleep. Can we do this another time?"

He looks dejected, but nods his head. "Okay."

"I'll call you..." I say.

"Wait," he interrupts, as though he was worried I was going to just end the call without even saying goodbye. "Don't go just yet." He pauses for a moment, then takes a deep breath. "I understand that you're tired, Grace, but..."

"Yes?"

"Look... are we... okay?" He's staring into the screen.

Are we? What is 'we'?

"What do you mean?" I ask, because I don't know how to answer him.

"Our... our friendship... is it okay?"

Friendship? Oh... Is that what this is?

"We're fine, Matt." Why do I feel so disappointed?

"You're sure?"

I think so... Except... *Friendship?* I guess, if that's what he wants... At least I didn't make a fool of myself; at least I didn't tell him about my past, when he only wants friendship. "Yes," I say.

"And we'll talk tomorrow?"

"Yes. I'll call you."

Lying in bed after a quick shower, despite my utter exhaustion, I still can't get off to sleep. I know why. I've got unfinished business. I should have spoken to him properly and, because I didn't, it's all still rattling around my head. Even if I'd just managed to explain my reaction at the hotel last night, it would have been something, and now I feel guilty, because the look on his face just before we hung up on each other was wretched. I did that to him, and it wasn't fair.

I glance at the clock. It's eleven now. In Boston it'll be six o'clock. Maybe it'll be easier to talk by text. At least I can't slip up that way. I reach for my phone and type:

— *Sorry to bother you again. Have you got a minute? G.*

His reply takes just a few seconds:

— *Of course. You're not bothering me. What's wrong? M.*

— *I wanted to explain about last night, at the hotel. I've got a few things on my mind at the moment, and it all got on top of me. I'm sorry. I should have been more understanding, and I apologise. G.*

— You're apologizing? Grace, I have no idea how tough things must have been for you lately, but you were so much more than understanding. Your words helped more than I can tell you. I don't need to forgive you, because there's nothing to forgive. I need to thank you. M.

Oh. I hadn't expected that.

— I don't think I did anything. G.

I feel embarrassed now.

— Well, you did. A lot. So thank you. But it's late. Why aren't you asleep? M.

He's changed the subject. It's like he knows I'm feeling self-conscious.

— Don't know. Really tired but can't seem to sleep. G.

— You could try some music? M.

— Any suggestions?

— I'm finding Elgar works well for me ;)

I smile. I prefer this tone. It's easier...

— Thought you were a Joe Cocker fan. G.

— What makes you say that? M.

— Er... It's your ringtone? G.

— You heard that?

— Yes. I was right outside your door. Why? G.

— No reason. M.

That's odd. I scroll quickly through to iTunes and look up Joe Cocker, then the track I'm fairly certain I heard. I let the sample play. Yes, that's the one. I listen to the lyric for a few seconds. That's his ringtone? How weird... I download it, so I can hear the whole thing, and leave it playing while I type:

— Can I ask a question? G.

— You can ask me anything. M.

— Your ringtone. Is that for all your callers? G.

It takes a little longer for him to reply this time.

— No.

— Who's it for then? Just personal calls? G.

Although I'm not sure why he'd put me in that category, when I'm really a supplier...

— *It's just for you, Grace.*

What do I say to that? The track is still on repeat. The words are... astounding. But surely, he can't mean this about me? Can he? At the very best, we're friends, aren't we? *Friendship*... That's what he wants. Is this a ringtone for a friend?

— *Is it a track you like then? G.*

— *Since I met you, yes. It's my new favorite. M.*

Really? *Come on, Grace, it's just a piece of music; a ringtone on his phone. Isn't it?*

— *Are you still there? M.*

— *Yes.*

— *You okay?*

— *Yes. How long has this been my personal ringtone? G.*

I'm intrigued.

— *A while now. But, I can change it, if you like, if it makes you uncomfortable. M.*

Do I want him to? I think about it. It's gratifying that he thinks of me like that. No-one else ever has, and to deny that seems wrong, unfair... to both of us.

— *Grace?*

— *I think your choice is strange, but don't change it. G.*

— *Good, because I wouldn't have done anyway ;) Why is it strange? M.*

— *Because I'm not.*

— *You are*

— *Er. I don't think so. We do have mirrors here, you know. G.*

— *So*

— *What does that mean?*

— *Beautiful*

Oh, I see what he's doing.

— *Stop it.*

— *To me.*

— If you're going to do the whole lyric, we'll be up all night.

— Sounds good to me. I like the sound of being up all night with you. And you are... so beautiful, that is.

Could this be any more embarrassing? Well, yes, I suppose he could be saying these things, repeating the song lyric out loud, standing in front of me, rather than by text message.

— I don't know what to say.

— You don't have to say anything. It's getting late. You should go to sleep. We'll talk tomorrow.

— Okay. Goodnight, Matt.

— Goodnight, beautiful. Sweet dreams... And I meant it, Grace... Thank you.

I've slept really well, which isn't surprising. I'm more relaxed and happy than I've been in months, or maybe years. It's a good feeling. I like it.

I'd turned my phone to silent last night, so I switch it back on and check it quickly to see if there are any new messages... Am I hoping for one from Matt? Yes, I am. I can't deny, I enjoyed our text conversation last night.

Sure enough, there's one from him, timed at four in the morning, so eleven in the evening for him:

— Just off to bed. Unless you're an insomniac, you'll get this tomorrow morning. Hope you slept well. I'll listen to Joe to help me sleep... then I know I'll dream of you. Talk later, beautiful. M x

I can't help but smile. I like the thought of him dreaming of me... and I especially like the kiss at the end.

There's a second message. I don't recognise the number, but the words...

— I'm watching you, bitch.

... make my blood run cold.

Chapter Ten

Matt

The last few months have been filled with equal measures of pleasure and pain. The pleasure has come in the form of numerous – sometimes daily, even hourly – e-mails, texts, phone calls and FaceTime conversations between Grace and I. The pain is because I haven't been able to see her in the flesh, or touch her… until tonight, that is. Work has been flat-out for both of us. Grace has been covering for Jenny and, with the launch of the new Amulet range, Luke and I haven't had a day off in weeks. I'm only here now because of the Fashion Shows, but it's a good enough excuse for me and I'll take it.

I'm in a cab on my way from the station to Grace's apartment. Luke and I got to London this afternoon, fitted in a quick meeting and had a drink at the bar before I caught the train to Richmond. I've left him flirting with the barmaid at the hotel, who's giving as good as she gets. I have no doubt they'll end up in bed before the night is out.

The cab drops me off at Grace's address. I was right, it's an old house that's been converted into apartments. I climb the few stone steps, and ring the middle of three doorbells, marked with her name. I hear her voice and she lets me in. She's on the ground floor and, as she opens the inner door, I'm once again a little breathless. She looks better every time I see her. Tonight she's wearing jeans and a light grey, oversized sweater. I'm standing here with my mouth open and she smiles at me, and now I know how good she feels in my arms, even if she was crying at the time, I'm damned if we're shaking hands. So I reach for her, pull her close and kiss her on the cheek, letting my lips linger, my hands resting on her hips. She feels incredible and I lean back a little to look down into her eyes. I want more, but I still need to take things slow with her.

"Hi," she whispers.

"Hi, beautiful." I let her go, realising a little late in the day, that I'm still holding her, although she didn't pull away.

"I feel guilty," she says, standing to one side and letting me into her apartment.

"Why, what have you done?" I turn to face her as she closes the door. I can smell something cooking. There's a definite hint of garlic and tomatoes.

"I know we said we'd eat out, but would you mind if we stayed here?"

Mind? I'm thrilled. "Of course not."

"I've cooked." She says it like she's trying to make amends, but she's cooked for me – how much better does it get? "Come on through." She leads me from the narrow hallway into the tiny but delightful living space. She's made it homely and comfortable. The candles in the hearth are lit, giving off a warm glow, and the small table has been laid for two. Since we're not going out anymore, I take off my jacket and tie, laying them over the back of her couch, then undo the top two buttons of my shirt, and start to roll up my sleeves, while she goes into the kitchen, opens the refrigerator and pulls out a bottle of wine.

"Would you like some?" she asks.

"Please." I join her, standing near the glass door that I can now see leads out onto a small walled courtyard garden, filled with pots of herbs and flowers. She comes over to me and hands me a glass of wine.

"Cheers," she says, clinking her glass against mine.

"Cheers," I repeat, taking a sip. It's ice cold and delicious. "What is it?" I ask her.

"It's Gavi. Some people say it tastes of cut grass, but I don't get that."

"No." I take another sip. "Pears, yes, but not cut grass."

"People can be very odd when it comes to wine."

"People can be very odd when it comes to all kinds of things." She smiles and turns back to her stove. On top of it, there's a large pan of boiling water. "I've just got the pasta to cook," she says, "and then we're ready."

I move a little closer, partly to be nearer to her, but also to see what it is she's making, because it smells really good. The other pan has a lid on top, so I'm not getting any clues there. While she fiddles with the pasta and checks something in the oven, I turn and lean against her countertop, watching her. She looks great in jeans. I hadn't realised until now, how fantastic her legs are...

"Okay, I think we're ready," she says, pulling me back to reality. "Have a seat." She nods towards the table and I obey... who am I to argue?

Within a few minutes, she joins me, bringing with her two bowls of linguine, topped with a rich tomato sauce containing mussels, clams, prawns and scallops, olives and, judging from the smell, more garlic than should be legal. She also brings a warm sliced baguette.

"I hope you're hungry. I didn't realise I'd made quite this much." She sits down opposite me.

"I'm ravenous," I reply, but after seeing her in those jeans, I'm not sure my hunger is for food anymore.

After we've eaten the delicious meal, we clear the plates together and Grace asks me to sit on the couch, telling me she's got a surprise for me... She takes something from the refrigerator, although I can't see what it is and I have this awful fear that she's made a dessert and I'm going to have to pretend to like it, because she's gone to so much effort.

"Close your eyes," she says from the kitchen, so I do. And I wait. Would it be wrong to say I'm finding this really arousing? "And open your mouth." Okay, arousing doesn't begin to cover it anymore. I'm rock hard as I feel the couch dip and she sits, or maybe kneels, beside me.

"Taste this," she says, and I feel a spoon being placed between my lips. God, this is so erotic. I close my mouth and she pulls the spoon away, and I taste... Wow! My mouth is filled with a soft creaminess but there's something crunchy too, and the textures are incredible together. But the biggest shock of all is the bitterness, the intensity. It's not really sweet at all. It's like a rich espresso in solid form, but there's something else there too...

"What the heck?" I say, as I swallow. "How's that even possible? Can I open my eyes now?"

"Only after you tell me what you think." I can hear the smile on her lips.

"It's bitter, but in a good way. And intense, like the strongest coffee, or maybe it's not coffee... Is it chocolate?"

"It's both."

I open my eyes and look at her. I was right about her smile. It's intoxicating. She's holding a small plate.

"Okay, so that looks like cheesecake... Chocolate cheesecake?" I say. I'm a little confused now. "So, why wasn't it sweet? And why did I like it?"

"Because it isn't sweet... and it isn't just a chocolate cheesecake. It's a coffee and chocolate cheesecake. It's got very little sugar in it, and it's made with lots of espresso and really good dark chocolate in the base." She offers me the spoon and I help myself to another mouthful.

"I can't believe how good that is."

"I'm glad." And she is. It shows in her voice, and her face.

"You made that for me?" She really did that? For me?

She nods her head. "It took some experimenting over the last few weeks, but I wanted to prove that you could like desserts, if they're made to your taste."

"Well..." I lean over to her. "You're very sweet." And I take another spoonful of cheesecake. "Unlike your dessert, which is very bitter. And I'm very pleased it's that way around." I wink at her, taking the plate and finishing off the slice.

I excuse myself and head to the bathroom while she makes us coffee. When I lock the door and turn around, I nearly laugh out loud. This has to be the smallest bathroom I've ever seen and I'm careful when I move, in case I break something. While I'm in there, I hear a cell phone beeping. It might be mine, but I can't check as I've left it in my jacket.

When I go back into the living room, I'm surprised to find Grace isn't there, but I assume she must be in the bedroom, so I check my phone. There's no message, so I guess it was Grace's. There are two cups of coffee on the countertop. I carry them over to the couch and sit, smiling as I remember our text messages about ringtones on the night she flew back here. I imagine she found that embarrassing, and I know I was taking a chance doing what I did with that Joe Cocker lyric, but I think that was a breakthrough moment for both of us and, certainly, since then, our calls, messages and texts have been very different to how they were… Grace can be quite flirty when she's relaxed enough, and I've enjoyed the way our relationship has changed over the last few months. I'm hoping we can develop that in person, now I'm here.

I wait for a few minutes, but there's no sign of her and I'm starting to worry, so I go down the hallway and knock on the bedroom door.

"Grace?" I call.

I hear a rustling noise and a slight coughing sound. "Yes?" she says. Her voice sounds odd… strained.

"Is everything okay?"

"Yes… I won't be a minute."

I go back to the couch and sit down and, sure enough, she reappears. One look at her face tells me everything I need to know. As she walks past me, I grab her hand and drag her down next to me, turning her to face me and pulling her close. She makes no effort to move away.

"You've been crying. What's wrong?" I ask.

"Nothing." Why do women do that? It's infuriating.

"Bullshit… Sorry, but that's bullshit. Something's wrong." She shakes her head. She's so damn tense in my arms but I'm not giving up that easily. "Is it something to do with me? Have I done anything to upset you?"

She leans back and looks at me, her eyes trying to read mine, I think. "No. Why would you think that?"

"Because you won't talk to me." Maybe she's worried about what might happen next? Doesn't she know that nothing has to happen… well, not if she doesn't want it to. "I can leave, if you want me to… If you're uncomfortable having me here." *Please don't say yes, Grace. Please don't let it be me.*

"I don't want you to leave," she whispers. Did I just hear that right? She doesn't want me to leave? *Good. I'll stay. I'll stay forever, if she'll let me.*

"Can I help?" I ask, but she shakes her head. "There's nothing I can do?" She looks up at me and I lean closer. She doesn't pull back. "Are you sure about that?" Our faces are just an inch or two apart. She glances, for a second, at my lips and I close the gap between us and cover her mouth with mine. I run my tongue along the full softness of her lips, just once, and she gasps, opening herself to me and I delve inwards, tentatively. I'm not going to rush this; she's like a tender flower, slowly unfurling and if I try to push too hard, she could easily break apart on me again. I can taste her. She's sweet, and for once, I like it. She's like ripe strawberries on a hot summer's day. Then I feel her fingers moving up my arms, coming to rest softly on my shoulders, and I hear a low growl resounding in my own throat. I place my hand on the side of her neck and nip gently at her bottom lip, biting and sucking it, and she arches her back, just slightly, so I can feel her breasts pressing into my chest. I'm so hard again, like steel, and reluctantly, I pull back before I forget how to and ruin everything. The connection between us is broken and I feel a little lost.

When I lean back and don't move in to kiss her again, she looks up at me. "What's wrong?"

"Nothing." *Absolutely nothing.*

"So why are you stopping?" she whispers. She seems unsure.

"I have to."

"Why?" Does she really not understand? The look on her face, the confusion and sadness in her eyes tells me she doesn't. I take a deep breath because I know I can't afford to get this wrong.

She looks down at her hands, now resting in her lap and I resist telling her that what I want, what I really want, is to carry her through to her bedroom, peel her out of her clothes, kiss every inch of her body, lay her down on her bed and make love to her, real soft and gentle, all night long… Except that's ridiculous. That's so ridiculous it's laughable. That's not gonna happen. I know it's not… because we wouldn't make it to her bedroom. Just one word, one look of encouragement from her, and I'd be unable to help myself from tearing her clothes off and taking her right here on the couch. And there'd be nothing soft and gentle about it. It'd be hard… real hard. Maybe, a little later, we'd make it to her bedroom… although the kitchen countertop looks tempting too, so maybe we wouldn't… My point is, that once I start with her, I'm never gonna be able to stop. Ever.

I hook my finger under her chin and raise her face. "I think we need to take things slowly," I whisper, calming my thoughts before I start acting on them, and I lean in to kiss her gently, on the lips.

Do I say the words? Do I tell her that I've fallen in love with her? Will that reassure her that I'm serious about this… Or will it scare her off. The uncertainty in her eyes tells me to hold back a little longer. And I do.

Today has been our show day, so it's been busy and I haven't had the chance to see Grace, although when we said goodnight on her doorstep last night, we made plans to spend tomorrow afternoon and evening together. Then I gave her a very chaste kiss, because if I'd done anything more, I think I could very easily have forgotten my pledge to take it slow.

Luke and I have a dinner meeting with a buyer once the show has finished and I've had my phone switched off all day, but as we climb into the elevator, I turn it back on. I've been hoping for a message from Grace, but there's nothing. I'm more than disappointed.

"What's up?" Luke asks.

"I thought she'd text, or e-mail."

"You only saw her last night."

"Yeah, but…"

"But what?"

"Well, we kissed."

"For the first time, you mean?" I nod. "Really?" He seems genuinely surprised.

We arrive at our floor and the doors slide open. We step out and head down the hall toward our rooms. "We don't all leap straight into bed with every woman we meet," I comment.

"Yeah, I get that not everyone behaves like me," he says, and I feel guilty.

"I'm sorry, Luke. I didn't mean——"

He shrugs. "It doesn't matter." We reach my room first. He puts his hand on my shoulder and turns me to face him. "Just tell her you love her, man. We both know you do. It's written all over your face."

I don't bother to deny it. Why would I? It's true. "It's not that simple."

"Why not?"

"What if she doesn't feel the same?"

"I've seen you together back home. She feels the same. Maybe she's finding it difficult, that's all. She might feel guilty about falling for another guy so soon after losing her husband." I let us into my room.

"That's exactly what I mean. That's precisely why I shouldn't push her too hard," I say, closing the door. "I told her we should take it slow."

"Then what the hell do you want from her? You can't have it both ways. You can't tell her you want to slow things down, and still expect her to call you all the time. Honestly, Matt…" He sounds exasperated.

"I didn't mean slow things down, as in 'back off'."

"I get that, but did she? I'm guessing that when you said this, you'd just kissed her?" I nod my head. "And did she understand what you meant?"

I don't know. Did she?

He sighs, shaking his head at me. "You're an idiot, Matt."

"Thanks."

"Well, you are." He walks over and sits down on the bed. "This taking it slow thing, is that for her benefit, or yours? Which of you isn't ready yet? In your idiot opinion, that is?"

"Stop calling me an idiot. It's about her."

"I thought as much. The thing is, you don't *know* she isn't ready. You're making that assumption... So, from her point of view, how do you think this feels?" He sighs. "I'll walk you through it, shall I? Her husband dies... She meets you. You get to know each other and she likes you – God knows why, but she likes you – and that's probably a big deal for her in the circumstances. She's nervous. She's uncertain... Then you go and do that cheesy ringtone thing—"

"How did you know about that?"

"Man, the whole damn office knows about your ringtone. Every time your phone goes off, which is like twenty times a day, all the girls are swooning, wishing their boyfriend or husband would do something that romantic for them."

Really? How don't I know about this? *Because you've been living in a bubble, apparently... you idiot.*

"I take it you've actually listened to the lyric of that song?"

I nod. "Of course."

"And so did she, once she knew about it. So she'll know exactly how you claim to feel about her."

"*Claim* to?"

"Yeah, claim to. Because, going back to her point of view, the moment she lets you in and you start getting close to her in *real life*, not just in a song lyric, you say you want to cool things off... Talk about mixed messages. What's she supposed to think?"

I start to pace up and down. Could she really be thinking like that? She knows it's much more than just a song lyric, doesn't she? I recall the look in her eyes last night – the hurt and uncertainty – and I suddenly feel sick. I try to look at it from her perspective. She's confused, she's mourning still, she's feeling guilty, she takes the risk of getting involved with another man, who claims that she's all he's ever hoped for and needed – even if he does only say it in a song lyric – who kisses her, just once, and without explaining why, tells her he wants to back off. I can only imagine how that made her feel. Pretty fucking lousy, I should think.

Luke gets up and walks over to the door, opening it. "I'll see you tomorrow," he says, shaking his head at me again as he leaves. He doesn't need to say anything else. He's right. I'm an idiot; a grade A idiot.

Today, I've dealt with our business meetings as quickly as possible. Yeah, I know I could have texted or e-mailed Grace, but I need to do this in person. So, as soon as I can, I leave Luke to finish up and make my way out to Richmond. I'm supposed to be picking her up at her office and we're going for a walk in the park. I've changed into stonewashed jeans and a white button-down shirt, with my black leather jacket on top. When I arrive, she's waiting outside the door at the side of the building. She's as beautiful as ever in a mid-thigh length cream dress, a chunky brown cardigan and matching suede boots. She's wearing her hair long. I love her sense of style. Of course I do. I love her.

I take her hand and lean down to kiss her. It's a chaste kiss, as she pulls away quickly. She still looks confused and hurt, and while we walk to the park, I resolve to change that.

Once inside the gates, I'm astounded by the size and splendor of the park. From where we are, it stretches as far as I can see. It's almost like being in the countryside and there's nothing to give away our proximity to London. We set off along one of the paths. It's a bright sunny afternoon, there are trees lining the pathway, their leaves just starting to change color, and I guide her over toward one of them, pulling her to a standstill beneath its wide branches.

I bend forward, but she stiffens and looks down at the ground between us. Luke really was right. I've screwed up. To hell with it. I raise her face to mine, cupping her chin between my hands.

"I'm sorry, Grace," I say. She doesn't respond, just looks at me like she doesn't understand. I lean down and capture her mouth. She tenses against me, but I flick my tongue across her lips and move my hands to the sides of her face, twisting my fingers into her hair and shifting closer. I put my feet either side of hers, then I change the angle of the kiss and she opens her lips, just a fraction. It's enough and I probe inside her mouth, exploring her, tasting her heady sweetness again. I feel her hands steal hesitantly around my waist, inside my jacket and I run one of mine slowly down her back. As my fingertips brush along her spine, she sighs into my mouth and it's all I can do not to flatten my hand on her back and pull her hard into me, to show her how much I want her. I'm not going to do that though; she might be horrified, especially as we're in public. But I'm not going to break the kiss either, not this time. As far as I'm concerned, we can do this until day becomes night, and night becomes day again. We can do this forever.

She eventually pulls back, just a little, her breath whispering on my cheek, her eyes on mine. "Why are you sorry?" she murmurs.

"Because I think I hurt you." I hold her in place, stroking her cheek with my thumb. "When I said the other night that I wanted to take it slow, I didn't mean that I don't want you." I kiss her neck, feeling her quickening pulse beneath my lips, and she moans, tipping her head back. "I meant the exact opposite. I want you, Grace, more than I've ever wanted anything. I just don't want to rush things," I say between the kisses that I trace along her jaw. "Because I want us to get it right." I look down at her upturned face. She has tears in her eyes. "What's the matter?" I ask. She shakes her head and leans forward, resting her forehead on my chest. I close my arms around her and hang on.

"I'm sorry too," she says after a while, resting back in my arms.

"Why are you sorry?" I ask.

"I'm… I'm not… I don't really know how to do any of this."

"Any of what?"

She waves her hand between us. "This."

"What are you talking about? You're amazing." I kiss her again then, taking her hand, I lead her back to the pathway. She leans into me and I luxuriate in feeling the heat from her body next to mine. I could keep her this close for all eternity and it wouldn't be long enough. It's with that thought that I recall I'm flying to Milan tomorrow. Then I'm moving on to Paris; and I have to be back in Boston by the beginning of October. I don't have an excuse to see her. I can't think of a single reason to come back here or get her to fly to the US in the next few weeks. Do I still need one, though? It's not like this is about business anymore...

I turn and, keeping hold of her hand, I walk backwards, facing her. "What are you doing, the first weekend in October?" I ask.

"The fifth?"

I think quickly. "Yeah, I guess."

"I'm not sure. Why?"

"Because I'll be back home by then. I want you to come to Boston."

"Oh? I didn't think there was anything new I needed to look at."

"There isn't. This isn't about work. I want us to spend the weekend together. Just us." She stops walking. So do I. "I'll book you into the hotel, as usual," I say, to reassure her I'm not looking to speed things up... not unless she wants me to. "What do you think?"

"It sounds lovely... It's just..."

"What?"

"Well, it's my birthday that weekend." I pull her into me, resting my hands on her hips.

"Really? But that just makes it better. Unless you have plans already?"

"Not that I know of."

"Then come to Boston. Spend your birthday with me."

She thinks for a moment, then smiles. It reaches her eyes and they sparkle. "Okay."

We while away the evening in a quaint pub, with great food, and a live band playing folk music, discussing our plans for her weekend in Boston. Her birthday is on the Saturday, so she's going to fly out on the Friday, and stay until the Monday. She says she can arrange to divert the business calls to Jenny's house; she's sure Jenny won't mind just for a couple of days. She seems excited, animated, and I'm thrilled.

We walk back to her apartment and, on her doorstep, after I've kissed her deeply, she invites me in for coffee. I shake my head. "I'd love to, beautiful, but I have to be going." Her head and shoulders drop, just slightly. "Hey," I say, placing my finger under her chin to raise her face to mine. "I've got to get back. I've got a plane to catch early in the morning and… well, I'm only human." She still looks sad and a little confused. "I want you," I say quietly. "If I come in with you, I'm gonna want to stay…" Her eyes widen. I think she's shocked, or surprised… God knows why. She has to know how sexy she is. "Oh, Grace… baby," I say, moving even closer, so her body is fused along the length of mine. I have to find the right words, so she'll understand. I stare deep into her glistening eyes, and all of a sudden, I know exactly the right way to tell her… "I'm in love with you, Grace." I hear her gasp. "But there's no pressure," I add quickly. "I don't expect you to love me back, or to want me… not yet. I know it's still too soon for you. I know you're still grieving. But I love you. I can't help it, and that's never going to change." I lean down and claim her lips. I feel her unfurling again as my tongue plays with hers and I know I've finally found the place where I belong. I belong with Grace.

I've just got on the train when my phone pings, announcing a new e-mail. I glance at the screen. It's from Grace. The subject is 'You're wrong'. I find that worrying, and I open it straight away, then feel a smile creeping across my lips.

> *'Matt,*
> *It's not too soon.*
> *I wish you hadn't left.*
> *I like your kisses.*
> *Grace x'*

I'm so tempted to get off at the next station, catch the train back, run to her apartment and take her in my arms, and then take her to her bed, but I'm not going to. That would spoil everything. I know it would. She says she likes my kisses, but I think she's telling me that's her limit right now, and that's okay, because I know she's worth waiting for. I hit the reply button.

'Grace,
I wish I hadn't left.
I love your kisses.
Can't wait to see you again.
Miss you already.
Love you,
Matt x'

ᴄᴏ᙭ᴏ

Grace

It seems to take forever to get through baggage claim and immigration, but eventually, I pass through into the arrivals hall and Matt's standing there. I've had such a rubbish couple of days, I want to run to him, and fall into his arms. I don't.

I've had time to think since he left London and, although I know I'm in love with him, and our calls, texts and messages have been fun and have made it very clear he's in love with me, I'm nervous. No, that's not true. I'm not nervous, I'm absolutely terrified, and Jenny's attitude didn't help much, but I'm not going to think about that... What's the point? When reality hits, when Matt knows the truth about me – which he's going to have to before long – everything will come crashing down anyway, so it won't matter what Jenny thinks about me.

I've spent the whole journey out here turning things over in my mind. I don't know if I'm ready to take things further with Matt yet. I know he'll wait until I am but, well, to be honest, I have no idea how I'm going to respond to him touching me intimately, no matter when that is. So the wait, however long or short, could be fairly pointless. I need to warn him, to prepare him for my reaction… but as soon as I tell him, I'll lose him. And that frightens me more anything. The idea of not having him in my life isn't worth contemplating. But what else can I do? He won't want me when he knows the truth… I've always known that no man could want someone like me. Oh God… I feel like I'm going round in ever decreasing circles… all ending in my own misery.

I'm standing in front of him now.

He pulls me to him, kissing me hard, regardless of the people milling around us. I drop my bag on the floor and – I can't help it – I run my hands up his arms and around his neck. He feels so good. How did I never realise it could be like this? *Dumb question, Grace.* His tongue finds its way into my mouth and, although all of this is a new experience for me, it's one I'm really enjoying. Whatever else I might fear, I can't deny how much I like his kisses. It's a while before we break apart and he grins down at me, his eyes alight with happiness.

"Hello, beautiful," he says, and picks up my bag. He puts his arm around my shoulders and we walk towards the exit.

"Do you want to rest at the hotel for a while?" he asks as we drive down the street in his car.

No, I don't want to rest there. What if he wants to 'rest' with me? It's too soon. I'm not ready yet. I need more time to think, even though I'm fairly sure I'll only end up going round in more circles, slowly driving myself insane. I do need to change my clothes, though.

"No, but I could do with a shower."

"Okay. I'll have a coffee in the bar while you freshen up." Can he sense my panic? Is it that obvious? "Then I thought we could go for a walk. We could go to Boston Common, if you like. It's not as grand as Richmond Park, but I like it."

"That sounds good."

"I'll leave the car at the hotel," he says. "We can eat there tonight, if you like. You can have the chocolate dessert again."

"I'll end up being enormous if I keep eating like that."

114

"I won't care." I look across at him and he's smiling, and I believe him.

The park is lovely. He's right, it doesn't have the grandeur of Richmond, but it's pretty and the trees are stunning; their colours are amazing. We've walked quite a long way, holding hands, and I'm starting to tire. The shower was good and perked me up a bit, but I've been awake for so long now, I could really do with some sleep. It's just after five and we start to head back across the common. Matt's telling me all the things he's got planned for the weekend, although he won't tell me anything about tomorrow – my birthday. We're laughing and it's refreshing after the worries of being at home; anticipating coming over here and facing the unknown with him, my argument with Jenny, the ever-present financial issues, and living like a hermit, because I'm terrified someone really is watching me. I thought that first message – the one I received back in May – was a joke, or a one-off, but they've continued on and off ever since. I daren't go out on my own at night, so I just go to work and back... and even then, I'm constantly looking over my shoulder. It's so nice to be out and to feel safe...

All of a sudden, it starts to rain, and I mean really rain. We're a long way from the hotel still, right across the other side of the park and, for a moment, we just stop, in the deluge, looking at each other. Then he pulls me with him, and we start running in the opposite direction.

"Where are we going?" I ask, half laughing. We're so wet, I can't really see the point in running, but it makes me feel alive, somehow.

"My place," he calls. "It's nearer."

My hair is stuck to my head, my shirt to my body and my jeans to my legs. My shoes are full of water and I wonder for a moment about taking them off, but I don't. It would take time and right now, I just want to get out of the rain.

We leave the park, cross a road and then enter a building directly opposite. It's a grand old building, red brick, with ornate windows and metal railings. The front door is half-glazed and inside the foyer is a uniformed man sitting behind a desk.

"Mr Webb," he says, nodding.

"Harry. This is Grace," Matt replies.

I wave a hand in Harry's direction, feeling guilty for dripping water all over the polished, tiled floor.

"Good afternoon, ma'am." Harry nods to me.

"Come on." Matt leads me to a lift at the back of the foyer, takes a card from his pocket and holds it over a scanner, then presses the 'up' button. The doors open immediately and we climb in. This must be what he meant about moving to an apartment with more security. After what happened to him, I don't blame him.

"This is very impressive," I say, but he just shrugs and presses the button for the 8th floor, which is the top one.

It takes less time than I would have thought before the doors open again, but there's a significant puddle on the lift floor. I look back as we get out and, as my eyes meet Matt's, we both start laughing. Ahead of us is a single door. He takes his keys from his pocket and opens the door.

Wow! I can't think of any other word. His apartment is enormous, and surprisingly modern, or maybe it just seems that way because there's next to nothing in it. There's a huge, L-shaped, soft, black leather sofa in the centre of the room and a coffee table, with a couple of large books set on top. A big wide-screen television is mounted on the wall and that's pretty much it. It's very spacious, and very masculine. The kitchen is off to one side, taking up the length of one wall, with dark grey cupboards and a pale grey granite work surface, and an island unit separating it from the living space. The windows in the farthest wall look out over the park, and the city beyond; the cloudy sky and the rain crashing against the panes create a dark and stormy atmosphere in the room. I glance around to my left, where there's a corridor, with another window at the end, and three doors leading off of it. I feel Matt's finger under my chin, pushing upwards and realise I've been standing with my mouth open. I look over to him and he's beaming at me.

"This is amazing," I say. I'm pooling water on the wooden floor. "I need to get rid of my shoes." I take them off and kick them to one side. He does the same, and takes off his soaking socks too. I pull my red leather cross-body bag over my head. It looks as though it's seen better days and I put it by my shoes and hope it will recover from its soaking. I look at him. Like mine, his jeans seem to have become glued to his legs, his t-shirt is stuck to his chest, showing off his muscles and his hair is even more dishevelled than usual. I dread to think what I must look like. A drowned rat, I imagine.

"We're wet," he says.

"No, really? You think?" He looks down at me, his mouth twisting into a smile.

"Yeah, a little bit." Just in time, I notice the change in his eyes. The smile fades and his expression becomes serious as he reaches out for me and pulls me closer, his fingers clasped around my arms. Then his mouth is crushed against mine, his tongue delves deeper than ever, and it all feels breathtakingly good. He turns us, pushing me back and, within seconds, I feel a cold, hard surface behind me. His hands drop, find mine and then he raises them above my head, moving closer still, his body pressing me hard against the wall... and I'm trapped. I go from pleasure to panic in a blink. I want to pull back, but the wall is behind me and I've got nowhere to go. My panic becomes breathless, agonising fear. I shake my head, trying to twist away from him...

He stops in an instant, lets go of my hands and stands back, giving me room.

"Grace?" he whispers, looking down at me. I pull my arms around myself, curling inwards. "Hey..." he says, and goes to touch me, but I shrink from him. "What is it?" he says. I can hear the concern in his voice, but I can't speak.

He waits for what feels like an age while I keep my eyes down. "Okay," he says eventually, although he sounds confused. "Come here." He steps back but holds out his hand and I look at it, then slowly up at his face. What I see there is love... nothing but love. "You can trust me," he whispers.

"Where are you taking me?" My voice is almost inaudible.

"You're freezing. I'll take you to my bedroom." I shrink away again. "I'll find you something to wear," he continues. "You can change out of those wet clothes and have a warm shower. I'll put your things in the dryer, and make us a coffee. How does that sound?"

God, I love him so much. I should tell him... before it's too late. But I can't.

I nod my head and put my hand in his, and he leads me down the corridor to the door on the right hand side.

His bedroom is big, his bed seems bigger – in fact, it's enormous – but I'm not going to think about that at the moment. There's a chair by the window, but other than that and a couple of bedside tables, there's no furniture in the room. There isn't a single picture or photograph anywhere. It's very impersonal. It feels like he moved in the basic things he needed to survive, but forgot to move himself in. He goes through into a room off to one side and returns with a white bathrobe. "It'll probably be a bit big for you." He nods to another room on the other side of his bedroom. "Go through there. Put this on and give me your clothes. Then I'll leave you alone to shower." He hands the robe to me and leans forward to kiss my cheek. It's a gentle kiss, but I don't really feel anything. I go through to the bathroom, peel off my wet clothes and change. I don't dare think, or look at myself in the mirror. I just do what he's told me to, bringing my clothes back to him when I'm finished.

"I'm sorry," I whisper, but he runs his finger down my cheek.

"Don't be. That was my fault..."

As he closes the door behind him, I stand in the middle of his room for a while, not moving. I don't know what to do. He's the most amazing person I've ever known. He's everything I could ever want, and he thinks this is *his* fault? I really have to tell him, at least some of it, some of the truth about what Jonathan did to me. I owe him that much... But Beth, the baby, the text messages that have haunted me, on and off, for months now...? No, I can't do all of it. Not all at once. As the enormity of all my problems, past and present, fills my head, I hear a sob and I realise I'm falling.

Chapter Eleven

Matt

Well, that was a disaster. I've thought of nothing but holding her, kissing her, tasting her, and maybe, just maybe – if she was ready – making love to her, for weeks. All the way around Europe, I haven't been able to get those thoughts out of my head, and the moment I get her into my arms, she freezes me out. I don't have a clue what that was about, but I guess I moved too fast. I know I'm not going to let her go until I find out what's wrong. I love her and somehow I need to get her to trust me enough to start talking.

I go through to the laundry room, grab some clean sweats and a t-shirt from the pile and change into them. Then I put her clothes and mine into the dryer and turn it on. In the kitchen, I fetch two cups from the cupboard. I'm just putting them on the countertop by the coffee machine when I hear a noise from my bedroom, it sounds like something falling. I drop the cups and one of them topples onto the floor and breaks, but I don't care. I take off in the direction of the bedroom. Without stopping to consider that she might be naked on the other side, I burst in through the door. Well, at least I know what fell now. It was Grace. She's lying on the floor. Did she faint? *No, dumbass.* She's sobbing. She's sobbing so hard, it's breaking my heart, let alone hers, and I go to her and pick her up, carrying her to my bed. I lie her down, her head on the pillow, and I sit alongside her. Should I hug her? Should I lie down next to her? Given her earlier reaction, probably not.

As I bend forward to move a damp hair from the side of her face, she opens her eyes. She looks up at me, leaning over her, and sits up, scooting across the bed. *What the hell?*

"Grace, I'm not going to touch you," I say. She's clasping the robe to her and that's when I see the real, genuine terror in her eyes. My blood freezes in my veins. Someone's done this to her. "Who hurt you?" I ask, instinctively.

She looks up at me sharply, and I know I'm right, even though she doesn't reply. I reach my hand across the bed toward her and she shrinks back again. "Who did this to you, Grace?" She won't respond and we sit like that for ages. She looks so small and vulnerable on my bed, it's killing me...

"Can I hold you?" I ask her. "I won't do anything. I promise. Seeing you like this... it hurts. I need to hold you, Grace... Please..." She looks at me, studying my face, then nods her head. I crawl across the bed, sit next to her, my back against the pillows, and take her in my arms, pulling her close and cradling her. This is better. She's where she belongs. I keep my arms tight around her, so she knows I'm not letting go, no matter what. After a while, I feel her breathing change and I know she's fallen asleep.

Alone with my thoughts, and with Grace in my arms, I try to work out what's going on. Something bad has happened in her past, something that makes her shy away from physical contact... but when we were in London, she liked my kisses; she said she did. I remember when we said goodbye, I felt she was putting a limit on us; that she wanted to keep it to kissing for now. Did she feel that, in pushing her back against the wall, I was pushing for more? Was that too much for her? Maybe she thinks, now we're here, in my apartment, I have different expectations. Maybe she doesn't feel so safe here? I let out a slow sigh, so I don't disturb her. I thought she knew by now, that wherever she is with me, she's always safe.

I remember how I felt after Brooke – that sense of insecurity and questioning about everyone I met. I also remember the letters I got, from women – and men – who'd been beaten by people who claimed to love them. They all spoke about how hard it was to trust, how hard they found it to talk about and share, even the ones who'd been lucky enough to escape the abuse.

I guess whoever hurt Grace made her feel the same. I guess I need to work a little harder at earning her trust. I'll do whatever it takes… I just want to help her.

I wonder who can have done this… It can't have been either of her parents, that's for sure. She's always spoken so fondly of them and their love for her. It has to have been a guy… a boyfriend…

Wait though… there's something about this that doesn't add up. She was married for four years, and she dated the guy for a while before that; surely whatever happened in her past, she'd have gotten over it during her marriage, wouldn't she? At least to the point where she didn't freeze up… And yet, her reaction was quite extreme; like the problem is still fresh in her mind, not something from her teens or early twenties, but newer. A thought crosses my mind and I try to dismiss it… I can't.

What if…? I feel my muscles tense. What if the guy who hurt her *was* her husband? But, no… that's stupid. That can't be. She's been grieving for him for months now; that's why we've been taking things so slowly. And Jenny acted like they were devoted to each other. Or did I read that wrong? She and Dan definitely told me what a great guy he was… But then I remember other conversations Grace and I have had, odd comments she's made, times when I've wondered about their relationship… That ABBA song…

She sleeps, with her head on my chest, for over an hour, before she stirs. It's getting dark now, and I lean over and switch on the lamp beside the bed. It gives off a soft glow.

I want to make things okay. Perhaps I can't, but it's a guy thing. It's in our DNA. When the woman we love is hurting, we have to try and make it right. As she surfaces from her slumber, I pull her up tight into my arms again, feeling her close to me and reminding my body not to respond, no matter how good she feels. That really wouldn't help right now. She looks up into my face, her eyes sleepy still, but there's something else there that gives me a small glimmer of hope.

"Was it your husband?" I ask. There's no point in waiting, or trying to avoid the necessary question. If I'm wrong, she'll just say, and maybe it'll encourage her to tell me the truth. She doesn't reply. I turn her over onto her back, lying beside her, not on top, and raising myself up on my elbow. Then, very gently, I place my hand on the side of her face. "I love you, Grace," I whisper. "I love you so much, and I want to help you. If I'm gonna do that, I need to know. Was it Jonathan?" There's the slightest nod of her head, which I might have missed if I didn't have hold of her. I feel my muscles clench. "Did he hit you?" Again, her head moves up and down, just once. I look at her. The fear is still there, in her eyes. "I'd never, ever hurt you, Grace. You know that, don't you? I love you." I guess he said things like that too though, probably just after he'd beaten the crap out of her. She needs a lot more than that from me. I run my fingers down her neck, accidentally nudging the robe across and exposing the top of her breasts. She tenses again and I glance up at her. She's terrified. There's more to this, I know there is. It's more intimate. And suddenly a horrible thought crosses my mind. "Was it more than hitting, Grace?" I ask. She doesn't respond, so I pull the robe closed, covering her, protecting her. I know where I'm going and I know what the next question has to be. I'm just really scared of how she's gonna answer me…

"Did he rape you?"

Grace

Thank God. I never thought I'd feel relieved, but Matt's guessed. I don't have to actually start the conversation now, do I? Not if he's guessed. That makes it easier for me. And I don't have to explain all of it, not yet anyway, just the bits about what Jonathan did to me. Of course, there's still the risk that he won't want anything to do with me, but something in his voice, his words, in the way he looks at me, in the way he's been holding me, gives me hope… *Please don't let me be wrong*…

"Yes," I whisper. It's the first thing I've said in ages and my voice is hoarse.

"Christ, Grace," he says and I know from his tone that he's shocked.

"Please don't hate me," I choke out. It's my greatest fear, so I can't help but say it.

He sits up, staring down at me. His eyes are burning. "Hate you? Hate *you*? I hate your fucking husband, but I could never hate you. Why on earth would I?"

"Well, it wasn't really rape, was it? I mean, we were married… And it was all my fault…" I sit up too and cross my legs. We're facing each other on the bed.

"Your fault? I'm guessing he told you that, didn't he?" He sighs and takes my hands in his, looking into my eyes. "He forced himself on you, right?"

I almost laugh out loud. "Yes."

"Then it's rape; married or not."

"But he told me…"

"I don't give a shit what he told you. If you didn't want it, it was rape, Grace. And it was *never* your fault. He had a choice. He could have chosen to love you like a man. Instead, he chose to rape you, and by raping you, he took away *your* choice, *your* right – and it is always your right – to say no." I suppose I've worked all that out for myself, especially since being with Matt, but I want to hug him for saying it, and meaning it. Jonathan beat it into me that all the things he did to me were his right as my husband; and if I didn't like them it was my fault. After months and years of it, I just couldn't fight back any more. "He hit you too?" Matt asks. He's struggling to speak now and I put my hand on his arm. His muscles are rock hard. He's too tense.

"It's okay," I find myself saying.

"No. No it's not." There's an edge to his voice and I pull away again.

"Please don't be angry with me."

He reaches for me and pulls me into his arms, twisting me so I'm sideways in his lap. "Oh, baby, I'm anything but angry with you. I just wish I'd been there."

"So do I." The words are out before I can stop them and he places his finger under my chin to tip my head back and kiss me, very gently on the lips. I'm surprised: it's just what I need.

"Do you remember I told you I find all this difficult," I say waving my hand between us.

"Yes. It makes more sense now. I wish you'd spoken to me about this sooner, but I understand why you didn't. It can't be an easy thing to talk about."

"No. I never have. No-one knows."

"Not even Jenny?"

I shake my head. "No-one. But…" I place my hand gently on his chest. "I think I want to tell you, at least some of it…" He takes a deep breath. "If you want to hear it, that is. You don't have to, if you'd rather not…"

"Hey… I'll listen to anything you want to tell me, but only if you're sure."

"I think I need to." I look up at him. "I think *we* need to. I think it's the only way for us to move forward…" He nods his head. I can do this – it's only part of it, after all. Maybe I'll be able to tell him the rest some day. But I have to start somewhere… It's the next step for me…

I look outside. It's dark. I nestle into him, curling up a little. This is good. I feel safe here, but he can't see my face as I speak.

"I don't know where to start," I say.

"Where did you meet… him?" he asks, helping me out.

"At work. I used to have a job at a big London design agency. They held a Christmas party, and he was there."

"How old were you?"

"Twenty-two."

"And him?"

I hesitate. "Thirty-five."

"That's an age gap."

"Yes, I know. But he seemed… more mature, more sensible than anyone else I knew… I'd never had a proper boyfriend…"

"He was your first?"

I nod my head. "He asked me out to dinner. He was charming. We met again a week or so later… and it went from there. We dated for two years, but not once did he try anything. He showered me with gifts, but everything was so proper; so platonic. I even wondered if he didn't like me very much."

"I'm guessing all that changed?"

"He asked me to marry him."

"Just out of the blue?"

I lean back a little into his arms, my fingers rubbing along the soft fabric of the robe, pooled in my lap. "Pretty much, yes. He never mentioned love or anything; just asked me to marry him. I should have realised then, I suppose, but my dad had just died. I was alone. I guess I thought of Jonathan as my knight in shining armour… You know? I thought he'd come to rescue me. After the engagement, I asked him why he hadn't made love to me yet, and he said he wanted to wait until we were married. He wanted it to be special… I thought it was sweet… Can you believe I actually thought that?"

"So you married him?"

This is where it's going to get more difficult. I pause for a moment before saying, "Yes."

"I assume it started off okay?"

"Oh, God no. It started exactly as he meant it to go on."

He sits up suddenly and I can feel all his muscles tense around me. "What do you mean?"

I breathe deeply. "On our wedding night, he… he took my virginity. He was rough. It hurt." I feel tears brimming in my eyes as I remember. "It hurt a lot. There was no preparation, he just…" Matt takes my hands in one of his.

"I get it," he says. I look up into his face and his eyes are stormy, so I look away again, down at our clasped fingers. I can't handle the expression on his face.

125

"Afterwards, he went to sleep. I didn't think it was meant to be like that. I mean, I knew there was supposed to an element of pleasure for me, so I assumed I must be doing it wrong, or something. The next morning, he wanted sex again, but I... I..." How can I tell him this part?

"What happened, baby? Tell me." Matt's voice is so soft, my breath catches in my throat.

"I... I was..."

"You were sore?" he guesses.

"Yes. I told him that. I said I was still hurting from what he'd done to me. I tried to get up out of bed, but he pulled me back, by my hair... and... he hit me hard, around the face, and then... and then he held me down..." I choke and Matt pulls me into his arms. "It carried on from there, really. Sometimes he'd tie me up, you know, to the bed... If I came in from work late, he'd be waiting... He'd force me up against the wall, or the back of the door... That was why..."

"Why you didn't like being held against the wall," he says, shaking his head. "I'm so sorry."

"You weren't to know... He used to tell me I should be enjoying it, but how could I? It was like he was punishing me, just for being a little late home from work."

"Can I ask something?" Matt says and I nod. "Why did he marry you?"

I smile. "I asked him that once, about three months after the wedding." I close my eyes for a moment, recalling the scene. "He'd been away for the first time since we got married, and I'd had such a peaceful time by myself. When he came back, he dragged me to the bedroom..." Matt's arm tightens again. "Afterwards, I asked him why he'd bothered to marry me if he hated me so much. He laughed. He told me it was 'convenient' at the time. I had no idea what that meant and I wasn't about to question him, just in case he did anything else to me. I know he inherited a lot of money when we got married, from his grandfather's estate, I think. So I've always believed it was something to do with that. As to why me, though, I'll never know. It made no sense." Matt strokes my hair with his hand. It's soothing. "Sometimes I used to think he was crazy. He'd tell me how bad I was in bed, how I could never satisfy him, or any man… and then, in the very next breath, he'd accuse me of sleeping around, usually with his friends, or my friends – not that I had many – or just complete strangers. That was the worst… If a man smiled at me, or even looked in my direction – just a man at a party, or even on the street – when we got home, Jonathan would go mad. But I never slept with anyone else. I knew what he'd do to me if I did. Besides, why would I? In my experience, sex is just about pain, not pleasure. Why would I go looking for more pain?" I take a deep breath. I'm getting near the end now, at least of this part. "He'd blame me for everything that went wrong. If I argued, which I did sometimes at the beginning, before I learnt to keep quiet, the beatings would be worse. But, after the first couple of years, it got better… well, sort of. The rapes suddenly stopped. He told me it was because I was so useless I didn't excite him anymore." I don't explain that I now know it was around that time he started seeing Beth. I don't want to talk about her yet. "He started going away more, but when he came back, if he found anything wrong, which he usually did, he'd hit me." I feel the lump rising in my throat, but I want to finish. "Just a few months before he died, he'd been away at a seminar and he came home to find Dan at the house. He assumed the worst, but Dan was just there for the evening because Jenny's mum was sick and she was visiting her. Dan came down for a coffee, just for the company. There was nothing going on, really there wasn't." I can hear the desperation in my own voice and it takes me back to that night, to lying on the floor of the living room, pleading with Jonathan… Matt turns my face to his.

"I know," he whispers. It's reassuring and I feel calmer.

"Jonathan played the genial host and waited for Dan to leave, and then turned on me. I… I thought he was going to kill me."

"Couldn't Jenny or Dan have done something?"

"They didn't know – they still don't."

"But surely there were bruises…"

"Jonathan was usually very careful not to mark me on my face. If he did, I just used to wear a lot of make-up, which is probably why I don't wear much now. Anyway, he went wild that night. My face was a mess… and I had a couple of broken ribs and lots of bruising. Being a doctor, he could treat my injuries, so no-one ever knew. I heard him call Dan and ask him to tell Jenny that he was taking me away for a week's holiday to make up for being away so much. I still had to wear heavy make-up when I went back to work, and long sleeves to cover the bruises on my arms, but Jenny didn't notice… No-one noticed…"

I feel Matt shift on the bed and I wonder if he wants to get away from me. I daren't look, I can't bear to see the disappointment in his eyes that I know will be there. "I know what you're thinking," I say, pre-empting his inevitable question.

"I'll bet you don't."

"You're thinking… asking yourself, why I didn't leave him. I used to wonder that too at the beginning, but then I stopped. You see, every single time he raped me, every time he hit me, or punched me, or kicked me, he told me – screamed at me – how useless I was, how disappointing I was; that I was no good in bed, no good at any of it; that he could get a better fuck from any street whore. Sorry to use those words, but it's what he said to me. He told me it would be no good me leaving him, because no other man would ever want me, would ever have me. And, trust me, when someone tells you those things often enough, until they're all you hear, it becomes really easy to believe you're worthless… I know you think leaving him would have been easy, but it wasn't…"

Matt hesitates, just for a second. "That's not what I was thinking at all." He sighs. "I was thinking that you are an incredible, brave, strong, beautiful woman and, regardless of what that piece of shit told you, as far as I'm concerned, nothing's changed. I want you so… damned… much. Every muscle in my body aches to be with you, but I ache so much more for what he did to you, what he said to you, and I wish I'd met you first, so you never had to go through that, and so I could have shown you that it should never, ever be like that between a man and a woman." He pauses for a moment. "Whenever you're ready, Grace, I want to show you that making love is not about pain. I want to show you how it's meant to be; how beautiful it can be." He reaches out, taking my face in his hands, lifting it and forcing me to look at him. Oh my God. There are tears in his eyes.

"Oh, no… What have I done?" I whisper.

"What have *you* done?" He seems incredulous and leans down, but then looks into my eyes, hesitates and moves back slightly.

Please kiss me. Please don't change… not now. "Please, Matt. Please don't… Don't let this affect us." Do I sound as desperate as I feel? I take a deep breath. I have to get him to understand. "Do you remember when I spoke to you about Brooke… at the hotel?" He nods his head. "Do you remember, I said that only you can control who and what you are… Well, when Jonathan died, I decided I wouldn't let his treatment of me determine who I am now and what I become in the future. I knew if I did, then he would have won. I wasn't going to give him that satisfaction."

"When I think back to that night," he murmurs, "I feel ashamed. You're so much stronger than I was… than I am."

"No, Matt. That's not true. I get my strength from you. It's only because of you that I've got to where I am. I'd be nowhere without you… absolutely nowhere. It may not always feel like it, but I've come such a long way since Jonathan died and that's all because of you… But, if you change towards me now…"

"I won't change, baby." He takes my mouth with his. His arms come around me and I know I'm safe. I've finally come home.

Chapter Twelve

Matt

Her tongue flicks tentatively over mine, like we're discovering each other for the first time, all over again… and it's sensational; like nothing I've ever felt. She's beyond words. Her strength, wisdom, humor, courage… I've never known anyone like her. Without breaking the kiss, I move us and push her gently down onto the bed so she's lying on her back again. What do I do now, though? Do I touch her? I want to so much and she's asked me not to change. If I was just being myself and that conversation had never taken place, I'd be caressing her, stroking her skin, feeling her softness, kissing my way down her body and tasting her. But what if it's too much for her? I can't just try it and risk a bad reaction; that might spoil everything. Man, this is hard. I pull back, raising myself above her, my hands low down, not by her head, so she doesn't feel trapped. I stare down at her. It's not exactly spontaneous, but, for the first time ever, I can't go with my gut. I need guidance and only she can give me that.

"I want you," I say, surprised by how my voice rasps. "But I don't want to do more than you can handle. If you like, we can just kiss for now… I need to know what you want, Grace… what you need, so I don't go too far too fast by mistake."

She reaches up and touches my neck, running her fingers down to my chest, then resting her hand there. "I want… I want you too," she whispers, and I think I've died and gone to heaven. "But I'm not sure how I'm going to feel when you…" In the dim lamplight I can see her blushing. "No-one's ever…" She looks at me like she's willing me to understand.

"No-one's ever made love to you." I say the words for her.

She nods her head. She's only ever been raped. So, how do I do this without bringing back those nightmare memories? I need to make it special… "I want what you said," she's saying. What I said… What the hell did I say? My mind's gone blank. "You said you'd show me how it's meant to be; how beautiful it can be," she reminds me.

I smile at her. Of course… *That's why it's called making love. I'm being an idiot… again.*

She presses her hand more firmly into my chest, getting my attention. "Just one thing, Matt."

"Anything."

"Will you please be gentle…"

"Oh, baby. Of course." I bend down and kiss her, nipping at her bottom lip, sucking it gently into my mouth, then I lean back slightly. "I promise I won't hurt you, and I'll make sure you never regret trusting me with this. Promise me something in return?" She nods her head. "If anything I do makes you feel uncomfortable, tell me and I'll stop." She nods again.

I claim her mouth again, exploring her with my tongue. She raises her arms, placing them behind my head, her fingers in my hair. It feels good. Then, I kiss along her jaw and down her neck, reaching between us and pulling the robe open. I don't look at her yet, but return my lips to hers and cup her breast in my hand; it's a perfect fit and her nipple hardens in my palm, so I softly rub it between my finger and thumb, feeling it tighten and lengthen. She moans, just faintly, her tongue moving slightly deeper into my mouth. I break the kiss and move down, and take her other nipple gently between my lips, then lick and suck on it until it stiffens to a hard peak and I feel her fingers in my hair again. I change the angle of my head and look up at her. Her eyes are closed, but the expression on her face is one to cherish for a lifetime.

Kissing my way slowly down her body, I arrive at the neat dark triangle of hair at the apex of her thighs. I pause. Her legs are slightly parted and I break the contact between us to kneel up between them. I sit her up and pull the robe from her shoulders and down her arms, before lowering her again.

"You're beautiful," I say, looking down at her naked body and taking her in for the first time. She has a flawless hourglass figure. Her breasts are soft, full and rounded, with hard, pink nipples. She has a small waist and flat stomach, flaring out to perfectly proportioned hips and those shapely, long legs. I gaze at her, enjoying her, then move down the bed. Leaning closer, I can smell her sweet, musky scent for the first time and, I blow soft breaths across her pubic hair. She sighs and I bend her legs up at the knees and spread them wider, exposing her fully as I kiss her inner thighs. I use my fingertips to part her silky folds and flick my tongue over and around her clitoris. I hear her gasp and glance up. She's staring down at me, at the place where my tongue is joined to her. She's biting her bottom lip and her eyes are filled with wonder. I continue licking her, teasing her, tasting her honeyed recesses, as her breathing becomes more uneven. Tiny moans and sighs escape her as I delve further, increasing the pace.

"Please," she whimpers, and she pulls her legs up a little further, raising her hips off the bed, and I carefully insert a finger into her. God, she's wet. "Yes… Oh, Yes," she hisses. I move my finger back and forth, circling around and around inside her, sweeping across the front wall of her vagina as I gently suck on her clitoris, nipping it with my teeth, and she bucks beneath me. She's nearly there, so I slowly remove my finger and kneel back. "Don't stop… Please," she whispers, her glazed eyes looking up at me.

I smile down at her. "I'm not going to," I say. I yank my t-shirt over my head and throw it to the floor, then stand and pull off my sweats, freeing my erection. I hear her gasp and look back at her. She's staring at me, her eyes filled with what looks like fear again.

I climb back onto the bed. "What's wrong?" I ask, lying next to her and caressing her cheek, running my fingers down her neck.

"That." She glances down. "I don't think I can…"

"I promised I wouldn't hurt you. I meant it."

"But…" Her eyes widen. "It's big. I mean, it's bigger than…"

I grin… I can't help it. "Don't worry about it." I lean down to kiss her again. She hesitates.

"Matt, you're going to taste…"

"Of you. I know. It's exquisite." She wrinkles her nose. "You don't like the idea of it? I can go brush my teeth, if you want?" She smiles.

"No, it's okay." She puts her arms around my neck. "I don't want you to go." *Good, neither do I.* I kiss her again and, as my tongue enters her mouth, she responds tentatively, tasting herself, for the first time, I guess. I run my hand down her body, and insert my middle finger into her, stroking her, while using my thumb to rub across her clitoris, creating small circles of pleasure. She's whimpering into my mouth, breathless, as I bring her back to the brink, then slow it down, calming her, before building again, over and over, until I break the kiss and remove my fingers from her, just as she starts to gasp into my mouth. "Oh, Matt," she whispers, "please don't stop." I lean across the bed to the nightstand and open the drawer, to grab a condom.

"I won't." I smile down at her.

"You don't need one of those," she says, looking at the small square packet in my hand.

"Really?"

"No. I'm on the pill."

"And I'm clean." I throw the condom back in the drawer and kneel between her legs again. "Do you trust me?" I whisper.

"Yes." Her eyes are still wide but I love that she didn't hesitate, not even for a second.

I lower myself gently until the tip of my cock rests against her entrance. She's staring at me. "Relax," I whisper. She nods her head, but she's still real tense. I lean down and kiss her. "You've gotta relax, baby." I keep my voice low and soft. I slowly inch forward until I'm just inside her. She gasps and I look at her. She gives me a nod and I push a little further. "You feel so good," I tell her, and she does. She's so tight. I calm myself, then push a little further, stretching her. I don't take my eyes from her face, looking for any sign she needs me to stop, but she's okay. Her eyes are locked on mine and I know it's more than just our bodies that we're connecting. I inch in gradually until she's taken my whole length, then I wait, letting her get used to the sensation. Slowly, I pull back out, and then in again, and again, and again, building a slow, steady, tender rhythm. After a while, she raises her hips, meeting me with each stroke. Her gasps each time I enter her become moans, and then cries.

"Oh, yes. Please... Oh, please, Matt!" She screams the last word – my name. *My name.* She's not quite there yet, but she's real close now; I know she is. One stroke more, another, and another and... she detonates around me, her head thrown back on the pillow, her back arched as she clenches around my cock in a grip so tight I think I might just die, but what the hell, I'll die happy. Watching her come apart is more than I can take and I explode. I'm vaguely aware of my own voice calling out her name as I fill her over and over, until I collapse, exhausted.

I surface slowly, remember where I am and that I'm on top of her, almost certainly crushing the life out of her, and turn us over. I don't want to disconnect us, not yet, so I bring Grace with me, keeping us joined together. She's covered her face with her hands, but I reach down and pull them away, desperate to look at her, to know she's okay. Her cheeks are streaked with tears, her eyes filled with more, brimming, awaiting her next blink. Shit! I promised I wouldn't hurt her... What did I do?

"Grace," I cry, pulling out of her and tugging her up into my arms. "I'm so sorry. Did I—?" She starts to flutter her hands in front of my face, like she wants me to stop talking. "What?" I say. "What's wrong?"

"It's... There's no... Oh, God." She's incoherent. This can't be good.

"What?" I'm getting really scared now. What have I done to her? I've never felt anything even vaguely as good as those moments we just shared, and if I've ruined it, she'll never let me near her again. The thought of never having her, never being inside her again is terrifying me. "Grace...please. I love you. Please talk to me." I have to know.

"I… can't," she pants between breaths.

"I'm sorry, baby. Whatever I did—" She starts flapping her hands again. I grab them. "What are you trying to tell me. Does it hurt? Tell me where it hurts."

"It doesn't." Her breathing is starting to calm at last.

"Then what's wrong?"

"I don't know."

"Look at me." She raises her face to mine. Her eyes are still filled with tears, but there's something there that isn't pain, or sadness, or fear, or even regret. No woman has ever looked at me like that before, and I don't know what to make of it. Could this… could this be what love looks like? God, I hope so.

"I'm sorry I cried," she says.

"Don't be. Just promise me you're okay."

"I'm fine. Well, I will be when I can breathe properly. That was beautiful, Matt. You were beautiful. I've never felt so much pleasure, so much joy… like waves and waves of it rushing over me. And then, there seemed to be so much emotion built up inside, tears were the only way out, I guess. I couldn't help the crying, but I didn't mean to scare you."

Relief floods through me. She's not hurt then. "That's okay. You cry as much as you need to, as long as they're good tears."

"Oh, they're good tears. Very good tears. Thank you, so much… for everything."

"Don't thank me. You never have to thank me."

"I can't believe how good that felt." She's still smiling. It's a blissful, contented smile.

"Neither can I."

She snuggles into me and I hold her tighter, grabbing the comforter to pull over us. She looks up. "But I'm so tired now," she murmurs.

"Then sleep, beautiful." I stroke her hair gently.

Her arm comes around me, resting across my stomach. It feels too good for words and I'm astounded that she trusted me so much, not just with her secret, but with her body. My heart expands into my chest and fills with love for her, and I kiss the top of her head. "I love you so much," she whispers… and my heart bursts.

❧

Grace

I open my eyes. It's dark outside, but the blinds are open and the moon and city lights enable me to see my watch. Four-thirty. I guess that makes it nine-thirty to my body and brain, which explains why I'm awake. I turn and come up against the wall of muscle that is Matt, and I can't help but smile. Last night was almost too good to be true. After everything Jonathan did to me, the years and years of pain, secrets, and lies, I can't believe I've been so lucky as to find this man. He's lying, facing me and I cuddle up to him. He moves slightly, bringing his arms around me as I nestle into his chest.

"You okay?" he murmurs, sleepily.

"Yes. Go back to sleep."

"Hmmm."

I'm not actually sure he even woke up then, not properly, anyway.

I lie still, listening to his steady breathing and his heartbeat, feeling his strong arms around me, expecting to wake up any moment and find this is just a dream and that I've been returned to my nightmares.

I must have drifted off to sleep again. Now, there is light on my face. Dawn is breaking and a pale sunlight is flooding the bedroom. I look across at Matt, still sleeping beside me. It's not a dream… it's real. It's very real, he's real, and he's absolutely perfect.

I glance at my watch. It's nearly seven o'clock and I realise I'm absolutely starving. We forgot to eat last night, so my last meal was on the plane yesterday and I have no idea when Matt last ate anything. Sliding out from under the duvet, I creep to the bathroom and close the door. First thing's first… brush my teeth. Except I have no toothbrush. I can't use Matt's… I open the cabinet and discover a

136

brand new one in it's pack, and there's toothpaste on the shelf, so I brush my teeth, and already I feel a little more human. Next, I walk into the shower and turn on the water, adjusting it to get the temperature just right, then quickly wash myself and my hair, using Matt's body wash and shampoo. I'm sure he won't mind. Stepping out, I take a large, white, fluffy towel from a shelf above the vanity unit and fold it round myself before it registers that I have nothing to wear. I don't know what he did with my wet clothes yesterday, and everything else is at the hotel. The robe I wore last night is still buried on the bed somewhere. Then I remember that Matt went to a separate room off his bedroom to fetch the robe. I guess that must be a dressing room. Maybe there's something I can wear in there? I wrap my wet hair in a smaller towel and open the door, tiptoeing across the bedroom.

His dressing room is vast – bigger than my bedroom at home. There are floor to ceiling cupboards lining the right hand wall, with a mirror covering the whole of the far end, and down the left hand side, a series of drawers and shelves. In the centre is a pale grey, leather chaise longue, with raised ends. It's very stylish. Feeling a little guilty, I open the first cupboard, to find suit jackets, all of them grey, or black. The next one contains the matching trousers, beyond which are shirts, all in white, hung neatly on hangers. On the shelves are some t-shirts, in white, grey and black. He's a very monochrome man. There's nothing for it. I remove the towel that's wrapped around me, grab a white t-shirt from the top of the pile, and pull it on. It comes down to my mid-thigh, which is just as well, as I've got no knickers.

Depositing the towel back in the bathroom, over the chrome heated rail, I slip out of the bedroom, down the corridor and into the main room. It's darker in here, as the blinds are closed, so I go across and open them, the sunlight streaming into the room. Then I make my way to the kitchen. On the living room side of the island are four leather chairs. There's a five burner stove with a wide oven beneath, and the sink is in the corner. I'm looking around, searching for the fridge, when I feel something beneath my foot and glance down. Wow, that was lucky. A piece of broken china is touching my heel, but I haven't actually trodden on it. I bend and pick it up, noticing several others, which I also gather. Once I've laid them out on the work surface, I see they were once a mug, a blue mug, the partner of which is next to a very technical-looking coffee machine. I gather up the pieces of broken mug and put them on the draining board, then go back to the coffee maker. There's no way I'm going to be able to do anything with that, but I've never seen Matt drink tea, either. I open a few cupboards, hoping he might have instant coffee, but no such luck. Neither does he have tea, but I do, however, find the fridge, which is integrated and enormous. He's got more food in here than I can fit in my whole kitchen and I find some eggs and bread. I can do that at least. Scrambled eggs on toast... except he doesn't appear to have a toaster, at least not one I can see, and if not, is there a grill in that oven of his? I feel so inept. Maybe I'll just start mixing some eggs. I open the egg box, then start rummaging through the drawers in search of a whisk.

"Grace!" I hear him shout and I nearly jump out of my skin.

"Yes?" I call. What on earth's wrong?

"Oh, thank God. You're here." He appears from the hallway, pulling up his sweatpants. He's bare chested and his hair is a mess, and he looks magnificent.

"Where else would I be?"

He comes into the kitchen and leans down to kiss me, just quickly.

"You weren't in bed," he says, holding me in his arms.

"I woke up hungry."

He glances around behind me, where I've left the eggs and bread on the side. "So you thought you'd take over my kitchen?"

I've got my head on his chest, so I can't see his face. Is he angry with me? "Um... yes. Sorry."

He pulls away and smiles. "Hey, why are you sorry? I like seeing you in my kitchen." *Oh, that's alright then.* "What are you making?"

"At the moment, not a lot."

"Oh? Why not?"

"Because I can't find anything." He laughs.

"What do you need?"

"A guide book would be good. Everything's so different. Especially your coffee maker." I look over at the enormous thing that dominates the work surface.

He pulls me into him again, then he yanks the towel from my head, letting my hair fall.

"Go dry your hair. I'll make breakfast. Fifteen minutes okay?"

I lean up and kiss his cheek. "Great. But... um."

"There's a hairdryer in the dressing room... third drawer down, I think. Despite appearances to the contrary, my hair isn't always messy. I do occasionally make an effort." I run my fingers through his hair, looking up at him.

"I like your hair messy," I say.

"Then from now on, I won't make any effort at all." I giggle, then go to turn away, but he grabs me and pulls me back, resting his hands on my shoulders. "Are you okay this morning?" he asks. I'm not sure what he means, but I'm hoping he doesn't want to talk about my revelations. I've had enough talking for a while.

"Um, yes."

"Sure?"

I nod.

"Not sore, or anything?"

Oh, now I understand. "I don't think so."

"Good." He leans down and kisses me, really hard, his tongue searching for mine and finding it. He breaks the kiss after a few minutes and pats my behind. "Now go, beautiful, or we won't get any breakfast."

When I return, two places are set on the kitchen island. There's orange juice in a big jug and blue mugs filled with steaming coffee.

"Just in time," he says, holding out a chair for me.

I sit, pulling his t-shirt down to cover a little more of my legs, before he joins me and, from the seat of the chair next to him, he reaches for a small square box and an envelope. "Happy birthday, Grace," he says, handing them to me, his eyes alight.

I'd forgotten it was my birthday, so much has happened since I got here. I open the black box, and my breath catches in my throat. I look up at him and see that he's watching me, uncertainly.

"Is it okay?" he asks.

"Okay? Matt, it's perfect."

"You like it then?"

"I love it." He takes the box from me and removes the tear-drop opal necklace, the exotic blues and greens enhanced by the intricate white gold lattice work which wraps around the gemstone. He stands behind me and, as I lift my hair, he clasps the necklace in place, letting the pendant fall into the 'v' of the t-shirt, just above my breasts. He sits again and looks at me, and it, then reaching forward, he touches the skin just below the stone with his fingertip.

"Yep… perfect," he breathes.

I know, from the size and quality of the opal that this will have cost him a fortune.

"It's too much…" I start to say and he raises his finger to my lips.

"Shhh," he says, his eyes serious. Beside my plate is the white envelope, and he nudges it towards me with his other hand. I open it and pull out the card that's inside, turning it over. I look at the image on the front and laugh, out loud, throwing my head back. It's a photograph of a DB9, in dark grey. It's not the most feminine card I've ever been given, but it has a significance to us.

Inside, the words he's written are even more special:

'Grace,
It's not about the past.
It's not about who hurt you.
It's about today, tomorrow,
and forever.
Together.
I love you,
Matt. xxx'

He must have got up after I'd gone to sleep to write this, after we'd spoken. Tears fill my eyes as I throw my arms around his neck and he lifts me across onto his lap. "Thank you," I mutter.

"You're welcome, baby," he whispers into my hair. "You know I mean it, don't you?"

We hug for a while, his hand rubbing up and down my back, while I rest my head on his shoulder. "As much as I'd like to sit here all day," he says eventually, "the eggs will dry out soon." I jump up.

"Sorry. I completely forgot."

"Well, considering how hungry you were, I'll take that as a compliment."

I touch his bare chest. "You should," I say. He clasps my hand in his and kisses my fingers.

"Now, sit," he says and gets up, going to the oven. He brings out two plates of eggs and bacon, and my stomach rumbles. He looks up. "Okay, so you are still hungry." He laughs.

"Guess so."

He sits down next to me again and we eat. I knew I was hungry, but it doesn't take long to finish the meal. It tastes really good and, as I place my knife and fork on the empty plate, I tell him so.

"Why thank you, Ma'am." He's using that good ole' boy accent again and I laugh once more. It's been ages since I heard him do that. The memories are good ones.

"I love to hear you laugh," he says.

"I love you." Saying it feels as natural as breathing and I know I waited too long to tell him.

He twists in his seat and turns me towards him, suddenly serious. "I love you too, Grace." His eyes are dark, fiery and I feel a shiver pass through my body. "Especially wearing my t-shirt."

"Yes, sorry about that. I didn't know where my clothes were."

"I might never give them back to you. Not when you look that good." He smirks, then leans over and kisses me. My mouth opens to his and our tongues meet. Not breaking the kiss, he pulls us to our feet. My hands are on his shoulders and his fingers are entwined in my hair. He keeps us locked together, but I can feel him moving us across the room, pushing me backwards, until I'm aware of the soft edge of the sofa behind me and he pushes me gently downwards, his knees between my legs, his hands behind my head, protecting me as I tumble. I moan into his mouth and arch my back so my breasts are forced into his chest and I feel my nipples tighten and harden in an instant. I can feel his erection pressing against me and I'm panting, I know I am. He breaks the kiss and raises himself above me, a questioning look in his eyes.

I nod my head, not letting him ask. I don't want this to be planned and calculated. I want normality; I want to feel his need, his desire… and I want to fulfil them. He kneels up and pulls the t-shirt over my head, throwing it onto the floor, before he stands and pulls off his sweatpants. Staring up at him, completely naked before me, I'm able to take in how gorgeous he is for the first time. Last night I was preoccupied with what he was doing, but today I can focus. And I'm focusing on perfection. His shoulders are broad, his arms strong, powerful… There's just a smattering of dark hair across his muscular, hard chest, and my eyes follow it down, over his taut stomach to his erection. I clench involuntarily, and then he's back, between my legs, spreading them, opening me up to him as he positions himself at my entrance. He looks at me again and I bite my bottom lip and thrust my hips upwards, just a little, so he knows it's okay, and he pushes slowly into me.

"God, you're so wet already," he whispers and I gasp at the feeling of fullness and wonder, just for a moment, if I'll ever get used to that, or his words when he's loving me. And then he's moving, taking me, and I'm going with him, stroke for stroke, as he creates a perfect rhythm between us. His hands rest either side of me, and I run mine up his arms, around the back of his neck and into his hair, pulling him down and into a deep kiss. His tongue swirls around mine, darting, caressing, the motions matching those of our bodies and I feel that same fluttering building, escalating, overwhelming me again as he quickens the pace, just slightly. I break the kiss. I need to breathe… to scream… Oh, God…

"Now, Grace. Now…" he pleads, and I explode, the spasms rippling through every muscle in my body as I scream and scream his name through clenched teeth. He groans loudly and stills, filling me, his whole body shuddering.

I'm vaguely aware of his weight on me. It's comforting. We're still joined and he's breathing heavily, like me.

He raises himself up, with some effort. "You okay?" he asks.

I nod my head, smiling up at him. "Hmm," I reply.

He kisses my neck. "You're stunning," he whispers.

"And you're incredible."

"I think we should just keep doing this until we run out of adjectives."

I think for a moment. "No. We'd run out before I could ever stop wanting you."

Much later, Matt goes for a shower and I pull his t-shirt back on and stack the plates in the sink. He's still saying that he won't give me back my clothes, but he's told me we're going out for lunch and he's got plans for us this afternoon, although he won't tell me what they are, so I'll have to get dressed at some point. I pick up the card on the kitchen island and re-read the words inside, running my fingers over the neat script. How lucky am I? I have very few good memories and he's creating so many new ones for me.

We've been lying on the sofa together for ages. It's almost ten-thirty and I should probably check my phone. I put the card down. I'm hoping Jenny will have left me a message, or a text. I remember the awkward discussion – well, argument, really – before I left. I had to ask if I could transfer the office calls through to her at home while I came over here and she was surprised that I'd be visiting Matt over the weekend, not understanding to start with that it's not a business trip. Once she worked it out, she was skeptical. No, she was downright insulting actually. Dan came home in the middle of our discussion, which was uncomfortable, to put it mildly. He sided with Jenny, but in a less vocal way, asking if I was sure about what I was doing with Matt. In the end, I walked out and sent a text later that night, just to verify that I'd be diverting the calls. Jenny replied with a curt, 'Okay', and we haven't spoken since.

With hindsight, I suppose I can't blame her, or Dan. They don't know the truth, so they think I was happy with Jonathan, and I'm being hasty, going into a new relationship so quickly. It was one thing to come over here on business, which of course, benefits our company, but a weekend here, with Matt, is something completely different. I haven't told Matt about the argument yet, because I don't want to make things difficult. I don't want him to think he's coming between me and Jenny, as I'm sure we'll sort it out eventually. Maybe, if there's no message from her, I can text her now, while he's getting dressed and he'll be none the wiser. In any case, I'm sure we'll be fine, and Matt need never know.

I go to the front door and pick up my bag. Some of the contents are still damp, but the phone is working. I check the screen. There are two new messages. I open the app and see neither of them are from Jenny, and my heart sinks, then plummets. I can feel myself start to shake. I've had so many of these texts over the last few months, but none for the past three weeks, so I thought they'd stopped. Evidently not. They're... frightening, and as I read the words, I know there's only one place I want to be.

Chapter Thirteen

Matt

The water cascades over my head and I'm smiling. No, I'm grinning. Last night was magical, but today was even better. We'd got past all the tension and fear, so this morning, it was just about need, and love… pure and simple. Grace is so… I don't even know the words anymore, which isn't surprising, really, since I forget my own name when I'm around her. Just thinking about her makes me hard again, and I wonder if we should forget my plans for this afternoon, and stay here… God, am I ever going to get enough of her? I chuckle to myself. No, of course I'm not. But then, I always knew that.

I step out of the shower and dry off, then run my fingers through my damp hair and smile at my reflection. She said she liked my hair messy, so messy it is. I brush my teeth and notice there's a new toothbrush by the sink… I like that she feels comfortable enough to help herself to my things. It means she feels relaxed here, and that's important to me.

I go through to the dressing room and put on some trunks, and find a pair of stonewashed Levis, throwing them onto the chaise, before grabbing a shirt out of the closet and shrugging it on. I smile as I remember the sight of Grace in my kitchen earlier, looking so damned hot in my t-shirt. Man, I'm going to get hard again if I don't get a grip. I haven't yet buttoned the shirt and I'm still rolling up the sleeves when I hear the bedroom door open and I turn just in time to catch her as she throws herself into my arms.

"Grace? What's wrong?" I hold her close. She's shaking, so I pick her up and she instinctively wraps her legs around me, which feels sensational. *Focus, Matt, for fuck's sake. She's upset.* Her arms are around my neck, her head on my shoulder, clinging to me as I carry her to the bed, sitting on the edge, still entwined and keeping her firmly in my grasp. "Tell me," I whisper.

She leans back and shakily hands me her phone.

"What?" I say, taking it and looking at her. She doesn't say anything. "Did someone call?"

"No. It's…" She takes the phone back, taps on the screen a couple of times and hands it back to me again. I'm looking at her message screen. My eyes widen and I feel a rushing noise in my ears. I swear to God, if she wasn't sitting on my lap, I'd get up and punch something.

In front of me are two messages from someone, it doesn't say who; the number's 'unknown'. The last one, which came in at three-thirty this morning, says:

— *I'm always watching you*

The one before that:

— *You'll never be good enough for him*

What. The. Fuck.

I scroll back and discover a whole series of texts, going back for months, all similar to this. There are gaps, none of which are very long, but on occasion, she's received as many as three or four of these messages in a day.

I can feel my grip tightening on the phone.

"Do you know who sent these?" I ask when I know I can trust my voice to sound calm.

"No," she says. "I've got no idea. I called my service provider when they first started, but they said there was nothing they could do. I don't think they took it very seriously, really… I–I didn't want to call them again…"

"And you didn't phone the police?" She shakes her head. "Why not?"

"The woman I spoke to at the phone company was so dismissmive... to be honest, I just couldn't deal with anyone else telling me I was over-reacting."

"Over-reacting?"

"That's what she said. She tried to make out it was just a practical joke."

"Some joke..."

Suddenly I remember that night in her apartment a few weeks ago... the text message that came in while I was in the bathroom, her tears, and her saying I couldn't help. Looking at the dates, these messages started way before that though... "Why didn't you come to me at the beginning?" I ask her.

"Because... because I didn't know what we were when I got the first ones... We were really just friends back then, so this was hardly your problem. Even now, it's not your problem..." *What?*

"Yes it is, baby. And even if nothing had happened between us, if we'd just stayed friends, you still could have told me. I'd have helped you. As it is... we're a lot more than friends, Grace, aren't we?"

She looks up at me through her long eyelashes and nods her head, and I lean down and kiss her gently, trying to reassure her.

"I'm here, beautiful and I'm yours, and that makes this very much my problem."

"Yes, but *I'm* only here for the weekend." A tear trickles down her cheek and I wipe it away with my thumb. "I don't see what you can do."

She has a point. "I'll think of something," I say, pulling her close again and holding on to her. "Trust me?" I ask eventually and she looks up at me and nods her head. "Good." I hold her just a moment longer. "It's still your birthday. And I'm not going to let this sicko ruin it. So, I'll finish getting dressed..." I stand us both up, looking down at her. "Then, I guess I'll have to give you back your clothes, and once you're ready, we'll walk back to the hotel and you can change. Then I'm taking you to lunch. And this..." I hold up her phone. "This stays with me for the day." I throw it onto the bed behind me.

"Thank you," she whispers.

While Grace is up in her hotel room changing into something other than the jeans and blouse she was wearing yesterday, I sit in the bar with a beer, going back through the messages on her phone. The idea that someone is watching her, if they really are, freaks me out a little. I look at the dates. They started back in May, the day Grace went home, and we texted each other about Joe Cocker… the day everything changed between us. They carried on continuously for a few weeks and then they stopped and started for a while, but from late July right up until the middle of September, just after I flew to Milan, they were incessant. I wonder… Is this why she didn't want to go out to dinner that night when I visited her? Is she so scared she doesn't leave her apartment at night? I wouldn't blame her, but she has to know I'd never let anything happen to her. I guess I'm not with her most of the time though… Up until now, she's been doing this on her own. *Not any more.*

I read through a few of the messages. They're cruel, threatening, vindictive, like the sick son-of-a-bitch who's sending them wants to really scare her. Who would do that? I only know of one person who's treated her like that, but it can't be him; he's been dead for months now. Who else would want to hurt her? I need to find out more, and one thing's for sure… she's not going back home by herself. Okay, so I can't stay in London forever, but I can go over there, help her sort out a new phone, talk to Jenny and Dan, maybe; get him to keep an eye on Grace, see if they know who this might be. Even if I can just be there for a few days to support her, settle her in and make her feel safe again, it's better than letting her go home to face it all alone. I pull my cell from my pocket and call Luke.

"Hey," he says. "What's up?" He knows Grace is here and I guess he didn't expect to hear from me until she goes back to London.

"I have a huge favor to ask…"

"Then ask."

"Grace is having some personal problems. I need to go to London."

"When?"

"I'm going to try and get on the same flight as her, on Monday. I probably won't come back until next Sunday, so I'll need you to take care of work for me."

"Okay."

"Can we meet tomorrow? There are a few things I need to brief you on... Sorry if that's a problem."

"It's fine. Do you want to get together at the office?"

"No. Can you come to the apartment? I don't want to leave Grace on her own."

"Okay..." He sounds confused, and concerned. "Is there anything I can do to help?"

"No, but thanks for asking. I'll see you tomorrow."

"Around ten?"

"Sure. Thanks Luke." I hang up, then go on to the Internet. I know Grace flew over with British Airways, so I go to their website and find their local number. It takes a while to organize and I put the phone back in my pocket just as Grace appears in the doorway, wearing a really pretty white dress, and carrying a pale pink cardigan.

"Hi," I say, getting up and going to her. "I've booked lunch at a little restaurant around the corner, but there's one condition..."

"What's that?" she asks, taking my hand.

I lead her out the door and onto the street. "You're not allowed dessert." I look down at her.

"Why not?" She's puzzled and I'm loving it.

"Because..." I smile at her. "It's a surprise."

Grace

Lunch was great. When we came to order, Matt suggested we should eat 'light', as he put it. I'm starting to think he's worried I'm gaining weight, after his suggestion that I shouldn't have dessert either. So, I ordered the shrimp salad, and he had oven-roasted salmon. It tasted amazing, but I spent most of the time wondering why he made such a big deal about not eating too much.

It's been a very odd day so far. It started so well, with his incredible gift and card, and making love on the sofa, then lying wrapped around each other afterwards; but the messages… Should I have shown him? I still don't know. I do know that I wanted to feel safe, and being in his arms was the best place to be. He's taken my phone now, which is a relief, as I don't have to worry about reading anything else, and he says he'll help but I know I've got to go home on Monday morning, and he'll be here, and I'll be on my own, trying to deal with it by myself again. Why do I feel like panicking whenever I think about that?

We arrive back at the hotel and I look up at him. I'm unsure what's going to happen next. He told me he had something planned for this afternoon…

"Come on," he says, pulling me through the doors and into the lobby. He takes me over to the reception. "Is everything ready?" he asks the uniformed man standing behind the desk.

"Yes, Mr Webb. If you'll wait just a moment…" He picks up the phone and dials a number.

Now I'm really confused. Matt keeps hold of my hand and turns towards me. "Curious?" he asks, smiling.

"Very."

After a few minutes, a man in a white jacket appears. "Monsieur Webb…" he says, coming over and shaking Matt's hand.

"André," Matt replies. "Grace, this is André."

André turns to me and, as he takes my hand, his eyes sparkle. "Tu ne m'as pas dit qu'elle était si belle," he says to Matt.

"You didn't ask," Matt replies and I stare up at him.

"Um… I don't understand," I whisper.

Matt laughs. "André was just telling me off."

"Oh? What for?"

"For not telling him how beautiful you are."

I can feel myself blushing.

"Hey," he says, "Don't be embarrassed. You are beautiful. I keep telling you… and André agrees, so it must be true." He leans over and kisses me on the cheek.

"I didn't know you spoke French?" I murmur, just to change the subject.

"I understand a lot better than I speak," he says. "Luke's the real expert."

"Are we ready?" André asks and, without waiting for us to reply, leads us towards the dining room.

"More food?" I mutter under my breath, so only Matt will hear.

"Kind of…" He's smiling at me as he lets me pass through the door ahead of him. André doesn't stop in the nearly empty dining room, but continues on, through a set of double doors and we follow, into the kitchens. I turn to look at Matt. *What's going on?*

He doesn't say a word, but just keeps smiling. André guides us through until we reach a quiet preparation area at the back. There's a long work surface forming an island, with an eight-ring stove behind. Two stools have been set up in front of the island and Matt takes me over and pulls one out, so I can sit down. I'm still bemused, but I take my seat and wait for him to join me.

Once we're settled, André comes and stands before us on the other side of the island unit.

"Now," he says, clasping his hands together and looking at me very seriously. "I understand you like chocolate."

"Thank you so much for arranging that," I say to Matt once we're back in my hotel room. "It was so good… but I'm not sure I'll ever eat again." I sit down on the bed, rubbing my hand over my stomach.

"I think André was just as impressed with you. He's really going to adapt your cheesecake recipe and put it on the menu, you know that, don't you?" He's leaning against the wall, his arms folded across his chest, looking down at me.

"It's a huge compliment."

"He's been trying to convert me to desserts for years. I think he's a little jealous that you managed it so easily. So, what did you like the best?"

"I learnt so much from his demonstrations, but to eat? I think the chocolate and peanut butter mousse cake was probably the best. That was wonderful… just the right amount of peanut butter. Although, I think the most enjoyable part of the afternoon was the look on your face when André made you eat the white chocolate parfait, just to please me. That was priceless."

"Really?" He walks over and leans down, his hands either side of me, his eyes serious. "Priceless, huh? The things I do for you…" I look up at him. He's so close I can feel his breath on my cheek. "And you're so damn worth it," he whispers. He closes the gap and kisses me gently on the lips. I put my arms around his neck and he deepens the kiss, his tongue entering my mouth, exploring, tasting. He lowers us down onto the bed, rolling us and pulling me on top of him, his hands running up my back. My hair forms a curtain around our faces and I can already feel his arousal against my thigh.

"What do you want to do?" he murmurs, breaking the kiss. I don't really know what he means. It must show. "Do you want to continue this here, or we can go back to my place now?"

"Your place," I say, without hesitation. I like being where he lives.

He kisses me again. "Okay," he says, then turns us over again so we're side by side. "Where's your bag?"

"My bag?" Once more, I'm clearly confused.

"Grace, I want you to stay with me for the rest of the weekend, so we'll get your things together now and take them with us."

"You… you want me to stay?" I remember what he said about never having women at his place.

"Of course. I'm not letting you out of my sight until I absolutely have to, not after seeing those messages." And there it is… the reminder that I've got to go home on Monday and face everything alone, again. He looks into my eyes. "But why wouldn't I want you to stay with me?"

I may as well say it out loud. "When you… when you told me about Brooke, you said you hadn't ever taken a woman back to your apartment. I assumed last night was a one-off and I'd be staying here tonight. With or without the messages, I don't want to tread on your toes, or make you uncomfortable in your own flat."

"Do you *want* to stay here?" he asks. I don't take my eyes from his; I just shake my head and he runs his finger gently down my cheek, letting out a sigh. "Well, that's a relief, because I'd really hate to have to kidnap you." We both laugh, then Matt says, "Grace, I want to share my space with you. I'll admit I've never wanted that before, but I do now, and as long as you're okay with that too, can we just pack up your stuff and get the hell out of here?"

And this time, I nod my head.

It's not really worth unpacking, so Matt just puts my bag on the floor in the bedroom and joins me in the living room, on the sofa. He leans in and kisses me.

"What do you want to eat tonight?" he asks.

"I don't think I can eat anything yet."

"I can order something in for later… How about Thai?"

"That's fine. Do you mind if I take a shower?"

He turns to face me. "You don't need to ask, Grace. You're not a guest. Just make yourself at home, okay?"

"Okay." I reach up and kiss him on the cheek, wondering how to ask him my next question. "Would you… um…?" It's too embarrassing. I can't do it.

"Would I what?"

"Nothing, it doesn't matter. I'll go for that shower." I get up, but he grabs my hand.

"What is it, Grace?" he asks, and stands too, facing me.

"It really doesn't matter."

"It does. What do you want?"

"I want you to shower with me," I whisper, so quietly I'm almost certain he won't have heard.

"You do?" he asks. *Okay, he heard.*

"Yes." My voice is fractionally louder.

"Can't think of anything I'd like to do more." He smiles down at me, his hands coming up to rest either side of my face. His eyes are on fire. "Well, I can... but maybe we can do that while we're in there." He winks and leads me to his bedroom.

Chapter Fourteen

Matt

I take my time, kissing my way down Grace's body as I slowly undress her. She's breathing heavily, her head rocked back and her mouth open by the time I've finished. I then quickly lose my own clothes and take her into the bathroom, turning on the shower and letting her set the temperature.

The water flows over her, running down between her breasts. I stand next to her and pull her close, feeling her soft body along the length of mine as I kiss her deeply. She sighs into my mouth, her arms coming up around my neck and her fingers into my hair.

I pull back just a little. "What do you want?" I breathe. I guess she might just want to shower… as in, wash… I really hope not though.

"You."

I smile. It's good to hear her say it. "How?" She shrugs. She doesn't know. Of course she doesn't. "Do you trust me?" I know I keep asking her that, but I have to be sure when I'm going to try something new that she's willing to put her faith in me, and embrace it. She nods without hesitation. I don't want to back her up against the wall: we're not there yet – we might never get there – but I still want to see her face. I reach down slowly, caressing her stomach, and moving lower until I feel her slick, swollen folds open to my fingers as she parts her legs a little wider. She's wet, real wet, and I kiss her again, as I circle inside her, feeling her tighten around me. As her breathing gets heavier,

I remove my fingers from her, and lift her up into my arms. Just like this morning, she wraps her legs around me and, supporting her with one arm, I use the other hand to guide the head of my cock to her entrance. Then, moving my hands to her ass, I slide her down onto me. She gasps, her eyes wide open and fixed on mine as she takes my length right into her core. "Hold my shoulders, baby," I mutter, and she does. Then, setting my feet firm, my legs braced, I lean back at a slight angle, on to the wall, and settle against the cool tiles, the water pouring down between us. I lift her again, almost breaking our connection, before I slowly lower her once more, all the way down my shaft. Again she gasps and I take her mouth with mine, keeping up the rhythm, the rise and fall of her body onto mine, speeding up, then slowing down again and, every so often, letting her rest on me, letting her enjoy the sensation of being full. She breaks the kiss, gulping in air. Her face is a picture of rapture, her eyes closed, her lips apart and set in a slight smile. I lift her higher, then plunge as deep as I can, repeating and repeating that, over and over, deeper and deeper, until my muscles burn and her husky cries fill the room, echoing off the walls. She leans back, clasping my shoulders, her head rolling, as she finally contracts, clenching around me and she screams out my name, then, with one final thrust, I convulse into her, holding her still, until my legs give way and I collapse, bringing her with me.

Slowly I become aware that the water is still running and our bodies are entwined. I'm slumped in the corner of the shower, Grace is on top of me, against me.

"Are you okay?" I manage to ask. "I didn't hurt you?"

"I'm fine," she sighs. "But how did you…?"

I sit up properly and pull her into my arms, holding her on my lap. "How did I what?" I kiss her forehead.

"How did you do that? Your legs… your arms…" She runs her fingers over my biceps. "I'm not that light… It must have nearly killed you."

"I can think of worse ways to go. Standing up might be a challenge, but…"

"Oh. So… you won't want to do that again?"

I look down at her and she's smiling. It's a shy, but sexy, tempting smile.

"Straight away?" I'm kinda scared she's gonna say 'yes', because I'm not sure I can, although I'll give it a damned good try if she really wants to.

"Not straight away, no. I'm turning into a prune here, and I could do with something to drink… but I'd like to think we could do it again… soon."

"Definitely. Very soon. You liked it then?"

She nods her head, all self-conscious. God, she's gorgeous.

Luke arrives at ten sharp. Grace is exhausted, so I've left her sleeping still, with the door closed so we don't disturb her.

We're sat on the couch, with coffee, going through the week's diary.

"I've only got three meetings booked for next week," I say. "And one of those is with Paul and Josh, so I could still do that by phone, as long as we time it right, so it's not the middle of the night for any of us." Luke nods.

"I'll fix it up with them," he says. "Who are the other two with?"

"You might be able to re-arrange one. It's with Felicity Harrison… that buyer from New York? Remember, the one you met at the show?" He nods his head again. "That's not booked until Thursday. Maybe get Mary to call her and re-arrange for another time. If it's not possible, you'll have to see her. Make my apologies. Say I've got a family problem, or something."

"Fine. And the other one?"

"That's with Frank Watson, but that's on Tuesday morning, so there's no chance of re-arranging that." He's an old client we've dealt with for years.

"He won't mind. I'll take him to lunch."

"Just make sure it's not a liquid lunch; you know what Frank's like."

"What else is there?"

"Nothing much that I can think of, unless Mary booked anything in on Friday when I wasn't there."

"I'll check with her first thing tomorrow."

"And can you let her know what's going on? I won't have time. She can call me if she needs to, but it would be better if you can handle things."

"Oh, she'll like that." Luke grins. He and my secretary don't get on too well. She's been with me longer, but Luke's a friend. It can get awkward sometimes.

"I don't care. Tell her I said you're in charge. If she's difficult, let me know."

"It'll be fine, Matt. I'm sure we'll manage not to do each other any actual physical harm, just for one week."

"I'd appreciate it. I really just need you to keep an eye on everything. It's probably best if we set up a regular time each day to call; then you can just text me if anything major happens. I'll keep my phone with me."

He waits for a moment. "These problems that Grace is having..." he says tentatively. "Can I help at all?"

"You are helping."

"You know what I mean, Matt."

I'm not sure I should tell him about it without Grace being here. It's her life, her story, not mine. "I don't think so." Being Luke, he doesn't push.

"And you'll be back next Sunday?"

"Yeah, and I'll be in the office on Monday."

"And what about——?" Whatever Luke was going to ask is interrupted by the sudden appearance of Grace at the end of the hallway. I didn't even hear the bedroom door opening and now, I'm wishing I'd warned her that Luke was going to be here. At least she's wearing one of my t-shirts... but that's all she's wearing and, as she sees him, she flushes bright red.

"Oh, shit!" she says. One hand goes to her mouth, while the other goes to the hem of the t-shirt, trying to pull it down and she turns and disappears again.

I can't help but laugh. Luke's grinning and shaking his head. "I'm guessing you forgot to tell Grace that I'm here?" he says.

"I didn't forget exactly. I just thought she'd sleep in." I get to my feet, walking toward the bedroom as I speak. "I'd better just make sure she's okay. Help yourself to more coffee. I'll be back in a minute."

Inside the bedroom, Grace is lying on the bed, face down.

"Sorry," I say, straight away, sitting beside her and resting my hand on her thigh. "I should have warned you Luke was coming here today."

"God, I'm so embarrassed," she mumbles into the comforter.

"Why? He couldn't see anything, Grace. Honest, everything's covered."

"That's not the point."

"What is then? Tell me…" I press.

"Well… Me being here, with you. Like this…"

I turn her onto her back and lean over her. "What the hell's wrong with that?"

"He'll know now… about us."

"He knew already."

"He did?" She covers her face with her hands.

"Yeah." *Was it meant to be a secret?*

"And he doesn't mind?"

"Why on earth would he mind?"

She lowers her hands and looks at me for a moment. "Because some people might think it's unprofessional. Some people might think I should have waited longer, after Jonathan…" The last few words are whispered.

I pull her up off the bed and into my arms. "Screw being unprofessional. We worked together, we fell in love… so what? That's our business. As for waiting longer. Given what Jonathan did to you… you owe him, you owe his memory nothing, Grace. Nothing. Do you hear me? Don't beat yourself up about that."

"I'm not, well not really. But other people don't know what he did. They have a tendency to judge."

"And does that matter?"

"Sometimes."

"Well, Luke doesn't judge. He's not like that." She nestles into me. "Come out and say hello to him," I say.

"Dressed like this?"

"Well, maybe put a few more clothes on first." I smile down at her and kiss her lightly on the lips. "He's easily distracted."

She climbs off my lap and goes to her bag, rummaging inside and pulling out a pair of jeans. "Why's he here?" she asks, taking off my t-shirt. Standing in front of me, naked, I'm tempted to tell Luke to leave, but we're not quite finished yet.

"We had a few work things to deal with."

"On a Sunday?"

"Yeah." She bends back down, rifling through her bag again. Her ass is divine and, if I'm ever gonna finish this meeting with Luke, I have to leave the room before I take advantage of that view.

Outside, Luke's still on the couch.

"Do me another favor?" I ask him as I go into the kitchen to top up my coffee and fetch one for Grace. "Don't mention anything to Grace about me going to London with her?"

"You mean she doesn't know?"

"Not yet."

"And when are you planning on telling her?"

"After you've gone. If I give her too long to think about it, she'll try and talk me out of it."

"So what am I officially doing here then?"

"We've just got some business to talk through."

"Okay... And can I assume you've stopped being an idiot?" I shoot him a look. "Well, I take it Grace hasn't been sleeping in your guest room..."

I smile at him. "No comment."

He smiles back. "I'll take that as a yes."

"Take it however you like... Can we get back to work now?"

"Sure. I was just going to ask, before your girlfriend interrupted us so charmingly, what about the new models? Did you want me to contact the agency, or leave it until you get back?"

While I'm still taking in the fact that Luke called Grace my 'girlfriend', and how much I like it, Grace reappears, fully clothed in jeans and a t-shirt of her own, with her hair tied up in a loose pony tail. I go to her and take her hand, bringing her over to the couch. I sit her down next to me and hand over her cup of coffee.

She looks slightly warily at Luke, and he gives her his most endearing smile. She shakes her head slightly and smiles back. She's got the measure of him.

"Hi," he says. "How are you, Grace?"

"I'm fine, thank you," Grace replies. "You?" Was she ever this formal with me, even when we first met in London? I don't think so.

"I'm good, thanks." He exudes charm, which usually has women eating out of his hand, but she's immune and I'm loving it.

"Where were we?" I ask Luke, dragging his attention back to me.

"The agency? The models?"

"Call them, if that's okay with you. We need two new guys, maybe three. The last couple we had weren't really right. You know what we're looking for. Same body shape, but less aggressive-looking."

"Okay. I think we've covered everything," Luke says. "How did yesterday go?"

"I got André to demonstrate some chocolate recipes," I tell him. "You enjoyed it, didn't you?" I turn to Grace.

"Yes, it was great. I had a lovely day." She gives me a stunning smile, then turns back to Luke. "André even got Matt to try some, not that he liked it." She leans into me. "He has yet to be fully converted to desserts."

"Yeah well, your coffee-chocolate cheesecake is one thing; that white chocolate concoction of André's was way too sweet for me." I kiss her gently on the lips.

"Sweet can be good," she murmurs and I suddenly wish Luke would go, so I can taste her own special sweetness again.

He coughs, grinning at us. "Well, if we're done, I've got a life too... somewhere out there." I let go of Grace's hand with a quick squeeze and stand, walking to the door with Luke. Once there, he turns, puts his hand on my shoulder and whispers, "I know there are problems, but I'm real happy for you – for both of you – that you've got together at last. You're... well, you're just right for each other."

"We wouldn't have got here without you."

"How do you work that out?"

"It was you that made me realize I was being an idiot."

He chuckles. "I think you'd have realized that all by yourself, eventually." He pauses. "Call me… if you need anything."

He's gone before I can thank him, but I know I don't need to. He gets it.

Grace

Lying on the sofa together, Matt asks whether I want to stay at the apartment for the day, or go out. It's not a difficult decision.

"It's our last day together," I say, trying not to think too hard about how much I'm going to miss him, or going home on my own and facing everything… the messages, work, Jenny, or the looming financial problem I've been trying to ignore. With Jenny not bringing any income in to the business, but still taking a salary, we're struggling. I've maxed out my credit card on this trip and I don't know how I'm going to afford to come back here any time soon, so who knows when I'll see Matt again. "I don't want to share you," I add and he squeezes me tighter and kisses the top of my head.

"About that…" he says and the tone of his voice makes me look up. He's staring down at me.

"What about it?"

He pauses for a moment. "Don't be mad at me…" he says, then waits. I'm not going to interrupt. I'm too interested to know what he thinks I'll be angry about. "It's not our last day together."

"Well, I'm flying home tomorrow, so it kind of is…"

"Except I'm flying back with you."

I sit up, looking down at him. "You can't."

"Why can't I?"

"Because… because you've got a business to run."

"That's why Luke was here this morning. He's taking over for the week."

"The *week?*" I exclaim.

"Yes."

"But you can't stay for a whole week. You have responsibilities, people depending on you…"

"Yes… you. You're my responsibility; you depend on me. At least I hope you do. Nothing and no-one else matters as much as you, Grace."

"But…"

"But what?"

"What can you do in London that I can't?"

"Well, I can go with you to buy a new phone, or at least get your number changed, for one thing. That should put a stop to the messages. They won't be able to contact you anymore."

"I could do that by myself. I don't know why I didn't think of it before…"

"You said they didn't take you seriously. Well, I'll make damn sure they do. Then I can spend some time with you, make you feel safer. I don't like the idea of you going back to your empty apartment by yourself. I can be there with you for a few days, just until you settle back in." This is so kind of him… again. I have to admit, it sounds almost too good to be true. "And I want to talk to Dan, ask him to keep an eye on you; and maybe Jenny too. I was going to see if they've got any ideas about who might be doing this to you…" Ah, there's the hitch. There had to be one. He's looking at me closely now. "What's wrong?" he asks.

"Nothing."

"That's bullshit, baby."

He always knows… How can I tell him what happened? Just open my mouth and say the words, I suppose. "There's a problem with Jenny," I say, "and maybe Dan as well."

"What kind of problem?"

"We had an argument."

"What about?"

"You."

He looks surprised. "Does this have anything to do with what you said earlier? About people judging you?"

I nod my head. "It was just before I came over. I had to ask Jenny if I could divert the calls to her at home, and she realised I wasn't coming over for business, but to see you. She… she got a little critical about my… morals." He sits up too now. We're facing each other.

"Excuse me? Your what?"

"My morals. She said I was being disrespectful to Jonathan's memory… She called me a slut."

"She did what?" He pulls me into a hug. "Jeez… Haven't you gone through enough?"

"She doesn't know about that."

"Well, maybe she should. What did Dan say?"

"He wasn't as bad as Jenny, but he did say he thought I was rushing things, that I should wait a bit longer and be sure I was doing the right thing." I pause for a moment. "Things haven't been right between me and Jenny for ages," I say. "Not like they were when we were at college together."

"Why?"

"To be honest, I don't know."

"Well, how long's it been going on for?"

I think back. "It's hard to fix a time, but not long after I married Jonathan, I suppose. She just became more distant, and more critical."

"And you didn't ask her what was wrong?"

"No. I think I probably assumed the problem was with me, that I must have done something to offend her. I would never have gone looking for confrontation back then, so I just left it."

"You need to have your friends around you, and know you can rely on them. I'll speak to them, set them straight."

"I've got the company to think about, Matt. I can't afford to upset anyone."

"I won't cause any problems." I can see he's thinking. "What about if I take Dan out for a drink… just me and him?"

"How much would you tell him?"

"How much do you want me to tell him?"

"Not about the sex."

"The rapes, you mean?" I nod my head. "We have sex. Jonathan raped you. Call it what it is, Grace."

"Okay. But, I don't think I want anyone knowing about that."

"That's fine, baby. I'll go along with whatever you want to do... Grace," he says, pausing for a second, "remember when you told me about it, on Friday night..." God, was it only Friday night? Just two days ago? "... You said you were going to tell me 'some of it'?" I nod my head. "Is there still more?" I nod again. I feel him contract, just a little, like he's in pain. "Is it worse?" he asks.

"Not worse, just different... more damaging, maybe."

"How can anything be more damaging?"

"You'd be amazed."

"I don't think I would. Not anymore."

"I'm sorry, Matt. I will tell you one day, just not yet."

"Hey, it's okay. I wasn't pushing. I just needed to know." I look at him, and I know the confusion shows on my face. "I'm trying real hard not to screw up, that's all."

"You haven't. You couldn't."

Chapter Fifteen

Matt

We stare down at the bed, then back at each other. My lips curl upwards and so do hers and then we're both laughing out loud, which is good, because we're completely exhausted, and fed up, and I think Grace could easily cry if anything else went wrong today.

We got to Logan early this morning to find the flight was delayed, then there was a mess-up over the seats, even though I'd paid to upgrade Grace to first class when I booked my ticket, so we could sit together. When we got to Heathrow, there was a rail strike, so there were no trains, and we had to wait in the rain to get a cab back to Grace's apartment. Apart from that, the journey has been terrific. It's after midnight and it feels like we've been travelling for days.

"I'd forgotten how much smaller it is than yours," Grace says. We're standing at the end of her bed, looking at it. She's right, it's tiny by comparison.

"Is this really meant for two people?" I ask, folding my arms across my chest and trying not to laugh again.

"Yes, it's a standard double bed, so it's four foot six across, and a little over… Oh." She looks up at me. "It's probably not as long as you are tall." She's stifling a giggle. "How big's yours then?"

I smirk. "My bed?"

"Yes, your bed." She pats my arm, playfully, but lets her hand rest there.

"It's six feet six inches wide, and just over eight feet long… Back home, we call it a Texas King, Ma'am." That cheesy accent always makes her smile… every time.

"Oh, you would." Her eyes are alight. "Show off."

I drop the accent. "That's me." I wink at her.

"So, how are we going to do this?" She nods in the direction of her bed.

"I guess, it has potential." I turn her and push her down onto the mattress and she squeals, then giggles, and moves up the bed until her head's resting on the pillows.

"Well, I'm comfy, but I don't know where you're going to sleep," she says, grinning up at me.

"I'll work it out." I climb slowly up on top of her, until my face is level with hers. My feet are still hanging off the end and I'm resting on my elbows, keeping most of my weight from crushing her. "How about here?" I whisper, pushing my hips into hers, so she can feel my erection.

"Seems reasonable." She leans up and kisses me. "But I need a shower first," she says. "I feel revolting."

"You look sensational."

"I'd like to suggest we shower together…"

I raise myself up onto my hands, looking down at her. "Grace, I've seen your bathroom. I think we can only shower together, if one of us can be out in the hallway at the time… which could get a bit messy."

"Okay… so my bathroom's small, I'll grant you that."

I roll off of her so she can get up. "You go ahead; I'll make us some coffee."

"There's decaf in the cupboard above the sink," she calls as she leaves the room.

"Don't swear at me," I say back to her. "Decaf?"

She pokes her head back round the door. "Well, make me a decaf then, please? I won't sleep if I have normal coffee at this time of night." I get up and walk over to her, pulling her into me.

"Who said I was going to let you sleep?"

The sleeping worked out okay, once we got around to it. In my bed at home, Grace had taken to lying with her head on my chest, her arm across my stomach, her leg bent across mine, while I slept on my back, with my arm around her. Here, in her bed, we spooned. It's made for an interesting early morning and I can see definite advantages to the smaller bed.

Grace is drying her hair, so I take advantage and look up Dan's number on her phone, copying it to mine. By the time she's finished, I'm ready to go.

The morning has gone well. Grace has cleared me a space in her office, so I've set up my laptop and have probably got more done here than I normally would at home.

At lunchtime, we head to the phone shop and, after putting the overly flirty sales woman in her place, we manage to change Grace's number. She's right, they don't seem to understand the problem, or take it too seriously. I save her new number onto my cell and, while she's picking up some sandwiches from the deli, I call Dan.

He answers on the third ring. "Hi Dan, it's Matt. Matt Webb." I start off friendly.

"Oh. Hello, Matt." His voice is suddenly cool, remote. That's just fine with me.

"I'd like to meet you," I say, making my tone businesslike.

"Me?" He's surprised.

"Yes. Are you free this afternoon?"

"Um… Yes, I suppose…"

"Good." I cut him off. "Tell me where and I'll be there."

"Well, where are you?" he asks.

I look up at the sign above the shop. "I'm standing outside 'Dominico's'."

"What, at the office? You're over here?" Would I be asking to meet up otherwise? "Sorry, that was a stupid question, wasn't it?" I don't reply. "I can meet you there, then. They serve coffee."

"At Dominico's? Okay. What time?"

"Say… four o'clock?"

"Fine. See you at four." I hang up, just as Grace comes out and I fill her in on the plan. She's nervous, I think, that I'll lose my temper with Dan, but that's not going to happen, despite my irritation with him. I need him onside as much as she needs Jenny in the business. That doesn't mean I'm going to let him off completely though…

I'm seated at a table when he arrives and I've already got a black coffee, steaming in front of me. He joins me and orders a latte and we sit in silence, waiting until it's brought over. If one of us doesn't speak soon, it's going to get a bit awkward. I've asked for this meeting, so…

"I need to ask you a question," I say.

"Okay." He sounds wary. *Good.*

"How much do you know about Grace and Jonathan's marriage?"

That surprised him. "Well… um… just what I've seen for myself and what Jenny's told me, really. I mean, Grace had already been married to Jonathan for a year or so before I even came on the scene." I'm just staring at him, my face impassive, letting him speak. I know it makes people uneasy and that's pretty much where I want him. "As far as I know, they were very happy, and she was devastated when he died."

"So, you'd be surprised, I take it, to learn that he used to beat the shit out of her."

His mouth falls open. "He… he did what?"

"He routinely beat the shit out of her," I repeat.

"How do you know this?"

Dumb question. "Because she told me." I see a look cross his eyes. "And don't even think about doubting her. She even took a beating because of you once."

"Me? Why?"

"Do you remember visiting Grace at home a few months before Jonathan died? I think Jenny had gone to stay with her mother?" He nods his head slowly. "Do you remember Jonathan coming home?"

"Yes…"

"And then do you remember him calling you later on, and asking you to tell Jenny that he was taking Grace on vacation, to make up for being away so often?"

"Yes, I do. Jenny said it was so typical of Jonathan, being so considerate."

"Considerate, my ass. Once you left, he accused her of sleeping with you; she denied it, obviously, because it wasn't true and he battered her nearly to death."

"But surely, she'd have left him, if…?"

"Yeah, that would have been real easy, wouldn't it? He ground her down so low, she had nothing left. As far as she knew, she had nowhere to go."

"She could have come to us…"

"What? Her supportive friends, you mean?"

He pales. "We didn't know."

"I appreciate that none of us knows what goes on in someone else's relationship, but did you really not see anything? Nothing at all? No bruises? Nothing in her mannerisms?"

"No. She's Jenny's friend, really, but if I had…" I'm calming down now. He seems genuinely remorseful. "God… I gave Grace such a hard time… about you."

"Yeah, I know."

"She told you?" I nod my head. "It was nothing personal, Matt."

"I don't care. I only care about Grace. She needs you guys. I'm three thousand miles away – or I will be from next Sunday. I'd like to think she has friends here, not people who are judging her decisions. Can I rely on you to look out for her?"

"Yes… yes. Of course you can. Look, I'm sorry. If we'd known…"

"You're apologizing to the wrong person." I pause for a second. "What about Jenny?"

"I think she and Grace probably need to talk it out between themselves."

"Maybe, but if that's the case, I'm going to be there when they do."

When I get back to the office, Grace is sitting at her computer screen, her head in her hands.

"Has something happened?" I ask.

"Jenny," she says, not looking up. *What now?*

"What about Jenny?" I go around to her side of the desk and turn her chair so she's facing me, then I place my feet either side of hers, looking down at her.

"She's just called... How did your meeting with Dan go, by the way?"

"It was fine. He says he didn't realize and he's sorry about what he said." She nods her head. "But tell me about Jenny."

"She wants to meet up."

"Well, that's a good thing, isn't it? Dan suggested it too. Maybe he called her once he'd left me? He thinks you two need to talk everything through."

"I'm not sure that's what she's got in mind."

"What do you mean?"

"She didn't sound very friendly. She said she needs to talk about the business, and she asked if I can go round there after work tonight. I said okay and she just hung up."

"Well, I'm coming with you."

"You don't mind?"

"Mind? Try stopping me. You're not going alone."

"Thank you."

I lean down, placing my mouth next to her ear. "I really, really wish you'd stop thanking me."

"But you're being so kind." I hear a crack in her voice and pull her to her feet and into my arms.

"This isn't kindness, baby... It's love."

Grace

We've decided to go straight to Jenny and Dan's from the office, rather than eating first. I'm not sure I could eat, with my stomach churning the way it is. I've still got no idea what she wants to talk about, but her tone was brusque, to put it mildly.

Matt rings the doorbell of their neat terraced Victorian house and Dan opens the door to us.

"Hi," he says, looking embarrassed. Is that because of his conversation with Matt, or because he knows what's coming? He stands to one side, letting us enter.

The hallway is narrow and we squeeze past him, and I take the first door on the right, which is their living room, with Matt following. It's a chilly evening for October, and they've lit the fire, which is warming. I love their home; it's cosy. Dan did the refurbishment himself and it's incredible. He's really talented. Jenny is sitting on one of the two-seater sofas, holding Lily, and music is playing in the background. It's something I haven't heard for years. It's a track called *Happy* by Lighthouse Family. It takes me back to my first year at Art School, when I met Jenny. I think it was a year or so old at the time, but we both liked their music and we listened to it a lot. Has she done this on purpose, to remind me? She clicks a button on a remote control and the room falls into silence, except for the quiet snuffling which Lily makes as she sleeps in her mother's arms.

"Hello," I say. Jenny looks up at me.

"Hello." Wow. Her voice is like ice. She glances at Matt, but doesn't say a word. She needs to remember that he's still a client, even if she doesn't approve of what he and I have become. *At least be polite, Jenny*.

"Good evening," Matt says and I turn towards him. He's staring at her, his eyes dark, and his voice when he spoke was frosty. This is going to be fun.

She just nods her head, then looks back at me, raising an eyebrow. I know she's querying why he's here, but I'm not going to justify anything to her. Dan moves a little further into the room. "Take a seat," he says, and we do, on the other sofa, opposite Jenny. Dan sits next to her.

"What did you want to see me about?" I ask. My voice is remarkably calm, considering how agitated I'm feeling.

"I'd rather have discussed this in private, but as you've insisted on bringing your... *boyfriend*... with you, I suppose we'll just have to conduct our business affairs in front of him."

"Yes, we will." The way she said 'boyfriend' makes me want to slap her. I've not thought of Matt in those terms yet, although I suppose that's exactly what he is, but on her lips the word sounds insulting.

"Very well." She shifts in her seat. "I want you to buy me out of the company."

Is she serious? "What?" The word is out of my mouth before I can stop it. "Why?"

"Because I'm not coming back to work. I want to stay at home and look after Lily."

"Since when? We agreed... I mean, you always said—"

"Things change, don't they?"

"Oh, for Christ's sake, Jenny. Is this because I'm with Matt now? Is this about our argument? Because if it is, there are things you should know..." Dan is staring at the stripped wooden floorboards, so I've got no clue as to whether he's already told her about his conversation with Matt.

"I already know everything I need to. I know a lot more than you think."

"Oh, really?"

"I know you didn't deserve Jonathan... You never did. I know you're spreading lies about him now he's not here to defend himself. I know he was far too good for you." The words spew out of her like gunfire.

"Jenny? What do you mean?" It's Dan who speaks first. "I explained earlier about..."

"Yes, you explained about *her*, and her lies."

"Grace isn't lying," Matt says.

173

"How would you know? Were you there?"

"Were you?"

"For some of the time, yes."

I'm confused; so is Dan. Matt isn't thrown quite so easily. "Not in their house you weren't, Jenny. You didn't see what Jonathan did to her."

"That's because there was nothing to see. She's making it up."

"No she isn't."

"She is. It's the only thing that makes sense… He wasn't like that. All the time he and I were together, he…" Jenny sucks in a breath. She didn't mean to say that. She glances at Dan, who's staring at her.

"What are you talking about?" he whispers into the mounting tension. I'd really rather be anywhere else but here.

She sits in silence for a moment – a long moment – then turns in her seat to face him. "Years ago," she says quietly, "I had a 'thing' with Jonathan…" She reaches across to him, but he withdraws into the corner of the sofa. "It was before I even met you, Dan. I broke it off with him as soon as I met you, honestly." She sounds desperate, pleading.

Dan's thinking, but I've already worked it out. It explains so much about her behaviour at that time – and since. "But…" He looks across at me. "But if you only broke it off with Jonathan when you met me…"

"Then Grace was already married to him?" Matt finishes the sentence.

Jenny nods her head, keeping her eyes fixed on Dan. Even from this distance I can see the fear in her eyes. "Jonathan tried so hard to please her. He did everything he could for her, but nothing was ever good enough. He was miserable with her. That's why he came to me, looking for someone he could actually have some fun with… and now… now… He's only been dead a few months and look at what she's done…"

"What *she's* done?" Dan is incredulous; his shock has turned to anger. "How could you, Jen? How could you do that to your friend?"

"You didn't really know Jonathan. He was… a very charismatic man."

"Yeah, when he wasn't beating the crap out of his wife, I'm sure he was great company," Matt says.

I feel like we should leave. Dan and Jenny have a lot to talk about.

"What do you want, Jenny?" I sit forward on the seat, making it clear we won't be stopping much longer.

She turns to look at me. "What I've already said. I want you to buy me out."

"I can't afford to do that. Jonathan left me nothing."

"I don't believe you. He wouldn't have done that."

"I don't care what you believe; it's the truth. I had to sell my car months ago, I live in a tiny rented flat; I'm working on Matt's projects, and we've got no other work, but you're still taking your share of everything I earn, despite not actually doing any work. You know all this. Where the hell do you think I'm going to get the money to buy you out?"

"I don't really care." She's so cold. "Borrow it."

"Against what? I just explained. I have no assets. No-one's going to lend me that kind of money."

I feel Matt's hand in mine. "Do you want to do this, Grace?" His voice is soft and I turn to find he's looking at me, his face serious. "Do you want to buy her out?"

"I guess so, but I can't…"

"What's the set up?" he asks. "Of the business, I mean?"

"We each have a fifty-fifty share." He nods and turns back to Jenny, but keeps a firm grip on my hand.

"I'll get someone independent to look at the finances as soon as possible," he says, talking to her while getting up and pulling me to my feet. "Then I'll pay you fifty per-cent of whatever they say the business is worth, and not another cent… sorry, penny." I feel him squeeze my fingers.

"And if I don't agree to their figures?"

"Tough shit. That's the deal; take it, or leave it."

Jenny hesitates for a minute. "Okay," she says finally.

Matt pulls me towards the door and Dan gets up. For a moment I wonder if he's going to leave with us, and so – I think – does Jenny.

"Where are you going?" she asks, panic in her voice.

"I'm going to show our guests out," he says quietly. "Then we're going to talk."

We're already at the door, but I don't look back at her. I can't feel sorry for her, or her predicament, but I do hope they're okay – for Lily's sake.

When we get to the front door, Matt opens it. Dan is standing behind me.

"I'm sorry, Grace," he says and I turn. He looks so sad.

"Don't be. It wasn't your fault. You weren't even around at the time."

"I mean I'm sorry I didn't see what he was doing to you," he admits.

"Oh, don't worry about that. He was good at hiding it."

"And I'm sorry about Jenny too."

I nod my head and let Matt lead me out into the night.

Chapter Sixteen

Matt

The walk back to Grace's place was silent. I think we both had a lot to take on board. There's the affair to start off with. I don't know how she's going to come to terms with that. And Jenny's betrayal is compounded by the way she's behaving over the business. At least I can help there. I wish I'd known money was so tight, though. I don't blame her for not telling me, but I'd have helped her out sooner, if I'd realized.

She lets us in to the apartment and we don't bother with the lights. We stand in the tiny hallway and she leans into me, her hands creeping around my waist and I pull her close. She's very still.

"Do you need anything?" I ask.

She shakes her head, but tightens her grip around my waist. I guess that means she doesn't need anything but me? Well, that goes for me too. I bend down and lift her into my arms, and carry her through to the living room, sitting on the couch and bringing her down, onto my lap. We stay there, for what feels like an age. I'm starting to think we'll never move again when she stirs.

"Can we go to bed?" she whispers.

"Sure." She goes to get up. "You okay?" I ask her. She stills but doesn't reply. "Grace? Are you okay?"

"No."

It's hardly a surprising reply. I pull her back down again. "Wanna talk?"

"Not really. Not yet."

"Okay."

"Just take me to bed."

I stand, taking her with me and carry her through to the bedroom, lowering her beside the bed. I undo her blouse, button by button, not taking my eyes from hers, the streetlights providing enough illumination for me to see her dazed face. She's beyond feeling, I think. Once I've peeled off her blouse, I remove her bra, then her jeans and panties, and pull back the comforter. She clambers into bed, curling up and I take off my clothes and climb in behind her, pulling her into my front, my arms tight around her.

"Shhh, baby," I say and she nestles into me.

"I'm sorry," she whispers.

"What the... I mean, what for?"

"For not telling you sooner."

"About the money, you mean?"

She hesitates for a moment, then nods her head. Is that what she meant, or was there something else? Something I haven't picked up on? I'm not sure now.

"I couldn't face it."

"How bad is it?"

"Not desperate. I can eat."

My muscles clench automatically and I try to relax. "And pay rent?"

"Just about."

"And Jenny's still claiming her share, even though she's not working?"

"Yes. We agreed that because she said she'd be coming back to work next month... only now... now..." Her voice breaks.

"It's okay. I'll deal with it."

"You don't have to."

"Yes, I do."

"It could be a lot of money. I have no idea how much the business is worth."

"I don't care how much money it is. I'll find an accountant in the morning and go over the figures with him – or her. It'll all be dealt with before I go home. I promise."

"How can I ever repay you though?"

"Repay me? You don't have to repay me. It's not a loan, Grace."

"I can't just take your money."

I take a deep breath. I don't want to fight with her about this. "Okay, but I don't want you to repay me. Can you do something for me in return?"

"What?"

I turn her around so she's facing me. "You don't have to do it right now, because I know it's hard, but when today's behind us and you're feeling better... I'd really like to see you smile again."

"You're going to buy out my business partner and, in return, you just want me to smile?" Even in the dim light I can see the tears brimming in her eyes.

"Just smile, baby, that's all."

"God, I love you," she says, and it's everything I need... Well, that and to see her smile again.

This morning, I've spent a little while on the Internet, finding a respectable-looking firm of local accountants. Grace assures me that she doesn't know them and they haven't provided any services to the business before, so they'll be independent enough to satisfy Jenny. I give them a call, speak to one of the senior partners and, although he tells me he's 'really busy', I arrange a meeting with him for just after lunch. It's amazing how loud money can talk when you let it.

Grace gives me all the accounts for the previous year and I take them with me to meet Christopher Austin, at his offices, which are on the other side of Richmond. In the cab, I have a quick look at the figures. It doesn't take a genius to see that the business isn't doing great and, I'm guessing that, without the work from Amulet, they'd be in even bigger trouble. This goes in Grace's favor, of course, as the value of the company will be less, but I had no idea things were so bad.

Christopher Austin turns out to be a little older than me, tall and thin, with glasses. A pleasant enough guy, he agrees to look over the figures and get back to me with a valuation for the business by tomorrow afternoon. He keeps reiterating how unusual the circumstances are, and how they'd normally take much longer to carry out an audit like this. I repeat how much I'm prepared to pay, which seems to appease him.

As I leave his offices, I switch my phone back on. There's a message from Grace.

— *Do you want to eat in or out tonight? Gx*

I reply straight away.

— *In. I'll cook. You can watch. You okay? Mx*

— *A little better. Watching you sounds good. Looking forward to it already. Gx*

— *Me too. Any requests? Mx*

— *Just you. Gxx*

— *You got it. Back soon. Mxx*

We closed the office early and Grace is sprawled on top of me on the couch in her living room. She's naked and I'm running my fingertips along her spine. It makes her shudder and I like that. I love her reactions; she's incredibly sensitive.

"Why am I the only one who's not wearing clothes?" she asks.

"Because I've still got to cook," I reply, smiling. "I bought steak... I could burn something important."

"That would never do." She wiggles her hips onto me.

"If you do much more of that, we won't get any dinner."

She rolls off of me, toward the back of the sofa. "Well, you'd better get cooking. I'm hungry."

"Yeah, so am I." I pull her back on top of me and kiss her. Hard.

While I sear the steaks, Grace – now wearing one of my t-shirts – makes a salad. This is really tough, because in her tiny kitchen, we're continually bumping into each other and it's all I can do not to lift her onto the countertop and bury myself in her. But, after yesterday, I want to make our next time different; special, memorable.

The steaks are good, although I say so myself, and Grace makes a mean salad. Over dinner, she tells me about the website designs she's been working on for the latest collections. I'm going to check them out with her tomorrow, but they're sounding really good so far. When we're finished, we clear away, then go straight to bed, sitting propped up, naked against the pillows. There are a few lit candles dotted around and I realize it's that kind of thing which is missing in my apartment. That, and maybe flowers? I need Grace to give it a touch of... something. A touch of Grace, I guess. She shifts down the bed a little, turning and resting her head on my chest. I'm already hard and, with slow, faltering moves, she runs her fingers down my stomach, then lower, until she's at the base of my cock. She's never touched me before and I'm suddenly aware that she's uncertain what to do. I want to let her find out for herself, at her pace.

"You can stroke me, if you want," I whisper, "but only if you want. You don't have to."

Little by little, she raises her hand, encircling me in her grip. She looks up at my face and I smile down at her, nodding, and she starts to move her fist gently up and down my length. Her eyes dart down to where her hand is steadily pumping me. I close my eyes, just for a moment, savoring her touch, her caress. I'm going to have to stop her soon, but it feels... it feels so... damned...

"Grace!" I hiss between my teeth, opening my eyes again.

"Hmm?" Her gaze is fixed on mine.

"Stop, unless you want me to..." She halts. Thank God. I let out a breath, and a thought occurs to me. "Wanna try something?" I ask. She's still staring at me and nods her head, just once, her eyes blazing. I pull her on top of me. "Do you want to try taking me?" I say.

"How?" Her voice is husky.

"Put one knee either side… so you're straddling me," I say, and she does. My swollen cock finds her opening like it's meant to be, and she rests, just for a moment, on the precipice. "Now, beautiful… it's your move."

Slowly, with her eyes closed, she lowers herself down until I'm buried deep inside in her. She lets out a sigh, then opens her eyes, gazing at me. I nod my head and, leaning forward slightly, she rests her hands on my chest as she raises, then lowers herself again. She feels so good, and watching her take me inside her is the best thing I've ever seen. She sits back a little, forcing me deeper, and gasps, her head rolling back as she rocks her hips, then starts a steady rhythm, riding me harder and faster, and I raise and flex my hips to meet hers. I reach out and capture her breasts, pinching her nipples gently between my thumbs and forefingers, and she moans softly. She's getting close but I can feel her thighs quivering with fatigue, so I sit up, her breasts crushed against my chest, and she shifts, wrapping her legs around me. With my hands beneath her glorious ass, I take over, raising and then lowering her onto me… over and over, harder, deeper, faster. She thrusts her fingers into my hair, her mouth over mine as her orgasm hits and her screams fill my throat. I plunge into her one final time, and then I'm filling her as she rides out the waves of pleasure. It's powerful, and intense. It's eternal.

She's lying on top of me, breathing hard, and we're still connected and I think I could stay this way… maybe forever. Unfortunately, reality hits with the beep of a cell phone.

"Yours or mine?" she murmurs into my chest.

"Probably mine," I mutter. "I guess it's Luke. It's around five at home, so he'll just be checking in."

"Where is it?" she asks.

"My jeans… back pocket."

"And where are your jeans?"

"On the floor, somewhere." She raises herself off my chest and leans over the edge of the bed, then sits up again. I'm still inside her and she seems to like it that way – she's not trying to disconnect us.

"I can't see them."

"Try the other side." I move us across the bed and she leans again.

"Oh, yes. Got them." She reaches over and pulls up my jeans, retrieving my cell from the pocket and handing it to me. I keep one hand rested on her thigh while I check my phone, but there are no new messages.

"Not mine," I say. "Where's yours?"

She looks down at me, half smiling. "Kitchen?"

"You're kidding me…" I run my hands around behind her.

"It's fine. I'll go."

"Like hell you will. I'm not giving you up yet. We'll go together." She squeals loudly, giggling, as I move to the edge of the bed, keeping us locked together, place my hands beneath her ass, and stand up. "Wrap your legs round, baby," I say and she does and settles onto my already hardening cock, bringing her arms around my shoulders.

I carry her through to the kitchen, where her phone is lying on the countertop. She reaches over, picks it up and, holding it between us, opens the message screen.

"No!" she howls. "No… Matt. Oh God, this can't be…"

"Grace?" I lift her off me, lowering her to the ground and, taking her phone, I read the message:

— *It's not that easy to get away, bitch*

And, as we're standing there, the phone beeps again.

— *I'm still watching you*

Grace

How is it possible for an evening to start so wonderfully and end so dreadfully? And how did they find me again? It's a new number, which only a handful of people even know yet. There's Matt, obviously, and he's given it to Luke; there's Jenny and Dan, because we've still got to communicate; a couple of regular freelancers and that's it. None of them would do this.

Matt held me all night, but I couldn't sleep; neither could he. Today's Thursday and he's going home on Sunday and I've never wanted anything more than I want to go with him. I honestly can't think of a single reason to stay here anymore. Even if the messages don't stop, at least I'd be with him. That's not going to happen though, so I've got to somehow face what's happening and try to work out who's doing this… and why?

It's still really early, but as neither of us have slept, we're up. Matt's skipping breakfast, apart from coffee, but I need toast, which is taking longer than usual in the grill. He's sitting at the table in sweatpants, his chest bare and beautiful, staring into his cup. I'm wearing one of his t-shirts again, because he likes me to.

"I know you're going to tell me I'm crazy…" he says, "but you don't think the messages could be from Jenny, do you?"

I'm shocked. "Jenny? No. She wouldn't."

"Would you have thought she'd have an affair with your husband?"

So many other women did, I suppose that doesn't surprise me much. "No," I say out loud, "but this is different."

"You heard her the other night, though. She was angry, vindictive."

He's right; she was. But she wouldn't do this, would she? I think back over the messages. Do they make sense for Jenny? She's not watching me; she's busy with Lily. And a lot of the messages are about my sexual inadequacies. How I'm not good enough for Matt. Why would she say that? She doesn't even want me to be with him. And there's another thing…

"The messages started before Jenny even knew we were involved. I mean, *I* didn't really know we were involved at that stage. She was still in hospital at the time; she'd just had Lily."

"She could still have got hold of a phone."

"But she was fine with me when I visited, just a few hours earlier. I really don't think it's her, Matt."

He hesitates. "Okay. I just thought…"

"I know."

I turn off the grill, and retrieve the toast, even though it's barely browned, and bring it over to the table with me. It would be easier if it could be Jenny; then we could ignore the messages, write them off as her petty jealousy and move on. As it is, not knowing is terrifying. I sit opposite him.

We stare at each other. "I checked out your finances," he admits, like he's telling me a deep secret, "when I took them to the accountants."

"Oh. So you know we're not exactly thriving then."

"Let's just say I'm glad we're keeping you afloat." He smiles across the table and then reaches over and takes my hand. "The thing is..." he continues, "is there any point?"

Well, I didn't expect that. He wants to pull his work now, on top of everything else? Why would he do this to me? "I don't..." I start to say, but my voice falters.

"Hey..." He gets up and comes round to my side of the table, crouching next to me. He's a blur as my eyes fill with tears. God, I'm sick of crying. I feel like it's all I've done for the last few months. "I didn't mean that I don't want to keep working with you, just that I think there's another way of doing it." He looks at the table, then stands. "Butter your toast, and we'll sit on the couch and talk. It's more comfortable."

I do as he says and he carries the coffees over to the sofa. I sit down next to him, my plate on my lap.

He turns to face me. "Let me talk for a minute, and tell me if I get anything wrong," he says.

"Okay." I take a bite of toast.

"You and Jenny have a business that used to thrive, but has hit harder times in the last couple of years, right?" He looks at me and I nod. "Jenny's not contributing anything now, but is still taking her salary, and you're the only person doing any work at the moment. You've got Amulet as a customer, plus a couple of local companies, who haven't given you very much to do for ages and seem to take a long time to pay their outstanding bills."

"That's one way of putting it."

"You both own a fifty per cent stake in the company and Jenny wants out, as of a couple of days ago, but you don't have the funds to buy her share."

"Yes, but I thought you said you were happy to…"

"Let me finish," he says gently. "Is there really any reason to keep this business going?" he asks.

"Um… only that it's my livelihood?"

"But you could close it up; cut your losses and start again… somewhere else."

"Like where?"

"Boston."

I stare at him. "How on earth would I do that? I can't just move to Boston." *Can I?*

"Well, it's not as easy as moving from here to… I don't know, Manchester, but it's possible. There are just a lot of forms to fill in; interviews, red tape, the usual government crap to wade through. I'd be your sponsor – if you want to do it, that is – so actually I'd be the one doing most of the form-filling."

"You've really thought this through, haven't you?"

"Not all of it, but I had a few hours' thinking time last night."

"Are you saying I'd start my own business out there?"

"You could, I guess. I'm not entirely sure how that works… I think you have to invest quite a large sum of money. I don't know how much, but I can look into it…"

"I don't have a large sum of money, Matt."

"I'd give you the money, if that's what you want to do."

"I'm not taking any more from you."

"Then why not let me be your sponsor and bring you into my company? It'll probably be quicker anyway."

"Work for you, you mean?"

"No, work *with* me." He stops, like he's thinking for a moment, then carries on, "I don't really care how we do it, Grace. I want you to come to Boston. I want you with me. We can iron out the details, can't we?"

"What about Jenny?"

"What about her?"

"She'll still want her share."

"Her share of what? If you close down the business, there won't be a share."

"That's sneaky. I'm not sure I'd feel comfortable doing that. It feels a bit underhand. Also, if she doesn't agree to closing the business, I'd have fight on my hands."

He leans over. "You're right. As much as I like the sound of doing it my way, it might be better if you buy her out. I'll pay her off, then once the company's yours, you'll have control, and you can close it down and walk away in your own time, with a clear conscience."

"You'd do all that? For me?"

"Baby, I'd do anything for you."

"I've had another idea," he says, almost as soon as I step out of the bathroom, wrapped in a towel, my wet hair dripping over my shoulders. He's lying on the sofa, clutching a half-drunk cup of coffee. "Being as we... you... well, we've kind of decided what to do about your company, and being as I'm really your only client at the moment... how about taking a couple of days off work? I mean, if you're going to close down the company anyway, what does it matter?"

"What would we do?"

"We could find a hotel and just get away from everything?"

"That sounds perfect."

"Okay. Why don't you use my laptop and find us somewhere to stay, while I grab a shower."

"You mean you want to go today?"

"I don't just want to go today, I want to go right now. As soon as we've packed." He jumps up and comes over to me.

"You like to be spontaneous, don't you?"

He leans down and kisses me. "I thought you'd have noticed that by now." He goes into the bedroom.

"Where do you want to go?" I call.

"I don't know. Your country... Your choice."

187

"Coast or countryside?"

"Um… Coast." He comes back out again, naked, but carrying his wallet, which he opens, taking out a credit card and handing it to me before going into the bathroom. I stare down at the piece of plastic in my hand.

"Any particular preferences as to type of hotel?" I ask, hoping for a clue as to the budget.

He sticks his head out of the bathroom door. "One with big beds?" He smirks at me.

"You did good, baby." The wind whips around us, catching my hair and he nudges it back behind my ears. "A great bed, *and* all this…" He stretches his arms out, then brings them around me again. "It's beautiful here." We're on the beach, watching the sunset at Durdle Door, a massive arched rock, on the south Dorset coast.

Getting here was a little chaotic, but well worth it. Fortunately the hotel had a room available; I found a local car hire company who were happy to help out and dropped off a VW Golf at my place, and then there was just packing. Super-fast packing. We arrived in time for a late lunch… and to try out the super-king sized bed, *and* the shower in the ensuite bathroom.

It's chilly in the wind, but we're well wrapped up. And I'm not sure I care anyway. I feel so happy. It's like all my problems have been lifted from my shoulders – well, most of them, anyway. Matt's got my phone again, so I don't have to be bothered by the messages, although I know there have been two more today. He hasn't let me see them, but his reactions tell me they've been unpleasant. I don't want to read them at the moment; it'll just spoil everything. We're going to change my number again when we get back home on Saturday, although neither of us think it will do any good.

Matt takes my hand and we stroll back in the direction of the car. The hotel's a few miles inland and, as the sun sinks over the smooth water, it's time to head back there.

"I have a question," he asks.

"Hmm?"

"When you come to Boston, where do you want to live?"

I hadn't expected that. Well, maybe I had, but I don't know the answer. I'd be lying if I said I haven't been thinking about it on and off during the day, but I haven't reached any conclusions, mainly because I don't know what *he* wants. I can hardly say I want to live with him if he's not ready for that yet. It's a big step for someone who used to shy away from even bringing anyone back to his place. And, in reality, we've only been together properly for a week — although that seems ridiculous — it feels like forever. "I don't know." I sense him stiffen beside me. "Where do you want me to live?"

"Wherever you feel most comfortable." He stops and turns to face me. "If you think things are moving too fast, I can find you an apartment near the office…" He looks away for a moment. The sun is almost gone and the dusk begins to settle around us. "Oh hell," he murmurs, turning back. "Move in with me, Grace… Please?" He moves closer. "I wasn't going to ask; I was going to let you decide, but the idea of you being in my city and living anywhere but with me… It's just wrong. Please, say you'll move in to my place?" I nod my head and curl my arms around his neck as he leans down, his mouth hovering above mine. "Is that a yes?"

"Yes. I—" I'm silenced by his kiss… And I don't care… I don't care at all.

Chapter Seventeen

∽

Matt

I've been surprised over the last two months that the biggest hold up hasn't been getting Grace a work permit, but dealing with the winding up of Richards Cole Design, which has taken weeks to organize. Even now, it's not completed, but everything from here on can be handled remotely. I paid Jenny off before I left London. I doubt she and Grace will ever speak again, which isn't surprising. It would be hard to forgive Jenny for what she did. I know I couldn't.

I flew Grace out here for Thanksgiving, but letting her go again was torture, maybe worse than ever. For the first time, she cried at the airport and I didn't want to leave her, or drive back home by myself. The apartment was too empty without her

From now on, though, she doesn't have to go back and we don't have to do airport goodbyes again. She's here, and she's here for good. Or she will be when her plane lands... I check the clock... in just over an hour. I need to leave for the airport soon.

I glance around. Everything is ready, or as ready as it can be. Not that 'everything' amounts to very much – I wanted to leave most of it until she was here.

She's actually in my arms, she's not going to leave again in a few days and I just want to breathe her in.

"Hi, beautiful," I whisper into her hair.

"Hi," she says, clinging on to me.

"You feel good."

"So do you."

"Shall we go home?"

"I like the sound of that." She smiles up at me and I bend down to pick up her case.

"Is this all you've brought?" I ask.

"The rest is being shipped." We start walking.

"But have you even got enough clothes here?"

"I've got enough for about a week."

I stop dead, so does my heart. "About a week?"

"Don't panic. I'm not about to leave again."

Okay. *Breathe, Matt, breathe.* "You had me worried. Why only a week's clothes?"

"Because it's all I could bring in one case. They're winter clothes. They're thick... heavy. I can wash things until the rest arrives."

"Or... we can go shopping." I smile down at her.

"I've cost you enough money already."

Hmm. That's not a promising comment, given what I've done. How's she going to react? I guess there's only one way to find out.

"We'll see," I say. "Let's go home."

Grace looks out the car window at the streets and shop windows decorated for the holidays; it's an abundance of lights and decorations. I'll bring her back out when it's dark, so she can see everything properly... but not tonight.

"Um... Where are we going?" she asks.

"You'll see."

"Matt..."

"We're nearly there. It's just around the next corner."

"I thought we were going to your apartment." I don't reply, but turn the corner and then pull in through the entrance, approaching the large red-brick building, pulling the car up in a parking bay at the front. "Why are we here?" she says.

"You'll see…"

"Stop saying that." I climb out of the car and open her door, helping her to her feet. "Matt, please…"

"Come on." I pull her away from the car toward the front door, which I open with a swipe card.

Inside the door, there are two elevators and I press the 'up' button. The right hand doors open immediately and I allow Grace to enter ahead of me, and press the button for the fifth floor… the top one. We ride up in silence, although she's staring at me and I'm trying real hard not to smile, but I just keep my eyes fixed on the doors until they open, revealing a hallway, with windows down one side, leading to a single door.

"What are we doing here?" she whispers.

I produce a key from my pocket, put it in the lock and open the door, then stand to one side.

"After you…"

She walks in ahead of me, but as she passes, I catch something in her eyes and it's not what I'd hoped for. I'd hoped she'd like it, well, love it actually. I'd hoped she'd see what I did, but she looks… disappointed. She only makes it a few feet inside the room, before she turns.

"Why, Matt?" she says. She's so sad. This isn't the reaction I'd expected.

"I thought you'd like it," I reply, going to her. She takes a step back.

"I do. It's lovely. But we agreed…"

"I know we did." Realization dawns. "Oh, wait a minute…" I smile down at her. "You think… you think I bought this for you? Just for you?" Well, I guess I did, but not in the way she thinks. "Oh, Grace, come here." I pull her into a hug. She comes, but stiffly, reluctantly. "This is for us." She leans back, staring into my face.

"But…"

"I thought we should have a fresh start… both of us… somewhere completely new. I didn't want you to think of anything as 'mine'. Everything here is 'ours'." I look around. "Except, there isn't much of anything to call ours yet." She leans into me, her arms around my neck. "You do like it, don't you?"

She turns, looking around properly for the first time. "It's amazing. Is it really ours?"

I nod my head, then reach into my pocket and pull out the spare swipe card and door key. "These are for you," I tell her, handing them over. "Now, let me show you around." I take her hand and lead her further into the main room. All four walls are of exposed brick, the pale varnished floorboards shine in the sunlight that's streaming in through the large windows that take up most of two sides of the room. There's an enormous oak beam above us, which bisects the room, dividing it into a living space and the kitchen and eating area. The kitchen itself takes up the whole of one long wall. The only thing on the countertop is my coffee maker; and there's space for a large table and chairs.

I turn her around to the wall behind us. There are three doors. The middle one opens onto a bathroom; the one to the left reveals the guest bedroom. Finally, I open the third door and allow Grace to pass through to our room. Again the walls are of exposed brick, and there are two large windows, looking across the Charles River. Set against the left hand wall, is the bed, which I made up earlier with pristine white sheets, but otherwise, the room is empty. There are two more doors, one leading to a dressing room, and the other to the ensuite bathroom, with a massive walk-in shower, and free-standing bath. I stand at the end of the bed and watch her as she turns, taking it in.

"Is that your bed?" she asks.

I nod. "It's the only thing I brought from my old apartment, well, that and the coffee machine."

"The jury's still out on the coffee machine, but thank God you didn't get rid of your bed."

"I figured you liked the Texas King. And it's not my bed anymore... It's ours." I walk toward her and reach out, running my fingertips down her cheek. "I want us to do this together, Grace. I want you to choose the furniture, the pictures, throws, rugs, candles... all of it." She rests her face into my open hand, closing her eyes and I move a little nearer. "I only brought the bed…" I whisper, "because I want to make love to you on it, right now, and then over and over… all afternoon and all night." Her eyes open and they're sparkling. "Tell me you're happy?"

She looks down at my chest, just for a moment, then up at me again. She takes a deep breath and when she speaks, her voice is trembling with emotion. "I didn't think it was possible to be this happy. Thank you."

"Don't thank me, baby."

"You don't understand. I had nothing, Matt. I'd given up on happiness, until you found me. I'd given up on a future, until you believed in me… and I'd given up on love, until you loved me."

I think that's about the nicest thing anyone's ever said to me. I take her in my arms and move her back toward the bed. "I'll always be here for you… I'll always believe in you… and I'll never, ever stop loving you," I whisper, as I lower her onto the soft mattress.

Grace

I've been here for nearly a week already, and it's just as well I didn't have to go to work – until tomorrow that is. It's been a whirlwind of shopping, deliveries, making arrangements and collections. We went out the day after I arrived and bought a sofa, which is enormous. It's cornflower blue and sits beneath the beam, dividing the living and eating spaces. Matt also wanted a couple of really deep armchairs. They took a little longer to choose, but we settled on pale yellow, with one on either side of the sofa, facing each other, and a large rustic driftwood coffee table in between. While I selected scatter cushions, rugs and throws, in various shades of blue and yellow, Matt disappeared to the electrical department. His purchases of a huge television and a really complicated stereo system, were delivered and installed the next day.

The dining table is reclaimed pine and seats eight. It fits perfectly between the sofa and the kitchen units.

In the bedroom, we've added bedside tables and a small white two-seater sofa, which sits under the window, with a large blanket box at the end of the bed.

Our only other purchase so far, is a new phone for me. Matt's optimistic that the messages will stop now I'm here, but I refuse to be encouraged. I changed numbers twice more before leaving the UK and still they started again within a few days. I suppose time will tell.

"It's like a different place," Matt says, looking around the apartment.

"Good different?"

"Oh, very good different."

We got into work early this morning, as it's my first day, so Matt could show me around before his first meeting, which is at nine-thirty.

"This is your office." He opens a door that leads into a large room, the far wall of which is made entirely of glass, looking out across the city. In front of this, facing the window, is a drawing board and to one side is a desk, with my laptop already set up. On the opposite wall to the desk, is an oak plan chest. The surface has an inlaid cutting mat and the six shallow drawers are ideal for paper, sketch pads and board. It's a beautiful piece of furniture, which would grace any home, let alone my office.

"It's perfect," I say, turning to him. He's holding my hand and I look down at our entwined fingers. "Should we be doing this here?" I ask.

"What?" he asks. "We're not doing anything, are we?"

"We're holding hands."

"I'm the boss. I can do whatever I like." He grins.

"I just don't want to start gossip, or cause you any embarrassment."

"You could never embarrass me." He leans down and kisses me, just as the door opens behind us and I spring away from him, dropping his hand and feeling my cheeks burning.

"Hi, Grace," Luke says, not batting an eyelid.

"Nice timing," Matt replies, but Luke ignores him, and comes over to me, kissing me on the cheek. I feel myself stiffen. I need to learn to relax more.

"How are you settling in?" he asks, not noticing my reaction, or ignoring it if he has.

"Here? Well, I've only just arrived…"

"And the new apartment?"

"It's incredible."

"You'll have to come over," Matt says, taking my hand again. "Grace has worked miracles. It actually looks like a home now."

"I'll take you up on that," Luke says, then turns to face Matt. "Frank Watson's just called…"

"What does he want?"

"He says he needs to see you before the holidays. He's in town tomorrow and Monday."

"Um… I'll have to check my diary, but I'm not sure I can do either of those. Can't you fit him in?"

"I can, but he says they want to double their order. He's looking for reassurance from you that we can handle it."

Matt runs his fingers through his hair. "Really? Double? Can we handle it? I mean, with the new orders coming in from Miami and Austin as well, we're already at capacity, aren't we?"

"Fairly close. And don't forget all the extra orders I picked up from Felicity Harrison as well. If we take this on, it'll be huge. I'm not…"

I cough and they both turn to me. "Why don't you take this up to your office?" I suggest. "I will be okay on my own, and then you can discuss the problem, actually check your diary, and find out if you can fit the man in tomorrow or Monday?"

"Common sense, brains and beauty," Luke says, smiling in my direction. "The perfect package." *Oh, someone please fetch me a bucket…*

"Yeah, and she's all mine," Matt growls and shoos him from the room. I can hear Luke laughing, and Matt joining in, as their voices fade into the distance and they head down the corridor towards the lift. Matt's office is two floors up from mine. I turn to look out of the window, taking in the view. It's breathtaking…

I jump, and let out a startled cry when I feel Matt's hands come around my waist. "I forgot to say," he whispers into my ear, "have a good morning." He bends down and kisses my neck and I lean back into him. "You know where I am if you need me." And he's gone again.

I put my jacket over the back of the chair, switch on my laptop and open my mail application. Matt's been on here – or someone has – because I've got a new e-mail account: grace@amulet.com. There's a message already in my inbox from Paul, asking me to look at some new designs he's working on, with a view to preparing a series of web pages. He's sent me through some photographs and told me to call him if there are any problems. I study the images for a few minutes, then gaze out of the window, thinking. After a while, I wander over to the plan chest, open the top drawer, and find a sketchpad, which I place on the drawing board. I take a pencil from my bag, because I'm very particular about using my own pencils, and set to work.

I guess I've been working for about an hour when the door opens and I turn my chair just as a woman walks in. She's got short blonde hair, cut in a bob style, and a pretty, round face. I'd say she's around forty years old, she's very neat and tidy, wearing a dark blue suit, and a white open-necked blouse and low-heeled shoes. I suddenly feel underdressed in my short grey-green skirt, cream top and patterned grey scarf.

"Good morning," she says. She's carrying a cup of coffee. "I'm Mary."

"Oh, yes." *Matt's secretary.* Although I've seen her when I've been to the offices on previous visits, I've always been with Matt, so we've never spoken, or been properly introduced. I stand. Even in my flat heeled boots, I'm a little taller than she is. "Hello, Mary. I'm Grace."

She nods her head in acknowledgement. "I know. Mr Webb asked me to bring you coffee," she says stiffly.

"You didn't need to do that."

"Well, he asked me to."

"That's very kind of you."

"It's no trouble." Except I kind of get the feeling it is, but I'm grateful to her anyway.

"Maybe you can tell me where the kitchen is, so I can make my own and bring you one next time?" I suggest.

"It's along the hall, third door," she replies. "There's a kitchen on each floor, so you don't need to bother bringing one up to me."

"Well, thanks for telling me." I take a sip of coffee. "This is delicious. Thanks again, Mary," I say, but the door's already closing behind her. *Friendly.*

I sit at my laptop and type out an e-mail to Matt.

> '*Hi,*
> *I know you're probably still in your meeting, but thanks for the coffee.*
> *G xx*'

Within a few seconds, I get a reply.

> '*You're welcome.*
> *My meeting finished about ten minutes ago. How's your morning going?*
> *M xx.*'

I hit the reply button.

> '*Good, so far. Your secretary was a little frosty. I'm working on something for Paul. How about you?*
> *G xx*'

Again, the response is quick.

> '*I'm shifting meetings around to fit Frank in tomorrow. It's important.*

Mary's always frosty. It's nothing personal. Ask Luke – she's positively glacial with him.
Don't let Paul drive you too hard. He's a bully.
Have lunch with me later? Please?
M xx'

I reply:

'Paul was very polite. I can work on defrosting Mary.
Of course I'll have lunch with you. Tell me when and where?"
G xx'

There's a delay this time. After fifteen minutes, he still hasn't replied, so I give up waiting and go back to my drawing board, glancing up occasionally to stare out of the window. The design is forming, slowly on the page, although something's not quite right.

"Twelve-thirty." He's right behind me. I can feel his breath on my neck and his voice hums along my nerve endings. "My office."

I twist but he's already walking backwards towards the door, his hands in his pockets, a broad grin on his face.

"I wish you'd stop creeping up on me like that."

"No you don't," he teases, and leaves.

A few minutes later, my e-mail pings and I get up and go across to my laptop.

'Sorry. I got interrupted by an urgent phone call, which I had to conference in with Luke, and then by the even more urgent need to be in the same room as you, even if only for a minute. Normal service has now been resumed.
See you at 12.30.
Love you.
M xx'

I can't stop smiling as I type *'Love you too.'* And I press send.

Chapter Eighteen

Matt

Christmas has been magical so far. We bought a massive tree, which Grace decorated with clear glass ornaments and white lights. It's really tasteful and understated, and I love it.

Grace wanted to cook me a traditional 'English' Christmas lunch, except we spent the whole morning in bed, so lunch became dinner. She'd even bought a Christmas pudding over with her. She made it a few weeks ago before leaving the UK, because, she told me, it needed to 'mature'. I was surprised, I actually quite liked it. It wasn't that sweet, not the way she made it anyway.

We avoided any embarrassment over money by agreeing to buy each other small gifts. Except she made mine… and I kind of cheated. She gave me a large framed photograph. The image is of a tree, bathed in early morning sunlight, thick mist draped around its trunk. The light and color are glorious. "It's our tree," she explained, once I'd opened it. "Where we kissed that afternoon… I went back there the next morning, really early." It reminds me of Grace. It seems too beautiful to be real, except I know it is. We're going to hang it above the bed. I got her a book of nineteenth century love poetry, which includes Byron's *She Walks in Beauty*. It's a first edition, which is the cheat. She lay with me on the couch for most of the afternoon, her head on my lap while the dinner cooked, reading aloud from it. We were surrounded by candles. It was very romantic.

Now, that we've eaten more than is healthy and drunk more than we should have done, I want to complete the day. I take Grace's hand and lead her into the bedroom, standing her at the end of the bed while I undress her slowly until she's naked in front of me. I kiss her, finding her tongue, caressing it gently with my own, then move down, licking her nipples, one at a time, until they're hard and swollen. I quickly remove my own clothes then, dropping to my knees, I kiss the tops of her thighs, and gradually run my tongue along her glistening folds, using my hands to open her up, exposing her clitoris to my delving, flicking motions. She pushes her hips forward and I feel her fingers in my hair, pulling me into her as I sweep my tongue across her hard nub, sucking it into my mouth and nipping her gently between my teeth. She's moaning, her legs trembling... She's getting close.

"Matt..." she breathes. "I'm going to... I'm..." And she comes apart. Her legs start to give way, and I hold her up as she bucks against me, my tongue driving her on, relentless, until she's spent.

"God," she sighs, eventually, sliding down next to me. "That was..."

"Yeah, it was." I smile. "You tasted divine."

She glances down at my erection, and without saying a word, takes it in her hand, rubbing it slowly. I sit down on the floor, leaning against the blanket box at the end of the bed, my head tilted back and my eyes closed, luxuriating in her caresses. She changes position slightly, moving in between my legs and she rubs a little harder, a little faster. I feel her shift again, her hand sliding down to the base of my cock, and then... I'm in her mouth. My eyes shoot open, my head jolts forward. She's kneeling over me, one hand on the floor, the other fisted around my shaft and she's sucking me, her tongue running over the tip of my cock, swirling in circular movements as she moves her head up and down. I don't move my hips at all, just let her do what she wants, at her pace, and it feels unbelievable. With each stroke, she takes me slightly deeper into her mouth and I know I won't last long: the sight of her taking me like this is too much.

"Grace," I whisper. "I'm gonna come..." She stops instantly, releasing me. I don't mind... not one bit. She moves up my body, straddling me, then lowers herself down, taking my length inside her and riding me fast, and hard. Then she slows for a while, grinding her hips down onto me, and sitting completely still as we kiss gently, before she speeds up again, her arms around my neck, her lips still on mine. I'm close, but I can feel her orgasm building… her breathing is erratic; she's trembling slightly and her moans are louder, becoming cries… so I hang on until we explode together. She screams something incoherent and I grab her hips and pull her down hard onto me, pushing my hips up, so I'm as deep as I can go when I pour myself into her.

It takes longer than usual to come back to reality. Grace is slumped on my shoulder, breathing hard, her hair draped across her turned face. I move it to one side and she breaks into a sexy smile.

"I don't think I can move," I say.

"We'll sleep here then," she mutters.

"Okay." I shift slightly trying to get more comfortable and she nestles into me.

"You alright?" she asks.

"I'm a lot better than alright."

She doesn't lift her head, but whispers, "What I did… was it okay?"

"It was more than okay, Grace. It was out of this world. I never thought…" I stop talking, but it's probably too late.

"Never thought what?" Her words are slightly slurred. She's exhausted.

I might as well say what's on my mind. "I never thought you'd do that."

She sits back slightly and looks at me, her face suddenly serious. "If I'm being honest, neither did I."

"Have you ever…?"

"Done that before?" She finishes my sentence. "Not like that." She leans into me again and I know instinctively what she's not saying.

"He forced you, didn't he?" I ask. She nods.

"He used to…" I move her away from me slightly, so I can see her properly. "He used make me kneel down in front of him. Then he'd hold me by my hair, and make me…"

"Shh. You don't have to tell me anything else. I get the picture." I wonder if this is the 'more' she was putting off telling me.

"I'm sorry I couldn't…" She looks down at my chest. "I'm sorry I couldn't let you finish." I raise her face with my finger.

"Stop. I won't have you saying sorry, not for anything."

"He used to… you know… in my mouth. He'd hold my jaw closed until I swallowed, and if I couldn't… he'd hit me." My muscles tighten. I want to hurt the guy… badly. "It used to make me feel sick," she continues. "I don't know if I'll ever be able to do that."

"You don't have to, Grace. You never have to do anything you don't want to… But at the same time, if there's anything you do want to do…"

"There is one thing…" she mutters.

"What's that?"

"Do you think we could get into bed now?"

Work has suddenly gone slightly crazy. Not only did Frank Watson double his order, but a couple of other clients have also increased their usual requirements, and we've got some new customers too, including one from Paris that Luke's literally just signed up. I've arranged a meeting this afternoon with Luke and a couple of the guys from the finance department, to discuss whether or not we should consider opening a second factory. I thought about putting it off until after the New Year, but Luke's found a potential site and we don't want to miss out, as the price is really good and he thinks they might even take a lower offer if we can move on it quickly enough.

Grace and Paul have been working hard on the new range, which is our best so far, without a doubt. She's fitting in really well and everyone seems to like her. As for me… well, I'm more in love with her than ever.

Grace

It's getting late. I've done as much as I can do for today; my back's aching and my eyes are itching from staring at my screen for too long. It's nearly six-thirty and Matt hasn't let me know that his meeting's over yet. I shut down my computer and delve into my jacket pocket for my phone and earphones, finding some music to listen to while I wait for him.

Buying the new phone seems to have worked. I haven't received a single message since I moved here… not that I've actually used the phone that much anyway. Matt's usually with me most of the time, and everyone else either calls my office line, or e-mails me. I think I've only received half a dozen messages in the three weeks I've been here, all from the service provider.

It's dark outside; the city's lights are twinkling and I wander over to the window, leaning against the wall and staring out. I'm not really a 'city' kind of person, but there is a beauty to this place which I'd never expected to find, especially at night.

The track changes to *I'm a Mess* by Ed Sheeran and I tap my foot to the beat, singing along in a whisper, just in case anyone can hear me. The track fades as a message comes in. It's from Matt, and I tap on it to open it up.

— ***Sorry, baby. I'm going to be here a while longer. I guessed you might have shut down your computer – hence the text. If you are finished, come on up to my office. Love you. Mxx***

I quickly tap out, **'Okay, on my way'**, grab my bag and jacket, turn off the light and go down the corridor to the lift.

Matt's office door is closed, Mary is nowhere to be seen; she's obviously gone home already… unless she's in the meeting too… so I knock gently and wait, my bag slung over my shoulder. Within seconds, the door opens and Matt is standing there. He's rolled up his shirtsleeves, his tie is loose and his top button is undone. He looks spectacular. He takes my hand and pulls me into the room.

"Everyone," he says, "this is Grace."

I look at the four people facing me. Luke stands, smiling at me, and I smile back... a friendly face, thank goodness. The other two men stand as well; Mary, who's sitting off to one side, doesn't.

"This is Peter Davis," says Matt, as the man with iron-grey hair and black-rimmed glasses steps forward, his hand outstretched.

"Hello," he says. His voice is low and soft.

"Hello," I reply.

"And this is Robert Hart." The fourth occupant of the room has a round, jolly face, and an amazingly luxurious-looking moustache.

"Good evening," he says.

"Hello." I nod.

"And you already know Mary."

We nod at each other. Matt pulls me back to him. "Give us a minute, guys?" he says and they all turn away, except Mary, who stares for a moment, then looks down at her hands.

"I'm going to be at least another hour yet," Matt murmurs, putting his arms around my waist. "What do you want to do? I can get you a coffee and you can wait here while we finish up, or you can take the car and I'll get a ride back with Luke."

Did he just say...? "Take your car? You mean... me? Drive it?"

"If you want to."

"You'd trust me to drive your car?"

"Of course. So, what's it to be?"

"Well, as much as I'd love to stay here and be with you... I'll take the car."

"Somehow I thought you might." His eyes twinkle and he kisses my forehead, then goes over to his chair, bypassing everyone else in the room. Peter and Robert are staring at him, Mary's still studying her fingers, but Luke's just sitting on the edge of the desk, tapping a message into his phone. Matt takes his jacket from the back of his chair and fishes his car keys from the pocket, returning to me.

"Here you go," he says, handing them to me.

"What about dinner? When do you think you'll be home?"

"I'll order something… Chinese okay?"

"Sounds good." I turn back to face everyone else. "I'll say goodnight, then." I raise my hand. They all say goodnight, including Mary. Matt pulls me into him, kissing me gently on the lips.

"Remember we drive on the right side of the road over here," he says.

"You mean the wrong side…"

"Yeah, okay." He kisses me again. "Take care, won't you?"

"Of me, or your car?"

"You… well, you *and* the car… Mostly you, though." His eyes glint as he smiles, and then he lets me go.

It's nearly nine by the time he gets home. I've showered and am just wearing a robe. After my shower, I watched some television, but found it mindless, so I've spent the last hour or so lying on the sofa reading. Luckily, I brought my Kindle with me, rather than shipping it. I miss my books, but hopefully it won't be long until my boxes clear customs and we can pick them up. I'm mid-way through a short *Father Brown* story, because I love G.K. Chesterton, when Matt gets home, and I lay my Kindle to one side. He comes straight across and leans over me, kissing my upturned mouth.

"I'm sorry I'm so late," he murmurs. He looks tired.

"It's okay." I reach up and run my fingers down his stubbled cheek.

"I phoned through an order for dinner. It'll be here in about thirty minutes. I'll just grab a quick shower." He stands up straight, stretching and pulling off his tie. "How did you get on with the car?" he says.

"Ah… well…" I lower my head and look up at him through my lashes, playing nervously with my fingers in my lap. "I didn't realise how difficult it would be to drive a strange car on the wrong side of the road at night… But it's not a *very* bad dent… If you know of a good bodyshop, I'm sure they'll be able to make it look like new…"

"Grace, what happened?" He drops to his knees on the floor beside me, taking my hands in his. "Are you okay? Are you hurt?" His eyes are searching mine and I can't carry on.

"Oh, for heaven's sake, I'm fine. Nothing happened." He looks confused.

"Then what the...?"

"I was trying to wind you up, but you're not even worried about your car, are you?"

"Of course I'm not worried about the damn car. I thought you might have been hurt. Don't do that to me." He sits back on his heels, heaving out a sigh of relief.

"You're a spoilsport," I say. "I was going to have so much fun..."

He gets to his feet and leans over me. "Fun?" he growls. His voice has suddenly lowered. "You wanna have fun?" And, before I know it, I'm in his arms he's carrying me in the direction of the bedroom, then straight on into the ensuite bathroom.

"Matt," I squeal, "I've already showered once." I can't stop giggling.

"Well, I'm going to make you all dirty again." And he lowers me to the floor, pulling the robe open as I descend.

I'm finding it really hard to concentrate today. It's nearly eleven o'clock and I haven't done anything yet. Images of last night keep invading my mind. The shower... the surging water, his strong hands supporting me, his eyes piercing mine, that exhilarating sensation of being filled by him, over and over. I shudder, recalling his need, his urgency, his words as he made love to me... He makes me feel so wanted. I never thought it could be anything like this. I sigh, again. I really need to focus. Paul's waiting to see this latest set of visuals...

My phone beeps. I haven't got around to putting ringtones on yet. It's Matt.

— *I'm struggling today. Mxx*

Oh. I know he's tired. I hope he's alright. He's got a lot on his mind now they've decided to go ahead and look at the second factory. We discussed it last night after our shower, sitting cross-legged on the bed, eating Chinese food out of the cartons. I've seen characters do that in TV shows and always wanted to do it myself... Matt thought I was 'cute' for getting so excited by the whole thing. I don't think he has any idea how much I'm enjoying each new experience he gives me. I tap out a quick reply.

— *Are you okay? Gxx*

His response is almost instant.

— *I can't concentrate, because I can't focus on anything but your body, your skin, your touch, your taste, your perfect breasts in my hands. I can't get enough of you. I want to feel you come on my tongue… and I need to be deep inside you again. Mxx*

My mouth has gone dry, but…

— *You just made me wet… again. Gxx*

I hesitate before pressing the send button, but I do. Why shouldn't I tell him the effect he has on me? It's true and I want him to know that he can do that, just with his words. I get up and go over to the window. It's a grey day, but I feel anything but grey or downcast. I feel so full of love for him, I'm not sure how to hold it in.

There's a slight delay before he replies this time.

— *Hold that thought. Mxx*

What does that mean?

— *Why?*

— *Because…*

— *Because what?*

"Because I want to find out for myself how wet you are." I spin round. He's standing, leaning back against the closed door, breathing deeply.

"Did you just run all the way down here?" I ask, trying not to smile.

"Hell, yeah." He walks over, slowly, deliberately, not taking his darkened eyes from mine. Without saying a word, he leans down and kisses me. My back is against the wall and he goes to turn me around, but I'm not afraid – not any more. I want this. I hold him in place, keeping my feet rooted. He breaks the kiss, leaning back slightly. "You sure?" he asks. We both know what he means and I nod and, without hesitating, he takes my lips again, raising my hands above my head and holding them there with one of his, pressing his body hard against mine, his other hand roaming down the side of my breast, my waist, my hips, moving lower, to the hem of my skirt and raising it, running his fingers over the damp lace of my knickers, moving them to one side, and rubbing along my now drenched opening, pushing inside me. I gasp.

"God, you really are wet," he whispers. I buck against his fingers, and he kisses me deeper, his fingers circling inside me. I'm starting to pant, and grind into him, when a loud beep sounds.

"That's mine," he mutters into my mouth, his fingers stilling. He hesitates, then kisses me again, but the phone beeps a second time. "Shit," he murmurs and, releasing my hands, he retrieves his phone from his pocket. He checks the message on the screen. "It's the realtor," he says, leaning into me, his fingers motionless. "I need to look at some figures. I'm going to have to go back upstairs." He groans. "I'm so sorry, baby." I cup his cheeks with my hands and raise his head.

"It's okay," I whisper and kiss him lightly. He pulls his fingers from me and straightens my clothes.

"We're not finished here," he says. "We'll conclude this later."

I feel a tingle running down my spine. "I can't wait."

"Good." He leans down and kisses me, just as his phone beeps again. "Give me a goddamn break," he moans, pushing away from me and going back to the door.

How on earth am I supposed to get anything done now?

Half an hour later, my phone beeps again.

— *We're seeing the new factory site tomorrow morning. Just got to have a quick meeting with Luke, Peter and Robert to finalize our offer. Should be finished by 12.30. Got time for a long lunch break? I think your boss will let you ;) And maybe, if you're still wet, we can conclude our other business... Mxx*

— *I'm definitely still wet and I'd really like that. Gxx*

— *I'll be down as soon as I can. Mxx*

I turn back to my computer. The photographs that Paul sent through are not doing it for me, so I fire off a quick e-mail asking if I can see the corresponding samples, then I sit back and stare at the wall, where Matt pinned me just a little while ago. That felt good — surprisingly good. It wasn't like before; I didn't feel trapped, but desired. It wasn't about control; it was about passion, need, love. I close my eyes and imagine Matt's hands on me, touching me; his fingers caressing me, inside me. The phone beeps again and I smile. I wonder what he's going to tell me now, but then my smile fades. I hope he's not going to cancel lunch. I open my eyes and pick up the phone... and my world crumbles...

— I'll never leave you alone, not unless you leave him alone. And I'll always be watching... Slut.

Chapter Nineteen

✧

Matt

Luke huffs out a breath. I can understand his frustration. I'm feeling it more than him. I'd far rather be back downstairs with my fingers – or better still, my cock – deep inside Grace than up here arguing… but… "It's obvious we shouldn't go in too high, Peter," he says. "The problem is, we're not the only people looking at this place, but right now, it's the only site that's suitable, so if we lose it, we'll have to wait for something else to come up, which could take months… and we don't have months. With the new orders I've just picked up, things are starting to back up already…"

Luke hates the bean counters even more than I do, but they serve a purpose; namely to act as the brakes if we need them.

"I understand that," Peter says, his voice calm… annoyingly calm. "But there's no point in bankrupting the company."

"Who's talking about bankrupting the company?" Luke raises his voice. "That would be a bit self fucking defeating, wouldn't it?"

"Okay," I lean forward in my seat. "This is getting us nowhere." I glance at Luke. The truth of the matter is, Peter doesn't really want us to go ahead with the new factory. Robert, Luke and I are in favor, but Peter is less certain. He's always more conservative, more reticent, and sometimes that's a good thing, but now isn't one of those times. We could lose some really big clients, not to mention future orders if we don't act quickly. I know we can afford this. I wouldn't take a chance on this if I wasn't absolutely certain it would work, especially not now Grace is in the picture. Luke and I have spent hours looking at it every which way. We know we're right. "Peter... I want you and Robert to work on the figures for me this afternoon." I rarely act the 'boss', but sometimes you just have to. "I need to know how high I can go with this offer; and I need it realistic, and on my desk before you leave today."

Luke looks at me, gives me a slight wink, then turns back to Peter. "Our meeting's—" His words are cut off by a loud noise coming from outside. We all turn at the sound of raised voices.

Before any of us can move, Grace bursts in, followed by Mary, who's glaring at her, red-faced and spluttering, "I tried to stop her, Mr Webb... I really did try, but she wouldn't listen..."

Grace looks bewildered, and terrified and I'm on my feet and make it to her, just as her legs buckle. I lift her into my arms and carry her to the couch in the corner. "Everyone out," I say. There's barely a moment's hesitation before Luke ushers everyone from the room, including a still protesting Mary. I'll talk to her later. I know she's protective of me, and there are times when I appreciate it, but if she ever tries to keep Grace out of my office again, I'll fire her... Luke shuts her up firmly, and closes the door behind him.

Grace is curled up in the corner of the couch, clutching her phone and I don't really need her to tell me what's happened. I know.

"Show me," I say, and she does. I read the message. This one feels more menacing, more personal, and it takes all my willpower not to smash the phone against the wall. I look down at her; she's so helpless, cowering like a hunted, wounded animal. I sit next to her, pulling her into my arms. "You're not leaving me," I tell her, "no matter what they threaten." She lets out a sob. "I want this to stop," I say and she snuggles down closer, "but I need help." I can feel her tense against me. "I need to tell Luke," I add.

"How much will you tell him?"

"At the moment, just about the messages."

She doesn't question me, just nods her head and relaxes against me in acceptance. Without moving her, I pull my phone from my pocket and send him a message:

— *Can you come back to my office? Matt*

He doesn't reply, but the door opens within a few minutes and he slips quietly inside. Without saying a word, he grabs a chair from near my desk and brings it closer, sitting down and waiting.

"I need your help... Well, I need Will's help." Grace twists in my arms, looking up at me.

"Who's Will?" she asks, her eyes wary.

"My brother," Luke replies and she glances at him, then stares back at me. "Why do you need Will?" Luke asks me.

"Because Grace is having problems."

"The same problems as before? The ones that took you to London in the fall?"

"Yeah." Where do I start? "A while back, she started getting text messages..."

"Who from?" he asks.

"That's the problem. We don't know."

"What kind of text messages?"

I show him Grace's phone and he reads. "Shit," he mutters under his breath.

"That's the first one on this phone; the first one since Grace got here, but when she was in London, they were a regular thing. We thought it was all over, but it seems not."

"What does... Will do?" Grace whispers.

"He works for the government," Luke explains. "Officially, he's some kind of analyst, but there's more to him than that." I'm surprised. He rarely, if ever, tells anyone about Will's job, for obvious reasons. He turns back to me again. "But I'm not sure what you think he can do?"

"I'm hoping he can trace the messages?"

"I have no idea if he can or not. I don't know enough about what he really does. It might be a walk in the park for him. You know Will: never tells me anything."

"Can you ask him?"

"Sure. You know he'll help if he can."

Again, Grace moves in my arms, turning round so she's sitting up. Her face is pale but she doesn't take her eyes from mine. "What's wrong?" I ask. There's something other than this latest message bothering her, I know there is.

"I've been thinking, about the messages," she says. She glances at Luke as though she's uncertain whether to continue, but then she relaxes. It's like she's decided he's okay, and she can trust him. I could've told her that, but I guess she needed to work it out for herself. "You don't think... you don't think it could be Jonathan, do you? I... I know that sounds crazy, but..." her voice trails away to silence. Does it sound crazy? After all, she's only voiced the same thought I had weeks ago, when she first showed me the messages.

"Wasn't Jonathan your husband?" Luke asks. Grace nods her head. "But..."

"Yes, I know he's dead... or at least, he's meant to be, but what if he isn't?" She moves slightly closer to me. "Think about the wording, Matt," she whispers. "It's just like him... He used to..."

"Did they identify his body?" I ask.

"I assume so."

"You mean you didn't have to do a formal identification?"

"No." She shakes her head and I suddenly feel icy cold.

"Why not?" Luke asks. "Surely..."

"His car hit a petrol tanker. It exploded. There wasn't much left."

"So how did they identify him?"

"I never bothered to ask."

We all stare at each other for what feels like a very long time.

"Call Todd," Luke says. "He'll know the answers; and if he doesn't, he'll know how to get them."

He's right.

"Is that okay with you?" I ask Grace.

"Todd's your policeman friend, isn't he?"

"Yes. I can get him to come over later on this evening, if you're going to be alright with that?"

"Yes. I want to know." She's shaking. She's real scared. I guess the kind of fear he ingrained in her doesn't go away that easily.

"He can't hurt you, baby," I whisper, holding her close. "I won't let him."

⌒∞⌒

Grace

Eventually I manage to stop shaking and Matt leans back a little.

"Can I leave you with Luke, just for a couple of minutes?" he asks me.

I nod my head. It's odd… while we were speaking then, I saw a different side to Luke. When he was talking about his brother, he changed… his demeanour altered, and I knew I could trust him.

"Where are you going?" I ask.

"I just have to speak to Mary." He turns to Luke. "Can I borrow your office?" he asks. "I need some privacy."

"Sure."

"And can you stay here with Grace?" Matt says to him.

"Yeah… I kinda got that bit." Luke smiles.

Matt leans down and kisses me gently. "Back in a minute," he says. Once he's gone, I turn to Luke. "What's that all about?" I ask him.

"I'm not entirely sure, but I don't think he's very happy that Mary tried to keep you out of here … I imagine he's telling her that—"

I jump up from the sofa. "No, he mustn't…"

Luke stands, blocking my exit. "Grace, let him do it. She's way too protective of him. She knows who you are. He's never hidden his relationship with you from anyone here. You were clearly upset and she overstepped the mark."

"But…"

He comes a little closer, but not too close. "Sit down," he says, softly. I hesitate for a moment, then lower myself onto the couch again and he perches on the edge of the coffee table in front of me. "I think Matt's probably struggling with this," he says.

"The messages, you mean?"

"The fact that he can't do anything about them, yeah."

"But he's done so much…"

"Not in the way he wants to." He looks at me. "A couple of years ago," he says, "Matt had a problem with one of the models we'd employed…"

"Are you talking about Brooke?

"He told you about that?"

"Yes."

He sighs. "Then you know it was a bad time for him." I nod my head. "But the worst part was afterwards, when the newspapers got involved. It was difficult enough when he only had to deal with the lawyers and suits, but the whole media thing made him feel powerless. He'd lost control of what was happening to him. And that doesn't sit well with Matt."

"But he doesn't need to take that out on Mary. That's not fair."

"He's not taking anything out on Mary. He's not like that. That's what I'm trying to explain… he's doing what he can, even if it isn't very much, to protect you. You needed him… Mary got in your way. He's gonna make damn sure that doesn't happen again, because right now that's all he can do… at least until I've spoken to Will and he's contacted Todd," he explains.

"But she was just doing her job."

"No, she wasn't, Grace. Mary can sometimes be a little over zealous. She guards him like a mother hen guards her chicks… except she's not old enough to be his mother, but you get what I mean. That's why she and I don't get along… because I don't take any notice of her clucking around Matt. But everyone else in this building is terrified of her. She needs bringing into line, and this has just given Matt the perfect excuse."

"I don't want to cause a problem." I can feel a lump forming in my throat.

"You're not."

"But Mary's important—"

He laughs. "You still don't get it, do you?" I stare at him, because I don't really know what he's talking about. He leans forward. "I've known Matt a long time. I've never seen him as happy or relaxed as he's been since he met you. You're good for him, Grace."

"Even so, this is his business…"

"Which he'd give up tomorrow if you needed him to."

The door opens and Matt comes back in. He looks pale and serious.

"Everything okay?" Luke asks.

Matt nods his head, comes over to me, sits down and pulls me into his arms. "It is now," he says.

"And is it safe for me to go out there, or is Mary gonna rip my head off?"

"As it's you, she might be tempted…"

"Same old, same old." Luke gets up and goes to the door. "I'll speak to Will and let you know what he says later on."

I've spent the whole afternoon on Matt's couch. He wanted to take me home, but I know he's busy, so he's worked, and I've been curled up here watching him. We haven't mentioned Mary… I'm not sure I want to deal with any more hassle right now. My head is just too full. My phone is on his desk, on silent, but I've heard it vibrate three times. He's checked it, and his face has become darker each time.

I don't really know where the thought that the messages might be coming from Jonathan originated. I suppose it could just be the language being used. It suddenly hit me when I saw the word 'slut' on the screen. He used to call me that – and worse – a lot; screaming abuse at me. It's made it all so real again. I need some time alone with Matt, in our space, away from the office…

We don't leave too late, because we're both really tired. Matt drives home through the rush-hour traffic and parks the car, helping me out of my seat and putting his arm around my shoulder as we walk to the front door.

Up in the apartment, he helps me off with my jacket.

"What do you need?" he asks.

"You." I put my arms around his waist and lean into him and he pulls me close, his chin resting on my head.

"I thought it was all over," he whispers and I nod. "How about a bath?" he suggests. That sounds so good.

"Yes. I'd like that."

"You go get undressed. I'll run it for you." He kisses me tenderly and lets me go.

Once I'm ready, I go through to the bathroom; he's filled the bath with rich foamy bubbles and surrounded it with candles.

"Thank you," I whisper, and he takes my hand, helping me climb in and lower myself into the warm water.

"I'll fetch you a glass of wine," he says. "Red or white?"

"Red, please." He goes to leave. "Matt?" He turns. "I love you," I say.

He comes back and bends over the bath. "I love you too, beautiful." And he kisses me.

He returns a few minutes later, with a glass of wine in one hand and his phone in the other, clasped to his ear. He puts the wine on the bath surround.

"It's about Grace…" he says into the phone. "Yes, my girlfriend Grace. How many Graces do you think I know?" He waits for a second. "Very funny." There's another pause in the conversation. "It'll happen to you one day, and I'm gonna laugh my ass off." He smiles down at me, puts his finger to his lips, kisses it and then places it on my mouth. I kiss it back and he leaves the room. "Enough already…" he says, and his voice fades as the door closes behind him.

A short while later he's back again. "That, in case you didn't guess, was Todd."

"Can he help?"

"I don't know. He had to take another call. He's going to get back to me. He's still at work." He sits on the edge of the bath. "Were you okay with that?" he asks.

"What?"

"Me calling you my girlfriend."

"Well, Jenny called you my boyfriend…"

"Oh yes, she did, didn't she? I'd forgotten about that."

"A lot has happened since," I sigh.

"So you don't mind?"

"Being called your girlfriend? Um… Hardly. It's my pleasure."

He puts a hand on either side of the bath, leaning over. "I hope so," he murmurs, just as his phone rings.

"Todd," he says, "Your timing always did suck." He gets up and leaves the room again, and I relax down into the soft bubbles.

I don't know how much later it is that Matt comes back in.

"Wake up, sleepyhead," he says and I open my eyes. He's changed into jeans and a black t-shirt. "You need to get out of the bath."

"Oh, do I have to?"

"Well, you do if you want to come and greet our guests. They're sure as hell not coming in here…"

"Guests?" I sit upright. "What guests?"

"Todd, Luke and Will are here."

"They're here? Since when? Why?" The questions pour out. I feel panicked, uncertain.

"They've been here about ten minutes, I guess. Todd agreed to come over staight away, then Luke called and said Will was happy to come and talk to you – well, happy might be putting it a bit strongly." He smiles. "That'll make more sense when you meet Will," he explains. "So, I thought we might as well get it over with at the same time. I've ordered Indian take-out for all of us."

"A curry?"

"Yes… do you like curry?"

"I love it." I stand in the bath and he takes my hand, helping me to step out.

"It'll be here in about twenty minutes."

"Okay." Matt takes a towel from the shelf and wraps me in it. "What will I say to them?" I ask.

"We'll just take it as it comes. They're all our friends, Grace. Whatever we have to tell them, they won't judge, I promise."

"They're not our friends. I don't even know them."

"Not yet, but you will… and I do. You can trust them." I nod my head. "See you in a minute?" he says, kissing me.

"Yes."

Suddenly I'm as nervous as hell.

Chapter Twenty

∞

Matt

I go back through the bedroom and into the main room. The three of them are sitting in the living area, Luke and Will on each of the chairs and Todd at one end of the couch, nearest Will, who's brought his laptop and has it open, his head buried already. He's tapping on the keys, intently.

"That was quick." Todd looks up at me, grinning. "You're slipping."

"That's what love does for you, I guess," Luke adds. "Takes the edge off."

"Oh, this I've got to see. Matt Webb in love…"

"Guys," I say quietly. "Can you behave when Grace comes out."

"What are you suggesting?" Todd says, feigning a hurt expression. "We're always perfect gentlemen."

"Yeah, right. I just mean drop the comments, okay? She's… Well, she can't handle it right now."

"We can be nice, and we'd never do anything to hurt a woman, Matt, you know that."

"I know. But even making remarks about me in front of her, could be… awkward. Just take my word for it, okay?"

"If you say so—"

The bedroom door opens and Todd stops speaking, turning his head toward Grace. I glance at her. She looks beautiful, as ever, in jeans and a pale pink sweater, her hair loose around her shoulders; then I look back at Todd, and smirk inwardly. His mouth is open, just slightly and his eyes have widened. He clambers to his feet. Luke's already standing and, a little belatedly, Will notices Grace's arrival, closes the lid on his laptop and gets up too. She comes to stand beside me, looking a little daunted, I think. It's hardly surprising. Will is just over six feet tall, and he's the shortest of all of us. I can imagine that we're a little intimidating when taken together.

"Grace, this is Will and Todd," I say, introducing them.

Will steps forward and offers his hand. "Pleased to meet you," he says, his voice quiet as usual.

Todd finally closes his mouth, only to open it again: "How do you do." *Such formality.* I look quickly in Luke's direction and notice that he's stifling a laugh, and it makes me wonder whether I should offer to pick up Todd's tongue for him, before he falls over it.

I step to one side to allow Grace to sit in the corner of the couch, at the opposite end to Todd. Will and Luke resume their seats, and I perch on the arm of the couch, beside Grace. She leans back into me and I put my arm around her shoulder. Will settles his computer back on his lap, opens it up again and looks at Grace.

"These messages," he says, getting straight down to the matter in hand. "When did they start exactly?"

"The middle of May," she replies. Her voice is muted.

"And they've continued ever since?"

"There have been breaks—"

"Any pattern to the breaks?"

"No…" She looks up at me. "I don't think so, do you?"

"No. It seems completely random. There would be short gaps, then several messages a day for a few days, and then nothing again for a while, but I can't say it resembled a pattern."

He nods his head, steepling his fingers and resting his chin on them.

"Can I have the phone?"

"Gladly," Grace says and I get up, fetching it from my jacket and handing it over. He starts pressing buttons, engrossed.

"Do you have your previous phone?" he asks, looking up.

"No. I got rid of it when I came over here."

"Shame."

"Grace?" Todd is speaking now and we both turn to face him, while Will continues with whatever it is he's doing on his laptop.

"Yes?" She's even more shy speaking to him. Maybe it's because Will is such a gentle giant, Todd seems more scary, by comparison. He is. He carries a badge and a gun, and he can more than hold his own in any situation, but what Grace doesn't know is that, of all my friends, Luke is the one you'd most want to have in your corner in a fight. He may look like a charming flirt, but he *really* doesn't like to lose.

"I understand from Matt that you're concerned the messages might be coming from your husband?"

Grace shifts on the couch. "I know it sounds ridiculous…"

"Not necessarily." Todd leans forward. He's being especially kind – although I've never really seen him at work, so maybe he's always like this with vulnerable women. "Can you give me some details about his death?"

She begins to fidget with the hem of her sweater, rubbing it between her fingers. "It was in February," she says, "February the 13th. I'd had a meeting with my business partner and Luke." She nods in his direction. "When I went got home, the police were waiting for me." I tighten my grip on her a little.

"What did they tell you about the accident?" Todd says.

"Just that his car hit a petrol tanker. It exploded." She pauses. "Then a little later I found out he was on the M4 motorway, just outside of Swindon… not that that's really relevant."

"But there was never any doubt it was him?"

"Well, I never thought to question it. It was definitely his car."

"Okay, let's assume for the sake of argument, that he faked his own death. That would mean he wanted to start again, a fresh life somewhere else… so why would he send you messages like these?"

Grace hesitates. "He… he always used to tell me… that I…that…" Her voice cracks. *Oh, baby.*

I take over for her. "The language in the messages – he used to speak to Grace like that. He used to tell her she was no good; that no man would ever want her…" I raise her face up to mine. "Can I?" I ask, she nods and I lean down and kiss her gently. "It'll be okay," I say, holding onto her. Then I sit back and face my friends, who are looking at me, bewildered. I take a deep breath. "Jonathan used to beat her," I say. Will stops typing and silence descends over the room. Luke sits forward, his hands clasped together and his knuckles white, but Todd moves back in his seat, right into the corner, giving Grace more room.

"Tell them everything," Grace mutters.

"No. We don't have to do that…" I start to say.

She twists in her seat and looks up at me. "I think we do though. I think my theory will only make sense if they know everything. You said I could trust them, Matt."

"You can… I promise you can. Are you sure about this?"

"Yes, but can you do it?" I nod my head.

I look up to find three confused faces looking at us. "He didn't just beat her," I say, my voice surprisingly clear. "He raped her, repeatedly, for the first two years of their marriage."

Luke gets up suddenly and walks over to the window, the tension pouring off of him.

Will closes his laptop and puts it on the floor. He stares at Grace, his mouth open slightly.

Todd runs his fingers through his short hair, his eyes dark, like thunder.

"He used to accuse me of having affairs," Grace continues, finding her voice. "I never did, honestly." She's got that defensive tone again, just like when she told me.

"They know that, baby," I tell her

"And he'd call me foul names," she continues, calming a little. "And then… afterwards… when he'd finished, he'd tell me that I was useless, that no man would ever want me. The messages on the phone are so similar."

Again, Todd leans forward, but his eyes have softened. The difference is remarkable.

"But those words, Grace; they're just words. Anyone could say that. It's not necessarily personal. It could be random."

"I know. But don't you think it's a huge coincidence?"

"It could be…"

Luke turns around. "I don't see why he'd have started sending them in May, though. You two weren't together then."

Grace and I look at each other. "There had been some text messages between us," I say, "right before the first message that Grace received. Nothing intimate. I guess you could say they were romantic, maybe, but not intimate… still…"

"If he was monitoring Grace's phone in some way, he'd have known." Will completes my sentence.

"Okay, let's just think this through…" Todd's thoughts are interrupted by the arrival of the take-out. I buzz them up, my mind racing.

∞

Grace

We've moved to the dining table and laid out the food and I just want to throw up. Matt and I are sitting next to each other. Todd is at one end of the table, to my left. Luke is opposite me and Will is facing Matt. I'm sure the food's delicious, but I can't taste anything. The few morsels I've put into my mouth, have resembled cardboard and I've chewed and rolled them around, then struggled to swallow them down.

Will, who's nothing like Luke at all, seems to think there might be something in my theory. Or at least that's the impression I get. He spent ages messing around with my phone, and tapping away on his laptop, but he's been focused on me since Matt told them about what Jonathan did to me. His eyes, which are deep, deep blue, behind his designer glasses, are soft and sympathetic, at odds with the flashing anger in Luke's pale blue eyes and the thunderous shadows of Todd's, which are a dark, molten brown.

"I understand where you're coming from, Will," Todd's saying, "but faking your own death is complicated; it's real hard to do. Before you go checking out who was monitoring the phone and how, it might be quicker to examine whether this bastard actually had a reason to want to pretend to be dead. There are usually a few standard motives for someone to fake their own death… why don't we look at those first…?"

I feel my blood turn cold. I hadn't wanted it to be like this. I'd planned to tell Matt, but not in front of his friends…

"Had you gone to the police about what he was doing to you?" Todd's asking me. "Were they taking action against him?"

I shake my head. "I didn't go to anyone."

"Not in the whole of your marriage?"

"No."

"Okay, so no imminent police investigations. What about money then? Was he in financial trouble?"

"No. Far from it."

"Okay. This is real awkward…" he says, and I know what's coming. "I hate to ask you this, but do you know if he had another woman?"

"We know he had one affair," Matt says, thinking he's helping me out. "With Jenny."

"What, your business partner, Jenny?" Luke asks.

I nod my head and hear a hiss of air escape him.

"Was that still going on?" Todd asks.

"No," Matt replies. "Jenny's married now. She had a baby in May. Her affair with Jonathan ended a few years ago, when she met her husband. That's what she says, anyway. I believed her, didn't you?" he asks me.

"Yes."

"Do you think there might have been anyone else? Someone more recent, perhaps?"

I take a deep breath. I can't not tell them… well, him. But like this? What choice do I have? If I ask to speak to Matt in private, I'll only have to come back out here and repeat it all…

"I know there was."

Matt's chair scrapes across the tiled kitchen floor as he turns to face me.

"Grace?" he says.

"I'm sorry... I'm sorry." I'm pleading with him, shaking my head. "Please forgive me... please, please don't..."

It's like there's no-one in the room but us as he leans forward, his face barely an inch from mine. "Shhh. It's okay, baby," he murmurs, interrupting me, and his hand comes up to cradle my face. "Is this the 'more' you didn't tell me about?"

"Part of it..."

"Only part? You mean there's something else?"

I nod my head and hear him exhale. I lean back and stare into his eyes, willing him to understand. He pulls me into him, then lifts me up and onto his lap, hugging me. "Tell us," he says.

I lock my arms around his neck, my head on his shoulder. "As far as I know, he had affairs throughout our marriage," I say, staring across the kitchen to a space on the furthest wall. I don't want to make eye contact with anyone. "And before it as well. Jenny was just one of many, many women." I can't help but give a half-laugh. "It was his way of proving to me that I wasn't good enough." Matt's arms tighten around me and he reaches down and raises my face up to his.

"You're more than good enough... I won't have you saying that about yourself."

I want to climb inside him for saying that... but for saying it in front of his friends... I run my fingers down his cheek, feeling tears prick behind my eyes. I have to finish this... at least this part. And then I'll tell him the rest when they've all gone. It's time.

"There was one particular woman though," I say, still looking at Matt. "The rapes stopped about two years into our marriage, because he fell in love with her. He had two lives really; the happy one with Beth, and the miserable one with me."

"Was he still involved with this Beth, when he died?" Todd asks, his voice very gentle.

I can't turn and face him, because don't want to look away from Matt; saying this is going to be so hard, it's going to tear me apart, again. "Yes, he was. She was pregnant... with his child." His eyes pierce mine, and I feel his hand moving behind my back in a waving motion, then everyone else gets up and they move into the living area. We're alone at the table, although they're only a few feet away.

"You knew this all along?" he whispers. I nod. "And you didn't tell me?"

"I couldn't. It's… so hard."

"I get that."

"Don't blame me. Please, Matt…"

He takes my face in his hands. "I don't, Grace. I just wish you'd told me, so I could've helped you better." *Better? How could he have done anything better?* He stops for a moment. "Is that it now? Is that everything?" I hesitate, then shake my head. "You mean…?"

"Not now… When we're alone; I'll tell you then… All of it."

"Okay."

He goes to get up, but I grasp his shoulders. "Matt?" I say. "You're not angry are you, because I haven't told you everything?" He settles in his chair again.

"No, baby, I'm not angry."

"Disappointed?"

"No, I'm not disappointed either."

"What then?"

He thinks for a moment. "I'm sad."

"I'm sorry."

"I'm not sad for me, Grace. I'm sad for you. No-one should have to go through what he put you through… I can't bear…" His voice cracks.

"Please don't…"

We sit for a moment, just holding each other, before Matt says, "Let's get this over with… then you can tell me the rest." He lowers me to the floor, and stands, leading me back to the living area.

Luke, Will and Todd are sitting in silence. I think they'll have been able to hear what we've been saying, but I don't really care. Like Matt, I want this over with, so we can talk privately. I need him to know everything now, and then, more than anything, I need to know we're going to be okay.

Chapter Twenty-one

Matt

I sit in the corner of the couch, bringing Grace down onto my lap and holding onto her, real tight. I'm not letting go; she needs to know that, and I don't care how many jokes Todd cracks at my expense. He's watching us closely. Will is buried in his laptop again; Luke just looks dazed. I should have taken his and Will's reactions into consideration, I guess, before mentioning the beatings Jonathan inflicted. It's bound to remind them of their childhood... but Grace has to be my priority. I'll talk to Luke later; make sure they're both okay.

"Grace," Todd says, "I'm sorry to keep asking questions, but I need to know as much as possible..." I can feel her nodding her head. "You said there were no financial problems... Did you inherit from your husband... or...?" He leaves the question open.

"No. Beth inherited everything." That explains the house and Grace's money issues. "The solicitor even demanded that I give back the necklaces and earrings that Jonathan had given me."

"He did what?" I can't help myself.

"I didn't mind. It wasn't like I wanted anything that was his." She nestles into me a little further and I like that.

Todd's brow is furrowed. He's thinking.

"Starting to come around to my way of looking at this now?" Will asks, not looking up from his keyboard. "The facts fit."

"Yeah, yeah." Todd says, still mulling over something. "I know..."

"What is it?" Will asks, slamming down his laptop lid and leaning forward. "The guy's a doctor; he could have done this. He has the medical knowledge to fake his own death, and probably access to everything he needed. It fits financially, emotionally, every way… And his personality… It tallies. Come on, man. At least get the British police to have a look at the death. I can't do that, not without things getting very awkwardly official, but you can."

"Oh, I'm going to, don't worry." Todd looks up at Will and, just for a moment, it's like the rest of us aren't even here. "There's just something that doesn't fit… only I can't put my finger on it."

"It's the timing," Luke says. "It would be a perfect fit, if the messages had started later in the summer… but May? Sorry, but it doesn't add up."

"He's cracked, Luke," Will says. "He didn't need to wait for Matt and Grace to actually get together, just the hint of a relationship from those initial text messages would have been enough. If he was monitoring her phone…"

"That's another thing," Todd cuts in. "He was a doctor. How would he know how to hack a cell phone?"

"He might have a friend…" Will's been talking about Jonathan in the present tense. He's clearly convinced. "Or you can just look it up on the Internet. It's not like he could go on practicing medicine, is it? He'd have time to learn…"

Grace sits up a little. "You're talking like he's still alive," she breathes. Damn, she noticed it too.

"Well, I think we have to assume that, until we can prove he isn't." Will turns to her.

Todd checks his watch. "It's ten o'clock," he says. "What time is it in London?"

"Three in the morning," I reply.

"I'm going back to the precinct."

"What, now?"

"Yeah. I can send over a request for the information we want. If I do it now, it'll be waiting for them when they get into work in the morning. If I leave it till tomorrow, that'll be midday their time… That's too much time wasted."

"What are you going to ask them to do?" Luke asks.

"At this point I just want clarification of the identification of the body. I'll keep it low-key and off the record, if I can. I think there's a guy in my department – Karl – who knows someone who works for the Metropolitan Police… I'll give him a call on my way back to work, and see if he can help. If they've got evidence it was Jonathan, that they checked the dental records were right, or they got DNA tests done, then we can be fairly certain he's dead. There's one other thing…" He turns to Grace. "I don't suppose… Sorry… I don't suppose you know where Beth is living now?"

"Yes. She and her son are living in Jonathan's house in Wales, in a place called Llangrannog. The solicitor confirmed it to me in one of his letters. I don't know why he thought I'd care. Do you need me to write down the name of the village?"

He smiles. "Yeah. Put it on my phone, if that's okay." He hands it to her and she taps in the name.

"Why do you want to know that?" Grace asks, handing the device back to him.

"I'm going to ask them to check whether there's anyone living with her – apart from her son, that is. If there is, I'll see if they can send a photograph."

I feel Grace shiver. It's suddenly become very real.

Todd gets to his feet. I move Grace onto the couch and stand. "I'll let you know as soon as I hear anything," Todd says, moving toward the front door. He turns as he reaches it. "Are you okay, Matt?" he asks, his voice real quiet. "This can't have been easy for you either."

"I'm fine. I just want this over with."

"Yeah, I know. Look, call me… you know, if you need anything."

"You're doing enough."

"Call me, Matt," he says, then leans in close. "And look after her. She's… well, she's too damn good for you, that's for sure." He smiles at me, then opens the door and leaves.

Back in the living area, Luke and Will are also getting ready to go.

231

"I'll need to keep your phone," Will says to Grace.

She waves her hand. "I don't care. I hate phones."

"I don't blame you," Luke replies. He looks at me. "Do you want me to handle things tomorrow?" He asks. Oh, shit! I'd forgotten all about the viewing.

Grace sits up. "No," she says. "Matt will be there."

"And you'll be with me," I say. "You can come and look round the site, can't you?"

She shrugs. "I don't have anything urgent to do, so I guess..."

"Okay. We'll see you there at nine-thirty. But once we're finished at the site, I'm taking the rest of the day off."

"Just let me know what needs doing."

"It's New Year's Eve, Luke. There's nothing that can't wait."

We start toward the door, but Will hangs back, going over to Grace, who's still curled up on the couch. He crouches down in front of her. He doesn't touch her, or get too close, just waits until she looks up, then holds her gaze.

"I'll do everything I can to find out who's doing this," he says. "I promise."

"Thank you." She smiles up at him and I feel my heart swell, just a little. I knew I only had to ask and my friends would help me... but they're not doing this just for me; they're doing it for Grace.

Will joins Luke and me and we go to the door.

"I'm sorry, guys," I say. "I probably should've warned you."

"Don't worry about it," Will replies and I'm surprised. He doesn't usually say much, and never speaks about their past. What little I do know is from Luke. "Listening to Grace's story... Seeing how she's handled it all... it's kinda humbling, really. It actually helps. She looks so fragile, and she's been through so much... but she's really strong... really strong." His voice fades a little and he coughs nervously, then adds, "I'll be in touch."

Luke's staring at Will, a smile on his face, then he takes a step forward. "See you tomorrow," he says to me, "but call me if you need to talk. Anytime."

My girlfriend seems to be having a positive effect on everyone.

Grace wanted to talk in bed, so we've left everything stacked in the kitchen, moved in here and got undressed. I've lit a couple of candles and left the blinds open, so there's enough light to see her. She's lying in my arms, her hand resting on my stomach, her head on my chest, and I'm propped up slightly on the pillows, feeling… well, scared, if I'm honest. I know, whatever else she's got to tell me has got to be bad, if she's kept it back till now.

"I'm sorry, Matt."

"Tell me," I say. I just want to know. Whatever it is, not knowing is killing me.

Her grip tightens around me, like she's worried I'm going somewhere. I'm not. It doesn't matter what she tells me, I'm not going anywhere. "When I'd been married to Jonathan for nearly two years, I… I discovered I was pregnant." I feel like I'm drowning, being sucked down into a deep darkness. "I was thrilled… and devastated. Jonathan was incandescent with rage. It wasn't supposed to happen, you see. I was on the pill, but I'd been sick with a virus, so it didn't work. He accused me of getting pregnant deliberately."

"You were already married, for Christ's sake. It wasn't like you were trying to trap him."

"He'd made it very clear he didn't want children." She pauses for a moment. "Not with me, anyway. He went crazy. He hit me and I fell…" She chokes slightly. "I fell down the stairs. He didn't push me," she adds quickly. "That part was an accident."

"Oh, really." I can't hide my skepticism.

"I think, deep down, he was probably hoping I'd miscarry, but he didn't push me, Matt."

"What happened?"

"I thought I was fine. I was bruised, I'd hurt my back, and I had a black eye from where he hit me, but I didn't bleed or anything. So I assumed the baby was okay. The next day, Jonathan started talking about an abortion…"

"He didn't make you…?"

"I refused to discuss it. He raged at me, ranting about how stupid I was… I think he would have hit me again, but the fall down the stairs

233

had shocked him as much as me, so when he realised I wasn't just going to back down, he walked out. I didn't know at the time, but he was seeing Beth by then, so I imagine he went to her. I felt quite triumphant; it was the one and only occasion I'd scored a victory over him. About two weeks later, he came back and told me he still wanted me to have an abortion, but I wouldn't talk about it, no matter how much he yelled at me. He packed a bag and left again. I had no idea when, or even if, he was coming back. It was wonderful.

"I had such a good time. I didn't have any morning sickness; in fact, I felt great and the pregnancy seemed to have given me some protection from him. I started to think about leaving him, for the first time. Bringing a child into that relationship would have been foolhardy to put it mildly, but if I could get away from him, I felt certain I could manage on my own. I know it sounds silly, but I used to have long conversations with the baby about all the things we were going to do together, all the fun times we'd have.

"Anyway, about three or four days after he left, I woke up in the early hours of the morning, in so much pain. I went to get up and fainted. When I came round, the pain was even worse... it seemed to be everywhere, my pelvis, my back, even my shoulders. I was so dizzy... I managed to grab the telephone from the bedside table and dialled 999, gave the address and passed out again.

"When I woke up, I was in the ambulance." So, she did have a miscarriage after all... She's choking back tears. I hold her tighter. "I won't go into the gory details of what they had to do, but the pregnancy was ectopic—" Okay, I know I'm ignorant...

"What's that?" I have to ask.

"It means it didn't develop in my uterus, but in my fallopian tube. The egg gets stuck, and fertilises there instead of in the womb and there's not enough space, so in my case, when it got too big, it ruptured, and I started bleeding internally."

"Oh God." She could have died.

"They removed my fallopian tube, and I spent a few days in hospital recovering. When I got home, Jonathan still wasn't back. He arrived about ten days later. I told him what had happened. He was... pleased."

The anger is too much this time. "I really hope your husband turns out to be dead, Grace," I say, my jaw set tight. "Because if he isn't—"

"He's not worth it, Matt."

"How can you be so calm?"

"I suppose I've had longer to get used to it." She reaches up, puts her arms around my neck and hugs me, and I run my hand down across her hip, feeling the warmth of her skin.

"Wait a second... You had surgery?" I ask, feeling a little stupid.

"Yes. Haven't you noticed the scars?"

"No."

"Well, they are tiny."

"And you're perfect." She looks up at me.

"No. No, I'm not. I only have one fallopian tube, for a start." I must be looking confused. I get that, because she said they removed it, but I don't understand what she's trying to tell me. "It reduces my chances of becoming pregnant again... not by much, but the doctor said I've got about a seventy percent chance... and I have about a twenty percent chance of it being ectopic again." She's blinking back tears. "Getting pregnant again would be something I..." She pauses and looks hard at me. "Something I..."

"*We*, Grace..." She's not on her own in this.

She smiles. "Okay, it'd be something *we'd* have to think very carefully about."

Grace

"Well, I hope we'd think carefully about it anyway. I told you, didn't I? Planned... but not too planned." He's smiling down at me.

"You don't seem to understand, Matt. We'd have to *really* think about it. If I get pregnant and it's ectopic again, and isn't treated early

235

enough, I could lose my other tube. And then our only chance would be IVF."

"I do get it," he says. "If I've understood this correctly, you could have died... so you can be damn sure we're going to think long and hard before making any decisions."

"Sorry... It's just that when I think about it, I go into a kind of tailspin. It's the fear of it happening again, I suppose."

"That's understandable. If we do make that decision at some point, I'm going to be scared too... until I know you're safe – so probably for around nine months, I guess." I reach up and kiss him. He doesn't understand...

"The ectopic bit doesn't take that long. We'd know after the first scan and, if it's normal, I'd just carry on like any other pregnant woman."

"I get that..." he says, kissing me back. *He does?* "Won't stop me being scared though." I smile up at him. He has a way of making me feel safe.

"I'm sorry I didn't tell you before. You had a right to know." I can't help feeling guilty.

"No, Grace. You have the right to your privacy. Losing a baby like that must have been hard, especially on your own."

"Yes, but... I mean, if you want to have children... I might not be able to do that."

"Well, I guess if it comes to it, I don't know I can father children. I've never tried – not yet anyway. Nothing is certain, not really. Having kids isn't a right; it's a privilege. Grace, I fell in love with you because of who you are, not for your ability to give me children. If we have kids at some point, that's great. But if we can't, I've got you and that's all I need." I can't believe this man. He pushes me down onto my back, leaning over me.

"I still should have told you," I say, as he brushes his lips gently against mine.

"Enough," he says and he raises himself up above me. "None of that matters now." He goes to kiss me, then stops. "I just have one question..."

"What's that?"

"Is that everything? There's nothing else…?"

"No. That's it. I've got no more secrets; nothing else to tell."

"Thank God for that." He claims my mouth, running his tongue along my lips and I open to him.

After he's made love to me slowly and gently, like I'm a piece of rare, fine china and he's scared he might break me, he blows out the candles and lies down again holding me in his arms.

"Can I ask you something?" he says and I feel him tense. "And please don't misunderstand."

"Okay…" This sounds ominous.

"When we first made love," he begins, "I told you I was clean. You didn't say anything, but I assumed you would be because… well, you made a point of telling me you were faithful to your husband. You said you didn't go looking for sex elsewhere because you associated it with pain, but…"

"But now you know he probably slept with half the women in Greater London, you're wondering if I was clean too?" He doesn't reply, but I know that's what he's trying to ask me. "I'm not a fool. After I came out of the hospital, I went straight back on the pill. I needed to protect myself from another pregnancy. But he never came near me again… not like that, anyway. I'd always known he slept with other women. He used to tell me about them in great detail; how much more satisfying they were, how they turned him on, about all the things they did for him so willingly. He never held back… So after about six months, when it became clear he really was leaving me alone, I realised it would be sensible to get myself checked over. It was humiliating, but at least all the tests came back negative." I twist in his arms and look up at him. "Matt, I love you… I'd never have put you in any harm. Surely you know that?"

"I'm sorry. I should never have doubted you. If I've offended you…"

"I don't blame you for wondering."

"No. I should have trusted you."

"Why? I've been keeping secrets from you all this time."

"Not secrets, Grace. Just things you weren't ready to share yet."

"Well, at least there's nothing more… except maybe a few details to fill in. Things that might not have made sense at the time, but which will do now…"

"Such as?" He turns onto his side, so we're facing each other.

"Oh, there's probably all sorts of things… I'm sure they'll come back to me in time…" I trace my fingertips down his cheek. "Do you remember when Jenny's baby was born?" I whisper into the semi-darkness surrounding us.

"Hmm. The phone call at the office?"

"Yes."

"I remember you crying like your heart was breaking."

"That was because Beth's baby… Jonathan's baby was due at the same time. Hearing about Jenny giving birth reminded me of what I'd lost…"

He pauses for a moment. "It makes more sense now. I was really worried that day. I thought I'd lost you…. After what I'd told you at the hotel the night before, I was scared you didn't want anything more to do with me."

"That's why I had to contact you; to let you know – or try and let you know – that my breakdown wasn't anything to do with you. I really wanted to explain it to you, but I didn't know what we were at that point. Then, later on, you asked about our friendship and I was glad I'd kept quiet. I couldn't have shared something so intimate with someone who was just a friend."

"I was scared of frightening you off if I told you what I really wanted us to be; how I really felt about you. I thought if I said 'friendship', you'd feel safer."

"Thank heavens for Joe Cocker."

We kiss for a while, both sleepy, and I'm starting to drift, thinking about those messages we batted back and forth that night and how they changed everything…

"Matt!" I sit up sharply.

"What? What is it?" He's instantly sitting with me.

"My phone… the messages."

"What about it, Grace? What's wrong?"

"Will… your messages… Oh God…"

"Baby, you're not making sense. What's wrong."

I turn to face him. "You sent me that message, about us… You said you wanted to feel me come… on your tongue, and you needed to be inside me… I said I was wet… Will's going to see all that." I bury my face in my hands. I feel so humiliated.

"Is that all?"

"All?" I look up at him.

"Grace, I'm allowed to tell you how great you are, how much I enjoy you, and how that makes me feel. You're allowed to tell me you're turned on by that. Okay, I'd rather my friends didn't know about it too, but if that's the only price we have to pay for putting a stop to this, then we'll pay it. Will might read it, but he's not going to show anyone else. He's a good guy."

He's right; I know he is. I feel like I can trust Will too. I relax down into Matt's arms and he pulls me close.

"Sleep, now," he whispers into my hair.

We're up early this morning. Matt's already showered and is preparing breakfast. I join him, with my hair just about dry. I'm wearing very tight cream coloured jeans, a pale green top and a long cream cardigan, with a green flowery scarf draped around my neck.

"You look… sexy," Matt says, from the stove, where he's scrambling eggs.

"So do you." I walk up behind him, running my arms around his waist and resting my head on his back. "I like you in a shirt and tie… and a suit… and jeans. I like you in pretty much anything, really."

"I got the impression you were getting to like me *out* of pretty much anything too," he smirks.

"Well, there is that."

He dishes up the eggs onto two plates and adds hot toast, bringing them over to the table.

"Where's the factory site?" I ask.

"About a half-hour drive away," he says.

"I can go to work, you know,"

"No way. Until we hear from Todd, or Will – or both of them – about what's going on, you're not leaving my sight."

It's the first time since his friends left last night that we've really mentioned this, but I still don't really want to talk about it. I don't want to think about the possibility that my suspicions might prove correct, and that Jonathan might be out there somewhere.

"Tell me about Will," I say by way of avoidance.

"Will?" He takes a bite of toast.

"Yes. He's very different from Luke."

"He sure is." There's a strange expression on his face.

"There's something you're not telling me."

"Because it's not my story to tell."

"Oh." I fork some eggs into my mouth.

"Luke and Will had a tough childhood," he says. I put down my fork and lay my hand over his arm. "They've reacted very differently to it…"

"It's okay. You don't have to tell me. I understand all about secrets. Better than most."

"Yeah, but I don't like keeping things from you."

"What's the age difference between them?" I ask – that should be fairly safe ground.

"Three years. Luke is older – although he doesn't always act it."

"And you met Luke at college?"

"Yeah. We had an apartment together. Will came to live with us before the end of our first semester."

"So he'd have been… fifteen?"

"Yeah."

"Did that cramp your style?" I smile across at him.

"I'm not sure I had a style then. As for Luke, he spent a lot of time helping Will, but then when he was sure his brother was okay, he got back to his usual ways again."

"He's a flirt, but is he really as much of a womaniser as he makes out?"

"God, yeah. Luke's a serial philanderer. He doesn't date, not like most guys, anyway... he just sleeps around."

"Really?" I can't help but feel a little shocked.

"To be fair, he's always completely upfront. He makes it very clear he's only in it for the sex; he never sees married women; he's never gotten a woman pregnant and he obeys my golden rule..." He suddenly stops talking.

"The one about the models?"

He looks down at his plate. "Yes. He did better than me on that score."

"It's in the past, Matt. Leave it there."

He reaches across, picks up my hand and raises it to his lips. "You're so good for me."

"Um... I think that should be the other way round..." I take another forkful of eggs. "So, why do so many women throw themselves at him?" I ask, returning to our original topic.

"You don't think he's good looking?"

"I suppose so, but he's not my type." I grin at him.

"Well, that's a relief... If I had to kill him, it would really mess things up at work." He gets up and plants a kiss on my forehead.

"What about Todd?" I ask, once we've cleared the city traffic on the way to the factory site.

"What about him?"

"Does he have a girlfriend?"

"Not at the moment." He's gone all serious again.

"Why? I mean, all three of your friends are very attractive."

"Oh are they now?" He smiles across at me.

"Obviously, they're nowhere near as good looking as you, dear."

"Hmm."

"So... Todd?"

"He dates..." Now he's sounding vague.

241

"Don't tell me he's like Luke…"

"No. He sees women on a more regular basis, but nothing long term."

"Why?

"It's ironic, really," he says, changing lanes. "His issues relate to his parents, but in a different way to Luke and Will."

I sit and wait, unsure if he's going to elucidate.

"Todd's dad was a cop too. He was shot and killed…" I gasp; I can't help it. He reaches over and puts his hand on my leg. "That was not long before I first met him. Todd had just started at the Academy, and I think he decided there and then that he'd never put a woman through what his mother suffered."

"So he refuses to get serious?"

"Pretty much."

"That's sad."

"Did he look sad to you?" he asks.

"Well… not really, but he might regret that decision one day."

"I'm not sure he looks that far ahead."

I suppose that's understandable. "How did you meet him?"

"We met at the gym when I was still at college. Todd and I used to work out; Luke didn't – Luke liked to run…"

"I suppose he needed to be able to get away from all those women?"

He chuckles. "Yeah, something like that. Anyway, after a while, Todd just kind of joined in with us, I guess. We all hung out together… and have done ever since."

"I like your friends." It occurs to me that I don't have any of my own… Jenny turned out to be the opposite of a good friend.

"They like you too," he says. I think he might have just read my mind.

Chapter Twenty-two

Matt

My mouth hovers over hers. "Happy New Year, baby," I breathe, and pull out of her just slightly, before pushing back in deeper, harder, then increasing the speed with every stroke... longer, faster.

"Happy... New... Oh... Matt..." she screams, her hands reaching out to the side grasping the sheets between her fingers. And I feel her clamp around my cock, as she throws her head back, her legs coming up around my waist, tightening... gripping me.

It's too much. I can't take anymore. I'm lost inside her.

The sun rose about an hour ago, but we didn't get much sleep last night, and Grace is still dozing. Watching her like this is one of my most favorite things to do now. When she's not curled up over me, she tends to lie on her side, facing me, and makes the cutest snuffling noises. I gently nudge a few loose hairs away from her face and she brings her hand up, as though to brush aside the minor distraction, a frown settling over her face. She's just adorable, and I can't help but kiss her pouting lips. Slowly, her eyes open and she smiles up at me.

"Good morning," she mumbles, her voice drowsy. She screws up her hands into fists, stretches her arms above her head and arches her back. Her breasts are exposed and I lean across and capture her erect nipple between my teeth, biting gently. She brings her hands back down, resting one on the back of my head, the other on my shoulder, holding me in place.

"That's... oh... that's really good." The drowsiness in her voice has been replaced by need, and I flick my tongue over her tight bud, then suck it into my mouth. "I really want to..." She squirms beneath me. "I really... Oh God." She's writhing, breathing hard. "Damn... I need to pee," she says, and I chuckle releasing her nipple, my head falling onto her breast. She slides out and runs for the bathroom.

"You'd better come straight back," I call out to her, just as my phone rings. I check the screen. It's Luke... at eight-thirty on New Year's Day? Something must be wrong.

"Luke?"

"Matt." His voice is serious and suddenly all the hairs on the back of my neck stand up. "Are you alone?" he asks. I glance up at the bathroom door, which is still closed. Grace could come out at any minute.

"Not really."

"Get yourself alone, now."

I jump out of bed and go through to the kitchen.

"What's up? You're scaring me."

"Good."

"Luke, what is it?"

"Will's been working on Grace's phone all day yesterday and last night. He got up about an hour ago, and he just checked the phone. There's a new message..."

My mouth has gone dry. "And?" I manage to say.

"It's much longer and worse than the rest... and there's a threat this time."

"Tell me."

"It says..." He pauses. "'You didn't listen. Now you're going to pay and when I'm finished he's never going to want to fuck you again.'."

I can't speak. "Matt?" I can hear Luke's voice on the end of the line, but my own has failed me. "Are you still there?" he asks. I nod my head slowly, dazed. "Answer me out loud, Matt."

"Hmm." It's the best I can do.

"She's safe while she's with you, but I think we should let Todd know."

"Yeah." At last, I've managed a coherent word.

"Do you want me to call him?"

"No, I'll do it." And a whole sentence. My brain and mouth are now coordinated. "Has Will got anywhere yet?"

"No. We worked till about three am... Well, he worked, I fed him coffee. So far, he can't find out that anyone's accessed her phone remotely. He had to admit, he's running out of options, but he's got a few more things to try before he admits defeat."

"You guys... I really owe you."

He goes quiet, then I hear him sigh. "Seeing Grace... hearing her story; it got to Will. It reminded us both of some of the shit my dad used to pull when Will was younger. We spoke about it on the way home and, to be honest, it's the first time we've talked properly in years. I think it was good for him. I think he needed it." He pauses. "How is Grace today?"

"A little better. We're going to spend the day here. We'll come into work tomorrow, to go over the offer details, but I want Grace set up in my office temporarily, especially after that message. I don't even want her two floors down, not until this is over."

"I'll arrange it before you get in."

"Thanks, Luke."

"Call Todd," he says and hangs up.

I find Todd's details and connect the call. I don't care that it's not yet nine am and he's probably still asleep.

"Matt," he answers and his voice is as clear as day.

"I didn't wake you then?" I say.

"No. I've been at work for an hour or two."

"You're at work?"

"We don't all get the same public holidays as you mere mortals," he says. "I was going to call you. I've just heard back from Karl's friend in the Metropolitan Police, in London. Do you want to put Grace on too?" No, I don't. Not with what I've got to tell him.

"No," I say. "I'll pass on anything you tell me."

"Okay. Well, Elliot, that's Karl's friend, contacted the police in Wiltshire where the accident took place, and they've confirmed that

245

they identified her husband's body using dental records, so they didn't bother with DNA testing."

"But he could have switched those, or faked them, couldn't he?"

"I guess. I don't want to push things too far at this stage. I'm still trying to keep this off the record… and Elliot owes Karl a favor, so I'm making use of it. I'm just waiting for him to come back on my query about Beth, and who's living at her property. That might take an extra day or two. Elliot has to wait to hear back from the local police in that village in Wales. If there's no-one but her, we might have to push the police in Wiltshire for something more on the identification. If there is a guy there, it might answer all our questions…"

"Yeah…" I'm trying to process what this means – whether it even changes anything.

"Why did you call me?" he asks.

"Oh… I heard from Luke."

"Right. And?"

"And there's been another message on Grace's phone."

"Okay…" He's waiting. "What does it say, Matt. You wouldn't be calling if it was more of the same."

"No." I take a deep breath. "It said, 'You didn't listen. Now you're going to pay and when I'm finished, he's never going to want to fuck you again.' I think that was it."

I hear a noise behind me and turn to see Grace standing in the doorway, wearing one of my t-shirts, leaning against the doorframe for support, her face as white as snow.

"Hold on," I say into the phone and throw it onto the counter top.

I stride across to Grace and pull her into my arms. She looks up at me, her eyes filled with tears. She's shaking.

"It's okay, baby," I say. "Come here," I guide her into the kitchen area and sit her at the table, then pick up my phone.

"Todd?" I say, sitting down next to Grace and taking her hands.

"You okay?" he asks.

"Yeah. Grace overheard."

"Shit. Is she alright?"

"Not really."

"Were any of the previous messages threatening in any way?" he asks.

"No."

"So, this is a complete turnaround?"

"Yes."

"Okay. How's Will getting along?"

"He's been working pretty much solidly, but Luke says he's still not found anything. No-one seems to have accessed Grace's phone. He's still on it though."

"Right. Do you want me to come by?"

"No, we're fine." I glance at Grace. She's staring into space.

"Okay. Don't let anyone in unless you know them. Which means me, Luke or Will. If anything suspicious happens, call me, or just dial 911."

It's worrying to hear him say that. It's a lesson I learned when Brooke pulled the knife on me, but this time it's Grace who's in danger, which makes it so much worse.

"Why?" Grace says for probably the hundredth time today.

"I don't know, baby. I don't understand any of it."

"I just don't see why he wants to do this to me. He's got the life he wanted. He's got Beth, their son, the money… all of it. Why won't he just leave me alone."

"We don't know…"

"Oh, please. Who else can it be?"

I don't have an answer to that.

We're both showered and dressed now. She doesn't want to be alone at all, so we showered together, got dressed together and we've been sitting on the couch all morning, Grace nestled between my legs, lying back on my chest. The longest we're apart is when I go to make coffee, or when one or other of us has to use the bathroom.

"Shall I make lunch?" she says, all of a sudden, as though nothing unusual has been happening all day.

"Sure, if you want. I'll help." We get up and check the refrigerator. Thank God we filled it a few days ago. The last thing we need is an impromptu shopping trip.

We decide on mushroom and goat's cheese omelettes and I chop and sauté the mushrooms while Grace beats the eggs and slices the goat's cheese.

"Do you like all cheeses?" she asks.

"Mostly, except blue." *Why are we having this conversation?*

"How can you not like blue cheese?"

I shrug. "I never have."

"I love a really good strong Stilton, or a ripe Gorgonzola – that's ever so good crumbled up on pizza."

"I'll take your word for it."

Silence descends and I continue stirring the mushrooms, uncertain why we had that little discussion. Her stifled sniff makes me turn and I see she's in tears, holding the knife tightly in one hand, while the other is clasped over her mouth.

I move the pan from the heat and step over to her.

"Come here." I take the knife and drop in on the chopping board, then pull her into my arms and hold her close.

"I can't do this," she says. "I can't pretend everything's normal, when I'm so bloody frightened."

"No-one's expecting you to pretend everything's normal."

"I just want to hide, Matt."

"Then we'll hide."

She half-laughs, looking up at me. "We can't. We've got to go to work tomorrow… and I'll be alone in my office. What if—"

"Hey… I've already arranged with Luke to have your computer and drawing board moved into my office. You won't be out of my sight. I've even got my own bathroom… You'll be begging for some time away from me before long."

She leans into me. "I don't think so." She pulls me down for a kiss. "Thank you," she says, breaking away again. "I think you must be wondering what you got yourself into, getting involved with me."

"No. I fell in love, it's simple."

"You think this is simple?"

"Loving you is, yeah." I want to take her to bed, but I don't think she's ready to make love, and I'm certainly not going to push her. Still, holding her, knowing she loves me, and she's mine... that feels more than enough for now.

Grace

It's odd working in Matt's office.

There's no peace in here, that's for sure, and I have no idea how he gets anything done. The phone rings constantly and people are forever coming and going. It's like working in the middle of Piccadilly Circus, in the rush hour.

Still, I'd rather be in here with him, than two floors down, on my own. I've blocked out the chaos around me by working with earphones in, and Ed Sheeran soothing me all morning.

Mary is still being off hand. Matt and I haven't got around to discussing his conversation with her yet; there have just been too many other things to think about, and I'm not going to tell him about the filthy looks she gives me every time she comes in here... I don't need any more trouble.

I've managed to come up with a few ideas for Paul, but I need to discuss them with him.

I fire off an e-mail to him, asking when he's free for me to pop down to him.

His reply is quick.

'Grace,
I'll come to you. 30 minutes.
Paul.'

That's curt.

"Matt," I say, pulling out my earphones and turning to face him.

"Yes, babe." He's studying some plans which are spread out on his desk. Luke's standing, looking over his shoulder. The deal for the factory site is going through, and there's a lot to do to get it set up and ready for production as quickly as possible.

"Have I done something to offend Paul?"

"Not that I know of. Why?"

"I just sent him a message asking for a time to meet, and he came back saying he'd come up here... but his reply was really abrupt. Normally he's quite friendly."

"That's my fault, not yours." He looks up for the first time. "I sent out a global e-mail this morning, telling everyone that you're working in my office until further notice and that if anyone needs to see you, they're to come here. Paul's a bit self-important." He glances up at Luke. "Don't get me wrong, he's a damned good designer, but he does think the company – well the world, really – revolves around him. I'm surprised he didn't argue."

Luke shifts awkwardly and Matt turns to him. "What's wrong?" he asks.

There's a slight pause as Luke looks from Matt to me and back again. "He sent me a message first thing, asking what the f—" He glances over to me. "Sorry, what the heck was going on. You know Paul, he went into one of his usual rants."

"You put him in his place?" Matt says, his face stern.

"Kind of..." Luke runs his finger along the edge of the desk. "I didn't bother to reply to his message. I just went and told him, in person, to do as you instructed..."

"I sense an 'or else', coming."

"There might have been. Sorry if I was out of line, but..."

Oh dear. I feel terrible. Paul's a big cog in the company... between him and Mary, it feels as though I'm making enemies here, and that's the last thing I need.

"You weren't," says Matt. "You did the right thing." Then he gets up and walks around his desk and comes to stand in front of me, crouching down. "Don't worry about it," he says, resting his thumb on my chin and easing my bottom lip from between my teeth. I hadn't even realised I was biting it.

"But he's important."

"Grace, he's nothing, not compared to you."

I have to tell him… "Matt, I feel like the people who work for you are starting to resent me."

"What are you talking about?" He moves to sit beside me. "Everyone likes you."

"Really? There was that trouble with Mary the other day… and now this. I don't like the idea that they think I'm treading on their toes."

He reaches over and turns me, so I'm facing him.

"Everyone in this place works for me, Grace. They're loyal, but that's because I pay them well. I'm under no illusions that if someone else came along and offered them a better deal, they'd be out the door tomorrow. Luke is the only person in this building that doesn't apply to… Luke, and you. If I had to, I'd close this place down tomorrow to protect you, and the three of us could just start again, doing something else."

I look over his shoulder to where Luke's still standing by Matt's desk. He raises an eyebrow and smirks. I half expect him to say 'I told you so,' but he doesn't.

"But what about Mary," I say. "She's loyal to you."

"Hmm, but her loyalty's misplaced. I've asked her to look for a new job."

"You've what?"

Luke comes closer. "Why?" he asks.

Matt looks a little embarrassed. He takes my hands in his. "I spoke to her the other day," he says. "I knew she was protective – sometimes a bit overly so – but I wanted her to understand that keeping you out of my office is unacceptable. It was just going to be a reprimand… What I hadn't realised was, her loyalty went beyond that of an employee. Almost as soon as I started speaking to her, she interrupted me. She told me she's in love with me and has been for years."

"What?" Luke says. I can't speak.

"I'm sorry, baby," Matt continues. "I honestly didn't know."

"Neither did I," Luke adds. "I always thought she was mothering you... not..."

Matt glances up at him. "Yeah, I know... that's what I thought too. It was real awkward. She was all over me..." He looks back at me, as though he's expecting me to react, but neither of them seem to have understood the significance of what Matt has said. "Grace?"

I look up at him. "The messages," I whisper. "Mary..."

He stares at me, paling.

Luke comes closer. "You think Mary might be behind this?"

Matt's shaking his head slowly. "It couldn't be her..." He sounds shocked.

"Why not?" I ask. "If she's in love with you, she wouldn't want me in the picture, would she?"

"But Mary knows nothing about phones... she has the oldest cell phone I've ever seen. Everyone laughs about it..."

"She might know someone," Luke suggests. "Someone more technically literate." He pulls his phone from his back pocket.

"What are you doing?" Matt asks.

"Getting Will onto it." He goes over to the window and starts talking.

Matt turns to me. "I really don't think it's her," he says. "But if it is... if I've caused this..."

"It's not your fault." I lean into him.

The door opens and Paul appears. Matt turns to face him.

"It's a door, Paul. Knock on it," he says... well, growls actually.

Paul stands still, looking sheepish.

"You okay?" Matt asks me. "Paul can come back later, if you need some time..."

"No... the distraction will be good." Matt leans down and kisses me gently then stands and returns to his desk. He watches for a few moments while Paul settles next to me, seemingly on his best behaviour, then returns to his work.

After lunch, Luke's gone into a meeting and Matt's a bit more available, so we sit together on the couch and I go through the layouts with him too. I think we're both avoiding talking about Mary for as long as we can. Paul liked one design in particular, but it's my least favourite. Matt agrees with me, and we bat it around for a while, but I don't want to antagonise Paul, so I decide I'll work up something that's more of a compromise.

"You shouldn't worry about him," Matt says. "Or anyone else…"

"Does that include Mary?"

"I still don't think she's responsible for the messages, if that's what you mean."

"Why didn't you tell me?" I ask him. "About your conversation with her…"

"Truth?"

"Of course."

"I was shocked."

"Why? Mary's very attractive…"

"I've never thought about her in that way. Besides, her behaviour was inappropriate." He pauses, looking at me. "She touched me…"

"She touched you?" He nods his head. "Where?" I'm almost afraid to ask.

"She put her hand on my cock, Grace."

I pull away from him. "Were you…?" I can't bring myself to finish that sentence.

"Aroused? Hell, no. I only want you, Grace." He looks down at me.

"But this just strengthens my belief that she's the one sending the messages… If she wants you that much…"

"I don't know. She was mortified afterwards. She said she'd misunderstood."

"What was there to misunderstand?"

"Nothing." He pulls me close again. "Nothing at all. I've never given her an ounce of encouragement. I only haven't mentioned it before now because… well… I was embarrassed, and we've been so wrapped up in other things. By comparison, it really didn't seem that important."

"But if she is behind the messages, it's more than important... and, whatever you said to her, she's still giving me filthy looks, Matt..." I know I wasn't going to tell him, but I feel like everything's changed now.

"Seriously?"

I nod my head. "Every time she comes in here."

He doesn't say anything for a moment, then he stands up and goes over to the door, opening it. "Mary, can you step inside, please." She enters, glaring in my direction. Matt sees the look she gives me and I notice his expression harden.

He goes across to his desk, sitting down in his chair.

"Please take a seat," he says. Once she's comfortable, facing him, with her back to me, he leans forward a little. "The other day, I asked you to start looking for employment elsewhere," he says. "How's that going?"

"I haven't started yet," she replies.

"Why not?"

"I... I haven't had time." It sounds like an excuse.

"Well, I'm gonna make that a lot easier for you." Matt's voice is harder than I've ever heard it. "I'd like you to leave today." I hear her gasp.

"You... you can't..."

He ignores her. "I'll give you six months' severance—"

Mary stands. "After eight years... eight years... you're pushing me out... for her?" She turns and points at me, and I feel myself shrinking into the corner of the sofa.

"What you did was unacceptable, Mary."

"And I apologised. I explained..."

"But I've also noticed how you behave toward Grace... I won't tolerate it."

"She's been here five minutes... five goddamn minutes—"

"That's enough!" Matt raises his voice. "It would be better for everyone, you especially, if you just left at the end of the day, but if you can't be civil, I'll get Luke to come along now, and escort you from the building…" He glares at her. "Do you want that? Or would you rather retain a little dignity?"

She pauses. "I'll wait until the end of the day," she murmurs.

"Fine. I'll have your severance pay transferred to your bank account this afternoon." He stares at her until she eventually bows her head and leaves the room. This time, she doesn't even look in my direction.

Matt takes a few deep breaths, then comes and joins me again.

"I'm sorry about that," he says, pulling me into a hug. "I probably shouldn't have done any of that with you present, but I don't like the idea of you being out of my sight."

"I'm glad she's leaving… I mean, I feel a little sorry for her—"

"You do?"

"Well, yes, in a way. She's in love with you… I can understand that. She can't help how she feels."

"No, but she can help what she does about it."

"That's why I only feel a little sorry for her. If she's behind the messages, making my life a misery just because of her misplaced affections isn't really fair."

"You're being very reasonable… a lot more reasonable than I'm feeling at the moment—"

The door opens and Luke comes in. "Mary just gave me the weirdest look," he says, "even by Mary's standards."

"That's because I just told her to leave… today. And threatened her with you escorting her from the building," Matt replies.

"Oh… was that wise?"

"Threatening her with you? She hates you. It seemed—"

"No, I mean… if she's responsible for the messages, isn't it better to keep her where you can see her?" he asks.

"I really don't think she is behind the messages… and having her here is too disruptive. Besides, thinking about it, if a male employee touched a female employee the way she touched me, I'd dismiss them on the spot. And they sure as hell wouldn't be getting severance pay."

"Fair point."

"It's great to see you and everything," Matt comments, "but was there a reason for you coming by?"

"Oh, yeah... Will called. He said to tell you he's run some initial checks on Mary. It seems she's got a cousin who works for an IT corporation on the West coast. Will's checking him out." Luke looks at us. "It doesn't mean anything..."

"But it might," Matt whispers.

"I'll keep you posted." Luke leaves again, closing the door behind him.

"This is a fucking mess." Matt puts his head in his hands.

"I'm sorry."

He turns to me. "Why are you sorry?"

"Your life must've been so much more straightforward before I came along."

"Not really..." He pulls me closer and hugs me. "And I wouldn't go back to that... not for anything."

We sit quietly for a while, just cuddled up.

"Are you okay?" he asks.

"Hmm... You were very... imposing."

"When?"

"When you were talking to Mary."

"Did that bother you?" He sounds wary.

"No." He leans over to kiss me. It's a sweet, gentle kiss. He's been sweet and gentle since yesterday morning. It's nice, but... well, I miss him.

"I won't break, you know," I whisper, looking up at him.

He stares into my eyes. "I know... I just..."

"I'm still me. I still need you... more than ever after all that's happened in the last couple of days. I need the reassurance, Matt. Ple—" His lips are on mine before I've finished speaking, and I open my mouth to his tongue, feeling the longing in his kiss. His fingers are in my hair, and I hear the groan in his throat as he turns, adjusting the angle to take me deeper. We're both breathing heavily, panting and I feel one of his hands move lower, coming around the front of my blouse, undoing the buttons. I break away.

"Matt... What if...?" I breathe, gasping for air, but looking at the door.

256

He grabs my hand and gets to his feet, pulling me up with him. "Come," he says and drags me across the room, to the door leading to his adjoining bathroom. Once inside, he locks the door, then he turns and claims my mouth again. Without breaking the kiss, he lifts me, sitting me on the wide vanity unit that takes up most of one wall. He stands between my legs, his hands on my thighs, pushing up my skirt. I reach forward and find his belt buckle, tugging on it. He laughs into my mouth.

"Let me," he says and undoes his belt easily before returning his hands to my thighs. I unfasten the button and zip on his trousers and they fall to his ankles. His tongue darts deeper still into my mouth as I pull down his trunks and his erection pops up into my hand. I stroke him gently back and forth and I can hear his soft groaning.

He pushes my skirt a little higher and pulls me forward, his fingers reaching the flesh above my lace-topped stockings. Then he moves further up, until he gets to the soft lace of my thong... the Onyx thong. Feeling it, he breaks the kiss and looks down.

"That's a surprise," he says. "I've never actually seen you wearing it."

"Well, you don't normally hang around long enough to notice..."

He laughs. "Yeah... You're right. But that's only because I'd rather get you naked..." He runs his fingers across the soft fabric again. "Feels good," he whispers, and lifts me off of the vanity unit again. He reaches behind me and undoes my skirt, letting it fall to the floor. Then he turns me around so I'm facing away from him, looking at us both in the mirror. His hands settle on my arms and he stares at me. His eyes are burning. "Stop me if you don't like this," he says into my neck. He waits. "Okay?" he asks and I realise he's waiting for me to respond. I nod my head, unable to take my eyes from his. "Bend forward," he says and I do, leaning over the vanity unit. He breaks eye contact with me, looking down, exhaling. His hands run over my exposed buttocks. "Beautiful," he whispers, then looks up and we lock eyes in the mirror again.

His hands continue their massage and he puts his feet between mine, pushing them a little further apart, and pulls my thong to one side. I can feel his erection rubbing back and forth, as he moistens the head against me. Then, he finds my entrance and pushes into me, filling me in one swift motion. It's glorious. My mouth falls open and I close my eyes, savouring the completeness of feeling him so far inside me. He stills. I open my eyes again and he's staring at me, waiting. I smile softly and nod my head and he begins to move, slowly at first, pulling out almost all the way before plunging back until we're deeply joined, our eyes, bodies and hearts connected. Then, he quickens the pace, taking me with him, and I start to feel the familiar sensation, the tingling, quivering deep inside me. He reaches around, insinuating his fingers beneath the soaking lace of my thong and rubbing my clitoris using hard, circular motions. With that, I'm gone… I force my eyes to stay open, as I ride the waves of my orgasm, watching him thrust hard into me one last time, his expression one of pure pleasure, as he fills me.

"I love you," he breathes as he finally shudders into me.

"I love you," I say to his reflection, our eyes still fixed.

"Was that reassuring enough?"

"Hmm." I nod my head.

Slowly, he pulls out of me, and turns me around to face him, pulling me into his arms and looking down into my eyes.

"Why did you need reassurance?" he asks. "Tell me what's wrong?"

"I just didn't like the idea of Mary touching you…"

"I didn't like being touched either. The only person who gets to touch me, is you."

"You are mine, aren't you?" I can hear the uncertainty in my own voice.

"All of me is yours, Grace… always. I belong entirely to you."

"*With* me," I correct.

"No… *to* you. You own me. There's been no-one in my head or my heart since the day I first saw you, and there never will be."

I let out a sigh… his words are so soothing, and he holds onto me, stroking my hair.

"Is everything okay?" he murmurs after a while, leaning back a little and looking down at me.

"Hmm."

"No. I'm serious, Grace. I mean… I know…" What's he trying to say? "I know he must have taken you like that," he says eventually. *Oh, I get it.* "I've been dying to do that with you for ages – not necessarily in here, obviously…" He glances around. "But I didn't want you to feel like…"

"Matt," I say, resting my hand on his chest, "Nothing that you do reminds me of him. You're so gentle, so loving. I can't possibly be reminded of him when I'm with you."

He leans down and kisses me.

"It's just, after that episode with the wall…"

"I thought we got over that, didn't we?"

He thinks for a moment. "Oh yeah. In your office…" He pauses. "Come to think of it, we never did get to finish that."

"I think we got side-tracked, if I remember rightly," I say.

"Well, I'm not getting side-tracked again." He leans down and picks up my skirt off the floor, pulling it back into place and re-fastening it. He kisses me again, harder this time. "Tonight… You, me, and the bedroom wall… Or maybe the living room… or both. Who cares."

I giggle. I can't help it. Everything feels a little better now.

Chapter Twenty-three

Matt

Taking Grace over the vanity unit, staring into her eyes while she watched me fill her, seeing the need, the consuming desire on her face, mirrored in mine, is beyond anything we've done so far. As soon as I entered her, I knew it would be good, but she takes me to new heights every single time.

Now, over an hour later, I still can't think straight and I don't care. With everything that's happening at the moment, I feel like our lives are in a whirl... out of control, but telling her that I'm hers was about the most steadying thing I've ever done. I like that feeling of being anchored, and I want to belong to her and I want her to know that I do.

I'm watching her sitting on the couch in my office, her laptop on the coffee table in front of her. Her head's swaying to the music that's playing through her earphones and her eyes are closed, like she's completely lost in the lyric, soaking it up and floating away on it. I want to know what it is, so I can understand the expression on her face. I also want to just go and sit with her, to kiss her, hold her, feel her. She fills me with a need that's like a raging fire, and I'll happily let it consume me. I get up, and my phone rings... *Damn*.

It's Todd. I glance up at Grace, but her eyes are still closed, immersed in the music.

"Todd," I say quietly.

"Are you at work?" he asks.

"Yes."

"What time are you going home?"

I glance at my watch. "We'll be leaving in about an hour, I guess. Why?"

"The Welsh police in that village I can't pronounce have come up trumps. I've got photographs." I freeze. This is it. Grace will know if it's Jonathan and then we'll all know what we're dealing with. "I can meet you at your place at six."

"You can't e-mail them?"

"I think we should do this together, don't you? It's not long to wait and I think it's best. If it is Jonathan, I think Grace might need the support of knowing we're all there to help." He's absolutely right. I know she'll go to pieces if he's still alive, and Will and Todd will probably be able to reassure her about what happens next far better than I can.

"Should I get Will and Luke to come over too?"

"Yeah, if possible. If it isn't him, Will might need to adjust what he's doing; if it is, he can probably stand down and I'll get the British police involved officially."

"Okay. I'll call Luke and set it up." It's only then that I realize Todd knows nothing about the situation with Mary. I quickly fill him in on what's happened.

"She touched you? Seriously?"

"Yeah."

"What did you do?"

"Jumped out of my skin. Then told her to remove her hand... It was really embarrassing... for both of us."

"I'll bet. I think Luke might be right though. I think you should maybe have kept her on... if only so you know what she's doing."

"It wasn't an option. Not with the way she was treating Grace. She's got enough to worry about, without my secretary giving her a hard time."

"I guess..." He sounds doubtful still.

My head's starting to spin again. "We'll talk about it later."

"Okay. See you at six."

He hangs up. I sit for a moment, feeling like I'm in a whirlwind. Grace still looks so calm and serene on the couch, but I feel like our whole world could be about to collapse around us... and there's nothing I can do about it. I call Luke and tell him what Todd's told me.

"I'll get Will to drive himself over and I'll come straight to your place from the office. It'll save time," he says. "Did Todd have any idea whether it's Jonathan or not?"

"No. He just said he's got photographs, that's all."

"Okay. I'll call Will. You sound odd," he says. "Are you alright?"

"No."

"What's up?"

"I feel... I feel so fucking useless. I've got you basically running the company; and Will and Todd are investigating Jonathan and Mary... What am I doing?"

"You're keeping Grace safe... that's your job."

"I should be doing more..."

"There's precious little point in any of us doing what we're doing, if you don't do that..."

"But... I was just thinking. Todd and Will... they're the ones who can really reassure her. When it comes down to it, what can I do, apart from hold her? I feel so fucking inadequate."

"Right... and it's never occurred to you that being held is what she needs most? Words from Todd and Will are fine, but feeling safe is about more than words, Matt. Only you can give her that. Only you can really give her peace of mind... so stop beating yourself up."

He's right. Again. "Okay," I say quietly. "Thanks."

"Welcome." I can hear him smiling.

I put the phone down and go over to Grace. She's still absorbed in the music, thank goodness. I sit down and she opens her eyes immediately, pulling out one earphone.

"What are you listening to?" I ask.

"Lighthouse Family," she replies. "I was reminded of them a while ago, when we visited Jenny... I've been listening to them on and off since then."

"Can I?" I indicate the dangling earphone and she hands it to me. I move closer to her and put it in my own ear, our heads almost touching.

"This is the track I've been listening to for the last hour," she says.

"What... the same track, on repeat?"

She nods her head. "It'll make sense in a minute."

She clicks on her laptop, starting the track from the beginning again... I notice it's called *Lost in Space*, which fits with my thoughts about her far-away expression earlier, but it seems an odd title. I listen to the lyric, because it's evidently made her contented, and lyrics seem important to us and, like Grace, I close my eyes. It seems to be about faith, although whether it's religious faith, or just faith in general, I've got no idea. And really, what does it matter? Either way, it's about having faith in someone, believing in them, and knowing you'd be completely lost without them. As the song progresses, knowing she can hear it too, I feel her move closer still, her head coming down to rest on my shoulder and I put my arm around her. When it finishes, I open my eyes, pull out the earphone and turn to her. She's staring up at me.

"That's how I feel about you," she whispers.

I feel a lump forming in my throat and I don't know what else to say except, "Thank you." She has no idea how much that means to me right now.

By the time I park the car outside the apartment, Grace is almost shaking with nerves. I check my watch.

"Come on," I say, helping her from the car. "You've probably got time to change, if you want." She looks up at me, her face full of doubt. "You don't have to," I add.

"Do I need to?" she asks.

"No." She looks beautiful.

"Then I'd just like a large glass of wine, and a hug."

I lead her into the building. "Okay."

Upstairs, I pour the wine while Grace sits on the couch. The door entry buzzes before I've even put the bottle back in the refrigerator. It's Will and Luke, who've arrived together, despite coming in separate cars, and from different directions. I press the button for them to come up, and open the apartment door.

They both want beers, so I fetch them while they sit with Grace. Todd arrives a few minutes later, and I make him a coffee.

Once we're all seated, Todd opens a large envelope.

"There's no point waiting," he says. "The sooner we know what we're dealing with, the better." Grace, who's sitting between Todd and me, leans forward as he pulls a handful of photographs from the envelope and spreads them out on the coffee table. Will comes and kneels to one side, and Luke stands opposite us, looking down at the display.

I quickly look at the images. In each one, there's a woman. She's pretty, but not beautiful. If Jonathan chose her over Grace, the guy must have been insane. She's got short brown hair, a wide mouth and a slightly turned-up nose. In some of the pictures, she's wearing glasses. The man, who's in every picture with her, is slightly taller, with blond hair. He's clean-shaven, sometimes wearing a suit and tie, although in most, he looks more casual. They give the impression of being proud parents, pushing a stroller, or with one or other of them carrying an infant. In one photograph, they're kissing. I turn away from the images and look at Grace. She's shifting the pictures, moving them around the table, her face pale, her mouth slightly open. I look over her head at Todd, who's studying her too. He looks worried. If this is Jonathan, I'm surprised. He seems younger than I'd thought, but also a bit out of shape. Somehow, in my mind, I'd pictured him as muscular, well-built. This guy seems—

"The lying bastard," Grace says and we all turn to her. "The lying, double-crossing, deceitful, corrupt bastard."

This isn't the reaction I'd expected. I'd assumed she'd fall apart.

"Grace?"

She turns to me. "That's Malcolm bloody Anderson," she says, like I'm supposed to know who she's talking about. The name Malcolm is familiar, but I can't… "Jonathan's evidently bent solicitor." We all look back at the photographs, then return our gaze to Grace. "I can't believe this," she mutters.

"I… I don't understand," Will says, taking one of the photographs and studying it.

"Malcolm Anderson was Jonathan's lawyer," Grace replies. "He handled Jonathan's will… his estate."

"And now he and Beth are… together?" Will looks shocked.

"It certainly looks like it, doesn't it?" Grace says.

"But what about Jonathan?" I ask.

"If this isn't him, then I think we have to assume he's dead," Todd puts in.

"Oh, it isn't him, trust me." Grace flops back onto the couch.

"The Welsh police sent through a report. They interviewed the neighbours. This… what's his name?"

"Malcolm Anderson," Grace supplies.

"Yeah… So, he's been a regular visitor since last spring. He's spent every weekend with Beth Jameson since the beginning of the summer."

"How can we be so sure Jonathan's dead?" Will asks, still studying the photograph in his hands.

Grace sits forward again. "Because there's no way he'd let Malcolm get his feet under the table, not if he was still around to do something about it." She looks up at me. I can feel her relief.

"I guess at least we know he's not sending the messages," she says.

"Does that help?" I ask.

"It helps me," she replies.

"I do have one other piece of news," Will announces. We all turn to look at him. "Mary's cousin. His job is in finance. He has nothing to do with the technology employed by the company he works for, and even if he did, I don't think it would help him… They manufacture robotic systems for the medical industry. It's all wrong."

"But she could've looked up how to hack Grace's phone on the Internet," Todd suggests. "You said Jonathan could've done that... the same thing applies to Mary."

"She could've, but I don't think so."

"Why not?"

"She didn't look anything up from the office computers..."

"How do you know?"

He looks at me. "Don't be mad... I hacked your systems. You needed answers. It was the quickest way in..."

"Why would I be mad?"

"Any number of reasons... firstly, it's illegal."

"I don't care. What did you find?"

"No-one in your office has accessed any form of instruction about phone hacking. Your data logs go back six months, so I guess she could've done it before then, but I seriously doubt it."

"Again... why?"

"We're talking about a woman who doesn't own anything more high tech than a coffee machine. She doesn't have a computer at home, her phone is out of the ark, and she rarely uses it... She just doesn't have the skills for this."

"And I'm assuming we really don't want to know how you found out all that information?" Todd asks.

"Nope."

"Are we saying it's definitely not Mary?" Luke says quietly.

"I'm as sure as I can be."

In a way, I'm relieved. I hated the thought that someone in my life was doing this to Grace.

"And we can be just as sure it's not Jonathan," Todd adds. "So what next?"

"I go back to square one," Will says.

"You're all doing so much." Grace sounds tired, but in a way stronger than she has for days. "I realize we still don't know who it is, but the fact that it isn't Jonathan makes me feel a lot better... I was so scared..."

I pull her close. "I'm still not letting you out of my sight."

"But surely…" she begins.

"Hey… Are you complaining about spending time with me?"

"No, of course not. But I don't want you to get bored with me…"
She stares into my eyes and I move a little nearer, my fingers brushing
up and down her spine.

"Well, that's never going to happen," I whisper.

"You two need to get a room," Todd says.

"We've got a whole damn apartment," I mutter, not moving, or
taking my eyes from Grace. "The problem is, it's kinda full right now."

"We can take a hint," says Luke, and Grace pulls away from me.

"No," she says. "Please, don't go. You're welcome to stay for
something to eat. We can order a take-away again."

"No, really," says Will. "I need to get back… I need to…" He runs
his fingers though his hair. He looks thoughtful, probably wondering
what to do next.

"And I'm officially still on duty," Todd adds, "for another two
hours."

"I feel like we're throwing you all out," Grace says.

"You're not," Luke says as they all head for the door, and Grace and
I follow, arm in arm. "Your boyfriend, on the other hand…"

I throw him a look and he grins at me.

Once they've gone, Grace turns and puts her arms around my neck.
"I feel guilty," she says.

"Don't. I'm sure Luke's got better things to do than sit around with
us; Todd's still on duty, and Will clearly wanted to get back to working
on your cell… And I want you to myself." I lean down and kiss her,
opening her mouth with my tongue, feeling her heat as she leans into
me, her breasts pressed against my chest. Without pausing, I walk her
backwards, putting my hand behind her head as her back meets the
wall. She doesn't tense; instead she moans, a throaty sound coming
from deep inside her, resonating through my body as she grabs my butt
and pulls me tight onto her, my hard erection pressing against her hip.

I lean down and nip at her neck, biting and licking her soft skin while she continues to grind into me.

"Now… I want you… now…" I mutter incoherently, stepping back and we strip urgently, ripping at our clothes. As soon as we're both naked, I gently push her back again, until the wall is behind her, then step between her feet, lifting her left leg up high over my bent right arm, holding it in place. She's open to me, my cock pressing against her entrance, and as she clasps my shoulders, I push up and inside her, letting out a rasping moan as I feel her clamp around me. I pull back, then plunge into her again, deeper and deeper each time, forcing her standing foot off the floor. It's frantic… feverish; a desperate release from the tension of the last few days' waiting. Her breasts rub against my chest and she nips at my bottom lip with her teeth. As I build up the pace, faster, harder, her nails dig into my skin, and she lets out a deep guttural groan with each thrust.

"Yes…" she screams. "Please, Matt. Now…" Her pleas send me over the edge and I can't hold back any longer. I let go inside her and my head rolls back as I cry out her name, my voice echoing off the walls.

I keep her supported, although I can feel her giving way, and slowly lower her bent leg to the ground.

She's flushed and breathing hard and it dawns on me, a little late, that I may have been too rough with her… again.

"That wasn't too hard, was it?"

"No," she says, catching her breath, gulping in air. "It was… probably… probably the most exciting thing you've done to me."

"Yet…" I add, smiling into the kiss I place on her lips.

She's lying in the bath, a glass of white wine beside her and I'm sitting on the edge, wearing jeans and a t-shirt, watching her.

"Do you want Thai or Chinese?" I ask.

"Chinese, I think."

"Okay. I'll order it in a minute."

She looks up at me, a little embarrassed. *What's this about?* I wait...
"And then can we try that again?" she asks, running her fingers up my arm, leaving a trail of fine bubbles.

"What?"

"What we just did..." *She wants more?*

"Sure..." I grin down at her. "That, or a variation of it. There's still the bedroom wall, remember?" I wink. "Did you like it then?"

She nods her head, looking kind of shy.

"Hey, don't," I say, placing my finger under her chin and raising her face. "There's nothing to feel uncomfortable about. I love that you're finally discovering your desires, your needs, your own sensuality... and, more importantly, that you're discovering them with me."

"You're a good teacher," she murmurs, her eyes darkening.

"I'm not teaching you anything."

"You're showing me, then."

"Only how to be yourself, baby." My phone starts ringing. It's in the kitchen, so I get up, give her a quick kiss and go through to answer it. The number isn't one I know, but I pick up anyway.

"Matt Webb speaking."

"Mr Webb?" says a male voice on the end of the line.

"Yes."

"I'm calling you from Mass General Emergency Room..." I feel a slight tingling pass over my skin.

"Yes?" I prompt.

"It's about Mr Luke Myers," the voice says and I move to the table to sit down.

"What about him?" I ask.

"I'm afraid he's been in an auto accident."

"Is he...?" I start to feel numb, but I'm trembling at the same time.

"He's in surgery at the moment."

"He has a brother, Will..." I say automatically. God, how's Will going to cope? He's relied on Luke for so long.

There's a pause. "Yes, Mr Myers was asking for him..."

"So, he *was* conscious... before the surgery?"

269

"Yes, when he was brought in, sir."

"Is Will on his way to the ER?" I ask.

"Yes, I believe so. But Mr Myers asked us to contact you as well."

He would. He'd know Will wouldn't cope on his own.

"I'll come… I'll come right away," I say.

"Thank you, sir." The line goes dead.

"Grace!" I call, running from the kitchen, through the bedroom and into the bathroom.

"What? What's wrong?" she says, sitting up, splashing water over the floor.

"It's Luke. He's been in an accident; he's in surgery. Sorry, baby, I have to go."

"Oh God. Of course you have to go," she says. "Is Will okay?"

"They were in separate cars."

"So, is Will with him?"

"He's on his way to the hospital."

I need to go… I'm standing at the side of the bath, staring down at her. I should probably wait, let her get dressed and take her with me, but the delay… Luke… and Will. Luke would want me to be there for Will…

"I can wait," I say, hovering.

"No." She's adamant. "I'm fine. Go. Will's going to be frantic. He'll need you." *She's worked that out already?* "Just call me as soon as you can, and let me know how Luke is. And take care." She grabs my t-shirt between her wet hands and pulls me down, kissing me hard.

Grace

I don't want to sit in the bath anymore. I'm too worried about Luke… and Matt. And Will.

He's nothing like Luke, or Matt. He's much quieter and more sensitive. Matt's told me a little of their childhood… I know their mother died when Will was twelve, but I don't know the details. Matt always says it's up to them to tell me, but I'm guessing it hit Will harder, being the younger child. He seems to rely on Luke a lot – so he's going to need Matt's help.

I dry myself off and go through to the dressing room. I want to get dressed; it could be a long night's waiting, and I feel that sitting around in a bathrobe would be wrong. I find a pair of leggings, some thick socks and a sweater and put them on, then go through to the living room, pouring myself another glass of wine on the way. The apartment seems empty without Matt, so I put on the television and turn down the volume, so it's just background noise. I'm not going to watch, but the sound is comforting.

I go over to the window. It's dark and it's started to snow. I'm not one of those romantic people who thinks snow is lovely. Personally, I can't stand the stuff: it's cold, wet, causes traffic chaos and is generally inconvenient. I much prefer a warm spring day, with flowers and blossom on the trees, to a blanket of snow.

Watching the flakes fall outside the window is a little mesmerising, though and I'm still standing there when the doorbell buzzes, and I jump.

I go over to the entry phone and press the speaker button.

"Hello?" Why do I sound nervous? I'm in my own home, for heaven's sake.

"Delivery from Ginger and Chilli, Ma'am," says a disconnected, rather bored sounding voice.

Oh. Matt must have phoned through the order from the car in case I got hungry. We'd agreed on Chinese, but I guess he forgot, and Thai is fine. It's so thoughtful of him, especially with what he must have on his mind.

"Come on up," I say as I press the entry button.

A few minutes later, there's a knock on the door and I open it.

And my heart stops beating.

Chapter Twenty-four

Matt

The traffic's been heavier than usual for this time of night. My first thought, that it might be because of the snow, was replaced by the darker one that maybe the accident Luke was in has caused the tailback. It was a horrible thought, and not one that was easy to dismiss. I've got no idea what's wrong with him; the guy who phoned didn't give me any details, but if he's in surgery it's got to be something fairly bad. I grip the steering wheel a little tighter. I just hope… I hope he's okay. For Will's sake… and mine. I don't really want to think about my life without Luke in it.

A drive that should normally take no more than ten or fifteen minutes at most, has taken nearly thirty, but I'm here at last and am just turning into the road that leads to the parking garage when my cell rings. It's Will. I take a deep breath and press the button on the steering wheel to connect the call.

"Hi," I say. "How are you doing? How's Luke?"

"Um… We're fine." He sounds confused. "Where are you?"

"I've just got here," I tell him. "I'll be inside in a minute."

"Inside where?"

"The hospital, of course. I'm just pulling into the parking garage."

"Why are you at the hospital?" I slam on the brake. Something's wrong.

"Because of Luke… his accident?"

"But Luke hasn't had an accident. He's standing here with me… Matt?"

I can't speak. My mind is racing… The guy behind sounds his horn.

I'm vaguely aware of Will's voice, calling my name again and then saying, "Luke, can you try talking to him?" Then I hear Luke's voice.

"Matt?"

It really is him. He's there…

"Matt, will you say something…"

"Luke," I mutter at last.

"Yeah…"

"You're okay?"

"I'm fine. What's wrong?"

Grace. I turn the steering wheel back out onto the street and floor the gas. "Fuck… It's Grace."

"That's why we were calling—" *What?*

"Call Todd," I interrupt him. "Tell him to get to my place."

"But I haven't even explained yet…"

"Explained what?" I take a left at the end of the road, the tires screeching loudly.

"About what Will found."

"Luke… Call Todd. Now."

"Okay. Will," he says, his voice a little muffled, "use my phone and call Todd. Tell him to get to Matt's place." There's a moment's pause and then he comes back on the line. "Matt, I need to tell you this," he says.

"Before you do… someone got me out of the apartment tonight. Grace is there alone."

"How did they manage that?"

"They told me you'd had an accident. I thought she'd be safe." *Oh God…*

"Where are you now?"

"I'm still on Charles Street, about ten minutes away. The traffic's…"

"Will's just trying to get through to Todd now. But I might be able to get there quicker then either of you… Hang on." I hear a scuffling noise. "Will? I'm going to Matt's place too." There's a pause. "No. You stay here, but get hold of Todd and get him over there." Then I hear a door bang. "Hang on," he says to me again. A few moments pass. The traffic I'm stuck in starts to move a little better. "Okay." Luke comes back on the line. "I'm in my car."

"Luke…"

"Don't think about it… just let me talk. There are things you need to know."

I'm frantic with fear. Whoever's doing this issued their threat and now they're going to see it through… Oh God. I can't… I can't lose her… *Stop it, Matt.* I need to focus on driving… on getting back to her.

"Matt!" Luke shouts.

"What?"

"Are you listening to me?" I hadn't even been aware he was talking. "Will's found something…"

"On Grace's phone?"

"No… on yours. Look, whoever's doing this isn't monitoring Grace's phone… they're monitoring yours and using your messages, to get Grace's details… Will decided to up the ante. I didn't know about this, but he got official, because of the threat to Grace and he contacted her service provider in the UK. He requested her old records, but they've taken a while to come through. They were waiting for him when we got back from your place, and he noticed that each time Grace changed her number, she didn't start getting any of these texts until after you and she had exchanged at least one message. "

"But none of her friends know me, except Jenny, and we kind of ruled her out…" There's a gap in the traffic ahead and I step on the gas again.

"I don't think it's one of Grace's friends, Matt."

"Then who? Surely not Mary…?"

"Once Will found out it was your phone, I had a hunch… so I got Will to check something." He pauses for a second. "Matt, I think it's Brooke."

"It can't be... she's still in prison."

"That's what I got Will to check... She was released on New Year's Eve."

I'm trying so hard to focus on driving, I'm not sure I'm even hearing him properly. "But how?"

"Don't worry about... Fuck it."

"What?"

"I just hit traffic... no, wait, it's getting going again."

"If it's Brooke... I don't get it. How could she do all this?"

"Don't think about that for now; just concentrate on getting back to Grace. We both need to drive, not talk... I'm gonna hang up," he says.

"Wait! Brooke's insane, Luke. You should stay away... this is my problem."

"I'm gonna pretend I didn't hear that."

"I mean it."

"So do I."

"You can't even get into my place without the entry card."

"Seriously? It's just a fucking door, Matt." He hangs up before I can tell him to watch his back.

The silence is deafening. I think I preferred it when I had someone to talk to.

This is my fault. All the time we've been looking for someone from Grace's past, and worrying about Mary, when we should have been looking at *my* past, and the most dangerous person I've ever known, who – if Luke is right – now has Grace...

I can see the intersection ahead and I speed up again.

I can't lose her.

275

Grace

My hands have gone numb. The woman who's standing in front of me tied them so tight behind my back, she's cut off the circulation.

She's hardly said anything since she barged in, the gun pointing at my chest. I still don't know who she is, or what she wants. She just told me to sit on this chair in the kitchen, facing the door to the apartment, tied my hands behind my back and my ankles to the legs of the chair, and then said I wasn't to speak. Since then she's been stood there, her back to the wall, the gun in her hand, looking at me, with a contemptuous, leering smile on her face. It's unnerving. Well, and bloody terrifying, of course.

God, I hope Matt comes home soon. I could be here all night with this woman.

I study her... There's nothing familiar about her. I'm absolutely certain I've never seen her before. She's tall and very thin, with long blonde hair, tied up in a pony tail. Her skin is pale and she's got large green eyes, that are just staring at me, as though she's trying to work something out, like I'm some great mystery.

Finally, she pushes herself away from the wall.

"You've got no idea who I am, have you? Even though I've been sending you messages for the last eight months," she says. For someone with such a pretty, delicate face, her voice is slightly jarring; it grates on my nerves. I shake my head. "So he didn't tell you about me?"

Realisation dawns. "You're Brooke?" I say, astonished. A smug smile brushes across her lips and she nods her head. "But I thought..."

"You thought I was still in prison? Afraid not. I was released a few days ago."

I was terrified before, but now...

"But... if you were in prison, how were you able to watch me?"

"I wasn't... I haven't been watching you... not until recently, anyway."

"But your messages…"

"Jeez, you're easily fooled… easily scared too." She laughs. "Matt'll be back soon," she continues.

"No, he won't."

"Yes, he will. Once he realises there's nothing wrong with Luke."

Oh shit… *shit*. It was a hoax. And yet she wants him here? So why go to all that trouble to get him out of the apartment?

"I had to get him out of the way, so I could get in here. He'd never have let me in." Obviously not. "You on the other hand… You're far more stupid. You're even more stupid than you look." She sneers. Her tone is scary… kind of child-like and yet terrifyingly threatening at the same time. "And you look *pretty* stupid," she adds and takes a step forward. I shrink back into the chair.

"What do you want?" I manage to ask.

"I want him to suffer. I've spent years in prison because of him…"

"No." I sit up slightly, my anger coming to the surface. "You spent years in prison because of your own actions."

"It was his fault!" she screams. "If he hadn't done what he did, none of it would have happened."

"That's bullshit." I use Matt's phrase. "You made your own choices." She walks over, standing right in front of me.

"You don't know anything!" she yells and, I see her raise her hand and then bring it down again. It's like being back with Jonathan – that vague awareness of the impending strike and being unable to move out of the way… only this time it's not just a fist or a hand. She hits me with the butt of the gun she's holding. My cheekbone feels like it's exploding. Everything swims, hazy and blurred, but I don't pass out. I've been hit too many times before. She bends and puts her face next to mine. "I've just had such a good idea," she hisses in my ear. "My original plan was to cut you… I was gonna do some real damage to that ugly face of yours, so he'd never want to look at you again, but – like I said – I've been watching you together for the last few days. I've seen how he is with you, and I know Matt… he'd only end up feeling sorry for you. So then I thought maybe I'd just kill both of you…" Oh,

God... She really is insane. "But now... now I think, when he gets back here, I'm going to give him a choice." I swallow hard. I think I can taste blood in my mouth. "He can choose... Either he can fuck me, one last time, on the table here in front of you – just for old time's sake – and then I'll kill him, *but* I'll let you live. Or, I'll kill you in front of him... but I'll let him live. I know which he'll choose... and so do you, don't you? And you'll have to spend the rest of your miserable life, knowing the last thing he ever did was satisfy me..." She stands and runs her hand slowly along the table, laughing and throwing her head back.

And now I hope Matt never comes home...

Chapter Twenty-five

Matt

I pull up right outside the front door to the apartment block. There's no sign of Luke or Todd, but I know they won't be far behind me.

I jump out of the car, grab my briefcase from the back seat and run up to the door, open it with the card and wedge it open with my case, so Todd and Luke can get in.

I head for the elevators and, luckily the doors open straight away. Once inside, I press the button for the fifth floor and wait while the doors close slowly… *Come on…* Why's it taking so long?

Finally, the doors open on our floor and I approach the apartment, pull out my keys and take a deep breath. I've got no idea what's waiting for me on the other side… but as long as Grace is still alive in there, I can handle anything. I place the key in the lock and turn it, gingerly. It clicks and the door opens. I stare ahead and it's like my whole world stops spinning.

I can see Grace. She's tied to a chair beside the table in the kitchen. Her face is swollen and bruised on one side, as though she's been hit very hard. But the thing that scares me the most is the look in her eyes as they catch mine… I've never seen fear like it. It's a wild, frenzied stare. Then her head starts to shake. I put my finger to my lips. It's the only thing I can think of to calm her. It doesn't work. "No, Matt!" she screams. "Go… Just run! Please!" *Not a chance, baby.*

I step forward across the threshold, into the apartment and start to walk toward her.

"Stop there!" the expected, familiar voice says from behind the still open door. *I hope she doesn't think to close it.* "I was starting to think you were never going to get back here."

I turn to face her, but don't reply. Her gun is trained on Grace.

"Nothing to say?" God, Brooke's voice is really irritating.

I shake my head. I'm trying to work how to buy some time until Todd gets here. I want to get her away from the open door, and get the gun off of Grace.

"You will... in a minute," she says, moving a little further into the room. I move with her, twisting, so I've got both Brooke and Grace in my sights. This is a little better. "You see, I've been having a nice little chat with your slut here."

"Don't call her that," I say.

"Oh... so you can speak."

"Of course I can speak."

"Good, then you'll be able to tell me your decision," she smirks.

"Decision about what?"

She looks at Grace. "I think you should tell him... slut."

"I said..." I move toward her. She raises the gun a little, so it's pointing at Grace's head. I back down.

"Tell him," she says to Grace.

Grace looks at me, her eyes still filled with that same fear. But there's also something else... Love? Sadness? Desperation? I can't identify it.

"She... she's giving you a choice," Grace mutters. Her lip is bleeding and swollen on one side and she's also crying. It's hard to hear what she's saying. "She said you could choose whether to... to..." She takes a deep breath.

"Oh, just say it," Brooke interrupts.

"She said you had to choose whether to fuck her... one last time—"

I snort. "Yeah, like that's gonna happen."

"Wait," Brooke says. She sounds smug... There's something else.

Grace takes a deep, shuddering breath, then continues, "One last time," she repeats. "On the table here, while I watch... And then she'll... she'll kill you." She chokes on the words. Brooke's already

280

unappealing proposal just got so much less enticing. I really wish Todd and Luke would hurry up. Grace starts speaking again: "She says if you do that, she'll let me live… If not, she's going to kill me in front of you… but she'll let you live. Matt, don't…"

"Shut up!" Brooke says, coming to stand in front of me. I need to buy just a little more time. Todd can't be far away now… And Brooke's just given me the perfect opportunity.

"Well, that's the easiest decision I'll ever make," I say, staring at Grace. *Look into my eyes, baby. Tell me you understand.*

"You're gonna fuck me, then?" Brooke simpers.

"How do I know you won't just kill Grace later, once you're finished with me?" I ask her.

"Because I want her to know you spent your last moments on earth inside me. I want her to watch you make me come; I want her to hear me screaming your name… and I want her to have to live with that for the rest of her fucking life."

Grace shakes her head. "No, Matt!" she screams, "please…"

"God, I'm getting really sick of you," Brooke says and, she grabs a dish towel from the countertop, using it to gag Grace. "Now, shut up and watch."

She turns back toward me. "I knew you'd choose me," she says.

"I'm not," I growl at her. "I'm choosing Grace."

"Hmm… a lifetime of happy memories… how kind of you."

"Well, you're not giving me very many options, are you?"

"We're wasting time," she says. *Yeah, I know… I was just hoping you wouldn't notice.* The gun is still pointing in Grace's direction, as she moves across to the end of the table. "Come on, then."

I walk slowly over, keeping my eyes on Grace, but she's closed hers. Brooke follows my gaze.

"Slut!" she says. I feel the anger burning. "Open your eyes… or I'll make his death twice as painful."

Grace snaps her eyes open and they lock straight into mine. *Please understand… I'm not going through with this… Please.*

"Matt, look at me," Brooke says. I tear my eyes away from Grace. Brooke is standing with her back to the table. "Lift me up," she says, pouting. Does she think this is attractive? I put my hands on her waist and lift her to sit on the tabletop. She lies back and spreads her legs. The gun is still in her grip, but it's up by her head now, not trained on Grace. My back is to the door, blocking her view... I just need Todd. Where the hell is he?

"Touch me," Brooke mutters. I lean over her, my hand just inches from the gun. "Oh." She sits up a little. "And don't even think about trying to take this away from me." She waves the gun in front of my face. "Try anything and I'll shoot her." She nods to her right, in Grace's direction and I let out a breath. She lies back down again, a smile forming on her lips. "I want your big cock inside me, Matt... Make me come, real hard, like you used to," she purrs. I hear a sob from Grace, but I can't look at her. If I do, I know I'll have to stop this charade and go to her. "Now!" Brooke demands. I run my hands slowly up her legs, still playing for time. She squirms and lifts her hips toward me. I know I can't go through with this... *Come on, Todd...*

I don't touch her, not where she wants me to, but I start to slowly undo her jeans. Then something changes. I don't know what... but my spine tingles and the hairs on the back of my neck stand on end... And I know... I know Todd's here. I'm between him and Brooke, but she's still got a clear shot at Grace, who's sat off to my left.

I stand up straight and Brooke opens her eyes. "I didn't tell you to stop," she says, waving the gun at me again.

Everything seems to happen at once. Todd says my name, and I dive to my left, putting myself between Grace and Brooke, just as she raises the gun. The sound is thunderous, echoing around the apartment. The pain is sudden and agonizing, like nothing I've felt before. The floor is hard, colder than I'd expected. Grace's scream is piercing... The shadows are dark, imposing. *No.* This can't be happening. I fight to stay awake. *Please, don't let this be it... There's so much need to tell her...* And then everything goes silent and black.

Grace

No... No... No... No. Please... No.

Todd moves forward quickly, his gun still on Brooke, even though he's just shot her and she's lying completely still on the kitchen table. Luke follows close behind. He looks from me to Matt and runs to him, grabbing a towel from the work surface as he goes and dropping to his knees. He pushes the towel against the wound in Matt's side staring at the blood pouring pooling on the floor.

"Make sure you press down hard," Todd says.

"I got it." Luke glances up at me. "He'll be okay, Grace," he adds.

Todd already has his phone to his ear, calling for an ambulance while he checks on Brooke, pushing the gun away from her flaccid hand, then replacing his own weapon in its holster. He's so calm, so collected, but my whole world is disintegrating in front of me. He comes over to me and removes the gag from my mouth. I take in a gulp of air, then start to cry, sobbing Matt's name. He's lying face-down on the kitchen floor, and the cloth that Luke is holding against his side is already completely soaked with blood.

"Help him," I say to Todd. He moves behind me to untie my wrists. "Please help him."

"I will... Just let me..." He pulls at the rope binding my wrists. "There." He's freed me and I bring my hands around in front of me, then lean down and, despite my numb fingers, manage to pick at the knots binding my ankles.

"Help him," I keep repeating. Todd is now kneeling next to Luke. He feels Matt's neck for a pulse, and his face darkens.

"Hold on," he says quietly. Then he turns to Luke and they stare at each other. "Keep pressing down."

I know my legs won't support me, so I slide off the chair and kneel down, crawling across to Matt. His face is turned towards me, his eyes are closed. He looks like he's sleeping, but his face is completely white.

"Is he…?" I look up at Todd.

"He's got a pulse," he says. "It's kinda weak, but it's there."

I lean down and kiss his cheek, stroking his hair. Then I move my mouth next to his ear.

"Don't you leave me," I whisper, tears falling from my cheeks to his. "You know I can't do any of this without you. Stay with me, Matt… Please…" I kneel there for what seems like a long time, just saying his name, over and over, hoping he'll hear me and wake up.

I'm disturbed by a commotion at the door and Todd jumps to his feet. "Over here, guys," he says, then comes and stands above me. Luke gets up too, moving to one side, so the paramedics can have some space.

"Come on, Grace," Todd says gently. "Let them work on him." I don't want to move. I want to stay close to Matt, but I feel a pair of strong hands under my arms and then I'm being lifted out of the way, pulled to my feet, and turned around into a hug. I weep into his chest.

His arms are comforting, but they're not Matt's.

We've been at the hospital for hours. A nurse and a doctor have looked at my face in the ER. I've had an X-Ray taken and there's nothing broken or fractured. It's all just cuts and bruises. Now we're sitting in a waiting room. Matt's in surgery, and no-one has told us anything. Will has joined us. He's pale and Luke is sitting beside him. Todd hasn't left my side since the ambulance took Matt away from the apartment. Some other policemen arrived not long after the paramedics and Todd gave them some details and left them to deal with everything, then he drove us here in a police car.

"What time is it?" I ask. I'm surprised my voice still works, it's been so long since I used it.

"It's just after two," Luke replies.

"In the morning?"

Luke nods his head. "Do you want anything?" he asks.

"No, thanks." I look down. I've got dried blood under my fingernails. I don't know whose it is, or how it got there and I start to pick at it. I can't bear the sight of it. I try using the nails of one hand to clean the other, but it's not working, the blood has stained... I can't get rid of it... I start to rub harder...

"Come with me." Todd takes one of my hands in his and pulls me to my feet and along the corridor to the Men's room. He opens the door and calls out, "Anyone in here?" There's no reply, so he steps to one side and ushers me in. Then he stands me in front of a basin and runs some hot water, lowering my hands into it and then adding soap from the dispenser and washing them carefully until all the blood has gone. He fetches a paper towel and dries my hands between his, then leads me back out to the waiting room again, without saying a word.

He sits beside me once more, his leg crossed over his knee.

"Thank you," I mutter.

"Don't," he says, and I glance across at him. His face is a mask, but his eyes, when he turns in my direction, are bleak.

"Hey, this wasn't your fault," I whisper.

"Don't, Grace," he repeats.

I turn in my seat. "I'm not going to let you blame yourself, Todd."

He turns too. "Why? It is my fault. I was talking to my captain and didn't have my phone on me... I should have kept it in my pocket, like I normally do, then it wouldn't have taken Will so long to get hold of me... If I'd... If I'd just gotten there sooner."

"Then what? You'd have come in first. She was waiting behind the door. If she'd seen you – or anyone other than Matt – I think she'd just have shot you. And then where would we have been? She'd still have done what she did; she'd have carried out her threat, and there'd have been no-one to come to the rescue."

"That's your idea of a rescue?"

"Yes."

He stares at me... well, more through me, really.

"She's right, Todd," Luke says, but Todd just continues to gaze at me.

"Okay," I say. "You can't see it right now... but think about it, please. I don't blame you. Neither does Luke and neither would Matt... So that makes you the only one——" A doctor in green scrubs appears in the doorway.

"Are you all here for Matthew Webb?" he asks. I stand the quickest, but Todd is immediately by my side.

"This is his girlfriend," he says and the doctor looks to me.

He's smiling... Thank God... He's smiling. "He's going to be alright..." I don't hear anything else... Todd catches me and holds me, but the rest of the words mean nothing. Matt's going to be alright...

Chapter Twenty-six

⮜⮞

Matt

When I wake up, I feel like my head's not my own; and my body aches all over... but I'm alive. I want Grace. I need to know she's okay. I turn my head. *Shit, that hurt!* But I don't care... She's here, curled up asleep in a big chair next to my bed, with a light blue blanket over her legs. She's too far away to reach, so I just lie still and watch her, breathing in and out gently until I feel myself drifting off again.

The next time I open my eyes, she's awake and tears are streaming down her cheeks. "Don't cry, baby," I whisper, reaching out my hand to her. She clambers to her feet and comes over, climbing onto the bed next to me.

"I thought... I thought I'd lost you."

"I told you, I'm yours... I'm yours to keep. And a guy my size? How can you possibly lose me." She shifts on the edge of the bed, moving a little closer. The side of her face is red and swollen, her lip is split, her eye half closed, and she's still beautiful. "Does it hurt?" I ask.

"You're asking me?"

"Hey, I'm so full of painkillers, I can't feel a thing... Does it hurt?"

"A little." God, I want to hold her. "Why did you do it, Matt?"

"Why did I do what?"

"Why did you take up her offer? And why did you put yourself between me and her?"

I try to sit up a little. "I took up her offer to buy time... I knew Will was calling Todd. I knew he'd get there."

"But, what if he hadn't got there in time? You'd have had to... you know... in front of me."

"That was never going to happen, Grace. It would have been a physical impossibility." She looks confused. "I need to be hard, baby... And I was anything but." Now she's embarrassed. "Grace..." I wait for her to look at me. "I did *not* want her... not for one second. If Todd hadn't got there, I'd have tried to find a way to get the gun from her. I was never going to touch her, and I was never going to let her hurt you."

"But you put yourself between us... You got shot..."

How can she not get it? "Of course I did. For the same reason you yelled at me to leave. I love you. I'd do anything to keep you safe." Tears fall down her cheeks. "Please don't cry," I say. "I want to hug you... and I can't."

The door opens a fraction and Luke sticks his head around.

"Can we come in?" he asks. He looks exhausted and pale.

"Sure," I say. Grace goes to get up, but I manage to hold her in place, just about. Man, I'm so weak.

Will follows Luke through the door and I wait, expecting to see Todd, but he doesn't appear.

"Where's Todd?" I ask.

Luke looks at Grace and says, "He had to go back to the precinct." I can't hide my disappointment. I need to thank him. "I think he has to file a report," Luke continues. "Brooke's dead... Todd shot her... you know... there's paperwork."

"Is he okay?" I ask.

"Yeah, he's fine." That was a little too rehearsed, too cheerful, for my liking. "How are you feeling?" he asks.

"Like I've been shot."

"At least she missed anything vital... like Grace."

288

"Yeah, I've been very lucky." It could've been so much worse, if Todd hadn't shot Brooke... if she'd had time to get another shot off herself. I don't even want to think about what could've happened to Grace... I just know I owe him everything. As for the bullet that hit me... it passed through the side of my abdomen. I lost a lot of blood, but it looked worse than it was.

"We're thinking of heading home," he says. "It's been a long night." He looks at Grace, but seems uncertain what to say.

"Do you want to go home too?" I ask her. "Luke can take you... You could have a shower, get some rest and come back later."

"No." Her reply is abrupt, and she shakes her head. She won't look up at any of us.

I glance up at Luke. He shrugs, but Will sighs and moves closer to the bed. "Grace," he says gently. "Would you like to come back to our place?" *Of course. I'm an idiot.* "Luke can go and get you some clothes from your apartment. You can have a shower. I'll make you some breakfast, and you can get a few hours' sleep... And one of us will bring you back here later on."

Grace looks at me.

"Sorry," I say. "I should've realized you wouldn't want to go back to the apartment. Will's plan sounds good to me."

She nods her head, then leans over and touches her lips to mine. I let out a long breath. She pulls away far too quickly, then goes across to Will. He doesn't touch her at all, but they move toward the door.

"Will?" I call out to him. He stops and looks back. "Thanks for everything you did."

He looks at the floor for a moment, then back up at me. "Just do me a favor?" he says. "When you get out of here, change the passcode on your phone... and don't ever use your date of birth again... on anything. It's too damn easy." He guides Grace out of the room. Luke goes to follow but I call him back.

"Look after her for me. Make sure she's okay."

"Of course."

"And thanks..."

"Nothing to thank me for," he says. "I didn't do anything."

"Somehow I don't believe you..." He smiles.

"Will or I will bring Grace back whenever she's ready. And don't worry about work. I'll handle things."

"That's what I mean... You have a weird idea of having nothing to thank you for."

"It's a team effort."

"I know. Speaking of which, what's the story with Todd?"

"He had to leave."

"Yeah, and I'm Britney Spears... C'mon, Luke." I sigh.

"Okay... He feels guilty... responsible..."

"What for?"

"For what happened to you."

"But if he... if both of you hadn't got there when you did..." I falter, thinking about what might have been.

"I know that... you know that... Grace knows that. She told him, while you were in surgery..."

"She told him what?"

"To lay off blaming himself. He stuck to her like glue, Matt. He was incredible... like a different person."

"I need to see him."

"I'll try calling him... but don't hold your breath."

❧

Grace

It's been five days... Matt's so much better now. He's up and about, but he hates being in the hospital. I'm staying with Luke and Will, in their high-tech house. It's like something out of a James Bond film, hidden behind security gates, with a 'control room' as I've taken to calling it, where Will works in front of banks of screens. I've got no real idea what he does, but I've never seen so many computers and gadgets in one room.

They've both been so kind. Luke has now fetched Matt's car for me, so I can drive myself around, and he's brought me over lots more clothes. I can't face going near the apartment at all. I don't think I'll ever want to go back there again. I'm not sure where we'll live but it won't be there. Matt and I discussed it yesterday and he feels the same.

Today, Matt's asked me to bring in his laptop, I assume so he can stay in touch with Luke more easily. I know he'll do some work too and I don't mind really because I know he's bored and needs something to do, although there's a part of me wishing he'd just focus on getting well so he can come home... except we don't have a home...

When I arrive, he's sitting up in bed, looking out of the window. He turns as soon as I enter.

"Hey, beautiful," he says, smiling.

"Hi," I reply. "And I'm not beautiful." The bruising has come out and my face is various shades of blue and purple, although the swelling isn't anything like as bad as it was.

"You're beautiful to me," he says as I lean in to kiss him. At least my lip doesn't sting anymore, so kissing is easier now. "And this will soon fade." He gently touches my cheek with his fingertips.

"How's things?" I ask.

"Oh, you know..."

"That exciting, huh?"

"Yeah." He needs cheering up.

"I brought your laptop." I open my messenger bag and pull it out.

"Ah... good girl." He takes it from me and puts it on his lap, opening it up.

"Why do you need it?" I ask.

"You'll see." He shifts over to one side of the bed. "Sit down," he says. I perch next to him and he puts his arm around me. "I miss you," he whispers.

"I miss you too."

"When I get out of here..."

"You're going to rest."

"Like hell I am... I'm going to hold you... kiss you... touch you... Ahh——" He stops suddenly.

"What's wrong? Are you in pain?"

He shifts slightly and moves his laptop further down the bed. "I'm just a little…uncomfortable." I move to get up and he laughs, pulling me back into place.

"Not like that," he says and lifts the bed covers, nodding downwards. I follow his gaze…

"Oh! I see." He's feeling better.

"Yeah… And I only got as far as *thinking* about touching you…" He shifts again.

"Have they said how much longer—?"

"Maybe the day after tomorrow. I'm healing well, evidently."

I'm elated… and worried at the same time. "But… where…"

He pulls the laptop closer again. "That's what this is about," he says, opening up a browser. "We need to look for somewhere else to live."

I lean back onto the pillows while he taps in a search…

"Houses?" I say, looking at what he's typed.

"Yeah." He looks at me. "A house feels right, unless you want another apartment?"

"Not especially."

He scrolls through a few properties, dismissing them for one reason or another, and then clicks on one. The screen refreshes and a beautiful… a truly beautiful house appears. It's a 1930s colonial detached house with a grey panelled exterior. I glance at the description.

"Matt, it's got six bedrooms. What on earth do we need six bedrooms for?"

"Who knows…" He winks at me, then turns back to the screen and clicks on the photo gallery. All the rooms are oak panelled, the living room has a huge fireplace and there's a library… an actual library. The master bedroom has a balcony, which overlooks a lake. And there's a deck beneath it with the same view.

"It's spectacular," I say. "But where is it?" It can't be in the centre of Boston, not with that view.

"It's in Winchester."

"And where's that?"

"It's north of Boston."

"How far north?" I ask, nervously.

"About a forty-five minute drive."

"Oh, okay."

"Wanna take a look?" he suggests.

"How much is it?"

"Wanna take a look?" he repeats, smirking.

"How much is it?"

"Well... This could get boring."

"Matt, we can't just spend money."

"Why the heck not?" He pushes the laptop away again and twists towards me, wincing slightly, then takes my hands in his. "If we learn nothing else from what's happened, it should be that life's not a dress rehearsal. We get one crack at this... I'd kinda like to get it right."

I lean into his arm. "I know... I feel the same." He reaches behind my head and pulls me into a kiss.

"We have to stop doing that," he breathes after a few moments, and I can't help but giggle. "Just wait till I get home..." he warns playfully.

"What home?"

"Precisely. So... do you wanna take a look at this place?"

"Matt..."

He chuckles. "Okay, you win. It's just shy of two million..."

"Dollars?" I choke.

He looks at me. "Yes, dollars." *How much?*

"Matt, we don't need six bedrooms, or a library. We can easily..."

He leans over and kisses me again, muttering, "Be quiet."

He's phoned the agent and booked an appointment for after the weekend. He thinks he'll be fit enough to go by then, if I drive... I can't wait. It's going to be a reasonably long drive, and I'll get to put my foot down in his car, just a little bit.

He's still got his phone in his hand and is turning it over and over.

"What's wrong?" I ask.

"Todd," he says.

"He still hasn't been in touch, has he?"

He shakes his head. "I don't think we've ever gone this long without talking – except when he's gone undercover."

"Call him," I say. He stares at me. I take his phone from him, open up his contacts list and find Todd's details, waiting for the call to connect. He takes a while to answer.

"Matt?" He sounds nervous.

"No, it's Grace, but Matt needs to speak to you. Hang on." I hold the phone out to him.

He looks at me, and takes the phone.

"Todd," he says and I get up and leave the room.

I give him ten minutes before going back in, armed with a coffee for each of us. I hand him a cup.

"That's another reason to get out of here." He grimaces as he takes a sip.

"How did you get on with Todd?" I ask.

"He's coming over."

"When?"

"Now."

"Would you prefer it if I left?" I ask.

"No... why on earth would I want that?"

"If you need to talk to him..."

"I can do that in front of you."

"Well, if he's uncomfortable having me here, I'll make myself scarce."

He doesn't reply. I straighten the bed a little, prop up his pillows, top up the water in the flowers that have been sent by a couple of his clients, and then sit beside him on the bed and rest my head against his shoulder.

"I could get used to that," he says.

The door opens and Todd walks in. He looks exhausted.

"Hey," Matt says and I can tell from the tone of his voice that he's noticed Todd's appearance too.

"Hi. How are you?" Todd asks.

"A lot better than I was."

Todd stands awkwardly between the bed and the door, like he's looking to make a quick escape.

"Come and take a seat," I say, sitting up a little and motioning to the chair on the other side of the bed. He hesitates for a moment, then walks over and sits, perched on the edge of the seat, staring at the side of the bed.

The two of the them sit for a while... It's like they've both got something to say, but neither of them knows how to start the conversation.

"How have you been, Todd?" I ask, tired of waiting.

"I'm fine." He doesn't look up.

"Okay..." I say, "to quote my boyfriend... that's bullshit." They both look up at me. "Well, I'm sorry, but it is." The corner of Matt's lip curls up. "You two need to talk," I continue. "If you'd rather I left, Todd, I'll go... but only if you both promise you're not just going to sit here doing impressions of statues."

"You don't have to leave," he mutters, then turns to Matt. "I'm sorry," he says after a moment's pause.

"What the fuck for?" Matt replies.

"Getting you shot."

"You did *not* get me shot."

"I should have got there quicker and dealt with it better."

"Todd, you did the only thing I wanted of you. You stopped Brooke hurting Grace... That's why I've been wanting to thank you."

"Thank me?"

"Yeah, thank you."

"But I thought..."

"You thought I'd blame you? You couldn't be more wrong," he says. "I'll never be able to repay you for what you did."

Todd sits quietly, then turns to me. I raise an eyebrow, although it hurts a little.

"If you say I told you so, I'll..."

"You'll what?" I say.

"I don't know…" he says smirking at last. "I'm pretty sure the big guy won't let me do anything to you that involves handcuffs…"

"Damn right I won't," Matt says.

"Okay… I'll have to think of something else then."

"Maybe it's just best all round if I don't say I told you so?"

Todd shrugs. "A lot less fun, but you're probably right."

Matt shakes his head, but he's smiling and I can tell he's pleased to have his friend back on form again. "Do you know what happened yet?" he asks.

"We've got a fairly good idea." Todd sits back in the chair. "I don't understand the technical stuff, but Will's found that Brooke – or rather her brother, Tony, who it transpires is some kind of analyst – hacked your phone."

Matt takes a deep breath. "You're not to blame," I say to him.

"I'd listen to your girlfriend," Todd says. "She's usually right. You had no way of knowing."

Matt looks from Todd to me and back again. He's not listening to either of us, I can tell. There's a haunted look in his eyes that shouldn't be there. "I don't understand," he says, "why Brooke was released early. She still had several months to serve."

"She was able to earn good-time… I don't know how. She must have worked and attended some programs or classes."

"Sorry…" I can't hide my confusion. "What's 'good-time'? Is that like time off for good behaviour?"

"Yeah," Todd replies.

"Good behaviour?" I'm a little incredulous. "She was sending me vile messages and making my life a misery, and that counts as good behaviour, or 'good-time' or whatever you call it?"

"So it would seem. I'm not happy about it either. I've spoken to my captain about what she was doing, and mentioned the fact that she had a cell phone, but what he'll do about, I don't know. He gave me some bullshit about phones being banned from prisons… but that doesn't mean they're not available. We're interviewing Tony at the moment at the precinct. He's not being exactly forthcoming with information, but we'll get there eventually."

"And it was Tony who called, to get me out of the apartment?" Matt asks.

"He hasn't admitted it, but he was dumb enough to use his own phone for that. We've traced the call."

"Will he go to prison too?" I ask.

"Oh, yeah." I suppose that's something.

Todd and Matt chat for another half an hour before Todd says he has to get back to work. I stand as he's leaving and he comes and gives me a hug. He holds me close, but not too close and, putting his mouth next to my ear, he whispers, "Thank you," then turns and leaves.

"I'm not sure I like him hugging you," Matt says once the door's closed.

I sit down beside him again, leaning back on his pillows. "Don't be grumpy. He was very good to me, when you were shot. He looked after me," I tell him.

"Hmm... So Luke said."

"Well, it's true." I turn to him and kiss him. "He didn't let me out of his sight, he let me cry over him, he stayed with me in the ER... and he washed my hands."

"Okay..." He sounds confused.

I nestle down a little. "I had blood under my fingernails... It was bothering me... I was worried it might be yours. He took me and washed my hands. It was thoughtful of him."

"He's a thoughtful kind of guy. He's a tough cop on the outside, but underneath, there's a very different side to Todd. He doesn't show it often, but it's there."

"I gathered that."

I put an arm around him, resting my head on his chest. "Thank you," he says quietly.

I look up at him. "What for?"

"Getting him over here."

"I didn't."

"Yeah, Grace… you did."

I'm back at Luke and Will's and they've fed me lasagne, which was very good. Luke's brought my laptop home for me, so I can catch up with work for the first time since all this happened, and I'm sitting on the bed in the guest room, with it on my lap. Luke is on the phone in the living room, talking to a buyer on the West coast, and Will is in the 'control room'.

I fire up the laptop. My mail application opens automatically. It's not as bad as I'd thought. I've only got seventy e-mails and most of them are junk. I wade through them in order, replying to the two from Paul that require answers. I finally get to today's, and find one from Matt. The subject is *'Open me later…'*. Well, it's later, so I click on the message and read:

> *'Grace,*
>
> *Being away from you is killing me. It reminds me of when you were in London and I was over here and we used to communicate best via song lyrics.*
>
> *Plug in your earphones, close your eyes, and listen to this. I know it's really old, but they don't write them like this anymore and it says just about everything I've been trying to tell you for days… well since I met you really, only I don't have the words.*
>
> *I love you, beautiful.*
>
> *Matt xx'*

He's attached a link to a piece of music. I do as he says and plug my earphones into the computer, then put them in my ears and listen. Oh… how can that be? It's the song my parents used to play… It's their song. Matt's right, it is an old one, I guess from the 1970s. I don't remember who sang it… but I do remember the title: *It's Impossible.* Tears are already falling down my cheeks as the introduction plays, before the lyric even starts. I know all the words by heart and, with my eyes closed, I can see my parents dancing around the living room, my mum in my dad's arms, smiling up at him… so happy.

As it finishes, I hit the reply button.

> 'Matt,
> *What can I say? That was my parents' favourite song. They used to play it all the time: in the car, in the house, on holiday… everywhere; and I'd watch them dancing while it played, my dad holding my mum in his arms. They were so happy together.*
> *I can't tell you how much I love you; there are no words to express it… It's Impossible.*
> Grace xx'

I put the laptop on the bed and go into the ensuite bathroom to fetch a tissue. As I'm walking back, I hear the ping announcing I've got a new e-mail. It's from Matt. I open it immediately.

> 'Beautiful,
> *I know you're crying. Please don't. I can't bear it when I'm not there to hold you.*
> *When I get out of here and we buy that house, I'll dance with you to that song… and I'll dedicate my whole life to making you as happy as you make me.*
> Matt xx'

And he says he doesn't have the words.

Epilogue

Grace

The house is perfect. We've been here for just over a month now. We bought new furniture – including a new bed. I didn't want to bring anything at all from the apartment and Matt was fine with that. He even bought a new coffee machine... a much less complicated one. There are enough guest bedrooms for everyone to come and stay and it's so spectacular out here, Luke and Will have become regular visitors. Todd's stayed over a few times too, when work allows. He rides out on his motorbike at the weekends and I love having them all here, especially Will, who's like the brother I never had. I know why Matt wanted such a big house now. We've already got a big family, even if we never manage to have any children of our own.

They've all taken to confiding in me, except perhaps Luke. He's chatty – and still a little flirty sometimes – but he doesn't confide. He fools around, but when he thinks no-one's watching, a sad look settles on his face. I don't think he's as happy as he'd have everyone believe. He may be a womaniser, but I like him, and I trust him, and I think he appreciates the fact that Will shares his problems with me.

Will still hasn't told me much about his childhood, but we talk about lots of other things. I think he's lonely. His life is very solitary. Whatever it was that happened to him when he was younger, it's obviously had a deep effect on him. It'll take time for him to overcome that. I just hope I can help in some way.

Todd talks about work, mostly. He's really fed up, that much is obvious. He was affected by killing Brooke, but I've found out there was another shooting before, a few years ago. He mentioned it once, then clammed up. Maybe he'll open up again one day…

After Matt came out of hospital, we stayed with Luke and Will for several weeks, until Matt could close on the house. It was very generous of them and we had fun, the four of us together. I got used to living there and, when we moved out, I missed them a lot.

We're both fully recovered now. I can't in all honesty say it's like it never happened, because we both still get the odd reminder. I know Matt still feels guilty. He's very protective of me, because he feels he put me in harm's way. That's rubbish of course and he'll work that out eventually, but I'm not complaining; I like him being protective. I struggle with the image of him touching Brooke, even though I know why he was doing it. When he first tried to make love to me, not long after coming out of hospital, I froze, and then I freaked out. It was like going back in time. All I could think about were her words, her telling him what she wanted him to do to her, and I got this image in my head of the two of them together. It was hard to get rid of. He was so very patient. We talked it through, and he waited until I was ready. It took me a while, but we're back to normal again now, especially since we moved in here. I always felt a bit shy making love at Luke's place. I worried that he and Will might hear. Matt didn't care… Well, he said he didn't. Here, there's no-one to hear us, which is just as well.

Tonight is the first Saturday since we moved here that we're going to be alone. Will is working, and Luke and Todd have gone to an ice hockey match. It's another game I don't really understand and they wanted us to go along with them, but Matt said no. He explained that we really want to have some time by ourselves and, although they made fun of him remorselessly, they understood. I've promised we'll go with them to the next home game.

Tomorrow is Matt's birthday and everyone's coming here for the day, so I've got every intention of making the most of a peaceful evening… and night. With that in mind, I go up to our bedroom, which is beautiful, decorated entirely in white, with a balcony overlooking the lake. I open the doors and stand outside for a while, taking in the view and breathing in the fresh air. For the end of March, it's quite mild.

I'm so lucky. It's only a little over a year since Jonathan died… and everything in my life has changed. I have the kind of happiness I never dreamed possible, with a man who loves me… a man who tells me and shows me he loves me all the time. Matt and I have come through such a lot… and we have each other. And nothing else matters.

I've brought home some samples from the newest range of lingerie… It's not even been photographed yet. We're doing that in the early summer, once we've found the right model and locations, but I wanted something special for tonight and this is very, very special. I've never seen anything like it. Paul and Josh have been working on this for ages but, when I asked, they were happy to let me have the items I requested.

I undress and pull the bag from the wardrobe. Inside is a bra, a thong and a kimono. They're made from two layers of lace, one a metallic silver, laid over an antique rose gold. The fabric is baby soft to the touch and, as I pull the bra on, I can't help but feel sexy. Once I've completed the look, with the thong and open fronted kimono, I stand in front of the full length mirror. Wow! Even I have to admit, I look hot.

The only problem now is that Matt's disappeared. He's been gone since three o'clock. It's now nearly six.

I go, barefoot, back downstairs and have just reached the bottom step when I hear the car pull up in the driveway.

A few minutes later, he comes in through the front door and stops in his tracks, staring at me.

"You have remembered I got shot recently, haven't you?" he says.

"Yes." *What's his point?*

"Then you know you shouldn't be walking around looking like that. It would be very unwise to give me a heart attack… I'm probably not strong enough yet."

I walk up to him, very slowly, his eyes darkening with every step. "You're strong enough," I say as I get to him, running my hands up his arms. "You held me up in the shower last night, remember?"

"Yeah, but I had the wall to help me, and seeing you in this…" He reaches down and touches the fabric of the kimono, playing it between his fingers, then pulls it aside, exposing me. "Oh God, Grace," he breathes. "You're beautiful." He leans down and kisses me, pulling me in close, one hand on my back, the other on my neck, holding me in place. His tongue finds mine and he explores me deeply.

"Bed?" he says.

"Dinner?" I say at exactly the same time.

"I love your cooking, babe, but I think I preferred my suggestion." He laughs.

"We can do that later."

"You mean I've got to sit opposite you at the table, and look at you wearing that?"

"I can take it off, if you prefer." I turn and walk away, winking over my shoulder.

"I'll take it off for you…" he offers, following me into the kitchen, "very, very slowly."

"Well, that's one option." I say, moving around the centre island. "Or you could get the glasses out and bring them to the table."

He goes to the cupboard and reaches up to get the long-stemmed white wine glasses. By the time he closes the door, I'm bending over, taking the salad out of the fridge and I all hear is, "Hell, Grace… what are you trying to do to me…?"

Matt

"That was amazing." I lay my serviette down by my plate.

"I didn't do much," Grace says. "It was lobster and salad. It pretty much cooks itself."

"It was still amazing." I get up from the table, grabbing the wine and our glasses. "Let's go sit down," I say. She leads the way through to the living room and I follow, enjoying the view of her gorgeous body through the sheer material of the lace kimono. Either side of the wide fireplace are two enormous cream colored sofas, with a coffee table in between. I place the wine and glasses on the table and sit in the corner of the nearest sofa and Grace lowers herself next to me, leaning against my chest. I put my arm around her, feeling her warmth.

"I like this," I say, feeling the lacy fabric next to her skin. "Has it even got a name yet?"

"I think it's going to be Rose Gold."

"I'm not sure I want it to go into production now. I think I'd like to keep it just for us."

"It'll sell well."

"Yeah, I guess."

She looks up at me and I lower my lips to hers, claiming her mouth. She twists in the seat, straddling me and running her arms around my neck. I want her now, right here… But I've got plans for tonight and they can't wait. I break the kiss.

"Can you just hang on a minute?" I say.

"I guess." She looks a little disappointed.

"There's just something I need to go and get." She moves, allowing me to stand and I go out to the car and grab the box from my briefcase. I open it and smile. It may have been a long drive to pick this up, but it's worth it… I put the box firmly in my front pocket and return to the house. I go through to the dining room, and set up the music, which will play throughout the whole downstairs, and grab the remote for the stereo, put it in my back pocket, returning to stand in front of her. She's looking up at me, a little puzzled that I'm seemingly empty handed.

"I think I owe you a dance," I say, holding my hand out to her. She tilts her head to one side.

"There's no music," she says.

"Shh," I lean over and nod toward my outstretched hand. She takes it and I pull her to her feet. With my other hand, I pull the remote from my pocket and press 'play', the music starts and she gasps. She recognises it immediately. It's her parents' song. I sling the remote on the sofa.

"I made a promise," I say, twirling her around to the center of the room, "and I keep my promises." I pull her close and she rests her head on my chest as we sway in time to the music, the words echoing in both our minds.

As the music finishes, I place a hand on each of her cheeks and raise her face to mine, holding eye contact with her.

"Grace," I murmur, "There's something I've been wanting to say to you for ages, and I'm not waiting any longer." I take a deep breath. "When I was shot, even as I was falling and hearing you scream, my worst fear wasn't dying... it wasn't even that I might never get to see you, or touch you, or hold you again. As I hit the floor, all I could think was that I couldn't I die yet, because there was too much still to tell you; too many things I hadn't said yet. I knew I needed to get back to you and have a life with you, so nothing would ever have to go unsaid. To start with, I want to tell you how I fall in love with you just a little bit more every time I see you and that I will never take you or your love for granted, because I know how lucky I am to have found you." I reach into my pocket, pull out the box and open it. "I want to share everything I have, everything I am, everything I can ever be, with you..." I drop to one knee and look up at her. "Grace... please say you'll marry me..."

I can see the tears brimming in her eyes, and as she nods her head and blinks, the first one trickles over, cascading onto her cheek. I stand quickly, lean down and kiss it away, taking the ring from the box and placing it on her finger. "Yes, Matt. Yes," she whispers in my ear.

I never knew it was possible to feel this happy and I kiss her deeply.

"Can I take you up to bed?" I ask her, finally breaking the kiss.

"Of course you can." She smiles and I lift her into my arms.

"I think we should discuss the future," I tell her as I carry her up the stairs.

"The future?" She looks up at me.

"Yes. I don't know how quickly we can arrange the wedding, but I want it to be soon… real soon…"

"What's the rush?"

"It's one of the things I've been wanting to say to you for a while… one of the unsaid things that really needs to be said…"

"What's that?" She looks confused.

"I want us to have a baby, Grace." We've reached the bedroom and I sit down on the bed, holding her in my lap.

"Matt… I explained…"

"Yeah, I know. It might be difficult… I get that. But that's no reason not to try. I'll make sure you get the best care there is. I won't let anything happen to you and I'll be there every step of the way and… Look, I know I've just sprung this on you and, if you want to think about it, then that's fine, we can wait… but—"

"I don't want to wait," she says.

"You're sure?"

"I want to have your baby, Matt."

"Really?"

"Yes, really." Her eyes are alight.

I grin at her, lowering her onto the bed. "I know you're still on the pill, but I was wondering if we should have a practice…" I crawl up over her.

"You honestly think you need to practice?" She smiles up at me.

I shrug. "No… but it can't hurt, can it?"

"As long as I'm with you… Never."

The End

Keep reading for an excerpt from book two in the Series...
Finding Luke.

Finding Luke

Escaping the Past: Book Two

by

Suzie Peters

Chapter One

∽

Luke

Iturn the key in the lock, and open the door, trying to be as quiet as possible, so as not to wake Will. I can do without 'the look', the guilt-trip, the lecture, the inevitable argument, followed by the drawn-out silence, which if previous experience is anything to go by, could go on for days. Just because he's not getting laid… I shake my head. *No, that's not fair.*

The house is in darkness, thank God, and I make my way over to the kitchen to grab a glass of water. Opening the refrigerator, the bottles in the door clink together and I 'shush' them, placing my finger against my lips, then take the water jug and carry it across to the countertop by the sink. I get a glass from the cupboard, fill it with ice cold water and drink it down in one go, before re-filling it again.

"Thirsty?"

I jump, spilling water on the floor.

"Jesus, Will. What the…?"

"Where the hell have you been?" he asks from the hallway, turning on the main light. I wince against the brightness and put down the glass. He's standing, bare chested, shorts hanging low on his hips, leaning against the wall near my bedroom door, with a disappointed look on his face. "On second thoughts, don't answer that," he adds. "I know exactly where you've been, and with whom. Can't you have a little bit more self-respect, Luke? You and I both know why you do this, but don't you think…"

That's it. I've had enough. "Stop it! Stop acting like my goddamn mother," I yell and he stares at me just for a moment, his face white. *Shit! Way to go, Luke.* I've really excelled myself this time. "Will, I'm sorry," I call to his retreating back. I can't leave it – it'll eat away at him. I follow him down the hallway toward his bedroom at the far end, but he slams the door in my face. I wait outside for a minute, breathing deeply, before opening it and standing on the threshold. Inside, he's sitting on the edge of his bed, his elbows on his knees, rocking slightly. He looks like he's twelve years old all over again, like the intervening sixteen years never happened. He's still my little brother; he'll always be my little brother, and I want to go over to him and tell him everything will be okay... but it's never been okay for him, well not since he was twelve years old.

"She was *our* mother, Luke," he whispers. I walk over and sit down next to him.

"I know."

"Then don't talk about her like that."

"I'm sorry, man, okay? I just get sick of explaining myself."

He turns to look at me. I don't like the expression in his eyes. It cuts a little too deep.

"Well, if you didn't screw around so much..."

It's true... I can't deny it, but... "It's my life, Will."

"I know it is," he relents and hesitates, opening his mouth and then closing it again.

"What?"

"I just wish I thought you were happy, that's all."

I was happy enough an hour ago when I was buried in... what was her name? Monica? No, Michelle. No... Damned if I can remember her name. *Yeah, I was happy enough then...* But am I ever *really* happy these days?

"I'm fine," I say out loud, not wanting to admit the thoughts that are running around in my head – to him, or myself.

He continues to stare at me, like he can see right through me. It's uncomfortable.

"It was Matt and Grace's wedding, Luke," he says at last. He's really laying on the disappointment this time.

"No… it was *after* Matt and Grace's wedding. There's a difference. And we went back to her place…" *Whoever she was.* "It's not like I was screwing her on Matt and Grace's deck, while they were saying their vows; or in one of their guest rooms during the speeches." He grimaces. "Sorry," I say.

I shrug off my tux. I've got no idea where my tie ended up – it's probably still at Mandy's house… No, it wasn't Mandy… I know it began with an 'M', though.

"I'm going for a quick shower," I say, standing up again. "Then I'll get a few hours' sleep." I make my way over to the door.

"Are you going to see Melanie again?" he asks just before I leave. Melanie! That's it. I turn and look at him.

"No," I tell him. That's not how it works with me, and he knows it. "And how did you know her name?"

"She introduced herself before the ceremony," he explains. "She saw you with Matt and asked me if I knew who the best man was."

I nod my head, keen to escape, and wander down the hallway to my own room. Once inside, I close the door and lean back against it.

'Best Man'. I let my head drop to my chest. It hardly feels like the right title for a guy who can't even remember the name of the woman he's just made scream with pleasure, three… no, four times.

I guess that must be the reason why I feel like such a shit right now.

I douse my head under the shower. The water's hot and harsh, and it's good to feel something for a change. I stand, just thinking. I've lived like this since I was eighteen… Thirteen years of doing exactly what I please. No questions, no strings, and no commitments.

I've never dated a woman, not conventionally. One night stands are my specialty. I don't like the idea of relationships; someone asking questions, wanting to know everything about me. I've never been in love and I certainly don't like the idea of a woman being in love with me. I can't do the whole obligation, responsibility thing. I'm just not that kind of person. In a way, I admire those who are. I can see how Matt's changed since he met Grace and that's great… for Matt, but it's not for me.

I'm sure there are a few women out there who'd call me a complete asshole – some of them to my face, given the chance… but I'm always upfront. I let them know that for me, it's just about the sex, about having a good time together, and I'm not interested in a relationship; I always use protection and I never sleep with married women. Even I have boundaries

I turn to face the cascading water and run my hand up over my chest, recalling Melanie's fingernails scraping across my skin a few hours ago. She was exactly what I look for in a woman: hot as hell, and experienced. She knew what she wanted and she made it very clear at the wedding, she was only interested in me for tonight. She practically threw me out when we were done; no phone numbers, no contact details. That suits me fine. It was just sex; good sex – not great, but good. So, why do I feel like there's an absence of something? And what's the 'something'?

I shake my head, splashing water off the white tiled walls. What the hell is the matter with me?

"How was the honeymoon?" I look across the desk. Matt's tanned and grinning. "Actually, I don't want to know. It's written all over your face."

"Jealous?" he smirks.

"Of course." Grace is beautiful; any man with a pulse would be jealous. The door opens behind me. I turn and the lady in question enters. Her tan is slightly darker than Matt's. Her hair has also changed color, lightened by the sun. Her eyes are alight, satisfied and contented. Matt's a lucky man. I stand. "Hello, Grace," I say and go across to her, planting a kiss on each of her cheeks and placing my arm around her shoulders as we walk across to Matt's desk. "You look fabulous, as ever."

"Hi, Luke," she replies, giving me that 'look' she always does, which tells me she knows I'm flirting, she accepts it, and she's not at all impressed by it. I grin back. We get each other.

314

"The Cayman Islands agreed with you both, clearly."

"It was spectacular," Grace sighs, taking the seat next to mine, and across from Matt. She catches his eye and they share a look. I love the fact that they're happy, finally settled after everything they've been through in the last few months, but right now... I don't know... something's eating at me.

"Great," I say, wanting to break the spell that's binding them – not for long, just long enough for me to get out of their presence and back to my own world. *Yeah, my own world, where I'm so damn happy.* "Everything's been going well in your absence."

"I know." Matt leans forward, dragging his eyes from Grace and across to me. "I read your e-mails."

"At least you didn't reply to them."

"I was on my honeymoon, remember? And I trust you to run this place..." I know he does, but it's good to hear him say it. "So, production's at full capacity in both factories now?" he asks.

"Yes." We purchased a second factory site at the beginning of the year and it's now completely up to speed, producing our sportswear and lingerie ranges. Orders have been flooding in and business is doing great.

"We just need to discuss the launch of the new range," Matt says.

Grace had been working hard on this with Paul, our senior designer, right up until the wedding. Since moving here from England just before Christmas, Grace has been much more involved in the business, and with this new range in particular, and Matt and I have taken a back seat while we got the new factory up and running.

"Paul and I have come up with a new idea," Grace adds.

"Okay..."

"We've decided that, rather than having three or four girls modeling the ranges, we should have a 'face of' model. One girl, who we feel typifies the style of that season's designs. She'll do all the photography, and the promotional work and she'll lead the shows in September."

I think it's a really good idea. It fits in with where we've been taking the products, in terms of their exclusivity.

"I like it," I say. "Are we going to use a well-known face? Someone the public will recognize?"

"No," Matt says. "We want the exact opposite. We want someone new and fresh. Someone no-one's seen before."

"Paul came up with a short-list of models while we were away," Grace adds. "Ones who best fitted the styles. And Matt and I made the final choice this morning. She's a stunning girl. We've got the whole shoot arranged. Paul and I have worked really hard on coming up with ideas…" Why do I feel that there's a 'but' coming round the corner and it's aimed straight at me?

I look from Grace to Matt.

"The thing is," he says, "the shoot is going to take place on location."

"Not in a studio?" That's a departure.

"No," Grace sits forward in her seat and turns to me. "You've seen the designs, Luke. They're exceptional. I came up with the idea of shooting the photographs outside, in places that reflect, or represent the styles. Paul thought it was a good pitch, and we put it to Matt."

"And I agreed." *And where's this leading exactly?*

I sit waiting for whatever it is to fall on me. Almost certainly from a great height.

"The locations are all in France."

"France?" It makes sense, I guess. France is beautiful. I've spent enough time in Paris over the last few years to know that.

"Yes." She turns to Matt again. He gets up and comes around to our side of the desk, leaning against it, his legs outstretched and crossed at the ankle, his arms folded across his chest.

"The thing is…" he begins, "we feel that one of us should go on this shoot. The model we've selected – Megan – she's never done anything like this before…"

"Never? Not at all?"

"No. I said, I wanted someone completely new."

"There's new, and there's a modeling virgin. Guess you went for the modeling virgin."

"Yeah... Look, I need you to go, Luke."

"Surely, Grace should go," I say. "It's her idea."

"Grace can't go right now," Matt says, looking down at her. "She's got a new project to work on."

I'm not that surprised. I don't interfere with the early design processes. It's Matt's company and he's 'hands on' in all departments; I only tend to get involved later on, when we're looking at sales and marketing strategies.

"Paul's been doing some initial work on a range of maternity lingerie," Grace says. "He's moved it along while we've been—"

"I'm sorry," I splutter. "Did you just say 'maternity'?"

"Yes." I'm vaguely aware of Matt letting out a deep sigh, even though I'm looking at Grace.

"Maternity?" I repeat.

"Yes, Luke. Maternity. Pregnant women are allowed to look sexy too, you know." Her British accent is much more noticeable when she gets mad. She's not all the way there yet, but it's brewing.

"Yeah," I can't hide the doubt in my voice. "Yeah, sure they are."

"The designs are good," Matt puts in. "Look," he says, more seriously, "the point is, Grace can't go."

"Someone is going from the design team though, right?"

"Yeah. Paul's decided that Emma can handle the artistic side, so she'll be going along too." Emma's a really nice girl, good fun, very pretty, and very married to Nathan, who's a firefighter. She's also a great designer, so she'll be useful to have around. "But with an inexperienced model, I need someone there who can handle Alec. Emma can't do that."

"We're using Alec?"

"Yes." *Damn.* "He knows what we need, Luke. I know he's difficult, but he's a good photographer." 'Difficult' is an understatement, but he is good at what he does. "I need someone with seniority on this trip. I can't go either; it has to be you."

"When is this happening?" I ask.

"You'll need to leave at the weekend."

At least he didn't say 'tomorrow'.

"And how long is the shoot?"

"We've allowed just over three weeks," Grace says.

"Excuse me?" I turn to her. "Three weeks?" A studio shoot is normally completed in a few days.

"Twenty-four days, to be precise." She twists in her seat again. "There are six ranges to be photographed. We've allocated two days for each shoot, but then there's travelling, finding precise locations at each venue, checking for lighting… All of that will be down to Alec, but you'll have to drive between locations and some of them might take a day, maybe longer, to get to. And then there's a contingency of about four to five days, in case you have bad weather and can't work."

"And if we finish up early and don't need those extra days?"

"That's up to you," Matt says. "Alec can send the images back electronically. So you can either get an earlier flight home, or stay on over there and have a short vacation."

"Working with Alec, I'll have earned it."

Grace has gone back to her office and Matt and I have finished discussing everything else that happened while they were in The Caymans.

"This new range," I say to him. "Maternity… Are you sure about that?"

"The initial drawings are good," he says. "Why do you have a problem with it?"

"We're getting a good reputation for tasteful, sexy lingerie… I just can't equate maternity with sexy, that's all."

"Are you serious?"

"Absolutely."

"But, can't you imagine how incredible it would be to have the woman you love carrying your child… caring for it inside her, nurturing it? Hell, I think that's about as sexy as it gets."

I stare at him… He's *really* changed. Admittedly, it's a change for the better, considering where he was a couple of years ago, but… Hang on a second… "Grace isn't pregnant, is she?"

"No." He hesitates for a moment. "But, we're trying."

"You are? Already?"

"Yes, already." He shakes his head at me, but he's smiling. "We made the decision the night I proposed…"

"How romantic."

"There were reasons," he says, pauses and then continues, "Grace has some medical problems, it might not be that easy—" He stops. I had no idea.

"Sorry, Matt." I feel like a jerk now. "Is this to do with her first husband?" The guy raped and beat Grace for years before he had the good sense to get himself killed. It's a wonder she's as together as she is – and she's about the most together person I've ever met.

"Yes. He got her pregnant. It went wrong." He looks up at me. "I can't go into details, but she could've died." I can see the fear in his eyes. "It's her story," he says. "It doesn't feel right…"

"You don't have to tell me anything, except that she's okay." I don't need details, but I do care about Grace.

"In terms of her general health, she's fine. In terms of getting pregnant and carrying it to term…? We don't know, but we'll find out, hopefully quite soon."

I can't imagine being where he is… Grace means everything to him. We sit in silence for a while.

"Are you sure you're okay with this photo shoot?" he asks out of the blue. "I'm sorry to throw it at you. I know you never really enjoyed doing them, but Grace needs to be here… And so do I, for obvious reasons." He grins at me. I get it now.

"Sure," I say. "It's fine. How bad can it be?"

"With Alec?"

"Yeah, okay. It could be bad."

"Grace will go through the locations with you tomorrow. She's got everything mapped out; flights, car hire, hotels, everything. Grace and Emma have arranged it all already… You just have to turn up, make sure everything runs smoothly and Alec doesn't cause too much trouble."

"Okay. This model... Megan, was it? How old is she?"

He opens a document on his computer and reads. "She's... twenty-two."

"That's young."

"It's one of the reasons Grace wanted Emma on the shoot. It'll be some female company for her, but she's also a really good fit with the styles. I'm just waiting for the final contract to come back from the agency."

"And then she's ours for three weeks?"

"Yes, but only professionally."

"Of course."

"Luke," he says, his voice sounding the warning note I'm so familiar with.

"Yeah, I know. No fooling around with the models... or model, in this case."

"Alec's a bully, and you'll need to look out for her, but your responsibilities end at her bedroom door... got it?"

"Got it, boss." It's his golden rule, and one I've never broken.

In any case, there's more to this shoot than the model... and, if my previous experiences of French women are anything to go by, maybe the next three weeks won't be so bad after all.

❧

Megan

"You do understand, don't you?" The woman's voice on the phone is persistent, like she's talking to a three year-old.

"Yes." Nothing she's said so far has been that hard to grasp.

"If you accept this job, you have to commit to this photographic shoot, and the fashion shows in the fall." She's going to repeat it all anyway... because I'm clearly three years old.

"Yes, that's fine."

"So, you're happy with the arrangements?"

"What will I be modeling?"

"Well… they're sportswear designers, dear… I've told you this already." Her sarcasm isn't lost on me.

"I know, but it's not too revealing, is it?"

"It's sportswear," she huffs.

"Yes, right."

"So, can I tell them you agree? I have to get the contract back to them."

I think for a moment… and it only takes a moment. The job is very well paid. It's worth more money than I could have dreamt of earning working at Dexy's bar. I can't afford to say no. "Yes, that's fine." I say.

She hangs up, telling me she'll be in touch.

I twist my phone round and round, turning it over in my hand, staring at the blank screen. Have I just made a huge mistake? I gave up my job at Dexy's a month ago. I couldn't handle any more drunks trying to get into my pants. I'm more than familiar with drunks – I lived with one for too many years – but I'd had enough. I wanted to find a job with one of the museums in the city, but there's just nothing available, and I need to pay the rent, and send my dad some money, or I'll have to move back with him… and I can't do that. This will work… It's just a temporary fix to a temporary glitch. Three weeks' work now… another three or four weeks in the fall, and I'm set for six months… which leaves me plenty of time to find the job I really want to do. It all makes perfect sense.

I hear the front door open, then close and Erin appears. She's a little shorter than me, thin, with shoulder-length auburn hair and just enough freckles to look cute. She's already found a 'proper' job, at an elementary school near the city center, but she doesn't start until next semester, so she's taken part-time work in a pizza restaurant just around the corner. We've known each other since our first day at college; we moved into this small apartment at the end of our first year and we're best friends.

"Well?" she says.

"I got it."

"You could sound a little more enthusiastic."

"It's not exactly my dream job, Erin."

"No…" she comes and sits down next to me on our tiny couch. "But it'll pay the rent and keep you fed for a while."

"Us… It'll keep us fed." She gives me a hug.

"And it'll get your dad off your back…"

"I know. Just as long as he doesn't find out where the money came from."

"How's he ever going to find out?" She has a point. He'll just take whatever I give him, and then ask for more, like he usually does. "So, what do they want?"

"I've got to go to Europe," I tell her.

She turns and stares at me. "Are you serious?"

"Yes." I can't help but smile. "It's incredible, isn't it? Europe! As long as I can cope with the flight, I'll be fine."

"What's wrong with flying?"

"I don't know… I've never done it. I've always been a bit scared of it though."

"You'll be fine. You need to try new things. Besides, it's the chance of a lifetime. Whereabouts in Europe are you going?"

"France."

"Wow… How long for?" she asks.

"Three weeks."

"When do you go?"

"I'm leaving on Saturday. And they're sending one of the women from the company, as a kind of chaperone, so it's all perfectly okay."

"I told you this would work out. And to think, I passed it up." Erin saw the advertisement calling for models, in a magazine last week. It was a local agency and at first, we laughed it off, but I was having no luck searching for work, and money was already getting a little tight, so I went to see them. They signed me up and told me they had the perfect job for me, on the spot. It seemed too good to be true, but so far, it's all working out fine.

"The company I'm going to be working for are in sportswear."

"Oooh... lovely. Lots of Lycra. At least you've got the figure for it." She laughs and jumps up off the sofa. "Coffee?" she offers.

"Hmm, please. And I suppose I'd better think about what to pack."

"I've decided to turn my phone off," I say to Erin as we pull up outside the departure building. "I can't risk my dad calling while I'm over there... Just in case he overhears someone speaking in French or something. You can text me if there are any problems and I'll switch it on each evening and check my messages."

"Don't worry, just enjoy yourself. You don't get to go to France every day."

"I'll be back on July 2nd at the latest."

"I've got your flight details in my diary."

"And if my dad calls on the landline..."

"I'll just tell him your phone's off because you're working, and you'll be there to see him... when?"

"July 19th, as planned, but—"

"I won't say a word about where you are, or what you're doing. Just stop worrying, Megs, and go have a great time." She kisses my cheek and I hop out of the car, grabbing my bag from the back seat.

"Bye!" I return her wave as she pulls away from the kerb.

It's a warm, sultry, overcast day, and I welcome the air conditioning as I enter the building.

I pull a piece of paper from the pocket of my bag.

It says I'm supposed to meet Emma Conway and a guy called Luke Myers by the Delta check-in desk. I've got no idea what they look like, but hopefully the agency will have sent them my photograph, so they'll find me.

It's fairly busy inside but I find the desk easily enough. There's a pretty blonde woman standing to one side, searching the crowds.

"Are you Emma Conway?" I ask her.

"Yes. And you're Megan Ford." She shakes my hand. "Wow. Your photographs don't do you justice," she says.

I know I'm blushing but she either doesn't notice, or is polite enough to ignore my embarrassment.

"I hope I haven't kept you waiting," I reply eventually.

"No. We've only been here a short while. Luke will be back in a minute. He went to get coffee."

I nod my head. She's a very positive, bubbly person. She's shorter than me, but then a lot of people are, being as I'm five foot ten. She's wearing jeans and a red check shirt, with sunglasses perched on her head, holding her hair back from her face.

"You may as well check your bag in," she says. "We've already done ours."

"Oh, okay." I go up to the desk and go through the procedure, then return to her.

"I think Luke went to pick the damn beans himself," she says. "Either that, or he's found some poor, deluded..." I've stopped listening. Her words are just white noise, because behind her, out of the corner of my eye, I've noticed the most gorgeous man I've ever seen, walking through the concourse. He must be around six foot three or maybe four inches tall, broad shouldered, with a narrow waist. His toned muscles are evident through the tight white t-shirt that's plastered to his body, and his long legs are encased in light stonewashed jeans. He's carrying three coffees in a cardboard tray. For a brief moment, I manage to tear my eyes from him and notice that every other female in the vicinity is also staring at him, some with their mouths open. I wonder if he knows how good he looks and how much attention he's getting. Then I look back at him... Of course he does.

He stops for a moment, then stares in our direction, a confused expression on his face. It seems like he's forgotten something. He waits for a minute or two, then almost seems to shake his head, before he slowly moves toward us...

Escaping the Past Series
by Suzie Peters

Available on Amazon

Printed in Great Britain
by Amazon